COMMISSAR

'Stand down,' Flint ordered Lhor. 'Get moving. We're leaving, Vahn. If you want out, now's your only chance.'

Vahn and the green-haired woman exchanged words too quietly for Flint to overhear, then he waved the rest of the group forward. Satisfied that all of the convicts were moving, Vahn jogged after them, and soon the entire force was moving back towards the tunnel entrance. He gathered his convicts, ordering them to follow their liberators. Flint could scarcely miss the tension between Vahn and Skane, but the two men appeared to reach an unspoken agreement that whatever recriminations would be voiced would have to wait until they were all clear of the penal generatorium.

With the dozen dragoons and the three-dozen or so convicts moving away down the tunnel towards the vent, Flint was the last to leave the carceri chamber. With one last look, he cursed the place, knowing it was just one of twenty such chambers, all of which would be swarming with murderous rebels. This, he knew, was just the beginning.

'Welcome to Alpha Penitentia, commissar,' said Vahn over his shoulder as h̶e̶ ̶m̶a̶r̶c̶h̶e̶d̶ ̶a̶f̶t̶e̶r̶ his companions. 'Welcome ̶t̶o̶...'

D1254912

A WARHAMMER 40,000 NOVEL

COMMISSAR

ANDY HOARE

BLACK LIBRARY

To my wife, Sarah

A Black Library Publication

First published digitally in Great Britain in 2013.
This edition published in 2014 by
Black Library,
Games Workshop Ltd.,
Willow Road,
Nottingham, NG7 2WS, UK.

10 9 8 7 6 5 4 3 2 1

Cover illustration by Rhys Pugh.

© Games Workshop Limited 2013, 2014. All rights reserved.

Black Library, the Black Library logo, The Horus Heresy, The Horus Heresy logo, The Horus Heresy eye device, Space Marine Battles, the Space Marine Battles logo, Warhammer 40,000, the Warhammer 40,000 logo, Games Workshop, the Games Workshop logo and all associated brands, names, characters, illustrations and images from the Warhammer 40,000 universe are either ®, ™ and/or © Games Workshop Ltd 2000-2014, variably registered in the UK and other countries around the world. All rights reserved.

A CIP record for this book is available from the British Library.

UK ISBN 13: 978 1 84970 609 4
US ISBN 13: 978 1 84970 616 2

No part of this publication may be reproduced, stored in a retrieval system, or transmitted in any form or by any means, electronic, mechanical, photocopying, recording or otherwise, without the prior permission of the publishers.

This is a work of fiction. All the characters and events portrayed in this book are fictional, and any resemblance to real people or incidents is purely coincidental.

See Black Library on the internet at

www.blacklibrary.com

Find out more about Games Workshop
and the world of Warhammer 40,000 at

www.games-workshop.com

Printed and bound by CPI Group (UK) Ltd, Croydon, CR0 4YY

It is the 41st millennium. For more than a hundred centuries the Emperor has sat immobile on the Golden Throne of Earth. He is the master of mankind by the will of the gods, and master of a million worlds by the might of his inexhaustible armies. He is a rotting carcass writhing invisibly with power from the Dark Age of Technology. He is the Carrion Lord of the Imperium for whom a thousand souls are sacrificed every day, so that he may never truly die.

Yet even in his deathless state, the Emperor continues his eternal vigilance. Mighty battlefleets cross the daemon-infested miasma of the warp, the only route between distant stars, their way lit by the Astronomican, the psychic manifestation of the Emperor's will. Vast armies give battle in His name on uncounted worlds. Greatest amongst his soldiers are the Adeptus Astartes, the Space Marines, bio-engineered super-warriors. Their comrades in arms are legion: the Imperial Guard and countless Planetary Defence Forces, the ever-vigilant Inquisition and the tech-priests of the Adeptus Mechanicus to name only a few. But for all their multitudes, they are barely enough to hold off the ever-present threat from aliens, heretics, mutants - and worse.

To be a man in such times is to be one amongst untold billions. It is to live in the cruellest and most bloody regime imaginable. These are the tales of those times. Forget the power of technology and science, for so much has been forgotten, never to be re-learned. Forget the promise of progress and understanding, for in the grim dark future there is only war. There is no peace amongst the stars, only an eternity of carnage and slaughter, and the laughter of thirsting gods.

'The martyr never truly dies. Every blow he suffers is the touch of immortality, every prison he is incarcerated within is a heavenly mansion.'

– Chapter DCCCLXXIII, Verse XXIX, the *Dictum Commissaria* (underscored several times in Commissar Flint's personal copy)

Commissar Flint,

You are hereby requested and required to proceed with all haste from your current post to that of regimental commissar of the 77th Vostroyan Firstborn Dragoons, currently en route to Munitorum penal facility at Furia Penitens [Astrocartographica ref. attached]. Find attached record of the 77th, a regiment with 9,000 years of glorious service to Him on Terra until its destruction at the Battle of Golan Hole 833926.M41. The 77th is now fully reconstituted, but its officer cadre is untested and rank has been apportioned according to the traditions of the ruling Techtriarch clans of Vostroya. Your task is to ensure the regiment maintains the traditions of its forebears, adheres to the Offering of the Firstborn, and the stain of the defeat is erased.

Additional.
Sealed archive:
+++BATTLE OF GOLAN HOLE SUPPRESSED AFTER ACTION DECLARATION+++
Attached for your eyes only.

ONE

The Drop

'Group seven-nine!' the naval loadmaster bellowed over the roar of cycling turbines. 'Forward and embark!'

Commissar Flint's newly appointed staff section dashed forward from the muster line, a dozen heavily laden men pounding up the drop-ship's loading ramp. As they reached the top the crew took hold of their kit bags and unceremoniously flung them deeper into the vessel before waving the passengers to their positions. Only when the entire group was embarked did Flint start forward, waving Dragoon Kohlz, his hurriedly deputised aide, ahead of him. Kohlz was the only one whose name he had yet learned, the younger and distinctly less burly Vostroyan standing out amidst the older warriors with their drooping, waxed moustaches and gruff manners.

The flight deck was a riot of tightly coordinated activity. The space was enormous, the walls and ceiling constructed

Andy Hoare

of the heaviest grade adamantium now pockmarked and oil-streaked by centuries of service in the Imperial Navy prosecuting the Emperor's wars. The decking underfoot was gouged and scarred by the passage of countless boots, tracks, wheels and landing claws. Every inch of the vessel spoke volumes to Commissar Flint, stirring his heart with conflicting notions – he was at once essential to the carrier's mission of bringing the Emperor's judgement to the furthest star systems of the Imperium, and merely the latest in an impossibly long line of men to have done so.

Two-dozen drop-ships of various sizes squatted on the pitted hardpan, loading ramps swarming with troops. The vessels belonged to the Imperial Navy, but it was the personnel of the Imperial Guard they would be transporting to the world below. Those warriors belonged to a supposedly elite 'Firstborn' regiment, but in truth they were untested. In fact, these men, and the handful of women serving in the regiment, had yet to even breathe the air of a world other than Vostroya.

Though he'd been with them for but a few hours, Flint could already tell these troops were unprepared. As the warriors swarmed up the boarding ramps, Flint took a moment to cast an appraising eye over the scene. The Vostroyan Firstborn were almost exclusively male, and slightly shorter than average height. They were stocky and muscular, raised in the foundries and manufactoria of a world entirely given over to industry, in particular the production of arms and ordnance. Every one of them bore a weapon crafted to the very highest standards, forged as an act of penance on the part of the arms-smith for a sin his forebears had committed at some point in the Imperium's earliest history. Though he was well prepared for his appointment, Commissar Flint had been unable to discover the exact nature of that wrongdoing, but it appeared the Vostroyans took it, or its legacy, very seriously. They appeared almost literally weighed down by something. They might be equipped with the finest gilded armour, fur-lined coats and master-crafted weapons, but many of the warriors Flint was looking at seemed somehow burdened, despite their outwardly grim-faced stoicism.

As Flint mounted the boarding ramp, the loadmaster waved him forward with brisk hand signals clearly understandable even with the ship's engines at full power. From his vantage point, Flint was afforded a spectacular view of the five main drop-vessels, each large enough to ferry an entire line company including its transports and support vehicles. The remainder of the drop-ships were smaller, designed to transport around fifty men and their equipment. These would ferry the various elements of the regiment's command staff so that no single incident or accident could take out the entire chain of command in one go. Flint was glad to be performing planetfall in the smaller vessel as dozens of combat drops in the larger ships had taught him how vulnerable they truly were. He was still haunted by his first campaign on Gethsemane. There, Flint had seen such a vessel struck by the insurgents' hideous self-guided ordnance. Several hundred men had burned in a second and the stricken drop-ship had plummeted into the heart of the breakout zone, slaying uncounted more. At the loadmaster's respectful, yet unmistakably impatient gesture, Flint ducked inside and located his position. Another crewman grabbed Flint's kit bag from Dragoon Kohlz and slung it into a cargo cage, slamming the cover shut to secure the contents against the violence of the coming drop.

Flint's drop-station was located near the fore of the vessel behind the enclosed passenger bay. A small, armoured porthole allowed a view of the scene outside – the boarding ramps of the heavier ships slowly rising and red warning lights flashing.

'Strap yourselves in and get secure!' the loadmaster ordered. 'This is gonna be a rough one!'

Flint could hardly miss the relish in the Navy man's voice, but he knew what to expect. As sirens howled from outside on the deck, the vessel's boarding ramp rose on whining pneumatics and slammed shut, the engines cycling to full power. Flint's ears popped as the air pressure equalised and he strapped himself into the grav-couch, glancing around to ensure that his section had done so too.

Kohlz was attaching the last of his restraints, his bulky vox-set stowed in a cargo bin behind him. Chief provost Bukin sat across from Flint, his grox-ugly face with its long, Vostroyan-style moustaches an unreadable mask as he awaited the drop. The remainder of Bukin's provost section were just as silent as their leader and Flint could tell they were each trying to maintain an air of brusque confidence despite the dread that must be rising inside. None had undertaken a combat drop before, but they would soon learn.

Then came the long moment of tension and expectation as the flight crew completed their pre-drop ritual checks. Flint remained impassive and stony faced, but he caught the numerous furtive glances cast his way by his newly appointed staff. Each man was clad in the heavy, red and fur-trimmed uniform of the Vostroyan Firstborn. Each wore segments of armour handed down through the generations and no two sets were exactly the same. Many of the men wore the tall, shaggy headgear so distinctive of the Firstborn, despite the building heat inside the drop-bay. At least, it might have been the heat that made the provosts sweat; it might just as well have been their proximity to the first commissar their regiment had been assigned since it was reconstituted.

Commissar Flint kept his snort of amusement to himself as he prepared for the drop. Outwardly, Flint appeared to be in his early forties, though like most of his calling he had ten times the scar tissue anyone of his age had any right bearing. In truth, he *felt* ten times older, so much death and destruction had he witnessed in his service to the God-Emperor of Mankind. Quite apart from that, he'd undertaken numerous superluminary voyages throughout his career, travelling via the warp from one appointment to the next. As such, he'd technically been alive for many more years than he had actually experienced subjectively.

Finally, the lighting in the passenger bay changed to deep red and the loadmaster worked his way along the rows of grav-couches performing last minute checks. Satisfied that none of his charges would strangle themselves during the violence of the drop, the loadmaster found his own station on Flint's left and strapped himself in. With an inaudible word of command spoken into his headset vox, the loadmaster informed the pilot that all was secure and the vessel drop-ready.

A subsonic rumble rattled through the drop-ship's frame as the mighty hangar bay doors ground aside, the barren surface of the world of Furia Penitens filling the view beyond. With a metallic clang, the drop-ship's grav generator kicked in, causing Flint to experience a brief moment of vertigo as the vessel's field synced with that of the assault carrier, *Toil of Kossia*. Then the ship's engines cycled to full power and its thrusters fired up, the view through the port lurching as the vessel lifted several metres into the air.

'Looks like we're in the first wave,' said Kohlz from Flint's right, addressing no one in particular.

Bukin threw a sullen glance across at Flint's aide, but held his tongue. The man next to the corporal grinned cruelly and growled, 'Yes, we are the flak magnets.'

Flint met Corporal Bukin's eye and the provost got the message. 'Shut the hell up,' Bukin ordered belligerently. 'Where the hell else do you think the commissar's going to be?'

The man appeared ready to argue but any further discussion was stalled as the drop-ship lurched forward on its launch rail, the open hangar bay hatch looming in the viewport.

'Everyone stand by,' shouted Commissar Flint over the whine of the drop-ship's engines. 'This won't take long and

I need you operational dirtside. You all know your duty, so do it.'

As the drop-ship neared the launch, it lined up with several others of the same size and class. Some would be carrying members of the regiment's command cadre, others units of its support echelons. One would be carrying the 77th's scout platoon, which would move outwards from the landing zone and establish the tactical situation at the drop zone just outside of the target. As the last of the light drop-ships took its place in the line a dozen sets of engines screamed in unison and the launch cradles carried them through the hatch to suspend them in open space.

'Any last words?' drawled the man next to Corporal Bukin. Kohlz swallowed hard. Flint said a silent prayer to the God-Emperor of Mankind. Then, the bottom dropped out of the world.

For the first thirty seconds of the drop Flint felt like he was being spun in every direction at once in the heart of an industrial-grade centrifuge, the entire passenger bay shaking as the ship was subjected to stresses that would tear a lesser vessel apart in seconds. Flint continued his prayer, using it as a mantra to focus his thoughts inwards and distract them from the fury of the orbital insertion.

It was all Flint could do to force his eyes open, so great were the forces being exacted on his body. The drop-ship's inertial fields were clearly struggling to counteract the effect of plummeting at supersonic speeds through the outer reaches of Furia Penitens' orbital range, blackness encroaching the periphery of his vision. The superhuman Space

Marines of the Adeptus Astartes might be able to withstand such punishment, but the drop-ship's passengers were mortal men and even Flint, a veteran of dozens of combat drops, wouldn't be able to take much more…

'Interface!' The loadmaster bellowed at Flint's side, strain audible in his voice.

If the first phase had been rough, the next was hellish. As the drop-ship plummeted through the thermosphere its outer hull grew white-hot so that traces of flame whipped across the outer skin of the viewing port. As the ship crossed the Kármán line at one hundred and fifty kilometres above ground level the temperature soared further. Several times Flint blacked out, only to come to what must have been a few seconds later. Several of the provosts had passed out too, and a number had developed fearsome nosebleeds, red liquid splattering about the cabin as the force threatened to shake them all to atoms.

The vessel's regulators cycled to full power in an effort to counter the heat but still the passenger bay felt as hot as a furnace. Flint longed to cast off his heavy leather storm coat but he knew the drop would be over in minutes. Then he saw that the loadmaster had his hand pressed firmly to his earpiece and was shouting loudly into his vox-pickup.

'What?' Flint bellowed at the loadmaster, unable to reach across – so powerful were the forces pressing him into his grav-couch. The officer tapped his earpiece and held up three fingers to indicate that Flint should set his vox-bead to channel three.

Clipped and fragmentary conversation burst from Flint's

earpiece. '…locked. Repeat, target lock confirmed, over.'

Damn, Flint cursed inwardly as the pitch of the drop-ship's systems changed and he felt the vessel roll. 'Ground defences?' he yelled into the vox.

'Yes, sir,' replied the loadmaster, his voice distorted over the link. 'The rebels have control of one of the ground-to-orbit defence silos.'

Memories of Flint's first drop, the disastrous Gethsemane Landings, came unbidden to his mind, but with an effort of will he quickly dispelled them. There was nothing he could do except trust to the skills of the flight crew, the inexperience of the rebels controlling the defences and, most importantly, the beneficence of the God-Emperor of Mankind.

The drop-ship bucked wildly and the passengers were jolted hard in their restraints. Flint quickly scanned the faces of his staff to gauge their reaction to the situation. They had no idea what was happening and there was no point in telling them. Bukin maintained his steely expression, which Flint knew he felt compelled to do to keep up his position as top dog even though the rank brassard he wore at his shoulder was sure sign of it. The other provosts had their eyes screwed tight shut and their jaws set in a rictus grimace. Flint glanced sideways at his aide and saw that Kohlz was mouthing a silent prayer. Smart lad, thought the commissar.

The drop-ship bucked a second time and Flint felt it slew violently as it plummeted. He cast a look out of the port and saw that the barren wastes of Furia Penitens now completely filled the view. Jagged mountain ranges were visible through churning swirls of dark clouds, illuminated from within by pulsating electrical storms. Millions of square kilometres of hard ground rushed upwards as if to swat the drop-ship from existence or smash it to oblivion in an instant.

'Receiving confirmation from intelligence, sir,' the load-master said through the vox-link. 'The rebels have control of a single battery. It's too late to abort; we're going in as planned.'

'There's no other option,' Flint agreed as the drop-ship's descent speed increased still further. To divert the first wave because of a single threat would be unforgivable, even if he himself was in that wave and therefore at risk.

'Incoming!' the loadmaster called over the vox-link. Flint glanced outside, though he knew he had no chance of catching sight of a missile homing in on the drop-ship before it struck and killed them all. A bright explosion blossomed several kilometres fore of the ship. The rebels had fired a cluster warhead.

Lacking the ability to fire a missile with pinpoint accuracy, the rebels must have coerced one of the weapon's crew into launching a weapon that would scatter a wide area with deadly munitions. As the explosion faded, dozens of smaller points arced away on thick, black contrails. The fire of the detonation faded to be replaced by a dirty smear of turbulent smoke, and the drop-ship was plummeting straight towards it. Flint fought against a sudden sense of overpowering vertigo as the entire vessel powered nose first into the debris cloud. One of the cluster munitions zipped past at hypervelocity and an instant later the drop-ship was out of the remnants of the explosion and the world below resolved once more, the mountains and valleys of the surface now visible in stunning detail.

'What the hell was that?' shouted the provost beside Corporal Bukin, his voice only barely audible over the roar of air against the drop-ship's hull. 'Some bastard shooting at us?'

'Not *us*,' shouted Corporal Bukin, 'just *you*,' before the entire drop-ship shuddered violently and the restraints tightened in response, pinning the passengers hard into their grav-couches. Flint knew instantly that one of the cluster munitions must have clipped the drop-ship.

The vessel's engines screamed like a gargantuan beast in terrible pain and the air pressure in the passenger bay bled out rapidly. With a sudden rush, a blast of ice-cold air flooded the compartment and pressure masks dropped down from the bulkheads above each drop-station. The loadmaster reached up and pulled his mask over his face and in a moment Flint had his fitted too. He took a deep breath of the bottled oxygen then looked outside to judge the ship's altitude. The vessel shook violently as the pilot fought to bring its nose up and level with the horizon, a jagged spire surrounded by a halo of chimneys rose in the distance silhouetted against the grey sky. Flint guessed the drop zone was less than a minute away, if only the ship could hold together that long.

Flint lifted his mask and yelled, 'Everyone prepare for

rapid disembarkation!' He couldn't tell if any of the passengers heard him over the roar of the wind both inside and outside of the drop-ship. The sound grew louder still as the ship levelled out. Flint took a ragged breath of the cold air and found that the pressure had equalised enough for him to breathe normally.

As the drop-ship plunged through a rearing cloudbank it shook violently and Flint's ears were assaulted by the deafening sound of a section of the metal hull shearing away. The shaking increased to a continuous, bone-jarring tremor punctuated by subsonic growls and high-pitched, metallic wails.

'Ten seconds!' the loadmaster called out. 'Brace for impact!'

Flint knew the drill. He folded his arms across his chest and set his head firmly against the padded headrest. The provosts' training had kicked in too, regardless of their outward brusqueness. But Kohlz had loosened his seat restraint and was attempting to secure his vox-set, which was working its way loose of the cargo bin he had stowed it in.

'Leave it!' Flint ordered, grabbing Kohlz's wrist hard. At that very moment the drop-ship struck a tall rock spire and the world turned upside down. The illumination inside the passenger bay cut out, a bright spear of sunlight arcing through the small viewport. The vessel dropped what must have been a thousand metres in a second and rolled onto its side. It held its course for several seconds more before the deafeningly loud roar of tearing metal made Flint look left. A massive wound had appeared in the side of the vessel and the thrashing bodies of several passengers had already been sucked through it. There was nothing anyone else could do, either to rescue them, or to avoid a similar fate. The only possible course of action was to pray to the God-Emperor of Mankind, and hold on for dear life.

Seconds later, the drop-ship slammed into the hard ground with bone-jarring force.

Blinding light and the deafening screech of rending metal was overwhelming. The bulkhead right beside Flint was torn away as the drop-ship disintegrated further, bouncing along the ground and showering the interior with gravel and metal shrapnel. Flint realised through the shock and violence of the crash landing that he was still holding on to Kohlz's wrist and that his aide's entire grav-couch had been torn free and sucked out of the huge wound in the drop-ship's hull. It was only Flint's holding on to Kohlz's wrist that was saving the aide from tumbling out of the breach to certain death.

Flint hauled on Kohlz's arm with all of his strength and pulled him back inside the passenger bay as the drop-ship continued its juddering progress along the surface. The screaming of metal reached a howling crescendo and the ship bounced one last time and slewed violently onto its side. Finally, the drop-ship came to a halt, the hull rocking back and forth a couple of times to the sound of creaking metal and scattering gravel. At the last, a shocking silence descended.

Flint let go of Kohlz's arm and his aide dropped to the deck on all fours. His ears were still ringing from the violence of

Andy Hoare

the crash and for long seconds everything sounded dull and distant. He slammed a fist into the emergency release clasp in the centre of his restraint harness and forced himself to stand on unsteady feet. The sound of coughing came from across the deck as the surviving provosts stirred themselves. Chief provost Bukin had lit a stubby Vostroyan cigar and placed it in his mouth even before freeing himself from his restraints.

'Everybody out!' Flint barked as he looked about for the best way to exit the wrecked vessel. He was acutely aware of the danger presented by spilled fuel catching alight, damaged munitions being disturbed or plasma cell containment failure incinerating the entire troop bay. He turned to the loadmaster and saw that the man was very obviously dead, a length of spar having impaled his chest at the moment of impact. The rear of the passenger bay was a mess and the hatch leading forward to the flight deck was so buckled it was obvious that way was out of the question too.

Hauling the shaken Kohlz to his feet, Flint made for the massive wound in the drop-ship's flank. Shorn power conduits sparked and guttered at the wound's jagged edge and the light pouring through it was blindingly bright compared to the dingy interior. Looking along the drop-ship's outer hull he saw that the entire prow was staved in and there was no hope the flight crew might have survived. Bracing both arms against the ruined bulkhead, Flint pushed himself through the hole as his eyes adjusted to the glare.

The surface of Furia Penitens was a barren waste. The ground was rocky and pitted with ancient craters, all of a reddish-brown hue. Jagged mountains rose on the western horizon and guttering thunderheads reared in the grey sky high above. Flint's gaze tracked across the land and he saw exactly why the Munitorum had chosen such a place to construct a penal facility. It was obvious that even if any convicts could affect an escape they would be dead within weeks if they couldn't find a way of getting off-world. To the east he saw what he first took for a towering mountain, before realising it was in fact the rearing form of the Alpha Penitentia penal generatorium.

'Gather up the gear,' Flint told the nearest man, a provost who was doubled up as he vomited away the adrenaline shock the crash had inflicted on his body. 'I want everyone ready to move out in five minutes.'

The provost finished his retching, then staggered back along the passenger bay, kicking one of his companions still struggling with his restraints. Flint jumped the two metres to the ground and took his first steps on the surface of Furia Penitens.

'Kohlz,' Flint called up towards the breach, his aide's head appearing a moment later. 'Pass down the vox-set.'

Kohlz ducked back into the passenger bay and re-emerged a moment later with the bulky communications set. 'Don't know if it still works, sir,' he called down, his voice shaky from the shock of his near death.

'If it doesn't we're walking,' said Flint. In a moment Kohlz had handed the vox-set down to Flint, who placed it at his feet and turned to gaze out across the windswept wastes towards the distant spire and chimneys of Alpha Penitentia.

The central tower was a flat-faced keep rising hundreds of metres, its slab-sided flanks grey and imposing. Squat blocks and fluted cooling towers were clustered all around its base, each several times the size of the largest of Ministorum cathedrals.

This place would be the making or the breaking of the newly reconstituted 77th. Its inmates had risen up against their wardens when the Munitorum had demanded a Penal Legion be raised from the population, to then be shipped out to some far-flung warzone in the Finial Sector. The 77th was the nearest available Imperial Guard regiment and Flint's appointment as their regimental commissar had been expedited with almost unseemly haste so that he could be in attendance for their first mission. So much for the Munitorum's plans, he thought, estimating the time it would take to walk to the drop zone if the vox-set proved inoperable.

As Flint squinted against the cold wind he saw faint columns of smoke rising from several of the blocks; evidence, he judged, of just how widespread and destructive the uprising within the complex actually was. How much of the facility was now under the rebels' control was impossible to tell, but a question the 77th would need to have answered as soon as possible.

A crunching impact on the ground behind Flint signalled that Kohlz was down. In another minute or so the remainder of the section was out, Corporal Bukin's provosts gazing slack-jawed at the distant installation.

'Just like home,' one of them said with the false bravado

of one who has just narrowly escaped a gruesome death. Reaching into his fur-lined coat, the provost withdrew a small, copper flask and took a hearty swig of the contents, then stopped guiltily mid-glug as he realised Flint was watching.

'Ahh…' the provost started, before proffering the flask to Flint. '*Rahzvod*, sir?'

Not such a bad idea, thought Flint as he nodded his thanks and took the offered flask. He'd read something of the Vostroyans' native brew: a clear, highly alcoholic beverage peculiar to their home world. Ordinarily he'd frown on such vices, but needs must, he thought as he upended the flask.

Emperor's mercy! Flint fought with every ounce of his strength not to show any sign of the drink's effect upon him. *Why the hell would they drink this?* The burning was like the after-effects of the inoculations the Officio Medicae administered before service on a death world. In fact, it was almost as bad as the infections those inoculations were supposed to counteract…

'You like it, sir?' the provost said, a look of genuine respect in his eyes. 'You like more?

Flint shook his head and handed the flask back, forestalling any further conversation as he turned to Kohlz, who was working the controls on the vox-set. 'Any luck?'

Kohlz's face twisted in frustration as he held the horn to his ear then threw it down in disgust. 'Nothing sir, its frag… It's non-functional.'

'No dust-off then,' moaned another of Bukin's men.

'Get moving,' Flint ordered, folding his storm coat back to reveal his holstered bolt pistol. 'And Bukin? Keep your men in line, or else I will.'

TWO
Absolutio

A piercing scream echoed the length of carceri chamber *Absolutio*, the vault resounding to the murder of another claviger-warden. The cry ended as suddenly as it started, a man's death marked by a sudden tearing sound and a wet thud.

Argusti Vahn, a convict of Carceri *Absolutio*, waited as the echoes faded away. A wiry-framed man in his thirties, Vahn's eyes had once been compared to those of a feral sump-rat. His features had always been lean and sharp and since being incarcerated in this hellish place had become even more so. His hair had become matted into long dread-locks and his arms were decorated with tattoos. Some took the form of pious script and images of beatific saints; others far less wholesome phrases and images. One of the tattoos, applied to side of his throat, was still new. It was a twelve-digit convict identification number.

To Vahn, the claviger-warden's unseen death was an opportunity. The scream covered his footsteps as he sprinted the length of the high, steel gantry. As the sound receded Vahn ducked back into the shadows, his breathing heavy and his eyes stinging with sweat.

Vahn's breath sounded raucously loud in the sudden quiet. Pushing himself further into the shadows between rust-streaked conduits, he took a moment to steady himself and get his bearings. The carceri chamber was a vast space with cliff-like rockcrete walls stratified by gantries and countless cell portals. Heavy generatoria machinery reared from the cold ground like rusty stalagmites or clung from the barrel-vaulted ceiling like corroded stalactites. Another scream sounded, this one more distant. Vahn guessed that the rebel convicts had moved on to carceri chamber *Benefacti*. A bloodthirsty roar sounded as the scream faded away, confirming Vahn's suspicion. The murderers were moving east through Vestibule 12, away from *Absolutio*.

Life in the vast geothermal penal generatorium complex of Alpha Penitentia was no easy prospect, even before the uprising that had erupted around a month ago. Now, it was a living hell. The entire complex had descended into anarchy and bloodshed and Vahn had been running ever since. That thought brought Vahn back to the present and he quickly scanned left and right to ensure no other convict-workers were nearby. The gantry was clear, for the moment at least, and the vast expanse of the carceri chamber below appeared not to harbour any immediate threats. The hunched forms of other refugees lurked in the shadows between the vast engines, ragged and desperate not to get caught up in the madness that had gripped the complex. Emerging from the shadows and passing quickly along the length of the gantry, Vahn purged the other refugees from his mind. They were weak and they would die. Vahn was getting out of this hellhole, whatever it took.

Movement up ahead, near the portal to Vestibule 18. Vahn slowed his pace and cursed himself for a fool. He'd been crossing the vast floor of northern *Absolutio* and allowed himself to take the quickest path at the expense of keeping a bolthole nearby. This time, there were no shadows to melt into as the rebels showed themselves.

'Speak!' the nearest rebel bawled, his slurred challenge echoing down the vestibule behind him. Vahn studied the shadows beneath the portal and saw there, forty metres ahead, a small group of men. They were obviously rebels, for no refugee would have challenged him so boldly.

Vahn stood his ground and held his tongue, his gaze fixed on the rebel group.

'Speak!' the rebel repeated. 'Name your allegiance or go the way of the clavigers.'

Vahn had no intention of meeting any such fate but the vestibule the rebels were blocking led towards the central spire. He had no choice but to pass them. If he could gain entry to the spire he could make his way to the gate hall, and then freedom. There was only one thing for it.

'*Absolutio*,' Vahn answered. 'Let me pass.'

A brief pause followed as the rebels conferred amongst

themselves. Then the original speaker called out again, 'If you're *Absolutio*, what business have you in the spire?'

Maybe the rebel wasn't as stupid as he sounded, Vahn thought. Guessing how things would play out he loosened his stance and shook out the tension in his neck as he prepared to draw the crudely sharpened iron bar secreted in his hip pocket. Knowing he'd need to get close to the vestibule portal before things got out of hand Vahn started walking, slowly but with confidence, towards the rebels.

'Stop!' the rebel slurred, stepping forward with his cronies at his side. 'None are allowed this way except those Strannik gives licence.'

That made sense, Vahn thought. Strannik, a fallen noble and former Guard colonel, was the figurehead of the uprising. He'd already decorated kilometres of gantry with the corpses of the claviger-wardens and his many rivals. Any convict from *Absolutio* not serving in one of his gangs was automatically assumed to be an enemy and treated as such.

'I wouldn't know of that,' said Vahn as he advanced on the group, stalling for time before the inevitable outbreak of violence. 'Strannik said nothing of the sort to me.'

As the distance closed, Vahn got a clear look at the opposition. There were three of them front and centre and at least another three lurking in the shadows on either side of the portal. The speaker was a twisted and deformed individual with his scratch-inked tats declaring his unending loyalty to his home – the agri-world of Pan. The man's limbs appeared grossly mismatched as if each had been grafted on, having been obtained from a different donor.

'Strannik said nothing *at all* to you, stranger,' the man said. As Vahn closed the other's features were revealed. Though weasel-like in appearance, cold hard guile shone from his mismatched eyes. 'You'll halt right now.'

Vahn didn't. He continued his advance. Another distant scream echoed through the cloying air, followed by the sharp clink of iron chains. The men on either side of the leader stepped out wide.

Vahn stopped ten metres from the other man. The rebel sneered, revealing a set of incongruously pristine white teeth that must have cost him a fortune in pen-scrip or other favours. He leaned his head back as if bored of Vahn's behaviour but Vahn noted the glance the gesture was intended to mask. It was a signal to the others lurking in the shadows – be ready.

The man fixed Vahn with a dark glare. 'The colonel wants the likes of you penned up,' he leered. 'He wants you for meat, for them down below.'

Vahn reached into his thigh pocket and withdrew the iron bar. 'You can tell the colonel to find his meat someplace else.'

'Bad choice,' the leader sneered, then glanced towards the man at his left to issue an order.

Vahn had closed the distance in the time it took the leader to draw breath, the iron bar raised above his head. The other man saw his mistake a split second too late and could do nothing to avoid the blow that scattered his brains and his expensive teeth across the rockcrete floor.

Vahn barrelled onwards as the body crashed to the

ground, using the momentum of his charge to full advantage. The two cronies bellowed their outrage at the death of their leader and powered after Vahn. More shouts from further behind told him the rebels who had previously held back were now joining the pursuit.

Vahn dared not spare even a second to glance behind him as he sprinted towards the yawning portal of Vestibule 18. The rockcrete ground, ordinarily kept clear by punishment details, was strewn with the detritus of the uprising and Vahn was forced to slow his progress or stumble and fall. Moments later he was through the twenty metre-high portal and plunging headlong into the shadows of the passageway beyond. Each of Alpha Penitentia's vestibules was a corridor large enough to allow the passage of a thousand-strong labour shift or an entire squadron of the so-called 'witches' – armoured enforcement walkers. Most of the passageways joined the main carceri chambers, labour halls and other, secondary zones. Vestibule 18 however led to the complex's central core, the forbidden spire only accessible to the claviger-wardens and their bonded menials. The tunnel was two kilometres in length and Vahn had been counting on being able to breach whatever barrier waited at the far end. If he couldn't this would be the shortest and most abortive breakout attempt in the history of Carceri *Absolutio* and probably the whole of Alpha Penitentia.

More shouts sounded from behind as more of the colonel's murderers picked up Vahn's trail. Now he dared throw a brief glance over his shoulder only to see a mob of at least two-dozen pursuers silhouetted against the receding portal. Reinforcements were emerging from small service tunnels joining to the vestibule and each was baying for his blood. His heart pounding, Vahn spat a curse that would have earned him a stretch in the hard labour halls were any claviger-warden alive to hear it.

Then Vahn stumbled. His ankle turned as his shin struck something twisted, stiff and rotten sprawled across his path. The mob roared as it saw his plight but somehow Vahn kept his footing, pounding onwards through the gloom. As the portal receded the vestibule was plunged into ever-darker shadow. The majority of the lumen-strips that ordinarily illuminated the tunnel had been smashed, the remains of their glass casings crunching beneath Vahn's boots as he ran. He saw more of the twisted forms ahead and as he passed the first he realised they were the butchered remains of the claviger-wardens who had attempted to hold the vestibule when the uprising first erupted. Even in the low, flickering light of the surviving lumen-strips, Vahn saw the walls of the vestibule were daubed with obscene blasphemies in the wardens' blood. He had no doubt that he too would meet such a gruesome fate should the mob catch up with him.

Beneath the blood-daubed scrawls Vahn saw the remains of stencilled lettering. It told him he was approaching the halfway point in the tunnel. The mob had dropped back slightly, the undisciplined mass unable to match the speed of a single runner. Knowing that the remainder of his life would be measured in scant minutes if he couldn't shake his pursuers Vahn studied the darkness up ahead as he ran.

Would the gate into the central spire be open? He prayed it would, and he soon found out.

Vahn's heart sank as he closed on the end of the vestibule. He skidded to a halt, his boots kicking up sharp grit. He shouted a single-syllable curse word that echoed back down the vestibule to mingle with the roar of the pursuing mob. The portal was blocked by an armoured shield dropped from above, a defensive measure intended to seal the central spire from the carceri chambers and lock the claviger-wardens in until outside help arrived.

Hoots and whistles filled the tunnel as the mob saw Vahn halt. Their blood was up and they knew they had their prey cornered. Vahn looked about for an alternative escape route and saw several service tunnel entrances nearby. He moved sideways towards the nearest as the mob slowed their advance but as soon as he neared the mouth he saw movement inside. More rebel convicts waited within the service tunnel, blocking his last possible escape route.

Vahn hefted the iron bar. He tossed it spinning into the air and caught it one-handed in nonchalant, bloody-minded defiance of the mob. The first rank of rebel convicts slowed to a halt and those further back lapped around the flanks forming an impenetrable semicircle around Vahn. He glanced at the service tunnel entrance again as he weighed up his chances.

Two men stepped forward from the crowd. Vahn recognised them as the companions of the leader he'd slain earlier. One was a brute, his head bald and his nose little more than a squashed mass of scar tissue. The other was lanky and alert with black hair tied back into a tail and his face striped with dark red war paint. The latter was the first to speak.

'I reckon we'll take you living,' the man said. 'The colonel likes making examples…'

Nervous laughter rippled through the crowd as if its members felt relief in sharing a joke aimed at someone other than themselves. Vahn's mind was made up. He tensed his muscles and prepared to rush the entrance to the narrow service tunnel.

The taller of the two rebel convicts facing Vahn anticipated his move and leaped forward to block him. Vahn sprang past his attacker and twisted as he hit the ground hard an instant before a wickedly serrated shiv cut the air a hand's span from his face. The brute barrelled forward and shoved his mate out of the way in an attempt to stomp Vahn's face into the ground beneath his hobnailed boots. Vahn snatched his head aside and rolled forward towards the tunnel entrance. Another rebel convict appeared from out of nowhere with a length of spar, tipped with a coil of barbed wire held two-handed across his torso. Vahn continued his roll and ducked under the man's two-handed swing. He kicked upwards and crushed his adversary's jewels with his heel. The convict bellowed as he toppled to the ground and the route to the tunnel entrance was clear.

Vahn was up in a second and it wasn't a moment too soon. The mob was surging forward, an unruly mass of baying murderers intent on tearing him limb from limb despite its leaders' intention to drag him before the uprising's figurehead, Colonel Strannik. Vahn sprinted the last few metres to the tunnel entrance, readying himself to knock aside the figures he saw lurking there.

One of those figures stepped out from the entrance as he closed and levelled a crudely made firearm directly at his head. The weapon's barrel loomed large but there was nothing Vahn could do to avoid the inevitable blast.

'Get out of my way!' the bearer of the weapon ordered.

Acting on instinct, Vahn dodged to one side and dove into the tunnel entrance. The cramped space erupted in noise and smoke as the firearm discharged right into the mob. A cone of improvised pellets spat outwards to lacerate the exposed flesh of a dozen rebel convicts. While not powerful enough to kill outright, the weapon caused its victims to tumble screaming to the ground and those behind them to trip over the writhing bodies.

'Time to get moving!' Vahn's deliverer shouted. The small tunnel was dark and still filled with the acrid smog of the weapon's discharge. All he could see of the firer was a hulking shadow but Vahn sensed there were at least another three people in the tunnel with him.

Before he could respond the firer shoved him hard in the back and propelled him into the tunnel's depths. 'I don't have time to reload this junker,' the man shouted. 'Move now or stick around, your choice!'

Vahn wasn't used to being ordered around, not by other convicts at least, but the man was right. As he pressed on, three convicts ahead and one behind, Vahn called out to no one in particular, 'Anyone know where you're going?'

The convict in front answered, her voice strangely accented. 'Same way you were I reckon, but the clavies locked us out.'

'You got any sort of plan?' Vahn called as he ran.

It was the convict behind who answered. 'Didn't get that far. You coming along sort of interrupted us.'

Vahn would be having words with the man once they were clear of immediate danger. Angry shouts came from the tunnel entrance but Vahn guessed the pursuers had realised they had little chance of catching up with the fleeing convicts in the confines of the tunnel. As the group ran on, the sounds of pursuit faded away until Vahn was reasonably sure they were safe.

'Wait,' Vahn shouted as he slowed to a halt. 'We need to get our bearings.'

The tunnel bored onwards in a straight line, its walls lined with ancient pipe work and long-decayed cabling. The floor was under an inch of chemical spill and what little illumination lit the convicts' path was afforded by a combination of barely working lumen bulbs, as old as the complex, and the faint luminescence of the polluted liquid.

'Where are we?' said Vahn. 'Somewhere north of *Honourius*?'

The female convict he had spoken to earlier appeared from the shadows. She sported a mohican dyed acid green and her mouth and nose was covered with a matt black rebreather. The mask and general demeanour marked her out as one of the so-called chem-dogs, an anarchic bunch Vahn had encountered long ago in what seemed like a previous life. How she had ended up on Furia Penitens he had no idea, given that her home world of Savlar was itself one huge penal facility. 'Must be,' she said, her voice sounding through the grilles on her mask. 'But we don't know where this tunnel leads.'

Another convict stepped forward into the light. The man had the martial bearing of a former Guardsman, as did many of the convicts from carceri chamber *Absolutio*. 'It leads either to the spire or to Carceri *Honourius*,' he said. 'Either way, we need to keep moving.'

'Wait up,' said Vahn as he read the tensions in the group. Whoever these convicts were they hadn't been together long and they didn't have much of a plan. 'Have you heard anything from *Honourius*? Has it fallen too?'

The two convicts glanced uncertainly at one another and a third stepped forward. The man was short and wiry, his hair close-cropped and by the scab on the side of his head he'd recently lost an ear. 'All we've heard is the proclamations from the colonel,' he said. 'He's demanding the entire complex follows his orders, else we all get fed to the sump.'

'Then we have to get out,' said Vahn. 'I'm not following that bastard and his murderous goons.'

'Then it's the spire,' the woman said, with a distinct lack of enthusiasm.

'Vestibule 16,' said Vahn.

'And if that's barred too?' said the big man behind Vahn.

'Then we find another way in.'

And with that, Argusti Vahn assumed command of a handful of convicts desperate to escape the madness of an entire penitentiary installation consumed by the bloodiest uprising in its history.

THREE
Bridgehead

The trek from the site of the wrecked drop-ship to the regimental deployment area was a hard one, and it took Commissar Flint and the survivors of his staff section all night to complete. The men had remained sullenly quiet throughout most of the journey, and when they had spoken it had generally been to grumble incoherently in the Vostroyan dialect. Flint was well used to serving alongside Imperial Guardsmen drawn from different planets with different cultures, and he was well capable of unpicking the meaning of unfamiliar terms, most of them stemming from a common tongue. The word *khekk* was uttered frequently, an obvious Vostroyan curse, as was *chevek*, a term Flint suspected was being used to refer to him and meant something like 'stranger' or 'unwelcome'. A dark glance at the last man to have spoken it had forestalled any further use of the term, earning a resentful silence from the provosts that lasted several hours.

Night time on Furia Penitens was, they soon discovered, cold and windswept, the stiff breeze carrying a sharp, chemical taint the like of which Flint had only ever encountered on far more developed planets. He knew it to be the result of the power generation processes utilised in the massive penal generatorium of Alpha Penitentia, whereby a cocktail of liquids were pumped down into the bedrock at high pressure, where they were heated by the highly irradiated minerals far below. When those liquids were returned to the surface they were equally radioactive and the arcane systems of the generatoria utilised them as a relatively stable form of fuel. The one thing Flint had been unable to fathom was the purpose of the entire enterprise. There was nothing that needed the power Alpha Penitentia produced – the prisoners might as well be breaking rocks.

Around midnight, Flint had been gripped by an unsettling sensation, one he hadn't felt since his storm trooper detachment had been ambushed by dominators in the rad-zones of Obediah Nine. Within ten minutes he was certain of it – they were being observed. Whoever it was, they were keeping their distance, but certainly, someone or *something* was out there in the barren wastes, tracking the small group's progress through the night.

'Mutants, sir,' Corporal Bukin stated coldly, his gruff voice low and conspiratorial.

'What?' said Flint, his eyes fixed on the shadowy rocks and

craters that dotted the land. Any one of them could be hiding an ambusher.

'Can't you smell them, sir?' Bukin growled. 'Mutants, I know it.'

'*How* do you know it?' Flint replied.

It was a few more steps before Bukin replied, his grizzled face scanning the wastes as he appeared to choose his words carefully. 'This regiment might be new to war, commissar. But I am not.'

'So you served in the Vostroyan defence forces,' Flint replied. 'So did every other trooper. You have particular experience?'

'I do,' Bukin cast a dark glance towards the commissar as he spoke. His scarred face appeared even more lined in that moment, though it may have been a trick of the gloomy ambient light. 'I was not always in the militias, sir. I served the Techtriarchs in... other ways before I was indentured.'

Something in the chief provost's tone made Flint slow to a stop and round on the other man. 'If there's something I need to know about your past, Corporal Bukin, you had better tell me now, before things get unpleasant. Out with it.'

The other provosts halted behind Bukin, while Kohlz stopped behind Flint. This was no place to be having a confrontation, not if they were being shadowed, but Flint was well aware he had to stamp his authority on these men, right now, or the balance of power would be perilously skewed.

The cold wind whipped Bukin's long moustaches across

his grox-ugly face as the man glowered back at Flint, clearly weighing up how, or even if, to respond. A number of his fellows shifted uncomfortably, and Flint knew exactly what they were thinking. Who would doubt them if they claimed the regiment's newly appointed commissar had perished in the crash, sucked through the wound in its side that had claimed several of their own number. Evidently, Kohlz saw it too, the aide's stance suddenly tense.

'I was known for a hunter, for a killer, of men and of mutants in the ruined factoriums of Vostroya.'

That made sense. With much of Vostroya's surface turned over to the sprawling manufactory complexes of its armaments industry, entire regions must fall from use and come to be infested with outcasts of all types. Men such as Bukin were needed, and they were paid handsomely for every mutant or recidivist hide they brought back from the ruins.

'I've killed too,' said Flint, his steely gaze fixed on Bukin's. 'Men, mutants and other things you should pray you never have to see. I've faced orks, tellarians and dominators and I'm still here to talk about it. Plenty of things have tried to kill *me*, Corporal Bukin, but none have managed it yet. Understood?'

Bukin glanced sullenly off into the wastes, then back at Flint. 'It's gone now,' he said flatly.

'I said,' Flint snarled, '"Understood?"'

'I understand, Commissar Flint,' Bukin replied as the wind stirred once more.

'Good,' said Flint. 'Now, what's gone?'

'The stinking things that were tracking us, commissar. You scared them off, I think…'

'Good,' said Flint. 'Let's get moving before they change their minds.'

It was sunrise the next morning before Flint and his section arrived at the drop zone. The regiment's vehicles were mustered in a huge, chaotic laager out on the flats in front of the prison complex, and the weary group had seen the landing ships departing around midnight. The sound of more than a hundred armoured transports jostling into position had rolled across the wastes and the stink of their exhaust hung heavy in the air. When he saw automated perimeter defences in the form of Tarantula sentry guns tracking back and forth for a target, Flint called for a halt. Soon, a Sentinel walker clanked over the rim of a wide, shallow crater, the heavy bolter mounted on the side of its enclosed cockpit locked menacingly on them. After a moment, a side hatch popped and swung outwards, the pilot leaning out to look down at Flint.

'Commissar?' he said, looking over the ragged group.

'Genius,' growled Katko, one of Bukin's provosts who had remained sullenly quiet for the entire trek.

Flint felt no need to confirm the pilot's insightful observation. 'Point us towards regimental command and carry on, dragoon.'

'Straight ahead, sir,' the pilot responded, emphasising the direction with a wave. Flint dismissed the sentry and led the group off in the direction of the command post. As he walked, he observed the various units that made up the 77th Firstborn, Chimera armoured transports grinding forward into something only vaguely resembling a regimental deployment.

'Corporal Bukin,' he said, the man increasing his pace to catch up. He nodded towards the scene of two Chimeras faced off bow to bow against one another, the commanders standing in the hatches and each yelling at the other to give way. 'This deployment is distinctly sub optimal. Get it in order, now.'

Corporal Bukin grinned nastily and offered his version of a salute before striding off in the direction of the confrontation with his provosts in tow. Flint had no idea whether or not Bukin or any of his crew were rated as marshals or banksmen. Frankly, it was more about authority and the ability to bang heads together than organisational skill.

'Kohlz?' said Flint. 'You can stay, if you can find another vox.'

'Yes, sir,' said Kohlz, grinning. 'I'll catch up with you at the command post'

In a moment Kohlz was dashing off to find the regimental quartermaster's post and Flint was alone. Resuming his walk towards the command post Flint studied the activity all around. With Bukin and his cronies now marshalling the Chimeras something resembling order was slowly imposing itself on the formerly chaotic activity. The provosts appeared amongst the worst disciplined of the regiment but they knew how to impose their will on others, making them ideal staffers for a commissar. The roar of engines filled the air as armoured transports were marshalled into company columns, which in turn were divided into platoon groups. The regiment consisted of five Chimera-borne armoured infantry companies, each made up of four or five platoons, in addition to the headquarters and the support companies. It was an impressive sight, though Flint had witnessed entire army groups deployed for battle at the outset of the Gethsemane campaign.

An open-topped Salamander scout transport rumbled along the line and Flint stepped aside to allow it past. The vehicle was headed for the command post, which Flint could now see up ahead. The regimental commander and his headquarters group had established themselves in a hard-shell prefab shelter at the centre of the laager with five Hydra air defence tanks forming a ring all about. Flint doubted there was any threat from the air, but then again, no one had expected the rebels to be able to launch a ground-to-orbit defence barrage either. He could hardly blame the man for taking precautions.

'Commissar Flint?' a voice called out as he strode into the command post. 'Over here, sir.'

The man's uniform insignia identified him as the regiment's chief intelligence officer. His face was underlit green by the multiple pict-slates of the tactical cogitation array he was consulting, a three-dimensional plan of the complex's main structures slowly revolving on the central screen.

'Major Herrmahn,' the officer said, proffering a hand.

After a moment, the commissar shook it, weighing the officer's character as he did so.

'Commissar Flint, reporting for duty.'

'Yes, sir,' the major grinned. 'I heard you took the scenic route down.'

'You could say that,' Flint replied, deciding he liked the intelligence officer but not wanting to waste any time on pleasantries. 'What's the situation?' said Flint, removing his peaked cap and running a hand through his dishevelled, jet-black hair in a vain attempt to maintain standards.

'Graf Aleksis means to get the regiment moving once he's finished talking with the installation's governor,' said Herrmahn, nodding towards the centre of the command post. Flint followed the gesture and saw the graf, a Vostroyan noble holding the concurrent rank of colonel, engaged in what looked like a faltering conversation over an intermittent two-way vox-link. The graf was familiar only by the files Flint had read during the long voyage to this new appointment, the two men yet to meet.

'So the governor's still alive? He's still in power?' Flint asked, wondering how the convicts had control of an orbital defence battery if that were the case.

'The situation is still unclear,' Herrmahn replied. 'As best we can ascertain the governor and his wardens are holed up in the gate hall,' he pointed to the pict-slate and a structure on the outer limits connected to the central spire by a kilometre long tunnel. 'Here.'

'And the rebels?' asked Flint.

'Unconfirmed,' said Herrmahn. 'As far as we know they might have the run of the entire complex.'

Even with just a cursory scan of Alpha Penitentia's schematics, Flint knew that if the rebels had control of the whole facility the force required to oust them might be far greater than a single regiment could bring to bear. The combined power plant and prison was as large as a city and as such represented one of the most arduous and costly types of battlefield to fight across. Vostroyan regiments were considered highly capable city-fighters, but the 77th was newly reconstituted and rated suboptimal, hence Flint's appointment to knock them into shape. Having recently been rebuilt from the ground up, the regiment was hardly more experienced than one newly elevated from a planetary defence force. Given the 77th's current status, the regiment's line companies would be reduced to ragged street gangs within days. Alpha Penitentia would swallow the regiment whole if the 77th was forced to fight on the rebels' terms. Even a veteran regiment such as those Flint had served alongside at Gethsemane would be hard-pressed and the 77th was anything but veteran.

With a gnawing sense of foreboding, Flint asked, 'So what's the graf's plan, major?'

The intelligence chief didn't have the chance to answer Flint's question, as the second-in-command, Lieutenant-Colonel Polzdam, called the command post to order. Two dozen officers and their aides stopped what they were doing and turned towards the centre of the post, the only sound that of the cogitation banks churning away in the background. Graf Aleksis had terminated his vox conversation with the governor of Alpha Penitentia and stepped up onto an ammunition crate.

'Gentlemen,' said Aleksis, scanning the faces of the gathered officers. If he noted Flint's arrival he gave no sign. 'As you have no doubt gathered, I have spoken with Governor Kherhart and now have sufficient information to proceed. The governor assures me he has control over the installation and is mustering his wardens to mount a full incursion. I have offered whatever aid he may require, and although he has no need of a full regimental deployment at this time he has agreed to meet to discuss the matter in greater depth.'

Aleksis nodded to a number of nearby officers, including Major Herrmahn. It was then that he acknowledged Flint's presence. 'Ah, commissar,' said the graf. 'Good to meet you. Finally. Are you able to join us?'

Flint's eyes narrowed but he decided not to show any reaction to the commanding officer's tone and the slight it implied. He slipped his peaked cap back onto his head and straightened out his black storm coat, still scuffed and dusty from the crash and subsequent trek, before replying.

'Of course, graf,' Flint replied through gritted teeth. 'I would be delighted.'

Dragoon Kohlz's shoulder was killing him, his arm nearly having been ripped from its socket by the commissar during the crash. He was alive and had survived his first planetfall operation, though only because of the intervention of an outsider, and a commissar at that. Kohlz had only been told he'd be Flint's aide-de-camp a few hours before the new commissar's arrival on the *Toil of Kossia* in orbit over Furia Penitens, and the two had barely had time to exchange a word before the drop. Kholz's first impressions were reasonably good – after all, Flint hadn't yet put a bolt-round through anyone's head for looking at him funny, which was pretty much all the rank and file expected of the Munitorum's morale officers.

Rotating the painful joint to work some life back into it Kohlz pressed on along a line of idling Chimeras, the crews and passengers busy loading supplies, securing stowage and camo nets or completing last minute checks. The morning air was filled with the growling of engines and the clanking of tracks. The only sound audible over the armoured vehicles was that of Corporal Bukin's provosts barking orders as they marshalled more carriers into line.

A Trojan support vehicle trundled along the column towing a heavily laden tracked trailer. Quickly scanning the markings stencilled on the side of the trailer Kohlz saw that it belonged to the regimental quartermaster's section and was conveying supplies from the drop zone established the day before to a holding area at the regiment's rear. Kohlz jumped up onto the trailer's tailgate as it overtook him, wincing as his wounded shoulder made its displeasure known once more. Five minutes later he was at the quartermaster post and looking for the officer in charge.

The supply post was a large plot surrounded by hastily erected blast shields and crowded with row upon row of ammunition and cargo crates. Kohlz located a prefab shelter but his path was blocked as a group of soldiers ambled towards him. Their intent was all too obvious.

'Where you going?' growled their leader. It was 'Slug' Slavast, the hated regimental bully.

Glancing around the post, Kohlz saw several more men closing in on him, each having stopped what they were doing amongst the stores as Slug confronted him. This was going to hurt.

'Drawing a new Number Four for the new commissar, Slu… Slavast,' said Kohlz, emphasising the fact that he was on official business.

'You provost now?' Slug crowed as he came to a halt uncomfortably close.

'We all have our orders, Slavast,' said Kohlz. 'Nothing I can do about it.'

Slug's face twisted into a cruel leer and he cocked his head at an angle as he replied, 'Something that *I* can do about it, *boy*.'

Slug withdrew an iron crowbar from his belt. 'Got a little message for Bukin and your provost friends…' he growled, pressing forwards and driving Kohlz back towards his cronies.

Flint stepped out of the regimental command post and took a deep breath of the exhaust-tainted air. His first impression of the 77th's officer cadre wasn't an especially positive one, though it confirmed the briefings he'd read in transit to Furia Penitens. With the exception of the intelligence chief Major Herrmhan, the officers were conforming to type.

They were bound by common ties of blood and lineage so tight they excluded anyone from the outside. In particular, Graf Aleksis's manner had been downright insulting, though from the officer's file he was potentially an able commander. Flint was the outsider here – the *chevek* – and would have to gain the graf's acceptance if he were to do his job as regimental commissar. Failing that, should the issues degrade the regiment's combat performance he would be forced to relieve Graf Aleksis of command, lethally if necessary.

But Flint had rarely had to execute a senior officer and more often than not it was to punish and contain overt cowardice or incompetence. As far as Flint could tell Aleksis was neither a coward nor incompetent, though he would only know that for sure once the regiment was engaged in combat.

Waiting for Dragoon Kohlz, Flint considered the issue of the distinct lack of discipline in the ranks. It seemed there was an odd disconnect between the officers and the troops as if the two were separated by impassable gulfs of class isolation. The rankers were drawn from the workers of Vostroya's endlessly sprawling manufactoria and the officers from the ruling 'Techtriarch' clans and clearly the two were unused to working together. What the 77th was lacking, Flint could see, was an effective middle-tier of sergeants and other non-commissioned ranks that could bridge the gap. Flint made a mental note to address the matter once the issue of the penal uprising was concluded.

Checking his wrist chron Flint decided his aide was long

overdue. Graf Aleksis would be setting off to meet the governor in less than thirty minutes and Flint was determined to be there with him. He could go without his aide but he valued the contact with the rankers and would sooner have Kohlz at his side. Deciding he had sufficient time, Flint set off in the direction of the quartermaster's post, expecting to encounter Kohlz at some point along the line of armoured vehicles.

Kohlz leaped sideways as Slug came at him, the crowbar passing centimetres from his head. Slug's accomplices, each one of them a brute from the logistics platoon, well-muscled from lugging ammo crates around, came after him. Thankfully he was faster and he got clear of his attackers to win himself a few brief seconds of breathing space.

Unfortunately, Kohlz now found his back to a sandbagged revetment and Slug was advancing on him once more. 'You taking your beating like a man?'

'Had I asked for it, yes,' Kohlz stalled, looking about for an escape route. 'But not from you.'

Slug grinned cruelly and his cronies laughed out loud. Getting a beating was hardly unusual amongst the lower ranks but it was normally administered by the junior non-coms as a means of punishing minor slip-ups without involving the chain of command. Had Kohlz invoked the wrath of a sergeant he wouldn't mind but he saw no reason to accept a beating from Slug just because he was in the wrong place at the wrong time.

Slug's eyes narrowed. 'Too good for us now, eh?' The

cronies chuckled mirthlessly at their leader's jibe.

Kohlz didn't bother answering. Instead, he started working his way along the revetment, hoping to keep his enemies occupied until he was close enough to the gate to make a dash for freedom.

'No you don't,' said Slug. 'Grab him!'

Four of Slug's accomplices started forward with a speed that belied their size. The closest jabbed an elbow down hard towards Kohlz's head but he ducked and dove clear. The next kicked out hard with an oversized ammo boot that caught Kohlz in the ribs and drove the air violently out of his lungs.

Winded, Kohlz fought for breath as he rolled clear of a second kick. A pair of meaty fists reached for his collar and pulled him upwards but he punched out, slamming his fist into a rock-hard abdomen. With panic rising within, Kohlz realised that his attacker hadn't even noticed the blow.

'Now that is not nice,' drawled Slug as he dragged Kohlz up by the shoulders, his wound flaring in pain at the rough handling. 'Will all be over soon...'

Kohlz sighed and screwed his eyes tight shut, resigning himself to the beating. He just prayed it would be over quickly and not rob him of too many teeth.

Seconds passed and nothing happened. Kohlz dared open an eye. Slug and his cronies had turned their backs on him and raised their arms. Beyond them, Kohlz saw Commissar Flint standing in the gate with his storm coat thrown back to focus attention on his holstered bolt pistol.

Great, thought Kohlz. Saved by a *chevek* twice in one day.

Andy Hoare

He'd be better off just letting me take the first beating...

'Is there a problem here, dragoons?' said Flint, his voice low and dangerous.

'No problem at all, commissar,' said Slug, his words dripping sarcasm.

Flint's eyes flicked back to his aide. 'Kohlz, did you draw the vox-set?' he said.

Realising he'd all but forgotten his reason for coming to the quartermaster post in the first place, Kohlz shook his head dumbly.

'Then do so,' said Flint. 'And leave me with these gentlemen for a moment.'

Kohlz nodded before extricating himself from the scene as quickly as he could. A few minutes later he'd drawn a new vox-set and hurried off through the gate. As he passed Flint the commissar was taking off his storm coat with deliberate slowness, placing it on a crate and dropping his peaked cap down on top. The last thing Kohlz saw was the commissar rolling up his sleeves as he advanced on Slug and his thugs.

Flint advanced at his own, slow and steady pace, his steely eyes fixed on Slug's now colour-drained face. The man had made his choice, now he had to face the consequences. The busy logistics area turned suddenly quiet as the other troopers sensed imminent violence.

Slug's eyes darted from Flint to his friends, then back again. 'What's your problem?' Slug drawled. 'I didn't do anything you need to get involved in.'

Flint's expression darkened still further, but he didn't reply.

Now certain what was about to happen, Slug was faced with a stark choice. Face a beating like he had expected of Kohlz, or maintain his nigh suicidal defiance of the new commissar. Spitting at the ground in front of Flint, Slug made the wrong choice. Turning his back contemptuously, he made to walk away. He only got three steps.

In a single, fluid motion, Flint strode forward and grabbed Slug's shoulder, spun him around and unleashed a pile-driver punch right into his face. The blow was delivered with such force that the other man's features were split wide open in a shower of blood and teeth.

Slug hit the ground hard, the only sign of life the wet gargle of blood-flecked breathing.

Flint stood over the sprawled form of the defeated bully, daring Slug's cronies to make a move. None did.

'Understood?' growled Flint, shaking out his fist as he looked around at the closest of Slug's accomplices. Slug coughed and struggled to rise, one hand wiping the blood from his split lower lip.

Slug nodded dumbly, unwilling to meet Flint's eye.

'This is your first warning,' Flint continued. 'I've been unusually charitable, but let me make this absolutely clear for you. There won't be a second chance.'

Flint turned his back on Slug before the other man could answer, and retrieved his cap and coat. As he walked away he heard the coughs and cursing of the wounded man as his lesson sunk in. Dragoon Slavast was poison. The sooner the regiment was engaged in combat operations the better. Slug and his circle could either prove themselves worthy of the uniform they wore or condemn themselves to the full sanctions of the Commissariat.

If it came to that, Flint would have no qualms about enacting a field execution on Slug and any of his gang that wanted to join in. A swift bolt-round to the head administered in front of the ringleader's underlings was normally sufficient to impose order once and for all. It was a fine balance though, as his training and experience told him. Many commissars, especially newly appointed ones, overstepped the mark and made themselves so many enemies within a regiment that their actions actually made things worse. Straightening his cap, Flint glanced around at the passing Firstborn dragoons as he walked out of the gate. The regiment had a proud history indeed, but these men were no elite, not yet at least. Some would need discipline beaten into them while others would need an example to follow. As commissar, it was Flint's duty to fulfil both needs.

Shrugging on his storm coat, Flint found Kohlz waiting up ahead, the new vox-set slung over his back. The aide looked distinctly uncomfortable and Flint knew why.

'That was nothing to do with you, dragoon, understood?'

When Kohlz failed to answer, Flint halted and turned on his aide. 'Speak freely, dragoon,' he said. 'You're my aide-de-camp and I need you fully functional if I'm to do my job.'

'Yes, sir. I understand, but Slug holds grudges and he has support.'

Flint considered Kohlz's words for a moment, scanning the closest of the passing troops. 'How many?'

'Right now, sir?' Kohlz answered. 'Just a few meatheads in the supply platoon, maybe a couple more here and there.'

'But?' said Flint, knowing there would be one.

'But they will be more,' Kohlz continued. 'And that lot have never accepted Bukin and the rest of the provosts. Now we're here and people aren't happy about the mission, sir. It's not really what they imagined.'

Them too, thought Flint. As if the officers weren't bad enough the ranks were in on it too. Well, maybe that would give them something to agree on. If the officers and the ranks *both* wanted the chance to get stuck in and prove themselves, Flint just had to find a way of getting both sides to play nicely together. Maybe then they'd gel and act like they deserved the regimental colours they were honoured to carry.

But to achieve it the regiment would need a common enemy. Flint looked towards the central spire of Alpha Penitentia with its ring of chimneys and cooling towers, its form dark and imposing against the morning sky. He could understand why the officers as well as the ranks were uneasy about the mission. For the officers there was little glory to be had in such a deployment, and for the ranks it simply offered a myriad of ways of getting crippled or killed. Either the penal generatorium would provide them the motivation or he would.

'Sir?' Kohlz interrupted Flint's chain of thought. The vox-horn was at his ear, a message coming in from the regimental command post. 'The graf is ready to depart for Alpha Penitentia, sir.'

'Let's go then, dragoon,' said Flint. Let's see what this place has in store for us.'

Three hundred metres up the rockcrete central spire of Alpha Penitentia, Argusti Vahn stood at the edge of a rail-less ledge, the wind stinging his eyes and whipping his dreadlocks into a medusa-like halo. Despite the discomfort and the danger of falling, Vahn leaned out still further as he gripped the embrasure's frame, thrilling to the novel sensation of the fierce gust on his face.

But Vahn wasn't standing there just for his health. The night before, a sentry manning the vantage point had heard the unmistakable sound of heavy transports landing on the plain outside. Vahn and his band now consisted of three-dozen or so convicts, all of whom had refused to join the anarchy that had embraced the complex. Of the first four convicts he had met as he fled Carceri *Absolutio*, one, whose name Vahn had never even learned, had died while more had since joined his band. Vahn, Vendell, Skane and Becka had become the core of the outcast group but Vahn had remained very much at its head.

So much dust had been thrown up in the initial landings that the convicts had been able to see very little of the landing operation. But they'd seen the lights of the transports as they departed around midnight, the flaring jet wash visible as the huge vessels laboured back towards orbit. When the sun had risen Vahn had assumed his watch and now that the dust of the landings had cleared he was able to make out something of what was going on down below.

'Guard?' asked Vendell from behind Vahn, obviously uncomfortable approaching the ledge.

Before Vahn could answer, Skane cut in from further back inside the chamber. 'Who else you reckon it would be, Vendell?' sneered the big convict. 'Battle Sisters? Come to punish you for all those dirty thoughts?'

Skane pushed his way through and stood at Vahn's side looking down at the activity far below. Skane was an Elysian, late of the famous drop-trooper regiments and as such had no problem with the height.

Shading his eyes with a raised hand, Skane said, 'What regiment?'

'Armoured infantry,' said Vahn. 'Mission like this, they can't have come far.'

'Vostroya?' said Skane. 'Firstborn?'

'Most likely,' said Vahn, the distance making it impossible for him to make out any unit insignia.

'Unless they shipped a unit in from one of the subsectors north of Finial,' said Skane, though his expression told Vahn the other man was clutching at straws.

'No,' said Vahn. 'Firstborn, straight from Vostroya.'

Skane looked Vahn in the eye. 'You served with them?'

Vahn looked away, resuming his study of the mass of armoured vehicles slowly mustering into company columns below. A pair of Chimeras, flanked by ungainly Sentinel walkers, were crawling forwards towards the installation's gate hall. He had no desire to share the details of his military service, with Skane or with anyone else.

'Not recently,' said Vahn, 'been a little... sidetracked.'

'I hear that,' Skane grinned, evidently taking the hint. Though the burly Élysian was prone to acting the hard man with the other convicts, he seemed to have accepted Vahn as the group's unofficial leader, a fact for which Vahn himself was grateful. He would have taken Skane on had he needed to. 'So what now?'

In Vahn's opinion, the regiment deployed below was their only hope of survival but in what form he wasn't so sure. The Firstborn might simply kill everyone in the complex, not caring who had and who hadn't joined in the murder and chaos of the uprising. Alternately, Vahn's group might be able to link up with the Guard, but then what? Return to incarceration? Be put on trial? The only other option Vahn could think of was to crawl into a deep, dark hole and wait the whole thing out. That option was out – Vahn had never run before, a fact that, ironically, was at least partially responsible for his incarceration in Alpha Penitentia.

'Get the guys together,' said Vahn, pushing himself back into the chamber. 'We can get out of here, but the options might not look too attractive.'

The Chimera Flint was riding in ground to a halt with a rumbling of gears. Flint hauled on the rear hatch release and the back of the passenger compartment swung down to slam into the dusty red ground. The commissar was the first out, Kohlz and the line infantry squad assigned to headquarters security detail tramping out behind him.

Flint and his aide hadn't been invited to ride along with Aleksis and the command group. Frankly, he was glad.

'Spread out,' Flint ordered the men of the security detail as the second Chimera pulled up beside the first. The escorting Sentinel walkers fanned out wide, their chin-mounted multi-lasers tracking back and forth protectively. As the troops dispersed in a wide semicircle around the two armoured vehicles, Flint looked up at the vast bulk of Alpha Penitentia.

The complex's massive gate hall reared fifty metres high and more, its rockcrete bulk dominated by a mighty iron portal that seemed almost large enough for a Battle Titan to walk through. The gate was surrounded by clusters of wall-mounted spy-lenses and antennae trained on the ground in front. The corroded surface of the gates was embellished with reliefs depicting various scenes from the Imperial histories. Etched in letters three metres high was part of a legend, what was visible through the corrosion reading, …*and those who dwell below take vengeance on him who shall swear false oath*. Flint recognised the fragment as an allusion to a pre-Imperial text, all that remained of the writings of a scribe revered on old Terra. It was grimly apposite, given the setting.

'The signal,' Aleksis ordered his vox-officer.

The aide spoke into his vox-horn, a brief conversation passing all but unheard as the group waited. A cluster of spy-lenses mounted on the wall nearby whirred and clicked as some unseen operator zoomed in on the men waiting outside. Then the wailing of a distant klaxon started up, soon followed by a low grinding of ancient gears.

Flint felt the ground beneath his feet tremble before

a dark split appeared in the vast portal. The rumbling of huge machine systems grew almost deafening as the split widened to reveal the shadowed interior of the gate hall. It struck Flint that these gates hadn't been opened in many years, the join marred by corrosion which crumbled to the ground in powdery rivulets as the two halves separated.

The graf and his second-in-command waited patiently with heads raised as if the spectacle before them was nothing out of the ordinary. Though the gate hall must have had other, secondary portals, someone had decided that the delegation was of such status that the main gates should be opened like a triumphal arch awaiting the victory march of a returning army.

With a juddering motion, the opening of the gates halted with the gap between them only five metres wide. The screaming of tortured gears filled the air then disengaged just as suddenly before falling silent. Evidently, the gates hadn't been maintained well and opening completely had become impossible.

'Security detail forward,' Flint ordered, regardless of proper procedure. 'Secure the portal.'

'Really, Flint,' said Aleksis. 'I'm sure that isn't necessary.'

'With respect,' replied the commissar, drawing his bolt pistol and racking the slide for effect. 'This installation is all but under the control of an army of mutinous killers.'

Aleksis looked to his second-in-command and Polzdam nodded his agreement. Feeling he'd won a small victory of sorts, Flint strode forward to join the security detail. Its members had taken position within the shadowed opening with lasguns aimed cautiously into the darkness.

The inner edges of the gates were embedded with piston-like bars, which when locked would bolt the gates against the strongest of attacks. As he passed, Flint noted that the locks were intended to protect against an impact from within as well as without. The masons had evidently planned for all eventualities, including the need to lock an uncontrolled population of convict-workers inside. The legend engraved upon the face of the iron gates came back to Flint's mind. He'd seen the inside of some of the most secure penal facilities the Imperium maintained, including the gulags of the Lazuli Salient and the mass correction-plants of the Delphic Bastion Worlds. While all had been constructed to repel outside assault, none had been built to resist such a heavy attack from within. No convict should have been armed with any weapon weightier than an iron bar ripped from a cell window.

'Portal clear, sir,' reported the security detail's squad leader over his shoulder as he tracked his lasgun left and right. 'Proceed?'

Flint halted at the man's side. The sergeant was wearing the Firstborn's full battle dress – deep red, knee-length greatcoat with chainmail hauberk and gold-chased armour plating. He wore the distinctive shaggy fur headgear of the Firstborn and his face was obscured by a bulky rebreather. His goggles were raised and his eyes were all Flint could see of his face. 'Wait,' ordered Flint, acting on instinct.

A scuffing sound echoed out of the darkness beyond the

portal, followed by the tread of heavy boots. The sound got louder and soon Flint realised what it was.

'Stow weapons,' Flint hissed to the warriors around him as he holstered his bolt pistol. 'Now.'

'Sir?' said the sergeant, squinting into the darkness as his lasgun tracked the sound approaching.

'Do it, man!' Flint growled through clenched teeth. When the sergeant still failed to understand the gravity of the situation, Flint reached out and forced the lasgun down towards the ground. A moment later the man stowed it by slinging it over his shoulder.

'Sir,' the squad leader started. 'What's–'

'Halt!' ordered a deep, flat voice from the darkness. The sound of footsteps halted with a scrape of metal on stone and was replaced by the whine of whirring servos.

'Stay perfectly still,' Flint whispered.

A needle-thin beam of red light lanced out from the darkness and swept across Flint and the members of the security detail one by one.

'Weapons detected,' the voice intoned. 'Threat index zero-zero-sigma. Proceed.'

'Proceed where?' the squad leader whispered.

'Not us,' Flint hissed back. 'Just wait.'

The metallic clang of a large switch being thrown resounded through the portal and the darkness was dispelled in an instant as blinding arc lights were activated. For a moment, Flint could see nothing but blazing white light before his eyes began to adjust and take in the scene before him.

Flint and the security detail were standing in the entrance

to the gate hall, a massive reception building rearing so high that even the powerful arc lights couldn't illuminate the full extent of its interior. All Flint could make out of the hall's construction was the marble flooring, which although wrought with outstanding artistry was so obscured by grit and detritus its wondrous patterns were all but unreadable.

The speaker, Flint saw as his eyes adjusted to the glare, was the largest ward-servitor he had ever faced. A hulking torso, so bulky it must have been that of an ogryn, was enhanced with all manner of pneumatic augmetics, and one arm had been surgically replaced with a vehicle-grade heavy bolter. The other arm terminated not in a meaty fist but a multi-lensed augur pod, the source of the red beam that had swept the men for weapons. The servitor's half-metal face was expressionless, its surviving features slack-jawed and imbecilic as its single organic eye rolled back in its socket.

Despite the servitor's lack of intelligence or will, Flint knew that to show any hint of aggression would trigger a hard-wired response and cause it to unleash a torrent of explosive shells that would wipe the security detail out in a second.

'Stand down order,' a new voice came from behind the ward-servitor and beyond the glare of the arc lights. 'Proto-col helix.'

The ward-servitor's shoulders slumped forward with a hiss of pneumatics and its weapon turned barrel down towards the marble floor. The arm bearing the augur pod remained raised however and the single organic eye darted to and fro in its socket.

More footsteps sounded, but these were sharp and precise

where the ward-servitor's had been heavy and solid. A silhouette appeared against the arc-light glare and a figure stepped forward. The man was slightly shorter than Flint and clad in a form-fitting hardshell of glossy black. The figure's face was obscured by a featureless black visor plate which scanned left and right as he came to a halt.

'Commissar Flint,' the commissar said, his cold eyes boring into the figure's black visor face. All he saw was his own reflection. '77th Vostroyan Dragoons.'

The figure nodded sharply at Flint as the graf's command group approached from behind.

'I am Claviger-Primaris Averun Gruss,' the black-clad figure stated, his deep voice resounding from phonocasters secreted in the plates of his armour. 'Seneschal-Marshal to Lord Kherhart.'

Gruss bowed as Aleksis stepped forward next to Flint.

'Welcome to Alpha Penitentia.'

'Shut the hell up and settle down,' Skane growled as Vahn stalked into the chamber the outcast convict-workers were using as a mess hall. Most obeyed the burly Elysian without question, knowing full well the nasty streak that ran right through him. Those who didn't get the message straight away were soon hushed by neighbours who could see that something was up.

Vahn waited a moment as the last few stragglers sat down on the floor or one of the battered crates littering the chamber. The room had once been a medicae bay, the white tiles that had once clad its walls now cracked or shattered across the floor. Articulated gurneys were suspended from the ceiling, some bearing long-dead lumen bulbs, others the remnants of drill-head medical instruments of indeterminate purpose.

'Listen up,' said Vahn, his gaze sweeping the motley group. Every man and woman assembled before him was as scruffy as an underhive scum-blagger, their features drawn after weeks of hunger and tension. White eyes looked back at him from dirt-caked faces and each outcast wore a rough and ready assortment of ragged convict uniforms and salvaged workwear. Frankly, Vahn was grateful for the fresh breeze gusting through the open embrasure in the next chamber.

'What's happening?' called out 'Rotten' Stank from the front row. 'They coming for us again?'

'Depends who "they" are, Rotten,' Vahn replied, grinning as he answered. Despite the interruption, he liked Stank. It was hard not to like a man who had sniffed out three of Colonel Strannik's infiltration gangs and saved the entire group each time. 'Looks like we've got company out on the plains.'

'Space Marines?' said someone else and a round of nervous laughter rippled through the group. Vahn gave them a moment, despite Skane's frown, but kept his own expression neutral.

'This is serious,' said Vahn. By the tone of his voice they could tell it was. 'It's the Imperial Guard.'

The laughter cut out at that, to be replaced with a hushed murmur. 'We're fragged then!' someone shouted from the back rank, drawing a chorus of agreement. At times like this Vahn was hardly surprised this lot had been booted out of their regiments and washed up in a Munitorum forced labour penal facility. Vahn saw Skane's expression darken and decided to get a grip before the big drop-trooper busted some heads.

'It's the Imperial Guard,' Vahn repeated, this time injecting a note of cold authority into his voice. 'And that raises questions.'

The crowd quietened down a bit and Vahn pressed on. 'Way I see it, we got two choices.'

Now the crowd fell totally silent, three-dozen dirty faces trained on Vahn. 'We hide from them, or we join them.'

By the darting glances that passed between many of the convicts Vahn could tell that neither option was especially attractive. There was no easy way to say it, so he pressed on. 'If we hide, they'll find us, or just burn the whole place down around us. If we join them, chances are we'll end up somewhere just like this place.'

'But we'll be alive,' Vendell spoke up.

'Either way,' said Vahn, 'it's a gamble.'

'You've already decided,' said Solomon, a gangly man from the world of Jopall. Clever guy, thought Vahn.

'I know which I'd prefer,' said Vahn. 'But we're all in this together and we need to agree before we do anything.' Vahn left it unsaid that the whole thing might go completely to hell and he didn't want to cop the blame if that happened.

'If we join them,' said Rotten, 'we get a second chance. We could leg it later on.'

'Possibly,' said Vahn. 'But getting to them without getting slotted is likely to be hard enough.'

'And they'll be going in hard on Strannik,' added Becka, her arms folded across her chest as she leaned nonchalantly against the wall behind Vahn. 'The crossfire's gonna get messy.'

'I say we risk it,' said Stank. 'Better that than wait here for them or Strannik to wheedle us out.' Others nodded, the idea of for once taking control of their lives finding favour over the thought of hiding while it all went to hell.

'My thoughts exactly,' grinned Vahn, and Skane, Becka and Vendell nodded in agreement. In truth, the four of them had already agreed which option they preferred.

'Which means we'll need to fight our way out,' he continued before he could be interrupted. 'We hit the perimeter hard and we don't stop moving. Even,' he added gravely, 'if not everyone makes it.'

'So,' said Solomon as the gravity of the situation sank in. 'We voting?'

Looking around the faces of the convicts, Vahn said, 'Looks like we're agreed.'

'Time to look lively then, people,' growled Skane. 'We got work to do.'

FOUR
Complication

Claviger-Primaris Gruss stepped aside as the regimental command group entered the audience chamber of Governor Kherhart, lord of Furia Penitens. Flint allowed the graf to enter first, having decided to hang back and observe for a while and only intervene should he deem it truly necessary. He had a feeling there was more at play here than the briefings had communicated and he wanted to gauge just what sort of an officer Graf Aleksis really was. Short of standing at his side in battle, that was a difficult judgement to make, even for a commissar as experienced as Flint.

The chamber appeared part office and part throne room. A stone plinth three metres high dominated the room. On it was set a huge bureau made of ancient wood. Behind the bureau was a high-backed seat padded with worn leather and on that seat sat the robed and periwigged Governor Kherhart, a parchment held up to his face obscuring his features. The chamber itself was lined in panels of the same wood used in the construction of the bureau and faded, gilt-framed paintings showing portraits of stern-faced past governors looked down at the visitors. Every flat surface in the chamber was strewn with scrolls, tomes and parchments and the scent of spilled ink hung heavy in the dusty air.

'My lord,' said Claviger-Primaris Gruss, his armour's phonocasters projecting his voice louder than before. 'Our visitors.'

There was an awkward silence during which Flint and the officers of the 77th studied the back of the parchment obscuring the governor's face. A moment later the parchment was discarded to a pile on the bureau and the governor's face was looking down at his visitors, blinking in mild surprise.

'What?' Governor Kherhart barked, his voice almost as loud as Gruss's.

'Our visitors, my lord,' said Gruss, his phono-casters turned up even louder.

'Ah!' exclaimed the governor loudly before groping about the chaotic surface before him. At length he found a bulky, brass-rimmed optical lorgnette that he held up by its long handle before his eyes. Suddenly, Kherhart's formerly myopic eyes appeared huge and threatening as he glowered down at the officers. Switching his gaze towards Gruss, the governor said, 'Proceed, then.'

'My lord Callistus Kherhart,' Gruss announced formally, his machine-enhanced voice almost painfully loud. 'Master of the Alpha Penitentia facility and Imperial Commander

of the world of Furia Penitens and her associated sys-
tem domains. Lord High Designate of the Departmento
Munitorum,' he continued, 'Scion of Vostroya, third Heir-
Presumptive to the seat of the Anhalz Techtriarch clan.'

Flint's eyes snapped across to Aleksis, who he knew from
his briefings to be a member of the same noble line. The
graf stepped forward to the base of the plinth and bowed
deeply to the governor, who glowered down at him, his
eyes appearing huge and threatening through the lenses
of the lorgnette. 'Graf Klass Aleksis, also of the Anhalz, my
lord.'

'Ah!' said Kherhart again, pulling a sheet of parchment
from a pile before him and holding it at arm's length as he
scanned the lines of spidery text inscribed upon its surface.
'Cousin?'

'Third cousin, I believe, my lord,' demurred Aleksis. 'Once
removed, at least.'

'What?' said Kherhart. 'Speak up, man!'

'Third cousin, sir!' Aleksis repeated twice as loud.

'Hmm,' said Kherhart. 'The Dzerzhinsky Anhalz, I take it?'

'Indeed, my lord,' shouted Aleksis, bowing slightly as he
answered.

'Good,' said Kherhart, turning his gaze from the graf as
if noticing the presence of the rest of the delegation for
the first time. His grotesquely exaggerated eyes scanned
the officers, settling on Flint with a scowl. 'And you bring
companions?'

'Yes, my lord,' replied Aleksis as loud as he dared. 'As you
know, we must speak of reclaiming your generatorium.'

'Ah,' said Kherhart. 'Yes, that.'

Flint's eyes narrowed in suspicion.

'All under control now, thank you, cousin.'

Aleksis blinked rapidly but did a sterling job of masking his confusion. Meanwhile, the governor returned his attention to the parchments before him, lifting one at arm's length as he started to read.

Aleksis coughed with obvious intent. 'My lord?'

Governor Kherhart lowered the mechanical lorgnette and brought the parchment he was reading right up to his face as he squinted at the text.

'My lord?' Aleksis repeated.

'What?' Governor Kherhart exclaimed, raising the lorgnette to his eyes once more. 'Ah, yes,' he shouted.

'Dismissed!'

The door to the governor's audience chamber closed with a resounding boom and Flint turned on Aleksis. 'What the hell just happened, colonel?' he demanded.

'Graf,' interjected Lieutenant-Colonel Polzdam. 'You may not address–'

'Yes, I *may*,' said Flint through gritted teeth. 'And I will. That's why I'm here. *Graf*?'

Aleksis raised his chin to look down his nose at Flint before shaking his head in obvious frustration. 'It's fine,' the graf said to his second-in-command. 'The commissar has every right to know.'

'Know what, graf?' said Flint, softening his tone slightly.

Aleksis glanced around the panel-lined antechamber,

his eyes lingering on a number of faded portraits hung in nooks along its walls. 'Lord Kherhart outranks me,' he said.

Flint blinked in confusion before realising that the graf wasn't talking about the military chain of command. 'Go on.'

'He's Techtriarch,' said Aleksis. 'Anhalz, like me.'

'And?' said Flint.

'You have much to learn of this region of the Imperium, commissar,' said Aleksis. 'We're of the same Techtriarch clan,' he continued. 'And, by the dictates of familial quartering, he is my senior and I am bound to obey him.'

'I see,' said Flint. 'Even above the Munitorum chain of command?'

Aleksis smiled indulgently at the question, though the expression was devoid of malice. 'The line of ascendancy and the chain of command in this region are one and the same, commissar.'

Military rank allotted according to aristocratic rank, just like the files had warned. There were feudal worlds across the Imperium that utilised such systems but it was generally limited to local forces. Some of the most ancient families of the Imperial Navy bought their commissions, and of course the rogue trader clans purchased status with the writ granted to them by the High Lords of Terra. But to see the system in place across the administration of an entire region consisting of scores of systems was unheard of in Flint's experience. He sighed inwardly, knowing things had just got a lot more complicated. 'So what now, graf?'

'That remains to be determined,' said Aleksis. Flint could

see the man's hands were tied by the very binds of nobility that had elevated him to his rank. 'An appeal to a higher tier, perhaps.'

'That'll take time, graf,' said Flint. 'I need not remind you that we have a mission to complete. The longer we delay the pacification of the rebel population of this complex the harder it will become.'

Aleksis nodded as his expression darkened. The officer was confronted with a dilemma he hadn't had to face before. His loyalties were split between his familial line and his duty as a senior commander of the Imperial Guard. As a commissar, one of Flint's responsibilities was to ensure that such tensions didn't interfere with the regiment's ability to fulfil its task. Whatever obstacle he found, from brawling troops to incompetent commanding officers, Flint was sanctioned to enact whatever course of action he deemed necessary to maintain discipline, doctrinal purity, morale and combat effectiveness.

Flint turned at the approach of Claviger-Primaris Gruss as the chief warden caught up with the command group. 'Might I suggest, graf,' said Gruss, 'a limited perimeter deployment, for now at least?'

Flint studied the man's featureless black visor, unable to read anything of his intentions.

'Perhaps,' said Aleksis.

'My men are capable of containing the uprising and retaking the complex,' pressed Gruss. Flint had seen little evidence of that being the case but he saw a chance to move things forward.

'I concur,' said Flint. 'For now at least.'

'Agreed, then,' said Aleksis. 'Until further arrangements can be made.'

Flint lingered a moment to watch the officers as they strode away. He would allow Aleksis time to settle the matter according to the traditions of the Vostroyan nobility, but if that wasn't possible he would have no choice but to intervene, however the regiment's command cadre took it.

The perimeter of the convicts' sanctuary was a maze of debris-strewn passageways that Vahn had ordered patrolled every minute of every day. Colonel Strannik had sent repeated infiltration gangs through the wall into the central spire in an effort to flush them out, but thanks to Trooper 'Rotten' Stank's tracking skills not one had made it through the third barricade. The corpses of each enemy gang had been flung down the central cooling flue as a warning to others attempting the climb, not that it had deterred them. The rebel convicts were more afraid of their leader than they were of Vahn's group and willing to risk even death over the colonel's vengeance.

The battles had been vicious and brutal with very few on either side equipped with firearms. Those few who were had either scavenged them from the bodies of slain clavigers or, like Skane, fabricated crude weapons themselves. In both cases ammunition was scarce and husbanded against the need to make a last, desperate defence. The most bloody and bitter of the fights had been fought with the convicts' bare hands, improvised clubs and shivs and, when necessary, teeth.

A no-man's-land had come into being beyond the last barricade, consisting of a corpse-strewn void between the spire's outer shell and the geotherm towers, vestibules and chambers. Vahn had to lead his convicts through that dead zone, penetrating as deep as possible before they were discovered. If he could, Vahn would lead his followers out without confrontation, but they all knew how unlikely that was. Vahn had split the three-dozen convicts into three groups in the hope of minimising the chances of contact and each was currently picking its way through the labyrinth of service conduits and pipes that ran through the spire and into the no-man's-land beyond.

'Down,' hissed Vahn, shrinking into the shadows as he detected a faint shift in the flow of stale air passing along the conduit. The geotherm venting scrubbers had stopped functioning soon after the uprising and all the conduits were achieving was the circulation of the stink of rotting corpses drawn from the carceri-chambers below.

Becka melted out of sight an instant before Vahn hissed his warning. Being from the world of Savlar she was well accustomed to such dangerous places. The other ten convicts in Vahn's group followed the example and quite suddenly the conduit appeared empty of all but debris and sump-rat crap. Vahn looked across the conduit to make eye contact with the chem-dog, who was kneeling pressed against the metal wall with her legs drawn up tight to minimise any silhouette she might present to an enemy. Her eyes, just visible above the mask of her rebreather were narrowed as she studied the darkness up ahead. Vahn followed her gaze and there in the shadows he saw another, deeper patch of darkness.

Becka looked across to Vahn and he subtly nodded, hefting his improvised metal club and moving forwards as quietly as he could.

The conduit was circular in cross section and lit only intermittently by the guttering lumen bulbs overhead. Every twenty metres or so a side passage led off towards another zone of the spire, while the main tunnel continued towards the outer shell. One of those side passages was only ten metres ahead and Vahn had little doubt that an enemy convict was lurking in its dark mouth. It was one of the forward sentinels the rebels had seeded throughout the network of conduits, lookouts set to guard against the very sort of intrusion Vahn was undertaking right now.

Nothing for it, Vahn thought to himself. Rising as swiftly and as stealthily as he could, Vahn dashed forward along the conduit wall. By keeping to the edge he avoided kicking up the debris that had collected along the centre of the pipe. His target had no idea he was even there until he was bearing right down on him.

The man's eyes widened in horror as he realised he'd been looking the wrong way as death closed from behind. Vahn dove forwards as the enemy grabbed for a chunky stub gun tucked into his belt but his hands never reached its pistol grip. They both went down in a mass of sprawling limbs as Vahn's hands closed around the other's throat and he squeezed with all his strength.

The enemy convict tried to cry out but Vahn's grip was so tight nothing more than a hoarse croak emerged. Then it struck Vahn that if his enemy were trying to shout a warning there must be someone else nearby to be warned.

Vahn's only warning was a glint of light reflected from a soot-dulled blade, but it was enough to save his life. A cleaver as long as an arm scythed in from overhead and Vahn yanked the convict he was struggling with upwards in response. The cleaver missed Vahn's head and came down with a meaty *thunk*, embedding itself in the head of his opponent. Vahn's eyes were instantly filled with the convict's blood and he flung himself backwards to avoid the next attack, which he knew he would never see.

As he rolled he heard a dull thud and a grunt, followed by a splash as something or someone toppled into the water pooled around the passageway mouth. Blinking the blood from his eyes he found himself looking right at a pair of thick-soled, iron-studded high boots.

'You just gonna lie there?' said Becka. The Savlar proffered a hand and in a moment Vahn was upright. Behind Becka sprawled the broken form of the second attacker, a stiletto blade Vahn hadn't even known Becka owned lodged hilt-deep in one eye.

'Get the others forward,' Vahn ordered as Becka pulled the blade from the rebel's eye socket with an audible slurp. Then she was gone.

Vahn studied the darkness in the passageway the lookout had been hiding in. He'd intended to take his group along the main conduit towards the breach in the spire's outer skin but now he was reconsidering. Strannik's men were well aware of the breach and it was likely that way was guarded. He knew he'd have to face the enemy in strength at some point but perhaps this side passage offered another route. He took a few steps along the passage, his eyes adjusting to the scant illumination provided by only a handful of overhead lumens.

'Hey!' Becka hissed from the mouth of the passage. 'Where you headed, Argusti?'

'Change of plan,' Vahn whispered back. 'We're taking a detour.'

'I don't like detours,' said Becka. 'And neither will Skane or Vendell.'

Good point, Vahn conceded. The other two groups would have no way of knowing that Vahn had led his a different way and if either other group got into more trouble than it could handle there'd be nothing Vahn could do to intervene. Nevertheless, every one of Vahn's combat instincts were telling him this was the way to go.

'Neither do I,' said Vahn. 'But trust me. This is the way.'

Becka cocked her head for a moment as she gazed quizzically at Vahn. Then she nodded and said, 'Fine. Have it your way, but don't say I didn't warn you.'

'A moment please, graf,' Flint said to Aleksis as the command group disembarked the Chimera at the regimental laager. Polzdam made to object but Aleksis indicated with a curt gesture that the lieutenant-colonel should leave him and the commissar alone for a moment.

'Very well,' said the graf, pneumatics hissing as he pulled the lever to close the hatch. 'Speak, commissar.'

Flint folded his arms across his chest and said, 'Governor Kherhart.'

'What of him?'

'Your cousin,' said Flint.

'What of him?' Aleksis repeated.

'If he won't allow this regiment to complete its mission, he can be removed,' said Flint, his voice low and threatening.

Anger flashed in the graf's eyes but he held his tongue. 'He cannot. He holds the rank of Imperial Commander. And besides...'

'No,' Flint interrupted, holding up a hand. 'That rank is honorary and subject to the mandate of the Munitorum. This world is not a sovereign realm and neither is it his personal fiefdom. He can be removed or recalled to other duties. As a commissar, I can make this happen.'

'That may be the case in other sectors, Flint, in other war zones. But in this region, the Techtriarch clans of Vostroya have a long reach. As I have said, things are handled differently here.'

Flint was getting sick of hearing that, but he gestured for the graf to continue.

'Every commission in this region, from second lieutenant in a planetary militia to logister-general is made according to the rules of ascendancy of the Techtriarch clans, don't you see? There is no authority you could appeal to that would approve your request, Flint. Not one, do you understand?'

Flint sighed. 'I am a commissar, graf. A *regimental*

commissar. It is my Emperor-given duty to ensure that missions such as this one are carried out according to orders and free of let or hindrance. If I have to, Aleksis, I'll remove your third-cousin-once-removed from office myself. Do *you* understand?'

Flint left another threat – that he could very easily remove Aleksis from command too – hanging. It would in fact be easier to do so than to remove Governor Kherhart from his position, but ultimately less conducive to the mission. Doing so would just make Flint the enemy when really he needed Kherhart in that role. If the officers of the 77th could see that the governor was standing in the way of the glory Aleksis had promised them, the mission might have some chance of success and the morale and integrity of the regiment itself would benefit.

Not for nothing were commissars sometimes referred to as *political* officers.

'Do what you must, Commissar Flint,' Aleksis replied, a note of weary resignation in his voice. 'Do what you believe is right to get this mission underway, but do not take the rules of ascendancy lightly. If you cross the Techtriarchs, I assure you, you'll regret it. We all will.'

Vahn led his group of convicts through another three kilometres of labyrinthine passageways before passing under a wrecked scrubber valve and into the upper galleries of Carceri *Didactio*. The carceri was one of the largest of the dozen geotherm plant chambers radiating from the central spire and was large enough to house many thousands of inmates.

The interior of Carceri *Didactio* resembled a vast hybrid of monumental architecture and capital engineering. Vertical planes of rockcrete intersected with surfaces resembling the outer faces of engine casings, all rendered hugely out of scale. The chamber's dimensions reduced the human form to utter insignificance: the empty, weightless voids of space pressing downwards on the inmates with unbearable, crushing pressure. Kilometres beneath the chamber, the geotherm sinks plunged deep into irradiated mineral deposits, the decay heat from which the generatorium used to produce power. It was an irony of tragically epic proportions that the vast reserves of power were put to no actual use – the toil was the punishment.

The vaulted ceiling was lost to smog and darkness high overhead, even though Vahn's group had emerged into one of the highest galleries. Vast chains hung from rusted gurneys high in the vaults and narrow metal gantries cut across the void, intersecting seemingly at random. Each walkway was strung with further chains as well as lifeless sconces and cracked lumen bulbs.

'Keep low,' hissed Vahn as he moved out along the gallery, Becka and the other convicts following behind. The gallery was little more than a corroded iron scaffold, the levels beneath visible through the rusted mesh decking. Vahn drew his sharpened iron bar as he came to an opening in the rockcrete wall, the door to one of the hundreds of cells set into the rockcrete wall of the chamber.

Gesturing for silence, Vahn edged towards the cell door to

peer around the doorjamb. It took his eyes a few seconds to adjust to the darkness inside and to discern its contents. When they had, Vahn wished they hadn't.

Vahn snapped his head back from the doorway as he suppressed a wave of disgust and nausea. Memories of the first few hours of the rebel convicts' uprising flashed to mind, staccato images of men and women tearing one another apart in an orgy of violence. The strong had dragged the weak off into the shadows to perform the most barbarous acts that years of incarceration and forced labour had bred within their souls. The cell was one such shadowy hole in which such barbarities had been enacted.

'Pass it along,' Vahn whispered to Becka as she sidled up. 'Keep clear.'

Becka studied Vahn for a moment then nodded her understanding. As she passed the instruction back along the chain, Vahn crept silently to the edge of the scaffold and looked downwards towards the distant floor at least a hundred metres below.

The hard rockcrete ground was obscured by a miasma of foul air, no doubt the result of the fires unleashed during the uprising. With the disabling of the geotherm scrubbers the air was dank and still, the smog hugging the ground instead of being sucked away and cleaned. Through the greasy haze, Vahn could just make out a line of figures winding from a distant entrance towards a portal on the other side of the chamber, herded along by dozens of rebels. The clink of chains drifted upwards, underpinned with the low, mournful wailing of the rebels' prisoners.

'That portal,' said Becka as she set herself down next to Vahn. 'The one they're coming from?'

'Yup,' said Vahn.

'That's where we're going, right?' she said.

'Uh-huh,' said Vahn. 'It's the only way through to the gate hall.'

'Somehow I knew you'd say that,' sighed Becka. 'So what's the plan?'

'Wait 'til the line passes through, then we go in,' he said. 'Any guards still down there, we take them out.'

'What about the prisoners?' said Becka, indicating the snaking line.

Vahn sighed, not wanting to play the callous bastard but knowing there was little choice. 'Best we can do for them is get through to the Guard and get this done with. Either way, we can't help them right now.'

'Understood,' said Becka. Reading her eyes Vahn saw that she meant it. Life was tragically harsh in Alpha Penitentia and it had got a thousand times harsher since the uprising. Despite himself, Vahn was glad she thought no less of him.

'Best get moving then,' Vahn said as the last prisoners in the line passed out of the chamber entrance. There were still dozens of guards left milling around the portal, but Vahn had known all along that his small force would have to fight its way through at some point. Estimating how much time had gone by since he'd led his force away from the agreed route through the conduits, Vahn guessed that Skane and Vendell's groups should be nearing the gate soon. They, however, would be appearing on ground level within a few dozen metres of the portal. For the attack on the portal to be coordinated between all three groups, Vahn's would have to be down there as soon as possible.

Vahn gestured to the other convicts to duck down into the shadows before setting foot on the debris-strewn ground of the chamber floor. The descent through the levels of the scaffold had taken longer than he had intended, the group slowed up by the need to tread carefully or have the creaking of rusted metal tread plates betray them to the rebels guarding the chamber entrance. By the time Vahn's convicts had reached the lowest gallery the line of bound prisoners was all but gone having disappeared through the stinking smog that clung to the ground level. Though the prisoners had been led away across the chamber towards the next vestibule, several dozen guards had remained to watch over the portal.

Vahn had anticipated that this portal would be well guarded, for beyond it was the route towards the gate hall, the last vestige of the governor's control over Alpha Penitentia. If the convicts who refused to join or surrender to Colonel Strannik managed to escape the entirety of the complex would be under Strannik's control, only the gate hall and a few insignificant out structures remaining in the claviger-wardens' hands. Vahn had no way of knowing what might lie beyond the portal but it must be better than waiting to be caught by Strannik's murderers.

The guards milling around the portal looked like the worst sorts of scum Strannik had recruited. Only the brutes of his personal bodyguard were more muscular or cruel. The guards were all large men, for they'd spent the years of their incarceration coercing food rations from weaker prisoners. Every one of them had served in the Imperial Guard and been consigned to Alpha Penitentia for some transgression not quite bad enough to earn a death sentence but too serious to be dealt with by their regiments' own commissars.

They carried an array of crude weaponry, mostly iron clubs and hatchets. But one of them, Vahn saw as he watched from the shadows, was carrying a combat shotgun, prized no doubt from the dead grip of a slain warden. The man carrying it must have been a Catachan or else born on some similar world. His frame was almost grotesquely over-muscled. The high gravity death world of his birth bred the very strongest of men and women and other Guardsmen serving alongside its famous jungle fighters sometimes referred to them as 'baby ogryns', though never to their faces. Just like the brutes the nickname referred to, the man was a mountain of iron-hard muscle, but unlike ogryns, Catachans were quick-witted and intelligent – they had to be just to survive more than an hour on their hellish birth world.

The Catachan was clearly the leader of the guard detail and the others were visibly cowed by his sheer physical presence. The slightest growl from his thuggish lips and the other guards obeyed without question. Barking an order to a group of around two-dozen rebels, the Catachan pointed towards a nook in the chamber wall and the men moved across to take up position inside it. Vahn's eyes narrowed in suspicion and the hairs stood up on the back of his neck.

The Catachan crossed to another nook and Vahn realised the two positions were on either side of the entrance to a small service tunnel leading into the chamber. The tunnel was the one his own group would have entered the chamber from had he not felt the need to take a detour. Worse still, Skane and Vendell's groups would soon be emerging from the tunnel. They would be walking right into an ambush.

FIVE
Infiltration

The return journey from the gate hall to the regimental laager had passed in silence, Aleksis apparently brooding on what had passed between himself and his regiment's new commissar. Upon reaching the laager, Flint followed the graf and his staff back into the command post and was greeted by the shouts of several junior officers. As Aleksis and Polzdam made for their tactical stations to ascertain what was happening, Flint headed for the intelligence chief, Herrmahn.

'Just in time, commissar,' the officer said, not taking his eyes from the flickering data-slate in front of him.

Flint removed his cap and passed it to his aide. The tri-D representation of the hybrid power and penal facility revolved on one of Herrmahn's screens, but the main image was zoomed in on one particular generatoria zone, labelled *Didactio*.

'You've achieved machine-communion with the installation's systems?' said Flint, surprised and mildly suspicious that the intelligence chief had access to the complex's security grid.

'Strictly speaking,' said Herrmahn, casting a sideling glance at Flint, 'no.'

Flint decided not to press the issue further, even if it was technically a crime Herrmahn could be consigned to the Penal Legions for. 'So, what's happening at *Didactio*?'

'So far as I can tell, some localised disturbance,' said Herrmahn. 'Could be trouble between rival factions within the uprising, or it could be a sideshow to get us looking.'

'A diversion?' said Flint. 'If that's the case, what don't they want us looking at?' he mused.

'Can't tell,' said Herrmahn. 'This is the best resolution I can achieve. If you really want to find out what's happening in there you'll have to confirm it yourself. Terran-pattern, Mark I eyeball. It's the only way to be sure.'

'No, commissar!' said Aleksis, looking up sharply from his command station. 'Absolutely not.'

'With respect, sir,' said Flint, fighting to keep his tone level despite his frustration, 'my mandate grants me the command authority.'

Aleksis glanced at his second-in-command and Lieutenant-Colonel Polzdam nodded subtly in reluctant confirmation of Flint's assertion. Seeing his opportunity, Flint pressed on before Aleksis could object further.

'If I lead a scouting party in and find out what's really going on in there, we can get this mission on track. It's on my authority as regimental commissar, so you don't have to worry about ascendancy or upsetting the in-laws, Aleksis. It's on my head, it's my call, and I'm taking it.'

Aleksis sighed, the staff officers gathered about the command post not daring to meet his gaze. 'You'll not be able to take a line company,' he said. 'You know that, commissar?'

'I know that, graf,' said Flint, getting somewhere at last. 'I'll take my provost section. We'll travel fast and light, find out what's happening, then get out.'

'Then do so, commissar,' said Aleksis. 'Needless to say, I cannot help you in this, you understand?'

Recalling the conversation earlier and the talk of lines of ascendancy and patronage of the Vostroyan Techtriarch clans, Flint nodded. 'I understand. Thank you, graf.'

'Good luck, Commissar Flint,' said Aleksis. Flint threw him a salute and received one back in return.

Flint spent the next hour assembling an infiltration force from amongst the regiment's flotsam and jetsam. Denied access to the line companies, he was forced to scour the various headquarters and support platoons for individuals skilled enough to undertake the reconnaissance mission he had planned. Fortunately, the Firstborn were the product of the cyclopean manufactoria of Vostroya and Alpha Penitentia wasn't so alien an environment to them. After ex-loading Major Herrmahn's tri-D plan of the complex to his personal data-slate Flint was able to plot a course towards carceri chamber *Didactio* easily enough, or so he thought until several of his newly recruited team corrected

Andy Hoare

his planning and suggested a far quicker and more secure route.

The team he selected consisted of Dragoon Kohlz, who Flint was beginning to trust as a capable aide, Corporal Bukin and his goons, a combat medic named Karasinda, Dragoon Lhor and two other huge men from the logistics platoon. Flint had consulted with Kohlz on the selection to ensure that no fractious elements were allowed to slip through. The last thing he needed on the mission was a disagreement, fight or even a desertion attempt with the enemy so close at hand.

The medic Karasinda represented something of an exception in the ranks of the Firstborn. By ancient tradition the people of Vostroya rendered their firstborn sons to service in the Imperial Guard, but the daughters weren't subject to that oath. The very few women serving in the Firstborn regiments were volunteers and they were regarded by their peers with a mixture of suspicion and respect.

Karasinda put herself forward for the mission as soon as word got out that Flint was looking for volunteers and he had been suspicious of that fact to begin with. Speaking to her however, Flint had found Karasinda to be a curiously intense woman and he was soon convinced that genuine duty compelled her to volunteer, not just for his mission but for service in the Imperial Guard itself. Such spirit was rare indeed amongst the rank and file of the 77th Vostroyan Firstborn and Flint was loath to discourage it. Besides the fact of her volunteering for the duty, Karasinda was by her own, modestly advanced account, a highly capable medic who, unlike many amongst her peers, had actually seen combat. Karasinda claimed to have served in an expedition into the ruins of the vast Derzhinsky tank manufactorium when she had been indentured to the Vostroyan planetary defence force, taking part in a three-month long campaign to rid its southern reaches of a population of mutant scavengers. Though not a first line combatant, Karasinda had earned a higher kill-rate than any other member of her company and received high commendation for her service.

Having selected his team, Flint ensured they were properly equipped for the mission. Dragoon Lhor had drawn a heavy flamer from the quartermaster's post and the two fellow logistics platoon members were assigned as his assistant and his ammo-lugger. Flint sincerely hoped that he would have no need to order the huge weapon's use, for to do so would be a sure sign that things had gone badly wrong. Nevertheless, it paid to be prepared. Raw muscle would be provided by Bukin's provosts, and Flint hadn't had to order them to arm up. They did so themselves, each man equipping himself with a heavy Vostroyan-pattern Mark III combat shotgun. The weapons were crude and as ugly as the provosts but supremely effective in the cramped environs the team would be moving through.

At the last, Flint dispatched Kohlz to requisition a set of night vision goggles for each warrior. The quartermaster staff had objected strongly to the request until Flint's aide informed them on whose authority the requisition was being made. The storesman demanded the goggles be returned intact when the mission was over. Kohlz had considered reminding the man that a commissar hardly cared for such things but found it easier to lie through his teeth that they would be returned safely.

Three hours after the mission had been devised, Flint was leading his small team out from the laager. The sun was setting and the group was moving on foot and already the air was getting uncomfortably cold. Despite the discomfort Flint couldn't afford to move the team in by armoured transport, there being a need to keep the mission secret from Governor Kherhart's surviving forces. It was unlikely the rebels would detect the presence of a single Chimera rumbling across the wastes but Kherhart's men most likely would and that would just complicate things. Once again, Flint cursed the fact that the regiment seemed more focused on politics than the mission.

'Sir?' said Kohlz, following close behind Flint with his heavy vox-set on his back.

Realising he must have muttered his curse out loud, Flint shook his head. 'Nothing, dragoon,' he said, looking up at the grim façade of the nearest of the complex's subsidiary structures. Carceri *Didactio* was less than an hour's march away and was one of the vast geotherm plant chambers arrayed about the central spire and joined to it by knots of huge pipes and armoured vestibule tunnels. The grey rock-crete caught the last light of the setting sun, the numerous small cracks and fissures etched on its surface giving it the appearance of aged leather. Columns of smoke still drifted up from several of the blocks, evidence of the destruction the rebel convicts had unleashed within.

'Nothing,' Flint repeated as his aide drew up beside him. 'Anything on the vox?'

'Channel is not good, sir,' said Kohlz, 'but the governor's staff are telling the graf everything is fine and there is no need to send anyone in to help.'

Flint smiled grimly at that. 'Any response from Aleksis?'

'Odd, that, sir,' said Kohlz. 'Seems the graf just can't get a clear channel. Every time Kherhart asks for an assurance that we aren't sending anyone in to intervene, the channel goes down.'

'That *is* odd, isn't it,' said Flint, glad that Aleksis was playing along. How long the graf could keep his deception going was another matter of course. Flint was painfully aware he wouldn't have long to complete his reconnaissance and get his team out again before the governor got suspicious.

'Pick it up,' Flint said to Corporal Bukin at the thought of the mission's time constraints. 'Double time!'

'You heard the commissar,' said Bukin, his words slurred around the unlit Vostroyan cigar in the corner of his mouth. 'Double time, ladies!'

It wasn't long before the laager was lost to view behind the jagged craters and boulders scattered about the wasteland around the generatorium, though the sky above glowed with the reflected illumination of the camp's numerous arc lights and the sound of its generators grumbled across the land. As they marched, Flint was reminded of the trek from the crashed drop-pod to the laager the night before, and was suddenly aware that he hadn't slept a wink since planetfall. Despite that, he was wary, and he saw that the others who had undertaken that trek were too.

'You see anything, Bukin?' Flint asked the chief provost as they marched, keeping his body low. Bukin evidently shared his concerns, his cold eyes scrutinising any position an enemy could be lurking in.

'See something, sir?' Bukin growled as he marched, his heavy shotgun braced across his chest ready for action. 'No, sir. But I can *smell* them…'

Flint was instantly alert, though he tried not to give the fact away by reacting to Bukin's warning. 'Report, corporal.'

The provost's nose wrinkled in an exaggerated display of distaste before he replied. 'Last night, it was just a handful, sir, and they were keeping their distance. Now though, the closer we get to this place, the closer they get to us, and there's more of them. A lot more.'

A mix of disgust and dread rising within him, Flint studied the lengthening shadows, alert for any sign of danger. But as hard as he looked he saw no sign of whatever it was Bukin claimed to be able to detect. Maybe it wasn't his sense of smell the chief provost was using, but some previously undisclosed psychic power manifesting itself under stress, he considered, but an instant later, he detected it too.

'You smell that, sir?' said Bukin. 'That is the smell of filthy, dirty mutants.'

Bukin was correct, there was no denying it. The wind had changed direction and carried on it a truly vile taint that was nothing natural or wholesome. It was a blasphemous cocktail of the chemical and the biological, like distilled pheromones held in some irradiated suspension. It was unspeakably… wrong, calling to mind images of filth-ridden things copulating in dark holes far from the eyes of sane men.

'Everyone, stay alert,' Flint snarled into the personal vox-net linking each of his troops. 'Pick up visual scanning and watch your arcs.'

The remainder of the journey passed without incident, but Flint grew increasingly certain the wastes about Alpha Penitentia were not so empty as they appeared to be. Whatever was trailing the group, it was nothing human and it appeared not to be interested in engaging the small force. Perhaps it was some native creature, Flint thought, some autochthonous life form beneath the notice of the astrocartographic surveyors whose task it was to catalogue such things. In Flint's experience, the galaxy was teeming with life of every conceivable, and numerous inconceivable varieties, only a tiny fraction of it discovered or observed. Yet somehow, Flint knew whatever was out there it wasn't an animal of any kind. Bukin was correct in his assertion it was a mutant, Flint could feel it deep down, and the very thought utterly sickened him.

Of the rest of the infiltration group, only Karasinda appeared to share the provost's apprehensions. The medic hadn't needed to be warned, but had cottoned on to the fact that they weren't alone by herself. Her drills were flawless as she led the group forward in the point position, scanning every possible hiding place for signs of an ambush and calling her companions' attentions to potential danger spots with a series of rapid hand gestures. Clearly, this Firstborn

Andy Hoare

daughter had paid attention during training, while the First-born sons had been found wanting.

By the time the infiltration group had reached the outer limits of Alpha Penitentia, the sun had set and the blasted land was plunged into a darkness made all the more total because the starlight was all but obscured by its rearing form.

Having consulted his data-slate to get a fix on his position, Flint craned his neck to take in the sheer enormity of the complex's outer surface. The structure was as bulky as any Munitorum ordnance silo and taller than a Ministorum cathedral. Up close, the outer surface of the carceri was largely featureless, a stark contrast to the ornamentation on the iron portals of the gate hall. Looking closer however, Flint could see that the weathered walls were studded with heavy-duty vents and access hatches that must have been sealed shut from the outside centuries ago. One such vent was nearby at ground level and guarded by a rusted grille that looked strong enough to keep a bull grox out.

'Get to work,' said Flint, motioning Dragoon Hannen, one of Lhor's companions forward. The members of the logistics platoon appeared to conform to one of two types – they were either weasel-like clerks or hulking meatheads: bean counters or ammo-luggers. This individual was most certainly the latter.

Hannen grunted and unslung a canvas sack as he squared up to the grille.

'Perimeter defence,' ordered Flint to the remainder of the team. 'You know the drill.' At least, he hoped they did.

Hannen went about his task as the other warriors tracked their weapons back and forth into the darkness. The Vostroyan was already assembling his portable plasma cutting rig, screwing the photonic cell into the main assembly as Flint peered into the vent through the rusted grille. The blades of the vent were visible and it was immediately apparent that they hadn't revolved in some time, the fins visibly corroded and broken.

Flint drew his bolt pistol as Hannen ignited the plasma cutter. An incandescent tongue of violet energy lanced forth several centimetres from the nozzle and Flint looked away just in time to avoid being temporarily blinded.

'Sorry, sir,' said Hannen, who had already lowered a photochromatic work visor. As the man got to work Flint took advantage of the sudden illumination to squint further into the vent's innards. The conduit beyond the broken blades was visible by the flickering violet-hued light and Flint was grateful that the plasma cutter gave off next to no sound beyond that of bubbling liquid metal splashing across the dry ground. He kept his pistol trained on the darkness all the same, wary for any sign of movement.

Hannen worked fast and within another few minutes was on the last cut. With a gesture, Flint gathered the infiltration team around the opening ready to move as soon as Hannen was done. He was gratified to see two of Bukin's men continuing to cover the darkness with their ugly Mark IIIs, moving backwards with combat shotguns raised as they prepared to pass through the vent as soon as it was accessible.

'Almost there,' warned Hannen as the plasma cut through

the last few centimetres. Molten metal spat and hissed as it ran down the rusted grille. 'Brace.'

Bukin motioned for two of his provosts to take hold of an edge of the grille each and just as the plasma cut through the last bar they lifted the whole structure to stop it falling noisily to the ground. Grunting, the two men shifted their weight and moved sideways, leaning the severed grille against the rockcrete wall beside the now open vent.

Flint motioned for silence and strained his ears for any sign of activity. After ten seconds he made a second sharp hand signal and Dragoon Lhor stepped forward into the opening, his heavy flamer raised. Flint lowered his night vision goggles, activating them with a turn of a brass dial. The goggles powered up with a brief, just-audible ultrasonic squeal and the scene was rendered into grainy green-grey.

No time like the present, Flint thought, making a downward chopping motion with his free hand.

Lhor was the first to move forward, the nozzle of the heavy flamer tracking left and right as he trod carefully along the tunnel. The weapon's blue pilot flame was a ghosting will-o'-the-wisp in the blackness. The floor was strewn with gritty debris, the dried effluvium of several centuries of neglect that crunched underfoot as the team advanced. Flint was painfully aware of the sound resounding with the step of every warrior apart from Karasinda.

'You hear that?' slurred Corporal Bukin.

'Shh,' said Kohlz, earning a dirty look from the provost leader.

His aide's warning echoing away to silence, Flint strained

to listen to the ghost of a sound coming from somewhere up ahead. The tunnel made the sound indistinct and nigh impossible to pinpoint, as if it could be coming from any one of several directions. Then the sound came again and this time Flint couldn't mistake its source. It was undoubtedly the sound of anger and pain.

'Get ready,' said Flint, raising his bolt pistol in one hand and loosening his power sword in its scabbard with the other. 'Lhor, keep going, but be ready. Do nothing unless I tell you.'

As the group approached a turn a sudden crack of gunfire sounded from just around the bend. The report was deafeningly loud in the confines of the tunnel and it bounced around the cold walls like a ricocheting slug round. As one, the team members ducked back against the wall or hit the deck, weapons raised towards the bend.

The sharp smell of a primitive and badly mixed propellant struck Flint's nostrils as a hazy blue cloud drifted into the tunnel from around the corner. A harsh shout followed, telling Flint that whoever had fired the crude weapon was scant metres beyond the turn. Bukin rose up with his combat shotgun raised to his shoulder but Flint waved him back.

As the sounds of combat continued, Flint listened intently. There was no more gunfire but plenty of improvised weapons clashing, crude iron striking flesh and bone, telling Flint something of the two parties fighting one another.

'Two rival groups,' Flint whispered to Bukin, who was knelt down next to him in the dark. 'No coordinated or sustained fire, so the wardens aren't one of them.'

Shifting his cigar from one corner of his mouth to the other, Bukin replied, 'Convict scum. Let them kill each other, sir?'

'I want to know who's fighting who, corporal,' said Flint. 'And why. And I want some idea what we're up against.'

'*Then* we let them kill each other, sir?' Bukin grinned wickedly.

'Maybe,' said Flint, seeing Bukin's pantomime expression of disappointment. 'Wait a moment.'

Flint peered around the bend, first one eye and then both as he strained to make sense of the shadows. His goggles rendered the view static-shot and green-grey, the blurry images slowly resolving as the goggles registered the scene.

There was an opening into a massive chamber just ahead and the first thing Flint saw was a number of figures silhouetted against it, with more dashing to and fro in the space beyond. Two members of the dozen or so strong group were engaged in an animated argument. Flint couldn't hear what they were saying but he could tell from their gestures and body language they were on the verge of a physical confrontation. More of the group were ducked inside the tunnel, several of them looking back towards Flint's position as if considering fleeing.

'Looks like an ambush,' Flint whispered just loud enough for Bukin to hear. 'They must have come this way and been jumped as they emerged into the chamber.'

'Then why don't they head back this way, sir?' whispered

Bukin.

'Looks like one of them's asking just that,' Flint replied as the two men near the entrance squared off against one another. One was a huge brute and by the ugly firearm held in one hand it was he who had fired the shot before. Scanning the other members crouching in the shadows, Flint confirmed that was the only such weapon they carried.

A shotgun thundered and pulverised rockcrete showered the two men facing off against one another. Both ducked back to opposite sides of the tunnel, shouting loudly at one another despite the danger they shared.

'Sounded like a Navy piece,' said Bukin, edging as close to Flint as he could without exposing himself around the corner.

'Or something looted from a warden,' replied Flint. 'Hang on…'

The shorter of the two arguing men stood and strode hurriedly away from the other. The larger man shouted something, but the only response he got was a crude gesture.

'One of them's coming this way,' he hissed. 'Take him, alive.'

Bukin looked hurt but the expression changed to one of nasty determination as he spun his shotgun in his grip, wielding it like a club. 'How alive, sir?' the provost sneered.

'*Talking* alive,' said Flint. A second later the convict rounded the corner at speed. Before he could even register the infiltration team's presence the butt of Bukin's shotgun slammed down on his neck and he collapsed in a crumpled heap.

'I said "alive".'

The convict moaned and tried to roll over but Flint restrained him with a gloved hand to the shoulder.

'He *is*,' complained Bukin. 'And he'll be talking too in a minute, sir.'

'What…' the convict spluttered as his eyes struggled to focus on Flint. Realisation dawned as the man took in Flint's peaked cap and black leather storm coat.

'Commissar?!' he coughed, his voiced filled with horror. It was immediately evident to Flint that coming face to face with a commissar in the depths of a penal generatorium taken over by rebels was almost too much for the man to comprehend.

Deciding to capitalise on the man's reaction, Flint raised his bolt pistol and racked the slide. 'You've got ten seconds to explain yourself – to me or to the Emperor. Your choice.'

Bukin almost guffawed, but Flint's cold expression forestalled whatever insolent quip he was about to make.

'Five seconds,' said Flint, lowering the bolt pistol towards the man's temple.

'Solomon, sir,' the man blurted. 'Indentee-trooper, weapons platoon, D Squadron, 71st Jopall.' The man reeled off a hugely long code that could only have been an Officio Munitorum troop serial number. He was Imperial Guard, or had been once, and the name, rank and number response was so ingrained in him that being confronted with a commissar had caused it to come tumbling out of his mouth unbidden.

'Time's up,' Bukin sneered.

The man's eyes darted towards the provost chief, then back to Flint as if he couldn't decide who to be more intimidated by.

'Who are you fighting?' growled Flint. 'And why?'

'The rebels, sir,' replied Solomon. 'We were trying to break out.'

'Out?' said Flint. 'Out of where?'

Solomon looked all around him, the gesture indicating he meant the entire complex. 'Out,' he repeated.

Bukin chipped in before Flint could respond. 'Getting too hot for you in here?'

'Shh!' Flint hissed. 'Where did you think you were headed?'

Something resembling realisation formed in the trooper's expression, and he looked around again, this time focusing on the warriors around the tunnel. Most had their rebreathers raised and their night vision goggles lowered, so he could see little of their faces. 'To the Guard,' he stammered. 'To you?'

Bukin's eyebrows raised with exaggerated incredulity. Lifting his bolt pistol clear of Solomon's head, Flint said, 'Why were you heading back this way?'

The trooper's face darkened before he answered. 'We were ambushed on our way to the main gate. Someone must have sold us out, so I was for finding another way round.'

'And the other, he disagreed?'

'Skane,' Solomon named the larger man he had been

arguing with. 'He wanted to fight through to Vendell's lot. They're in the gak, and we can't reach them.'

Flint's mind raced as he considered the situation. If there were convicts who hadn't rebelled against the complex's authorities and they were fighting for their lives right now, honour demanded he aid them. But the mission parameters would be best served by him cuffing Solomon and taking him back to regimental command right away. Flint was in no doubt the man would be able to offer up potentially vital intelligence about the rebels' strengths and dispositions, and, by the looks of him, he would do so willingly.

Then, things changed again.

'Sir!' Bukin hissed. 'Company!'

Another convict turned the corner. 'Solomon?' the man called out before his eyes penetrated the dark and registered the presence of several large calibre weapons pointed directly at his head. 'Solomon, what the hell…'

'Freeze!' ordered Flint, and the man skidded to a halt. His wide eyes focused on the bobbing blue pilot light of Lhor's heavy flamer.

'Solomon?'

'Silence!' Flint barked, his bolt pistol aimed right between the man's eyes. 'Solomon,' he continued, not taking his eyes from the newcomer. 'Stand up and join your friend here.'

Movement in the periphery of the view through his night vision goggles told Flint that Solomon was obeying his command, and a moment later the convict was standing alongside his companion. Another shotgun blast resounded from outside, and the two convicts shared a wary glance.

Flint's mind was made up.

'Bukin,' he said. 'Get everyone ready. We're ending this, now.'

'Sir, the mission...' Bukin protested.

'Has just changed,' Flint spat back. 'If there are loyalists in there, I want them on our side. We *need* them on our side. Get going.'

'You two,' Flint rounded on the two convicts 'You are at a crossroads. I need your help and you need mine. In a moment we'll all be rounding that corner, but you'll be going first, understood?'

The second convict, who was shorter than the first and blessed with a staggeringly ugly face only the Emperor could love, nodded in instant understanding. 'We're the messengers,' he said. 'Just hope we don't get shot.'

'Let's get on with it then,' said Flint. 'Move,' he waived the two convicts off with a flick of his bolt pistol.

Rounding the corner at the same time as the convicts, Flint and Bukin strode straight forward towards the group of men and women sheltering near the tunnel mouth. The nearest convict turned, and immediately shouted a warning. The big man, who Solomon had named Skane was ducked inside the entrance reloading his bulky firearm, which he raised one-handed as he spun around in response to the shout.

'Don't shoot!' shouted Solomon. 'It's me!'

'I see that,' growled Skane, his weapon trained on Solomon but his eyes squinting into the darkness behind his fellow convict. 'Who's with you?' His voice was deep and powerful, but laced with suspicion. 'You sold us out?'

'We've done this already,' Solomon replied through gritted teeth. 'We were trying to find the Guard, right?'

'Right,' said Skane, clearly expecting a trick.

'Well,' said Solomon, '*they* found *us*.'

Skane's eyes searched the shadows behind Solomon, but it was clear he could see nothing more than the suggestion of the infiltration team's presence. The crudely made firearm swept left and right, and Flint decided to take matters into his own hands.

'Skane?' Flint called out. 'Solomon's telling the truth. He hasn't sold you out. We're here to restore order.'

'Then step forward, where I can see you,' said Skane, though Flint could tell the man was still expecting a double-cross. 'Nice and slow.'

Holstering his bolt pistol despite Bukin's disapproving look, Flint stepped out around the two convicts and started up the tunnel towards Skane. As he did so he pulled his night vision goggles down around his neck and straightened his peaked cap.

'Commissar...' Skane snarled. Though the other man was silhouetted against the opening of the tunnel and his features cast in shadow, Flint could see his face forming into a bitter scowl. 'Your type don't help no one,' he barked.

Another shot was fired somewhere outside in the carceri chamber, and the sound of angry shouting drifted into the tunnel. 'Sounds like your people are dying out there, Skane,' said Flint. 'I'm here with the 77th Vostroyan Firstborn. I'm here to help.'

Skane's eyes bored into Flint's, the man's hatred of

commissars clear to see. Obviously, he had been on the wrong end of commissarial justice at some point, probably accounting for his presence in the penal generatorium. The man's eyes darted back towards the tunnel mouth at the sound of the shouting, and Flint could read his desire to aid his companions.

'Help who?' said Skane, forcing Flint to suppress his rising frustration at the man's bloody-mindedness. The shouting outside was getting louder and more urgent, as if a pitched battle were reaching a tipping point.

'I'm not here to haul you off to the stockade, Trooper Skane,' said Flint. While not totally sure that the man had been in the Imperial Guard, he had to try something. 'You're not on any charge. I can see you're not a rebel, and it's my duty to persecute those who are.'

Moments of silence punctuated by the sounds of distant battle followed, before Solomon spoke up. 'He means it, Skane. It's the only way. We don't have any other choice.'

'Okay, commissar,' Skane said as he lowered his firearm. 'What happens now?'

Flint let out a breath he hadn't realised he'd been holding. 'You tell me what we're up against, and we go make a difference, trooper.'

'Corporal,' said Skane, his eyes locked on Flint's. 'I was a corporal. Ninety-ninth Elysian.'

'Bukin?' Flint hissed at the provost. 'Arm Corporal Skane's men.'

'Sir?' the chief provost said, a protest forming.

'Share out your side arms,' Flint ordered.

Kohlz was the first Vostroyan to obey, unholstering his laspistol and passing it butt-first to the nearest convict-worker. The man reached for the weapon, uncertainly at first, then as his hand closed around the grip, with conviction. But Kohlz held on to the weapon for a moment, before Flint nodded and he released it in to the man's possession.

With obvious reluctance, Bukin unholstered a bulky autopistol from his belt, one of three side arms the provost carried, and handed it to a nearby convict. Within moments, Bukin had cajoled his fellow provosts into relinquishing their own personal weapons, and the convicts were all armed.

Skane nodded his thanks to Flint, and edged towards the tunnel mouth. Flint followed, and for the first time was afforded a view of the interior of one of Alpha Penitentia's mighty generatoria chambers.

Lifting his gaze from the floor towards the distant, haze-shrouded vaults, Flint saw that the chamber was impossibly vast. But he didn't have time to take in the full extent of the architecture, as the sound of another shotgun blast snapped his attention back to ground level. He was peppered with rockcrete shrapnel, and as soon as the powder-haze had cleared he located the firer.

'Who the hell is that?' growled Flint as he ducked back into cover. The biggest man Flint had ever seen was crouched in a nook forty or so metres down the wall from the tunnel entrance, his shotgun, obviously taken from a warden, raised before him.

'That,' said Skane, 'is Arnil Khave. Biggest, ugliest Catachan you'll ever see, and that's saying something.'

The Catachan swung his weapon around towards a massive and unidentifiable piece of machinery and unleashed yet another volley. A shower of sparks erupted from the machine as hundreds of metal shotgun pellets struck what looked like some form of engine casing. Flint heard shouts from behind another, similar piece of machinery, and guessed that several more groups of convicts were pinned down by the Catachan's fire.

'Who's he firing at,' Flint shouted back to Skane. 'Yours?'

'Mine is one of three groups making for that vestibule portal,' he pointed towards a distant section of wall made indistinct by the smoky haze that seemed to cling to the chamber floor. 'He's firing at Vendell's lot.'

'And the third?' said Flint, raising his voice as the Catachan bawled an order to an unseen underling.

Skane didn't answer. 'Tell me, corporal,' Flint ordered.

'Vahn,' he said. 'He's what you might call our leader.'

'But?' Flint pressed.

'He should have got here before us,' Skane said. 'Before both of the other groups. But Vahn's not here, and *he* is.' Skane emphasised the subject of his statement with a nod towards the Catachan. Now things were starting to make some sort of sense, thought Flint, in a chaotic sort of way.

'This Vahn, you think he's sold you out?' asked Flint. 'You think he's bought his freedom and you're the blood price?'

Anger flashed across Skane's face at so overt an explanation of what might have happened, but it was replaced a moment later by bitter resignation. 'I'm not saying he has,'

Skane began. 'But this doesn't look good.'

'No,' said Flint. 'It doesn't. But regardless,' he continued, looking out towards the huge mass of geotherm machinery. 'We need to extricate the other group and get everyone back to base.

'Listen up,' Flint addressed both the dragoons and the convicts. 'This is what we're going to do.'

'Move!' Vahn hissed urgently as the Catachan fired another volley towards Vendell's hiding place. Vahn's group was still too far away from the action to intervene, and closing on the ambushers would mean crossing the open chamber floor and exposing themselves to the Catachan's fire.

That wasn't an option.

Vahn ushered Becka and the rest towards a mass of corroded pipework that sprawled across the ground, reminding him of an abattoir floor.

Angry shouts sounded from behind the cover where he knew Vendell and at least half a dozen of his group to be taking cover, followed by more from behind other scraps of corroded machinery. Vahn moved quickly and by the time he reached the mass of twisting pipes had almost overtaken the convict in front.

'What now?' asked Becka as she peered cautiously over the pipe. 'We're still too far away.'

Vahn rolled over onto his front and lifted himself up on both arms so that he too could see the action. Becka was right; they were still too far from the action to intervene and too far from the vestibule portal to escape. To make things worse, the enemy had the firepower, and was using it to pin the escapees down. Ultimately, Vahn knew that Vendell's group would be outflanked and exposed to a lethal cross-fire; it was only a matter of time.

'Hang on,' Vahn told Becka as he squinted into the haze that half-obscured the scene. Part of it was the smoke of gunfire, but without the air scrubbers the vast carceri chambers were filling with condensation. Thick white clouds were gathering in the vaults and creeping fog cloaked the ground. The air felt damp and oppressive, like a thunderstorm was building up.

'Maybe we could use the fog,' Vahn said, half to himself. 'Head to the left and cross the floor under cover of the haze.'

'That'll bring us up behind the Catachan,' said Becka, a nasty glint in her eye.

'We deal with him, then link up with Skane in the tunnel mouth. Cross towards the portal and round up Vendell's mob on the way, dealing with any more of Strannik's scum as we go.'

'Catachan's the deal-breaker,' said Becka. 'Won't be no pushover.'

'No one ever said breaking out of an upsilon-grade Munitorum installation would be easy,' Vahn grinned.

'Go!' Flint hissed, patting Bukin on the shoulder as he moved out at a stooped run followed by his provosts.

The provost section crossed fifty or so metres of hazy, yet open, ground before the Catachan fired. Flint had timed his order to coincide with the enemy reloading his weapon, and Bukin's group had almost reached the cover of a large thermal transfer mechanism before the Catachan was able to fire again.

The ground at Bukin's feet erupted in a hail of dust and shrapnel as hundreds of shotgun pellets tore into it, the provosts charging through and throwing themselves behind a huge, cog-toothed brass wheel. One didn't make it, his broken form reduced to a torn, ragged mess by the blast. As Bukin ducked into the cover, he spun as a rebel convict appeared twenty metres away, firing his Mark III from the hip. The blast threw the rebel backwards and left only a fine red mist floating in the air where he had been. A moment later, another rebel appeared, and this time three of the provosts opened fire as one, scattering the bloody chunks that had been their target across the wall behind.

'Go!' Flint shouted to Skane and the recently armed convicts. The instant they appeared in the open the Catachan stood and levelled his shotgun right at them. Bukin and his companions fired from between the cogs of the huge gear wheel, peppering their target's cover with a churning storm of pellets and rockcrete shrapnel. The Catachan ducked back into his nook with an audible curse, and Bukin's group waited on overwatch for him to show himself again.

'Our turn,' said Flint, raising his bolt pistol in one hand and drawing his basket-hilted power sword with the other. He activated the blade's lethal power field with a flick of his thumb, tasting the bleachy tang of ozone as the air around the sword burned. Flint stepped out of the tunnel mouth, feeling instantly incredibly vulnerable.

'Sir!' a woman's voice shouted from somewhere along the wall behind him. Her tone was so sharp Flint responded on instinct, ducking down and throwing himself against the rockcrete. An instant later, a bolt of searing lasgun fire burned the air not a metre from Flint's head and a figure he had not even seen dropped heavily to the ground.

Turning back, Flint saw Karasinda lowering her lasgun, a wisp of vapour wafting from the barrel as the heat of the discharge bled into the damp air. Before Flint could thank her, she turned and jogged after Bukin and the other provosts.

'Putting the *combat* into *combat medic*, eh sir?' Lhor said as he caught up.

Flint ignored the comment, too intent upon facing the Catachan.

'Vendell!' Flint heard Skane bellow across the hazy chamber floor. 'Move!'

Hearing Skane's order, the Catachan peered out of his cover. Seeing what was happening he bawled for his followers to attack and then ducked back into the nook before the provosts could open fire. While Skane and his convicts were heading west along the chamber wall towards the vestibule portal, Flint and the heavy flamer team were heading east, towards the Catachan, covering the escape and hoping to deal with the enemy leader.

The white smog beyond the Catachan's hiding place grew dense with grey shadows, and Flint knew that more rebels were closing in, as he had expected them to. 'Get ready,' he growled, patting Lhor on the shoulder.

More shouts rang out from behind the various oversized machines around the chamber floor as Vendell's groups coordinated their dash for freedom with Skane and Bukin's. Flint didn't turn, but kept his bolt pistol trained on the nook where the Catachan was still sheltering.

After a few more seconds the first of the grey shadows resolved into a solid figure. It was a rebel convict, wearing fragments of glossy black hardshell torn no doubt from the body of a slain claviger-warden. The man was wielding a length of serrated iron bar. Lhor grimaced in disgust at the sight of the cruel weapon, and raised his flamer, but Flint warned him off. 'Wait.'

A few seconds later, more rebels emerged from the smog, each carrying an improvised weapon as cruel and inventive as the first man's. They saw Flint and immediately recognised him as a commissar, breaking into a chorus of hateful invective that echoed around the entire chamber.

'Now,' said Flint.

'With pleasure, sir,' said Lhor.

A jet of chemical fuel arced from the nozzle of the heavy flamer, igniting into blinding orange fire as it passed through the hissing pilot flame. Intense heat erupted all around, and even though Flint was standing on the other side of the weapon's business end he felt the exposed skin on his face singed by its force. Lhor had set the valve to fire a long, narrow blast, and the flames lanced through the smog, parting it before enveloping the lead rebel in burning fuel and transforming him into a raging column of fire, his rapidly disintegrating form collapsing to the ground. The man hadn't even had time to scream.

Lhor cut the roaring flame off as the survivors faltered, some backing off into the all-enclosing smóg.

'Stand!' the Catachan bawled from cover. 'Or I'll kill you myself!'

'Easy for him to say,' Lhor drawled, preparing to fire a second burst.

Seeing that Skane's group were all clear, Flint decided it was time to get moving after them. 'One more blast,' Flint ordered. 'Just to put them off following.'

A second lance of flame arced outwards, Lhor washing it left and right to catch as many of the rebels in the snaking burst as possible. Even over the roar of the weapon's discharge and the stink of its promethium fuel, Flint heard the banshee wail of burning men and smelled the stink of roasting flesh. Even for a battle-hardened commissar, some things were hard to watch, but he forced himself to continue aiming his bolt pistol at the Catachan's position.

He was glad he had, as the huge rebel leader powered out of his hiding place with his shotgun raised and unleashed an un-aimed blast towards Flint and his companions. At the very same instant, Flint fired his pistol and both attacks hit home at once.

The Catachan's volley blasted one of Lhor's fellow logistics troops to the ground as dozens of pellets tore into his right arm and shoulder. Flint's bolt shell grazed the Catachan in the meaty flesh of his upper left arm, but it exploded too late to inflict its full potential of damage. The Catachan was so tough and heavily muscled that he fought on, bellowing a curse at Flint.

Backing away, the Catachan raised his shotgun one-handed, his wounded arm hanging limp at his side. Flint lined up a second shot, this one aimed straight at his enemy's head, when the man spun on the spot and fired his weapon into the smog to his left. Flint's aim was spoiled, but Lhor was ready to fire again.

'Hold fire!' said Flint.

'I have them, sir,' Lhor complained, his face now blackened and sooty from the heavy flamer's backwash. 'I can take the whole *khekking* lot!'

'I said *hold*,' Flint repeated as the Catachan retreated into the smog, treading through the smouldering remains of his dead followers and scattering still-burning cinders across the ground. One more shot boomed out of the fog, this time muted by the heavy moisture in the air. The grey figures the Catachan had been firing at emerged to Flint's right, improvised weapons raised two-handed and eyes wild with a mixture of battle-lust and terror.

Lhor swept the heavy flamer back and forth, ready to incinerate the newcomers, but he held his fire as ordered.

Flint switched aim and pointed his pistol at the nearest figure. It was a woman, her clothes little more than rags stitched crudely around the curves of her body. She wore heavy, knee-high combat boots and a rebreather obscured the lower half of her face. She raised both hands as she skidded to a halt on seeing Flint.

A second figure emerged beside the woman, this one

clad just as roughly and sporting waist-length dreadlocks. He however did not raise his hands, and Flint brought his pistol to bear on the man's face.

'Vahn?' Flint called out, judging by his bearing that this was the leader of the third group of refugee convicts.

The two shared a quizzical glance as more convicts appeared behind them, spreading out but obviously nervous that more rebels would soon descend upon them.

'Guard?' said the man, flexing his grip on the iron bar he held in one hand.

'Vostroyan 77th,' said Flint as the sound of running footsteps rang from the fog beyond, soon accompanied by angry shouts. 'Your men are safe.'

Vahn nodded towards Lhor and the huge weapon he was still pointing towards the convicts. 'You sure about that, commissar?'

'Stand down,' Flint ordered Lhor. 'Get moving. We're leaving, Vahn. If you want out, now's your only chance.'

Vahn and the green-haired woman exchanged words too quietly for Flint to overhear, then he waved the rest of the group forward. Satisfied that all of the convicts were moving, Vahn jogged after them, and soon the entire force was moving back towards the tunnel entrance. There, Flint ensured that his entire infiltration party was accounted for, including the man wounded by the Catachan's shotgun blast. Vahn gathered his convicts, ordering them to follow their liberators. Flint could scarcely miss the tension between Vahn and Skane, but the two men appeared to reach an unspoken agreement that whatever recriminations would be voiced would have to wait until they were all clear of the penal generatorium.

With the dozen dragoons and the three-dozen or so convicts moving away down the tunnel towards the vent, Flint was the last to leave the carceri chamber. With one last look, he cursed the place, knowing it was just one of twenty such chambers, all of which would be swarming with murderous rebels. This, he knew, was just the beginning.

'Welcome to Alpha Penitentia, commissar,' said Vahn over his shoulder as he marched away after his companions. 'Welcome to hell.'

SIX
Integration

'So what is this?' snarled Corporal Skane. 'You pulled us out just to torture us?'

'Relax, corporal,' said Flint. 'No one said anything about torture. We just need to ask you some questions.'

Having extracted the convicts from the complex, Flint had brought them back to the regimental laager. Despite the fatigue and the post-battle comedown, Flint had known that he would have to segregate the convicts from the regiment until things could be squared with Aleksis, and so he had approached the intelligence chief, Major Herrmahn, and arranged the use of a number of habitents. The bulk of the liberated convict-workers were gathered in the largest, but Vahn, Becka and Skane had been separated and allocated a small side-chamber each. Flint had sensed that these three would have the most to tell him, whether they wanted to or not.

Now, Skane was seated in the centre of the habitent chamber that Flint was using to interview each of the segregated workers, the sole illumination provided by a portable lumen unit hung directly overhead. Major Herrmahn stood cross-armed behind the convict while Bukin loitered near the entrance, his Vostroyan Mark III rested nonchalantly over his shoulder while he chewed on the stub of his cigar.

'What questions?' said Skane. 'You said I wasn't on any charge.'

'And you're not, corporal,' said Flint. 'But we went in there to spy out the lie of the land, and we ran into you. We need to know how the rebels took over, how many there are and where they are. Start with *how*.'

Skane glanced around the bare habitent chamber, glowering at Bukin before looking back to Flint. 'Colonel Strannik,' Skane said. 'You know him?'

'Not personally,' said Flint. Though he had tried to access the data-stack archives on the former colonel, Flint had been unable to penetrate the cipher-seal placed upon them. He had considered asking for Major Herrmahn's help, but had decided against it until he knew the intelligence chief better. 'What do *you* know about him?'

Skane sighed, then answered, 'He was commanding officer of one of *your* regiments,' said Skane.

'I'm Commissariat,' Flint replied. 'You mean Strannik was Firstborn?'

Flint looked from Skane to Major Herrmahn, who shifted somewhat uncomfortably, then nodded subtly in confirmation.

'Yes,' said Skane. 'I don't know for sure what happened to him to end up in Penitentia, but there were sure some stories doing the rounds.'

'I bet there were,' said Flint, dismissing the comment. In all likelihood none of the stories Skane had heard bore any resemblance to the truth.

'Can't have been that bad though,' Skane added. Flint raised his eyebrows in response, and Skane added, 'Well, he wasn't executed, was he?'

That thought had crossed Flint's mind too. In all his years as a commissar, he had never seen a senior Guard officer who had committed a punishable crime sentenced to imprisonment in any sort of penal facility. Those charged with cowardice, gross incompetence or corruption were generally executed on the spot, while those with the clout to avoid such a fate were normally able to pull in some sort of favour that got them well away from the source of the trouble and any likely ramifications. Some fell back on past relationships with other officers now in a more senior position, calling in favours and buying themselves cushy appointments on the general staff or some backwater garrison. Strannik ending up in Alpha Penitentia was suspect indeed.

'What was he like?' Flint pressed.

'He ran the place like he was the governor,' Skane replied. 'Like it was his birthright.'

'And the other convicts, they accepted this?'

'Huh,' said Skane. 'They didn't have any choice. Anyone that didn't play along got strung from the upper galleries.'

'And the wardens, the clavigers. They allowed this to happen?'

'Oh yeah,' Skane sneered. 'They *made* it happen.'

Flint saw Herrmahn shift again, as if he knew all this already and had no desire to hear it again.

'How?' said Flint. 'And why?'

'Commissar,' Major Herrmahn interjected before Skane could answer. 'Might I suggest we pursue this line of enquiry at a later juncture?'

Flint nodded slowly, acceding to the intelligence chief's request. Herrmahn was perhaps his only ally on the regiment's staff, and not an officer he wanted to make an enemy of. Only by showing consideration to the convoluted politicking of the noble clans that dominated the region's military would he have any chance of fulfilling his duty as regimental commissar. Then something occurred to him. As commanding officer of a regiment of the Vostroyan Firstborn, Strannik must be, or must have been at least, part of that complex network of bloodlines and patronage. Perhaps, Flint realised, Strannik was a member of the Anhalz Techtriarch clan.

'Commissar?' Skane interrupted his chain of thought. 'We done here?'

'For now,' said Flint. 'Yes, we're done.'

Bukin stirred himself by the portal, and led Skane back to his makeshift holding cell. 'You want the next one?' he asked.

'Send in the Savlar,' said Flint, consulting his data-slate. 'Becka.'

Flint continued the interviews late into the night and well into the early morning, taking advantage of the convicts' fatigue to eke information out of them piece by piece without it seeming like an interrogation. He himself was well used to the technique and had little trouble staying alert even though he hadn't rested in what seemed like days. Nevertheless, Flint kept Kohlz on hand to fetch numerous cups of recaff. Bukin had nodded off several times, but had turned down Flint's suggestion he get an hour's sleep, his nasty streak compelling him to watch over every questioning session.

Becka turned out to be a former indentured labourer and erstwhile scum-ganger from the distant mining world of Savlar. While Flint hadn't heard of the planet, Herrmahn and Bukin both had, and they filled in what details the archives couldn't provide. Savlar's mines were served by recidivists, petty criminals and their descendents, and its population was generally held to be one of the most undisciplined in the region. By Herrmahn's account, the workers were so ungovernable they couldn't even be trusted to serve in the Penal Legions of the Imperial Guard. Instead, they were subjected to a brutal regime in which they were given the choice of working or starving, yet some, Becka included, still managed to escape. Flint got little out of Becka regarding how she came to be interred in Alpha Penitentia having escaped her home world, and he let the matter go for the moment.

He also discovered just why she wore her rebreather even when the atmosphere was perfectly breathable. The Savlars, it seemed, were forced to submit to their overseers' rule by keeping them addicted to a low level narcotic rationed out in canisters and inhaled via the facemask. Becka had replaced the regularly rationed chemical with whatever bootleg she could obtain in the seediest depths of Alpha Penitentia. Far from recreational, the continuous inhaling of the drug was probably all that kept her functional.

The Savlar had been unable to offer any more information on Colonel Strannik than Skane had and, in deference to Major Herrmahn, Flint hadn't pressed the matter. Instead, he concentrated on her accounts of the uprising itself in order to get some idea of the events that had led to the outbreak of violence. He already knew from the briefing stacks that the uprising had been triggered when the Departmento Munitorum had ordered the installation to render up a portion of its inmates to serve in a new Penal Legion, to be fielded against warp-slaved rebels preying on the outlying marches of the Finial Sector. The claviger-wardens had gone straight to Colonel Strannik and informed him that he would be responsible for deciding which of his followers would serve and which would be spared, and the complex had immediately split into two factions – those who Strannik sought to condemn to servitude and death in the Penal Legion, and his favourites who would stay behind. Inevitably, those loyal to Strannik were also the strongest and most brutal of the convicts, while those outside of his influence were the powerless and outcast.

Those Strannik consigned to the Penal Legion refused to serve, and driven to desperation rose up against him.

The ensuing battle was brief but deadly, and within hours hundreds of Strannik's enemies were dead, their broken corpses strung from the galleries and gantries of the carceri chambers. But the violence didn't stop there, for the colonel's followers took it upon themselves to punish all who weren't allied to them. They initiated a purge of the entire convict-worker population in a week-long orgy of bloodletting and senseless violence.

Perhaps realising that the violence would reduce the population so much that he would be unable to meet the Officio Munitorum's demands for a newly raised Penal Legion, it appeared that Governor Kherhart ordered the claviger-wardens to put down the uprising and to separate the warring factions. But that proved a grievous mistake, and one that Flint considered sufficiently dire to justify the governor's removal from office. Both sides turned on the wardens and the uprising entered a new and tragic phase. Within another week, the explosion of unfettered violence had resulted in the deaths of almost ninety per cent of the prison staff and untold thousands of the convicts themselves. The clavigers had been pushed back so that now they occupied the gate hall but no other parts of the complex, and as Flint knew only too well, the convicts had control of the defence batteries.

Having obtained a graphic picture of the violence of the uprising from Becka, Flint dismissed her and ordered Vendell brought before him. As Bukin ushered the man into the makeshift interrogation chamber, Flint caught glares of mutual dislike, as if the two men had decided within seconds of laying eyes upon one another that they would be enemies. Bukin seemed to have that effect on some people.

Flint's questioning of Vendell revealed that he was from the world of Voyn's Reach. Vendell had been a breacher in the 812th regiment of the world's heavy assault units, and had got himself into trouble with the Commissariat soon after his regiment's founding. In truth, Flint had neither the time nor the inclination to delve into the seedy details of every convict's fall from grace. Instead, he focused on quizzing Vendell on his knowledge of the rebels' numbers and dispositions. The Voyn's Reacher offered his best guess on both counts, estimating Strannik's followers to number in the thousands and that they were based in Carceri *Resurecti*, a generatoria chamber on the opposite side of the complex to the gate hall.

A plan began to form in Flint's mind as he questioned still more convicts. The ad hoc mission into the complex had achieved its objective, though not in the way Flint had originally intended. In liberating the convict-workers he had discovered more about the rebels than he may have been able to by way of a simple reconnaissance. Yet, it seemed that each convict he questioned had a different notion of the rebel's capabilities and their true agenda. Solomon, the man Flint had encountered first in the tunnels leading to Carceri *Didactio*, seemed to think the rebels numbered in the hundreds of thousands and that the colonel was planning on taking over the entire world of Furia Penitens and proclaiming its secession from the Imperium with him as its king. It was clear to Flint that Solomon's outlook was somewhat… limited.

With Solomon dismissed and returned to the holding area, Bukin brought the last of the convicts, bar Vahn himself, before Flint. Hailing from the feudal world of Asgard, Stank, called 'Rotten' by his companions, was as ugly as Corporal Bukin and just as surly. The man was missing his right ear, the wound still angry and red, as Stank had clearly not had access to proper medicae facilities since losing it at some point during the uprising. Stank voiced his opinion that the uprising was hiding something far more sinister, something heretical and unclean. Though Flint couldn't dismiss the possibility, he suspected that something of the culture of Stank's home world was coming through, the myths and folklore of Asgard's forest-dwelling communities retold and re-imagined through his exposure to the horrors of the galaxy at large. The conversation provided little in the way of genuinely useful information, but did serve to solidify Flint's growing belief that another mission, in larger force and deeper into the penal generatorium complex, was required.

As Bukin ushered Stank away, Flint and Herrmahn were left alone in the starkly lit habitent chamber. Flint had kept an eye out for Herrmahn's reaction whenever Colonel Strannik had been mentioned, and decided to broach the subject before Bukin returned with the last convict, Argusti Vahn.

'We've questioned almost three-dozen convicts,' Flint began. 'And still we know little of this Colonel Strannik or his motivations.'

'I would have thought you'd have guessed some of it by now, commissar.' Herrmahn said. 'You've certainly heard some truth amidst the nonsense these convicts have gabbled tonight.'

'I believe I have,' said Flint. 'But I prefer to deal in facts. Strannik was Firstborn, yes? And I'm guessing that he is related to Governor Kherhart by way of the Techtriarchs of the Anhalz clan. Am I correct?'

Herrmahn looked down at his feet as if considering how much of a truthful answer he should give. 'You are correct in that much, commissar,' he replied.

'But there's more, isn't there,' said Flint. It wasn't a question. In his mind's eye Flint could already see the labyrinthine genealogy chart spreading out before him, and he really didn't like the look of where the lines were meeting, or who they were joining together.

Herrmahn sighed. 'Yes, commissar, there is more. But it has to come direct from–'

'Last one, commissar,' said Corporal Bukin as he led Argusti Vahn into the habitent chamber.

Vahn was wiry to the point of emaciation, though Flint suspected that even in better times he was prone to leanness. His hair was formed into waist-long dreadlocks and his intense eyes gleamed with an almost feral light from the midst of his filthy face. Vahn wore a ragged assortment of clothes combining the basic uniform all of the convicts were issued upon their incarceration with whatever scraps he had obtained since, crudely stitched together in a fashion that reminded Flint of the attire worn by the hardcore of the Gethsemane rebels.

Despite Vahn's vagabond appearance, Flint could tell there was something more to the convict. He had after all asserted himself as leader of the refugee group, and apart from a few underlying tensions most of them appeared to have accepted him in that station. As a commissar it was one of Flint's duties to be aware of the ebb and flow of informal power that sloshed around Imperial Guard units, and the majority of the convicts he had questioned so far appeared to be ex-Guard, planetary defence force or militia. Even those like Becka who hadn't served in a formal sense had probably run with the hyper-violent gangs they grew up around.

'So,' Flint said to Vahn, gesturing for him to sit in the chair in the centre of the chamber. 'What's your story?'

Vahn cast a suspicious glance at the seat. Seeing that it was nothing more threatening than a standard-issue folding camp chair and therefore no immediate threat he sat, though he remained obviously distrustful of his surroundings.

'My story?' said Vahn. 'Can't really say I have one, commissar.'

Flint's eyes narrowed and he folded his arms across his chest. 'Come on, Vahn,' he replied. 'Everyone's got a story. Let's hear something of yours. Where you're from, for a start.'

Vahn snorted as if recalling a joke he had heard a long time ago. 'I'm from Alpha Penitentia, commissar. You?'

Flint didn't answer straight away, but scanned Vahn for any scrap of a clue he could use to his advantage. Vahn's arms were bare and covered in an intricate tracery of tattoos. Those on the right arm were fairly standard for many Imperial Guardsmen, depicting holy images and reams of votive text. Those on the left were less standard and of a more lascivious nature, but not unlike those sported by long-serving Imperial Navy ratings. Was Vahn either of these?

'Originally?' said Flint, going along with it to gain some degree of common ground, 'Orana, more or less. Then Progenium and the storm trooper regiment based out of Cirillo Prime.' Vahn looked blankly back at him, as if he hadn't heard of the place Flint's company had been based for the best part of three years. 'Then the Commissariat, and eventually Gethsemane.'

Still nothing. Vahn shrugged, unimpressed by Flint's credentials. Perhaps the direct approach would work better, he thought.

'I'm assuming you weren't born in the generatorium,' said Flint. Though tinged with sarcasm, the question hardly stretched credulity. Those penal facilities that didn't segregate the sexes or enforce routine sterilisation might have substantial populations of inmates born into incarceration, literally condemned for the sins of their fathers. Flint doubted this was so in Vahn's case however.

'No,' said Vahn, his expression suggesting he found the suggestion mildly insulting. 'I wasn't born in that place.'

'Fine,' said Flint. There was definitely something about Vahn that made Flint suspicious, though he wasn't any closer to uncovering just what it might be. Perhaps changing the subject would uncover more details hidden between the lines. 'We're here to flush this whole place clean, purge these rebels and restore order. I need your help.'

Vahn's eyes flashed to Flint's as the commissar seated himself opposite the prisoner. 'How so?' said Vahn.

'We need to know what we're up against,' said Flint. 'We've spoken to all of your people, but we're not getting much of any use.'

Vahn smiled at that, then said, 'I'm not surprised. Most of them had never left their own carceri chamber before the uprising. The complex is a big place, commissar, and a lot goes on most Emperor-fearing people really wouldn't want to know about.'

'So I've heard,' Flint replied, pleased to be getting somewhere at last. 'And we're here to stop it.' Then, he added, 'To stop *him*.'

'You mean the colonel,' said Vahn flatly.

'I do,' Flint replied. 'I mean to execute him by my own hand.'

Vahn's eyes flashed savagely at Flint's oath.

'You want to help?' Flint pressed.

The feral grin that split Vahn's dirty features was all the answer the commissar needed.

SEVEN
Advance Guard

By the time Flint had concluded his questioning of the liberated generatorium convict-workers, the sun was up and the red-brown wastes around the laager were aglow, casting everything from the regiment's armoured vehicles to the faces of its troops in an infernal blood-red hue.

Stepping from the portal of the makeshift interrogation unit, a memory of another time and place flashed across Flint's mind. It was his first battle against the rebels on Gethsemane, and he had sustained a vicious head wound during the initial breakthrough. Not long out of the storm trooper regiment and only a few weeks into his first appointment with the Commissariat, Flint had been given a classic junior's job – watching over the morale of a second line support unit. A group of insurgents had infiltrated the supply depot in the early hours and launched a brutal assault against the unsuspecting Imperial Guardsmen. The

young Flint had rallied the survivors and in time repelled
the attack, and at some point in the battle one of the frenzied rebels had struck him a vicious blow. Flint had fought
for an hour with his forehead split open and the blood
blurring his vision and tinting everything red, just like sunrise on Furia Penitens.

The unpleasant memory was dispelled in an instant by an
equally unwelcome present. Through the stink of the fuel,
exhaust and oil of the regiment's numerous vehicles came
a gusting taint of that abhorrent stink that had so dominated the wastes. Then it was gone, carried away on the ever
present winds.

Though bone tired, Flint dismissed his fatigue and set
about formulating his plan and the pitch he would make
to the regiment's commanders. He had ordered Bukin to
get a few hours sleep, for the man was practically dead on
his feet. He had made the same demand of Dragoon Kohlz,
but his aide was determined to perform his duty regardless
of his own tiredness, further confirming Flint's decision to
keep him on.

Flint's aide proved himself still more able as he fended off
several attempts from regimental headquarters to summon
Flint to brief Aleksis on the details of the mission. The graf
had received only a brief summary of events and was growing increasingly impatient. Kohlz understood that Flint
needed time to formulate a proposal for the next move, and
that the commissar wanted to keep politics at bay as long
as possible.

Over several cups of recaff, Flint had considered the

situation and how he would overcome it. The reconnaissance mission had learned little first-hand, but in liberating the convicts had gained a useful source of local knowledge.

Locked in the darkness of his personal habitent, Flint sought to block out the raucous sounds of milling Guardsmen and the to and fro of armoured vehicles. Until they knew more of the rebels' disposition, all of those Guardsmen and all of their mighty armoured vehicles were next to useless. While the 77th could simply drive in through the massive iron doors of the gate hall, Flint knew that to do so would be tantamount to suicide and a negligent waste of resources. The rebels were on home ground and would be well able to avoid the Chimera armoured transports.

The regiment could dominate the floors of the massive carceri chambers and labour halls, it could even launch sweeps of the larger vestibule tunnels, but Flint had learned from his questioning of the convicts as well as details provided by Major Herrmahn that the complex was riddled with thousands, perhaps hundreds of thousands of kilometres of vents, flues, pipes, access tunnels and service conduits. Ordinarily, such rat-runs would have been denied to the inmates, accessible only to the claviger-wardens as they moved from one zone of the penal generatorium to another. Since the uprising, the rebels had mastered these tunnels, and could use them to move around the entire complex at will.

No, thought Flint as the morning had dragged on. It was too soon to launch a major assault. The enemy had to be found and fixed in place before it could be brought to battle and destroyed.

His mind made up, Flint called Kohlz from the annex of his shelter. 'Request a command conference,' he ordered. 'And get me some more recaff.'

The regimental headquarters was crowded with officers and aides as Flint entered, Kohlz in tow. It looked like the entire command staff had been gathered to hear Flint's report, with tactical stations doubling as makeshift seats as the 77th's officer cadre packed into every available space.

The crowd parted as Flint made his way towards the throng of officers that represented the highest level of command – Graf Aleksis, Lieutenant-Colonel Polzdam, the adjutant, Major Skribahn and the chief of operations, Lieutenant-Colonel Karsten. While the officers' own personal aides scattered before the approaching commissar, the officers themselves appeared distinctly unimpressed, even haughty and arrogant as they looked up from their discussions.

'Commissar Flint,' said Aleksis. 'We are most glad you could spare us the time.'

So that's how you want to play it, Flint thought as he slowed to a halt before Aleksis and his fellows. The reasonable Aleksis, the man he had spoken with in the aftermath of the meeting with Governor Kherhart, had been supplanted by the aristocrat, the noble scion of the Anhalz Techtriarch clan for whom maintaining face in front of the *chevek* was all. Flint recognised that moment for what it was – the tipping point on which his standing as regimental commissar would be defined.

'My apologies, graf,' said Flint, Aleksis grunting dismissively in response. 'I seem not to have made myself clear.'

'No need to apol...' the graf began, before something in Flint's tone brought him up short. 'What?'

It was almost a repeat of the scene that had played out with the goons of the logistics platoon, and then once again with Bukin out on the wastes that first night. Flint stood like some lone gunfighter facing down a mob of frontier town bullies, his coat hooked back to reveal his bolt pistol at his belt. Aleksis's eyes narrowed as his glance flicked to the weapon, the most direct and potent symbol of a commissar's authority, then back to Flint's.

'You mean to threaten me, in my own headquarters...?' the graf stammered incredulously. 'You think you can...'

'Stop,' Flint ordered, holding up a pointing hand as if to transfix the other man. 'Say nothing more, until I have explained things to you in a manner you might understand.'

When no one dared utter a word, Flint continued.

'I have been appointed regimental commissar of this unit to ensure that the mistakes that led to its predecessor's destruction are not repeated.'

The gathered officers gave an almost inaudible gasp at the mention of that which none dared speak of, and Flint continued.

'The 77th was destroyed fighting the Asharians at Golan Hole. It was wiped out, *utterly*. The glory of ten thousand years, and the eternal debt of Vostroya, was reduced to ashes.' Anger swelled in Flint's heart as he spoke, for his reading into the tragedy of Golan Hole had left him with a poor view indeed of the traditions of Vostroya's so-called noble classes.

'Your forebears,' he snarled, not even trying to conceal the anger he felt as he recalled the suppressed accounts of the battle, 'Allowed themselves to fall prey to hubris and arrogance. The Techtriarchs that rule you sent the 77th to war against a foe they had no business engaging, and entirely for their own interests. The officers of that – of *this* – regiment were too enslaved to their own ideals of honour to object!'

Flint was all but shouting his denunciation of the officers of the last iteration of the 77th Firstborn, his anger and disgust twisting his features into a snarling mask of bitterness.

'Does not the *Tactica Imperium* counsel that a commander who wastes lives for no gain risks failure? "*Loss is acceptable*"', he quoted the holy text, '"*Failure is not!*" These are the words by which a thousand generations of officers have lived, fought, served and died – never for themselves, always for the Imperium! For the Emperor!'

He took a hard breath as he looked from one officer to the next, none of them able to meet his steely gaze.

None, apart from Graf Aleksis.

'Your point is well made, Commissar Flint,' said the commander, and Flint saw genuine contrition in his eyes. 'Those… mistakes shall not be repeated. That is my word, given to you upon my honour.'

Flint nodded slowly, then covered his bolt pistol with his

black leather storm coat once more. 'Then I accept your word, Graf Aleksis.'

The moment passed and the tension leeched out of the air as officers began conferring with their neighbours once more, though few still dared glance in Flint's direction. 'Carry on with your duties,' said the commissar.

'Thank you,' the graf said, something of his old bluster returning, though undoubtedly tempered by Flint's words and what had passed between them. 'Would you perhaps present your report?'

'I would,' replied Flint.

'Then let us call this conference to order,' said Aleksis. The graf's second-in-command looked relieved as he nodded to a tacticae operator, who worked the dials of his station. A large, tripod-mounted pict screen nearby flickered to life.

The image on the pict screen resolved into the face of Governor Kherhart, his head tipped back against the padded leather of his high-backed throne. The man's mouth was slightly open and his eyes were shut, and it was obvious to all that he had nodded off while waiting for the conference to begin.

What is it, Flint thought, *with Imperial Governors? Was it just the aristocracy of the Vostroyan Techtriarchs, or did they all conform to such a type?*

Lieutenant-Colonel Polzdam spoke softly into his vox-pickup, and a moment later the sound of a cough sounded through the pict screen's phono-casters. Flint recognised the sound, and guessed that Claviger-Primaris Gruss was just off-screen. Kherhart came awake with a start, his periwig slipping backwards to reveal a liver-spotted, bald pate.

'About time,' the governor barked. 'Get on with it then!'

'Gentlemen,' Flint began. 'Having thoroughly questioned the convict-workers liberated from the complex and collated all tactical debriefings, I am now in a position to recommend the next phase of our mission to Furia Penitens.'

'Excuse me,' interjected Polzdam, holding up a hand as he spoke. 'We don't even know if there will be a *next phase*. The Lord Governor remains confident that he can...'

'The Lord Governor has lost control,' Flint growled back at the lieutenant-colonel.

'What?' said Kherhart, his face expanding as he leaned into the spy-lens. 'What did he say?'

'By our best estimates,' Flint pressed on, 'the rebels have control of more than ninety-five per cent of the Alpha Penitentia generatorium facility. Worse, they have freedom of movement between zones and we have no real idea of their numbers.'

'There might be just a few hundred,' Major Skribahn cut in.

'There might be just a few hundred *thousand*,' Major Herrmahn said before Flint could answer the adjutant.

'Alpha Penitentia was constructed to house several hundred thousand convict-workers,' Flint continued. 'It's almost as large as the smaller manufactoria on Vostroya, so you all know what that means in terms of population.'

'What did he say?' Governor Kherhart said again as he squinted right into the spy-lens.

'Ordinarily, I might recommend gassing the rebels out, but that would render the entire facility unusable for some years, and as I understand it, the Munitorum's demands for the foundation of a new Penal Legion still stand.'

'They do,' confirmed Captain Rein, the 77th's chief liaison officer.

'Then we are faced with the need to capture the installation intact, and to limit casualties.'

'Limit casualties?' said Polzdam. 'We're talking about rebels here, commissar, not innocent civilians.'

'I've spoken to the convict-workers we extricated from Carceri *Didactio*,' Flint went on. 'And I believe we should deal with this insurrection the same way we would any other issue of discipline and morale.'

'You mean shoot it through the head,' said Polzdam. 'Isn't that how the Commissariat deals with most "issues of discipline and morale"?'

Flint glared darkly at the lieutenant-colonel. Polzdam had the truth of it in many ways, and Flint was glad to see the officers of the 77th hadn't missed the irony. 'As regimental commissar of this unit,' Flint continued, 'I do have certain... powers.

'But,' he continued before he could be interrupted, 'I see no reason to invoke them, not yet at least. Instead, I wish to propose a course of action.'

'Go on, commissar,' said Aleksis. Unlike his senior officers, the 77th's regimental commander appeared unphased by Flint's mention of his powers as commissar. While a minor point, it did confirm to Flint that the graf wasn't beyond redemption. 'I would hear your counsel.'

'Thank you, graf,' said Flint. 'I propose a second mission

into the complex, using the convicts' knowledge to locate the uprising's centre of power. We engage them, then call in the remainder of the regiment to deliver the killing blow. We bring the leaders to justice, and the Munitorum gets its fresh meat.'

'I forbid it!' barked Governor Kherhart, his overly loud voice metallic and distorted as it blurted through the phonocasters. 'The situation is in hand, I say!'

Flint ignored the outburst and fixed his gaze on Aleksis. 'I am only *suggesting* this course of action,' Flint growled. 'I am not *ordering* it.' Not yet at least. 'I leave that to you as regimental commanding officer. Do I make myself clear, graf?'

Aleksis visibly paled as he glanced from Flint to the image of Governor Kherhart on the large pict screen. Flint was well aware that he had placed the graf in a difficult position, in effect forcing the man to choose between his duty to the Emperor and his fealty to his Techtriarch clan. Should he repeat the sins of his father, Flint would step in, performing a field execution right here, in front of the entire officer cadre.

The threat hung heavy in the air of the suddenly quiet headquarters, every officer knowing that should he decide that their commander had made the wrong decision Flint could force him out of office, and worse.

'I understand, commissar,' Aleksis said finally. 'And I am in agreement with your plan.'

Governor Kherhart's face became suddenly grim as he leaned back in his throne. Flint was aware of powerful lines of influence and patronage shifting before him. He had no doubt that the graf had made an enemy of his own kinsman, and so too had Flint.

'If you plan to enter my beloved generatorium,' said Kherhart, his tone suddenly changed to one of conciliation, 'then at least let my men participate. Is that too much to ask?'

'It is not,' said Aleksis before Flint could answer. 'It is only fitting, in fact.'

'Then Claviger-Primaris Gruss and his best wardens shall accompany you,' said the governor. 'And this whole sorry business shall be concluded.'

Flint was less than keen about suffering the presence of the wardens, considering them a means for the governor to interfere. He knew that Vahn and his people were unlikely to react well either, but he set the issue aside for the moment.

'What do you need, commissar?' said Lieutenant-Colonel Polzdam. 'I assume you have drawn up a plan of action?'

'I have,' replied Flint, relieved to be moving on to a more mundane topic, but aware that his next suggestion might meet with some objection from the hidebound officer cadre.

'Firstly,' he continued, 'I want the convict-workers liberated from the complex indentured to the 77th for the duration.'

'You want criminals to join the ranks of my regiment?' spat Graf Aleksis. 'Surely, they're just–'

'Every one of them, as far as I can ascertain, is a trained Guardsman,' Flint cut Aleksis off. He'd known the graf would object and was prepared for it. 'In fact, most have more combat experience than your own dragoons.'

Several of the gathered officers appeared disgusted with the suggestion that convicted recidivists should join the ranks of their regiment, in particular Major Lehren, who held responsibility for the 77th's training and indoctrination. Flint ploughed on before Lehren or any other officer could voice an objection. 'And in addition, they have far more knowledge of the layout and the situation inside the complex.'

'Gruss and his men know as much, surely,' said Aleksis.

'I'm sure they do,' Flint conceded, 'and their presence will no doubt be a benefit. But they can know nothing of the situation since the uprising. We need the convict-workers.'

'Will they serve?' asked Aleksis.

'They aren't being offered a choice,' said Flint. 'They'll serve.'

'This way, ladies!' Bukin waved the liberated convicts into a wide area surrounded by sandbag revetments. Vahn's first reaction was suspicion, the place looking like an ideal killing ground for a regimental firing squad. He glared at the chief provost as he led the line of convicts through the makeshift gates, seeing that it was in fact a quartermaster's marshalling yard filled with cargo crates and busy logistics staff.

Vahn looked around as he waited for the three-dozen convicts to file into the yard, tilting his head back and looking up at the sky. The sight of so much open space was quite alien to him now, his incarceration in Alpha Penitentia having robbed him of the feeling of standing beneath an open sky for so long. The sky was the same colour as the penal generatorium's rockcrete walls – slab grey and dirty. Distant black clouds boiled, and the strobing of internal lightning told Vahn that a storm was brewing to the east. Turning on the spot, Vahn's eyes followed the jagged mountains that bit into the sky along the western horizon, and he judged the tallest were at least three kilometres high. The red-brown ground all around had been transformed into a sprawling Imperial encampment of the type he had seen a hundred times before on a dozen different worlds.

With the convicts' arrival, the logistics staff lugged over a number of crates and dumped them unceremoniously on the dusty ground before them, casting surly glances before shuffling away to the prefab habitent to one side.

'What is this?' said Vahn, growing rapidly tired of not being told what was happening around him.

Bukin grinned widely and pulled out a lighter from a pocket on his webbing. Having lit the cigar that had hung from his mouth all the way to the yard, he drawled, 'You are in the Guard now, son. You call me corporal, chief or lord, your choice.'

Vahn stepped towards the provost, his fellow convicts gathering behind him. As Bukin puffed out a billowing cloud of blue cigar smoke, the other five provosts stepped up to his side. They were a nasty crew, each with the look of a thug, yet Vahn and his people had survived the worst Alpha Penitentia could throw at them and lived. He could take Bukin, if he had to.

'I said,' Bukin leered, 'you are Guard now. You do as you are told.'

Vahn eyed the other man suspiciously and flexed his fists.

He missed the reassuring weight and mass of his iron bar, but he knew how to use his fists. 'You'd better quit messing me around,' Vahn growled as Bukin squared up to him. 'Tell me what's happening or I'll…'

'What's happening,' said Flint as he strode into the yard, his aide not far behind, 'is we're heading back into the complex.'

'Told you,' Bukin grinned. 'You are Guard now.'

'Commissar?' said Vahn, pointedly ignoring the ugly little chief provost.

'I promised you I'd bring Strannik to justice,' said Flint. 'And I said I'd need your help.' Flint scanned the nearest of the cargo crates the logistics staff had set down nearby, then kicked it so the hinged lid popped up.

Vahn's dread at the thought of returning to the charnel house that was Alpha Penitentia warred with his desire to see Colonel Strannik and his murderous followers taken down. The latter won.

'How?' said Vahn.

'Well,' Flint replied. 'I'm assuming you all know how to use these?'

Flint set a foot on the lip of the crate and pushed it forwards so that its contents spilled out across the ground.

'Lasguns,' said Vahn.

'M40 Vostroyan-pattern carbine, Mark V,' drawled Bukin. 'Only the best for you, ladies.'

Vahn looked around at the remainder of the crates, noting the markings stencilled upon each. The Mark Vs were clearly old and battered, probably excess stock, but they were functional at least. One crate contained a variety of

Firstborn-issue armour consisting of chainmail hauberks and plates of metal-chased carapace. Another contained frag grenades, a third an assortment of field gear and a fourth a selection of different support weapons, each at least as old as the Mark Vs. The equipment was basic and old and apparently drawn at random, but it would do. None of it was anything like the gold-filigreed, artisan-wrought heirloom weapons carried by the dragoons of the Firstborn, but it was clearly functional, and that had to mean something.

'You trust us with these?' said Vahn.

'*I* do,' said Flint. '*He's* not so nice,' he added with a nod towards Bukin. The chief provost was carrying several side arms about his person, as were his men, but at least they weren't pointing them at the convicts.

'Fair enough,' said Vahn. 'Not sure I would either, but I guess we'll need them where we're going.'

'Then get to it,' said Flint. 'I'll be back in an hour.'

The convicts, now penal troopers Vahn reminded himself, gathered around the crates. At first they were suspicious and not all were sold on the idea of returning to the hell that was their former home. Yet, all knew that there would be a price for escaping Alpha Penitentia, and for most that price was worth paying. What happened afterwards was another matter though, and a subject that Vahn was already giving thought to. If any of them survived their return to the complex, what then?

Maybe the weapons would come in handy later, thought Vahn as his companions opened the other crates and started rifling through the contents. Lasguns were passed from hand to hand and bandoliers of power packs slung over shoulders. The weapons were definitely cast-offs, he thought, short-form carbines, not the long-form, lovingly wrought and maintained weapons carried by the Firstborn. Webbing was donned and pouches stuffed full of grenades and other items. The penal troopers strapped armoured shoulder guards, vests and shin guards over their prison rags, and some took up the tall, furred helmet and rebreather so characteristic of the Firstborn. Evidently intent on starting up some new trade venture later on when supplies started to dwindle, Rotten had stuffed his pockets with as much gear as he could carry.

Becka inspected the standard-issue breath masks with obvious disdain, deciding to keep her own unit. Vahn, herself and several others decided against the wearing of helmets and rebreathers, feeling they would reduce visibility in the already dark and cramped environs of the complex's twisting network of pipes, vents and tunnels.

Vahn heard Solomon give an exclamation of delight as he unwrapped a Vostroyan pattern long-las sniper rifle from its protective sheath. Solomon had always boasted he was a good shot, and by the way he cradled the rifle he was set on proving it.

Finally, the penal troopers had all armed and armoured themselves, and Vahn looked them up and down. Short of some sanctioned merc-house, he had rarely seen such a bunch of misfits bearing arms in the name of the Emperor. Vostroyan armour was mingled with torn rags, and even though the new troopers had been allowed to wash they still managed to look dirty. Casting a glance towards the distant spire of the complex, Vahn reflected that it would take a long time indeed to wash away the stain of that place.

'Don't you ladies look a treat,' slurred Corporal Bukin as he checked his wrist chrono. 'Now straighten up all of you,' he barked as Commissar Flint strode back into the yard. 'Attention!'

Most of the penal troopers had served in the Imperial Guard and at the sound of Bukin's bellowed order half-forgotten training asserted itself with a vengeance. Even those who hadn't had the training responded to the order, stamping their feet and standing ramrod straight. It was evident straightaway however that each of the ex-Guardsmen had learned a different drill, for no two worlds' regiments held exactly the same military traditions.

'You will have to learn Firstborn way, *chevak*,' said Bukin, 'But you'll do.'

'Thank you, corporal,' said Commissar Flint as he paced the line of penal troopers. 'Now listen up,' he said as he came to Vahn. 'We've got a mission to complete, and I mean for us all to come back in one piece.'

High atop the gate hall block, Lord Governor Kherhart, thirteenth Imperial Commander of Furia Penitens and proud cousin of the Anhalz Techtriarch clan entered a dark chamber, the walls lined with dull lead into which was engraved an impossibly complex pattern of hexagrammic and pentagrammic wards. The chamber was a last ditch refuge from where the sole survivor of a disastrous uprising could call for outside aid, whether in-system by high-power vox or, if he had the ability and needed to communicate over greater distances, with his astropathic mind-voice.

Kherhart stepped over the raised lip of the chamber opening, his ancient limbs protesting despite the numerous augment-procedures he had subjected himself to over the years. Once through, the Lord Governor turned and hauled on the wheel in the centre of the chamber's armoured door, straining a moment before it yielded and swung inwards upon massive hinges.

Having turned the locking wheel, Kherhart proceeded towards the centre of the chamber. It wasn't a large space, for it didn't need to be. It was designed to protect its occupant long enough for help to be called. Once the message was sent, no one really cared what happened to the sender. In all likelihood, he would be a shrivelled corpse before help arrived, but his survival wasn't the point.

The point, Kherhart mused, was retribution.

The centre of the chamber was host to a large vox-caster, its machine systems housed within a column that ran from ceiling to floor and was lined with snaking cables and chased with numerous glass meters and brass dials. Kherhart knew that the caster was powerful enough to communicate with a starship in orbit, and given the time for its machine-spirit to speak across the void, with one much further away. But the governor wasn't here to talk to a starship, in orbit or anywhere else. He was here to communicate with someone much nearer by, and he needed the privacy afforded by the refuge-chamber to ensure that he wasn't overheard.

'Now then,' Kherhart muttered to himself as he looked

over the complex array of dials and levers on the vox console before him. 'Strike the Rune of Initiation,' he mumbled as he recalled the proper ritual for awakening the vox-caster's slumbering machine-spirit. 'The rune...' he said as his rheumy eyes searched the console.

Finally locating a small, green-lit plate marked with the sacred machine-code inscription *Omega nu*, Lord Kherhart gingerly reached out a liver-spotted finger and depressed it according to the ritual. Nothing happened at first, but soon Kherhart could hear a high-pitched whirring like an atmos-purger spinning at full speed. Then he jumped in alarm as a multi-tonal chime boomed forth from a phono-horn mounted halfway up the column just above his head.

Forcing his breathing to a normal rate, Kherhart recalled the next part of the ritual. Locating a panel of brass alpha-numeric keys, he entered his personal cipher seal, one key at a time, and waited. A moment later, a pict screen in the centre of the console guttered to life as the sound of machine nonsense blurted from the horn.

'Are you there?' Kherhart said with trepidation. Then he spotted a pickup shaped like the shell of some sea-dwelling crustacean, and leaned in towards it. 'Hello?' he said.

'I'm here,' a voice replied from the phonohorn, 'cousin.'

'Good,' said the Lord Commander. 'Good. I shall make this brief. They're coming in. They intend to bring you to justice and ship your men out to fight some secessionist rabble. They want to make an example of you.'

Ominous silence stretched out, punctuated by burbling machine chatter. 'You couldn't dissuade him?' the voice replied, laced with threat despite the interference.

'I could not,' said Kherhart. 'Our kinsman appears to have made a poor choice.'

'Then we'll have to settle this another way,' the voice said. 'I take it you've taken the necessary precautions.'

'I have,' said Kherhart. 'One of my own is going in with them.'

'Good,' the voice said. 'I shall await his signal. Out.'

Lord Kherhart waited a long minute, ensuring the communication was done with. Then he located the Rune of Deactivation and powered down the vox-caster. As the machine-spirit entered its slumber state, Kherhart dared to imagine his precious installation would soon be his again, despite the interfering of the Imperial Guard and his treacherous kinsman.

Yes, he thought as he shuffled back towards the armoured hatch. It was all about retribution…

As sundown approached, the grey skies darkened to a deep, velvety purple, the sweep of the local galactic arm bisecting the entire vista. The 77th's provost section led the newly recruited – some preferred 'press-ganged' – penal troopers towards the staging point, where they would take their place in the assault force Commissar Flint had assembled. The provosts cajoled and harangued the troopers as they trudged along, making sport of their rag-tag appearance and questioning their ability to shoot straight with any of the weapons they had been equipped with. Vahn glowered at the thugs as he walked, promising they'd see just how straight he could shoot if he got the chance to show them.

The muster point was just outside the perimeter of the regimental laager, and Vahn found a small group waiting there. Flint and his aide was present, the dragoon fiddling with his over-sized vox-caster. Why the man didn't use a Number Twelve set Vahn had no idea, for the Number Four he was using was way too cumbersome for use in the cramped confines of the conduits and sluice tunnels. The aide appeared to be listening intently to a signal while attempting to tune his set in, but by the expression on his face he wasn't getting very far.

Corporal Bukin was there too, his shotgun rested over his shoulder and a cigar puffing blue smoke into the cold air. Despite the chief provost's outward brusqueness, Vahn was savvy enough to catch the tension in his eyes. The man was wary, not of the penal troopers, but of something else. His gaze was constantly on the move, panning the surrounding wastes like he was expecting trouble at any moment. Seeing the provosts arrive with the penal troopers, Bukin moved off to confer with his goons, revealing another figure who had been standing behind him.

Vahn halted and brought his lasgun up with a fluid, instinctive movement. 'What's he doing here?' Vahn demanded. As if being led by a commissar wasn't bad enough, they expected his people to suffer the presence of a...

'He's going in with us,' said Flint his tone the very model of diplomacy. 'You will stand down, all of you.'

The three-dozen penal troopers had followed Vahn's example, every one of them levelling his or her weapon at the hard shell-clad figure of Claviger-Primaris Gruss. Further back, a full squad of armed clavigers milled around, waiting for the order to move out.

The chief warden's blank-faced mask scanned the penal troopers, the simple action somehow conveying as much disdain as a full sneer.

'Put 'em down,' Vahn growled, lowering his own carbine to point at the dusty ground.

'Why?' Vahn said to Flint, his eyes not leaving the warden's mask.

'Same reason we need you,' said Flint. 'Inside knowledge. Now let's…'

'Wait,' said Vahn, switching his gaze to the commissar. 'Before we go back in there…'

'Yes?' said Flint, meeting Vahn's gaze and holding it unblinkingly.

'I want your word. We're coming out again. No tricks.'

'No tricks. If any of your people don't come back, it's because the Emperor had other plans for them, not because of me. Understood?'

Vahn let the question hang for a moment. Vendell grunted while Becka nodded subtly. Skane looked away with disgust written on his face.

'Okay,' said Vahn, his mind made up. 'Let's get this over with.'

EIGHT
Penitentia

Trooper Stank, called 'Rotten' by his mates, didn't trust the route the claviger boss had told Flint they should take, but he had little choice but to follow it. The Asgardian was on point, utilising his training to scout the way ahead as the assault force followed on a hundred metres behind. The force had entered through a service port carved through the sub-surface of the wastes, and having crept through the work bays infiltrated the ten kilometre-long tunnel that passed beneath the purgation chambers and joined the workings under Labour Hall 12.

Treading lightly as he advanced, Rotten scanned the route ahead through his night vision goggles. He'd never used such devices before – because the regiment he had served in before coming to Furia Penitens recruited from a relatively primitive society its members were considered incapable of adapting to such technological marvels. Well, Rotten had adapted very well to such things. He'd developed a taste for collecting useful gear, which had caused him to become something of an unofficial quartermaster in his old regiment – someone his fellow rangers could come to if they 'mislaid' their issued equipment and didn't fancy their chances with the logistics staff. Rotten had earned a small fortune with his enterprise, but he had also earned a charge, and been sentenced to imprisonment in Alpha Penitentia.

A shape appeared in the middle ground, the goggles rendering it a roiling mass as they sought to focus on and refine the return. Rotten halted and went down on one knee, his carbine resting across his thigh. Cautiously, he strained his ears, and hearing nothing other than the ever-present dripping of liquid as condensation built up with the crippling of the air-scrubbers, he raised the goggles.

Without the aid of the machine-magic of the goggles, the scene up ahead was a mass of shadows tinged a deep red by what remained of the overhead lumens. Rotten focused on the large shadow as his eyes adapted to the darkness and he finally worked out what it was. It was a wrecked Admonisher, a class of armoured vehicle used by the claviger-wardens to herd large numbers of convicts from one part of the complex to another, in this particular case, between Carceri *Resurecti* and Labour Hall 12.

Standing, Rotten glanced over his shoulder, looking to judge how far behind him the main force was, but he neither saw nor heard much to indicate he was anything but alone in the tunnel. He turned back towards the tank, unable to suppress the urge to take a look inside as he crept past it. You never know what might have been left behind, he told himself with a wry grin.

Lowering the goggles again, he saw that they were still having difficulty rendering the shape of the ruined tank, though he still needed the goggles to ensure no rebel convicts were lurking in the shadows nearby. Advancing along the wide tunnel, he veered towards the centre and the ruined Admonisher, the goggles finally getting a fix on it as he approached.

The Admonisher was a variant of the ubiquitous Rhino armoured transport used by many branches of the Imperium, but was open-topped to allow the wardens it carried to maintain overwatch on the convicts they herded. The huge, V-shaped man catcher mounted at the tank's front towered over Rotten like the prow of a warship as he approached, and he slowed as he spotted debris strewn across the rockcrete ground around the tank. Tracking back to the Admonisher's open side hatch, Rotten saw that someone else had got there first. It looked like someone had rifled through the interior of the tank, the litter scattered across the ground indicating that nothing valuable had been found.

He was about to continue on his way when Rotten caught a whiff in the stale, damp air of the tunnel. It was meat, burned meat, and his gorge rose as he guessed its source. Penal mass-refectories rarely served high-grade grox steak – the meat in question could only be from one animal.

Rotten swallowed hard as the stink filled his nose and oozed its way down his gullet. He felt nauseous, but the sensation still warred with curiosity. Deciding to take just a quick peek, just to be sure the tank contained nothing that might threaten the mission, Rotten approached the side hatch and hesitantly leaned in to peer into the troop bay.

He wished he hadn't.

Rotten had seen a lot of unpleasant things in his life; on his home world of Asgard and out in the wider galaxy in service to the Emperor. On the ocean world of Psamath, he'd seen a carnivorous sand clam bite Ranger Nandi in half, and on Klaranthe Station he'd seen an entire infantry platoon sucked into the cold void when a hangar bay integrity field malfunctioned. But both had been accidents, the sort of thing that just happened to the 'poor bloody infantry' in the course of their service to the God-Emperor of Mankind. What Rotten saw inside the Admonisher's troop bay was different. It was a whole lot different.

The tank had been overrun at some point in the uprising, its attackers swarming up and over its high sides to fall upon its passengers and crew. The battle must have been brief, though the rebels' ire looked like it had been stretched out over several hours, the clavigers being subjected to a degree of cruelty that Rotten had never before seen, even in a galaxy of wanton savagery and bloodshed. He couldn't even tell how many wardens had been caught within the vehicle, so mutilated and burned were their remains.

Rotten turned away, fighting the urge to throw up.

'Stank!' a voice said in Rotten's vox-bead, causing him to jump almost out of his skin.

'Stank,' the voice repeated. 'Where are you?'

'Frag!' Rotten cursed. 'Who the hell is…'

'Stank,' the voice repeated. 'This is Vahn. We have eyes on some sort of vehicle. You there?'

'I'm there,' Rotten gasped as he fought to bring his breathing and heart rate back to normal. 'It's a wrecked 'monisher. Passing it now.'

'Understood,' Vahn replied. 'Flint says to pick up the pace. How far to the terminus?'

Squinting through his goggles, Rotten could just about make out the far end of the tunnel. 'Another twenty minutes,' he replied. 'Moving out now.'

'So,' said Flint as he stared up at the structure coded Terminus R1. 'How do we get through *that*?'

Terminus R1 was in essence a huge revolving door, but unlike any Flint had ever seen: its four wings were made of heavy grade armaplas measuring ten metres to a side. Each of the four armoured wings was attached to and rotated around a central shaft, the entire assembly held within a tubular enclosure with an exit on either side. The terminus was large enough to allow an entire sub-shift of convicts or a single Admonisher to pass through and, because there was never an open path right through, no one other than those permitted inside the enclosure could make a dash for freedom. Flint could well understand the function, but his question, addressed to Claviger-Primaris Gruss, was aimed at the fact that the mechanism was entirely immobile because its power source had been crippled during the uprising.

Gruss turned his blank-faced visor from the terminus and

his unseen gaze settled upon Flint. 'We don't,' said the warden through his hard shell armour's hidden phonocasters. 'We go around it.'

'How?' said Flint, looking around the end of the tunnel for any sign of other passageways offering an alternative route. Lifting his data-slate and consulting Major Herrmahn's tri-D map, he saw no obvious way around the terminus.

'Not every route is marked,' said Gruss. 'I'm sure you can appreciate the need to keep certain access points hidden from the inmates, commissar.'

'What about the main force?' said Flint as Vahn stepped up beside him.

'They'll have the firepower to blast their way through, and they won't be concerned with alerting the rebels to their presence,' said Gruss. 'We do not have such a luxury,' he added.

'How?' said Vahn.

'My men will lead the way,' said Gruss, sidestepping the question.

'Where?' Vahn pressed, his voice a low growl.

Gruss turned on Vahn and Flint saw the signs of imminent confrontation. Moving between them, Flint said, 'Gruss, lead the way. Vahn, get your people ready. We have a mission to complete.'

As Gruss stalked away to gather his squad, Flint turned on Vahn. 'You need to drop the attitude, and quick,' he hissed low so no one could overhear.

'*He's* the one with the attitude, commissar,' Vahn replied, his voice equally low. 'If we're all such close friends now, why doesn't he want us knowing where their secret tunnels are?'

The same thought had occurred to Flint, but he needed the clavigers and the ex-convicts working together and so had to avoid fostering suspicion between the two groups. God-Emperor knows, he thought, there were enough reasons for them to be at each other's throats and he had no desire to give them more.

'Give him a chance, Vahn,' Flint replied. 'Old habits die hard. And besides,' he added, 'I'm keeping my eye as much on him as I am on you, got it?'

'Down there?' said Rotten, following the claviger's directions into what at first appeared to be the gaping, shark-toothed mouth of an articulated waste compactor. 'You can't be serious?'

'I'm serious,' said the claviger, his mouth set in a smug grin that Rotten wanted dearly to punch right out. 'It's not like it's powered up.'

Rotten leaned forwards into the compactor's mouth and looked down into its workings. The entire inner surface was lined with multiple rollers edged with a million tarnished metal teeth. When activated, he knew that the rollers would come together and the teeth start revolving, annihilating anything thrown down the chute from masonry to corpses. In fact, Rotten could swear there were scraps of dried flesh lodged between some of the teeth, like bits of a gigasaur's last meal. At present, the rollers were retracted into the chute's wall, leaving a drop between them leading down into the darkness.

'Not at the moment,' Rotten muttered, leaning back and taking the rope line Solomon passed to him. He could hardly miss the expression of sympathy barely hidden on the Jopalli's face. 'How far down?' he asked the claviger.

'Only twenty metres or so,' the warden replied. 'Why?' he added. 'Scared?'

Rotten sneered but held his tongue, making sure to memorise the claviger's face. It would be terrible if the warden was nearby when Rotten's carbine discharged negligently...

'What's the hold up?' Rotten heard Vahn call from behind the claviger. 'Rotten? You wimping out on us?'

Ignoring the jibe and the leering grin from the warden, Rotten fixed the rope to a spar just above the lip of the waste chute and twisting it around one hand, tested it would take his weight. Satisfied, he edged into the gaping metal maw and set his feet on opposite rollers, the black throat of the chute visible between his legs as he looked directly downwards.

'Twenty metres?' he said to the claviger.

'It's twenty to where you want to go,' the warden growled. 'The chute goes further, but you really don't want to follow it.'

Rotten swallowed hard but was determined not to show the slightest degree of trepidation, not to a claviger at least. 'Right,' he said. 'Thanks.'

Pulling the rope through the compactor's mouth, Rotten sent it plummeting down its shadowed throat. With the toothed rollers retracted the chute was a couple of metres in diameter; with them deployed it would be less than a millimetre. Securing the rope to a loop attached to his webbing, Rotten took it in both hands and began his descent, one foot at a time.

Fortunately for Rotten, the teeth provided excellent purchase, and they weren't sharp enough to trouble him. Yet, he could scarcely shake the thought of the rollers suddenly grinding to life and tearing his body to gristle as the chute contracted. He tried not to look at the teeth as he descended, especially at the debris lodged between them, yet he could hardly avoid catching the occasional glimpse. Most of the material was nothing more than long dried out scraps of food or torn ration wrappers. Yet, one piece looked like a man's scalp, hair and bloody skin knotted together, and another like fragments of a jawbone, the teeth still affixed to a shrivelled length of gum.

'God-Emperor on Terra,' Rotten mumbled as he sped up his descent, carrying himself past what he prayed was not the body part it looked like. 'Beati Khalus and Sister Ebrina too…' he added, invoking two of his world's patron saints as he screwed his eyes shut. It *was* the body part it looked like.

'Stop!' the claviger up top called out, and Rotten halted, setting one foot on a roller on either side of the chute. 'Twenty!' the warden called down, his head and shoulders barely visible as silhouettes against the bloody red light far overhead.

A burst of panic erupted in Rotten's chest as he looked

around for the side passage he was supposed to take. It wasn't there – all he could see was the rollers lined with row upon row of metal teeth.

The claviger laughed coldly, and Rotten knew with dread certainty what was about to happen. He screwed his eyes shut, praying it would be quick…

'Behind you, you fenker!' the claviger called out cruelly.

Rotten's breathing came hard and fast as he opened his eyes and slowly twisted around. Behind him, he saw the gaping mouth of a concealed side passage, its interior completely lost in shadow.

'Hah!' Rotten laughed, the relief welling inside him threatening to turn to maniacal laughter. Of course, he thought as he braced his hands gingerly against the rollers on either side and twisted his body completely around. At one point his boot slipped on a smear of fluid, but he caught himself before he could lose his footing. Having turned his body all the way around, Rotten stood over the chute facing into the side passage.

Suddenly, he was less than keen to be out of the compactor's throat, the side passage looking somehow even more threatening.

'Stank?' Vahn's voice called out from above. Rotten glanced upwards, and although he couldn't make out Vahn's features he could tell it was him by his mane of dreadlocks.

'Uh-huh?' he called back, trying to sound as unconcerned as possible. 'Here.'

'You found it?' Vahn called. 'Gruss says there should be a passageway leading towards…'

'Yup!' Rotten called back, 'I've found it.' Taking a deep breath, he added, 'Going in now.'

The mouth was the entrance to one of the clavigers' many hidden runs, the maze of secret tunnels they used to move about the penal generatorium without the need to enter the sealed carceri chambers, turbine chambers and cooling halls. The placement of the entrance in the throat of a waste compactor chute had ensured its continued secrecy, for not even the most desperate escapee would be insane enough to think of climbing into such a hellishly lethal place.

The tunnel beyond the mouth turned out to be less shadowed than it had appeared to Rotten from the throat of the 'pactor. As he advanced he discovered it was lit by low-level lumen bulbs that emitted a wan, sodium-yellow light just bright enough to allow safe passage. The tunnel was all but featureless, its sides cast roughly from poured rockcrete. Unlike so much of the complex's interior, the floor was free of the ever present debris that littered most areas, and as Rotten trod silently along its length his passing disturbed a carpet of dust that had lain untouched for decades, perhaps centuries.

Having pressed on another fifty metres or so, Rotten signalled that the route appeared clear, and the main body of the assault force began its descent, one trooper at a time. The clavigers came down first, their leader Gruss shouldering his way past Rotten to advance further along the tunnel. The Asgardian could tell that the claviger boss was jealous of the knowledge of the secret passages' existence and would stubbornly guard the location of any other entrances.

Next down were Vahn and the rest of the penal troopers, and Rotten saw straight away the pattern Flint had chosen. With the clavies down first and the provosts last, none of the former convicts would be tempted to leg it. Not that they had anywhere better to be, Rotten thought.

Finally, the assault force was all safely down and Vahn clapped Rotten on the back as he overtook him. 'Let Solomon take point for a bit,' Vahn ordered, sensing the strain the descent had placed on Rotten's nerves. 'Farmer boy there could do with learning some new tricks,' he winked.

The first stretch of the passage proved so dusty that the troopers were forced to don their rebreathers. The Firstborn provosts carried theirs as standard issue, and the clavigers had full-face helmets with inbuilt filters they could wear. But not all of the penal troopers had brought such items along and so Rotten was afforded his first chance to act as unofficial quartermaster. Flint had seen him hand off a spare rebreather to the highest bidding of his companions, bartering against future rations and equipment issues, but had not reprimanded him... yet.

The advance continued in single column, the tunnel too narrow for more than one trooper. Solomon took his turn on point, halting every now and then to train the high-powered scope mounted atop his rifle along the length of the tunnel ahead. Of course, such a weapon would prove useless were an enemy somehow able to jump out at Solomon from close range, and so one of Corporal Bukin's provosts advanced just behind, his shotgun raised over Solomon's shoulder.

After an hour or so of tramping through the billowing dust of the secret tunnel, Gruss raised a clenched fist and Flint signalled the column to a halt. With a nod of his blank-faced visor, the Claviger-Primaris indicated a slight recess in the ceiling up ahead. Flint nodded to Solomon, then ordered two of the nearby regimental provosts to link hands and give the penal trooper a boost up to the small, metal hatch set in the recess. The provosts' objection to aiding the former convict was plain to see, and Bukin was about to issue a complaint when the sound of gushing liquid sounded from above, beyond the hatch.

Flint moved along the column until he was standing directly below the hatch. He listened intently as the sound of rushing water grew louder and he could make out solid objects bumping along the surface on the other side of the hatch. After a minute the sound receded, fading away to a low gurgling before disappearing entirely.

'What's up there?' Flint asked Gruss. Though he guessed the assault force was below the target zone, Carceri *Resurecti*, the generatoria chamber in question was several kilometres to the side and they could be well off their intended course. And if they ran into trouble and had to call the main force forward prematurely, the chances of successfully linking up would be that much worse.

Gruss didn't reply straight away, but glanced at one of his clavigers as if seeking confirmation. Whatever passed between the two men, Flint couldn't tune in to it. 'It's the sluice-weir below *Resurecti*'s primary cooling plant,' Gruss answered, but Flint could tell something was wrong despite the distortion imparted by his armour-mounted phonocasters.

'But?' Flint prompted.

'The generatoria systems right across the complex were shut down or crippled during the uprising,' Gruss began. 'The weirs below each cooling tower are there to siphon off the moisture that builds up as condensation when the systems are offline.'

'That,' Flint indicated the hatch, 'sounded like more than condensation.'

'It was,' Vahn interjected, shoving his way past the two provosts blocking his path. 'I served three labour cycles in one of these chambers. These weirs can only handle a handful of cooling plants going down.'

Flint looked back to Gruss and asked, 'How many are down?'

'All of them,' Gruss answered.

'Then the system's overloaded,' said Vahn. 'The weirs are filling up too fast and backing up into the outflow.'

'Which that hatch opens up into,' said Flint.

'Yes, commissar,' Gruss replied. 'This is but one of several hundred secret access points built to allow warden patrols to move around the various generatoria chambers without the convict-workers' knowledge. Without such hidden locations, many of our duties would be all but impossible.'

'Pretty good place to hide it, sir,' Bukin interjected, chewing his unlit cigar. 'Right underneath a river.'

'Maybe too good,' said Flint. 'I'm guessing the channel's rarely used. Regardless, we don't have a choice.'

Flint ordered the column to make ready, and just over ten minutes later the weir flooded again and the overspill drained away via the channel overhead. Flint estimated that a little under twelve minutes had gone by, and if the assault force were to avoid being caught in the open and dashed away that was the amount of time it had to get through the sluice gate and into Carceri *Resurecti*.

As the gurgling overhead faded away, Flint said to Solomon, 'Ready, indenti?'

Solomon didn't look especially ready, but he nodded nonetheless. 'Ready, sir.'

Why me, thought Solomon as the two provosts boosted him up towards the hatch. Why is it always me? His rifle slung over his back, he reached up with both hands and caught hold of the locking wheel in the centre. The wheel was cold and damp, and he braced his feet in the provosts' cupped hands and twisted with all his might.

A gush of stinging, chemical-laced water crashed down on his face and just for a moment Solomon thought he had opened the hatch too soon and brought death down on the heads of all his companions. Blinking as he gasped for breath, he heard the sound of the provosts below him swearing colourfully and he realised that the torrent had stopped as soon as it had started. The truth was, if the torrent hadn't receded, he wouldn't have been able to lift the hatch at all.

As Solomon lifted the hatch on creaking, corroded hinges, a shaft of blinding light shot downwards into the secret tunnel, widening as he opened it as far as it would go. The hatch clanged against a rockcrete wall and, lifting his head and squinting into the light, Solomon saw that he was at the base of the drainage channel, right up against one side.

'I'm going up,' he called down, and hauled himself painfully upwards. Blinking in the suddenly bright surroundings, he looked around. He was at the very base of a huge, circular chamber, the tapered vaults open to the sky hundreds of metres overhead. As his eyes got used to the brightness, Solomon saw that the motionless blades of the carceri's scrubber bisected the circle of light. The glare was the morning sun passing directly through the small patch of sky, and it was reflected from the glistening, corroded surfaces of the tower's interior walls. It was something of a shock to Solomon to realise that the force had been travelling throughout the entire six hours of Furia Penitens' night cycle and the sun was up already.

'What's the problem?' Solomon heard Bukin call from below. 'You see something?'

'Nothing, yet,' Solomon called back down the chute.

'Then move yourself,' Bukin growled back, and Solomon stood upright and looked around the drainage channel.

The rockcrete surface was slick with corrosion, the result of long years of practically non-existent maintenance as the scrubber blades high overhead had sucked the air through the chamber. The corrosion extended right up the tower walls, what looked like crusted mineral deposits gleaming in amongst the moisture coating them. Pools of almost glowing liquid were scattered all about, and it took Solomon a moment more to orient himself. Then he saw the direction he should be moving in, and unslinging his rifle set out at a stooped run.

As Solomon dashed across the rockcrete channel bottom, his nostrils were assaulted by the sharp tang of the irradiated, chemical-laced water. It reminded him of the bleaching yards the Honourable Concern ran back home, where grox urine would be fermented for an entire year before being refined and shipped off-world for no possible reason anyone on Jopall could imagine. In fact, it was worse even than that, the vapours stinging Solomon's eyes and bringing tears streaming down his cheeks.

His vision blurring, Solomon pulled down his goggles as he ran, almost dropping his rifle as he struggled to get the device straight. Panic rose in him again as he almost tripped on an object bobbing along just beneath the surface of the glowing liquid, but he kept his footing and dashed onwards towards the base of the ramp leading up towards the first tier of the weir.

The ramp was at least forty metres long, and it rose at least four metres over that length. Ordinarily, the gradient wouldn't be a problem, but the ramp was coated in moisture and corrosion and Solomon had to climb not just it, but the next three in the next ten minutes or be washed away and drowned. Glancing back towards the chute and the concealed hatch, he considered heading back to tell Vahn and the commissar that this route wasn't viable.

Then Solomon realised he had no choice but to go on. Deeply ingrained conditioning bubbled up inside his mind and the doctrine of the Indenti of Jopall came back to him. Only by service and sacrifice could the blessings bestowed upon his home world be repaid. Most Jopallis repaid the Imperium one enemy life at a time, counting off their debt as their kill-count mounted. But there were other ways too, including the performance of bold deeds when only the Emperor was watching. Glancing around the interior of the scrubber tower one last time, Solomon judged that indeed, only the Emperor would know his fate if he failed now.

By the time Solomon had struggled to the lip of the highest level of the weir, he was covered in chemical sludge and his eyes were stinging and almost gummed shut. His skin tingled as he imagined what radioactive substances were mingled with the slime, the liquid pumped into the mineral deposits far below the facility to generate heat. Throughout the climb he had managed to keep one thing above the slime and actinic liquid slowly rising in each tier, and that was his precious sniper rifle.

Reaching out a hand to steady himself against the two metre high lip, Solomon heard a deep, watery gurgle fill the stinging air of the chamber.

'What now...' he muttered as he saw that the liquid held on the other side of the lip was lapping over its edge. He saw then that he had only minutes to reach the gate beyond the last tier and the relative safety of the carceri chamber beyond. Turning, he looked back down towards the floor of the drainage channel, and saw the assault force approaching the lowest level of the weir and preparing to climb over the first lip.

Waving towards a figure he assumed was Rotten, Solomon turned and climbed up onto the last lip. Grunting, he pulled himself erect and looked towards the distant gate.

There, looking directly at him was a rebel lookout. The two men stood frozen for a moment that stretched into what felt like hours. Then both acted as one, the rebel lifting some form of communicator to his mouth at the very same moment Solomon brought his rifle up and sighted through the scope.

'You,' he said as he squeezed the trigger – the rebel's head jerked backward, a small but lethal wound having appeared in the centre of his forehead – 'are number one.'

A shout rang out from further along the gate, and Solomon snapped his aim right and tracked the source. It was another rebel. He'd obviously seen his companion fall but, thanks to Solomon's rifle's silencer, hadn't yet realised why.

'Two,' Solomon intoned as his second shot trepanned the man's cranium with explosive force.

Before the second rebel's body had even hit the ground, Solomon was running along the narrow dam, the overlapping liquid splashing at his passing. He heard more shouts, this time coming from behind and below as the leading members of the assault force tried to find out what was going on at the top of the weir. Solomon had no time to answer them however, as he caught sight of a third rebel. This man had clearly seen him, and decided to make a dash for the gate to bring help.

'Three,' Solomon muttered as his third shot punched into the rebel's back and sent him crashing against the gate hatch he was about to haul open.

Now the chemical liquid was spilling over the lip of the highest weir, lapping Solomon's ankles, and he could see that time was almost up. Any moment now, the liquid would surge over the lip and set off another chain reaction in the lower tiers. Then, millions of litres of the stuff would surge down the drainage channel and drown anyone still crossing it.

'Hurry!' he shouted down. 'It's rising!'

Rotten was the closest member of the assault force, and on hearing Solomon's warning he relayed it back along the column. In moments, the entire assault force was swarming forward, Commissar Flint yelling commands to ensure a smooth cover-and-move advance despite the urgency of the situation.

With the assault force heading for safety, Solomon dashed along the dam, which was now almost entirely submerged as the liquid in the upper tier surged over it. Passing the bodies of the slain rebels he rushed towards the gate they had been guarding, finding the mighty iron portal half a metre ajar. He slowed as he approached, checking back over his shoulder and seeing that Rotten, Vahn and Skane were helping each other over the weir and climbing onto the dam. Edging his way towards the open gate set in the rockcrete wall of the chamber, Solomon peered cautiously through into Carceri *Resurecti*.

'*Pash...*' he swore in his native Jopalli tongue. 'Why me...'

NINE

Resurecti

Commissar Flint hauled himself up onto the dam, which by now was functioning as anything but. The stinging liquid in the upper level of the weir was flooding down over him, and it took all his strength to pull himself up against the torrent. Pushing himself up onto his hands and knees, he saw that Kohlz had waited for him, against his express orders, and was offering his hand to help Flint up.

Pulling himself up with his aide's help, Flint checked that no one was left behind on the sloping ramp of the weir, and waved Kohlz on to the safety of the gate area. Even as the two ran the liquid swelled upwards towards their knees and the chamber filled with the roaring of millions of litres of the stuff.

Reaching the end of the dam, Flint climbed up onto the lip around the gate, finally out of the stinging liquid. The assault force had reached the gate not a moment too soon, and as its members stood soaking around the portal, the tide broke over the upper dam.

A great swell appeared in the centre of the upper enclosure, the irradiated liquid chemical bubbling as if some gargantuan beast of the deepest ocean were rising to the surface. An unseen valve somewhere in the guts of the overflow was forced open and a column exploded upwards with the force of an artillery shell. Flint and his companions were forced back towards the gate, the sheer spectacle of the tower of surging liquid rendering them impossibly vulnerable.

When the mass came crashing down around the spout, the upper enclosure burst spectacularly over the dam. In moments, billions of litres of irradiated liquid flooded each level of the weir in turn and surged down the overflow ramp. The drainage channel the assault force had passed along scant minutes earlier was transformed into a raging watercourse as mighty as any natural river Flint had ever seen, obscuring the access point the force had entered by and gushing away into the brightly lit tower.

As the roar receded and the flow decreased, Flint took a deep breath and turned towards the assault force. Every one of them, from the provosts and the other members of the 77th to the penal troopers and the claviger-wardens were soaked from head to toe in actinic chemical and stinking slime. Dragoon Lhor was attempting to clear the nozzle of his heavy flamer and get its pilot light re-lit, while the combat medic Karasinda was tending to a minor wound suffered by one of the provosts. The Savlar, Becka looked thoroughly dejected, her mohican hanging in lank strands around her face. Bukin was lighting a cigar – Flint had no idea how he had kept it dry.

'Solomon,' said Flint, addressing the Jopalli by the gate. 'You're off point. Good work.'

Flint expected Solomon to express his gratitude or relief at being relieved of point duty but the man seemed barely to register the command. He was looking through the gap in the huge iron doorway he was guarding, and his face had turned completely pale.

Vahn had seen the man's face too. 'What is it, Solomon?' he said.

Seeing the man wasn't going to respond, Flint gently but firmly moved him aside and leaned into the gap.

'Damn...' said Flint.

'*Resurecti*,' said Vahn.

The vast, stygian void of Carceri *Resurecti* loomed beyond the gate, Flint's senses having difficulty translating the space into a reality his mind could make sense of. The largest of the carceri chambers, the floor stretched so far that the opposite wall was lost to atmospheric haze. Because he was already wet, it took Flint a moment to realise that a fine drizzle was coming down from far above, and he saw that the upper reaches of the vast space were smeared grey with dirty clouds. The complex's generatoria were crippled, but the liquid pumped down into the geotherm sinks was still circulating, Flint realised. Each carceri chamber was developing its own climate, and in Carceri *Resurecti*, it was raining.

But this was no ordinary rain. It was raining blood.

The space overhead was cut by dozens of precarious iron gantries, and along these walkways were mounted the shrivelled remains of hundreds of corpses. The drizzle falling above was washing the bodies, their fluids mixing with the water droplets and staining the air below pink. Flint's gorge rose and some of the very first prayers he had ever been taught came unbidden to his lips. It was almost as if dark forces were converging on Furia Penitens, drawn by the vile deeds of traitors and murderers. Even as he walked the halls and chambers it was as if these forces were reshaping reality to better resemble their own blasphemous patterns...

'Strannik,' Flint said coldly as he looked away from the vile spectacle with open disgust. He'd seen anti-Imperial insurgents desecrate their enemies' remains in a less blasphemous manner. The rebel colonel who had led the uprising was clearly an individual of exceptional depravity to have ordered the bodies, or what remained of them, strung up in such a way.

Tearing his gaze from the bodies, Flint swept the chamber for signs of more rebels. The immediate area seemed clear, yet the haze as well as the dark forms of machines looming out of it obscured much of the view. The nearest of the gantries cutting overhead was clear of enemies, while the others were too far distant for Flint to be sure that no lookouts were stationed on them. In fact, such a lookout could be lining Flint up in his gun sights right now and he wouldn't know about it.

The centre of his forehead suddenly itching, Flint ducked

back inside the gateway and found the members of the assault force looking back at him dejectedly.

'What?' said Flint.

'Some of these ladies are not too happy, commissar,' Corporal Bukin drawled, his shotgun held across his chest. 'Some think they don't get paid enough for this *khek*.'

'Service is its own reward,' Flint quoted the *Dictum Commissaria*.

'Solomon told us what's out there, sir,' said Vendell. 'We don't want to join them, that's all.'

Flint didn't answer straight away, taking a moment to gauge the situation instead. The slime-streaked faces that looked back at him were more fatigued than mutinous. He'd stared down the most determined of turncoats in his time and he knew the signs well. There were plenty of commissars serving in the Imperial Guard who would have drawn a bolt pistol and shot Vendell through the head as an example to the rest, but Flint was more experienced and knew that while such field executions had their place, this was not it.

Instead, he passed over Vendell's comment and addressed Vahn. 'Twenty minute layup,' he ordered. 'Get your people cleaned, fed and watered.' Then he turned to Bukin. 'Corporal, perimeter security detail. Get on it.'

Bukin grumbled and his provosts cast jealous glances at the penal troopers, but the tension was broken and if there had been any genuine threat of mutiny it was dissipated, for the moment at least. In showing favour to the penal troopers over the provosts, Flint had demonstrated empathy for the ex-convicts, and earned a modicum of trust. No doubt Bukin would resent it, but Flint didn't care.

As the chief provost chivvied his section into action setting up guard points around the area and disposing of the corpses of the rebels Solomon had dropped, Flint took the opportunity to clean up himself. His storm coat was coated in a fine layer of chemical residue, and his high boots caked in sludge. He struggled to shrug the coat off without getting more of the irradiated muck on the cuirass he wore beneath it.

'Let me, sir,' Dragoon Kohlz said, appearing behind and taking hold of the heavy coat and pulling downwards.

'Really, Kohlz,' Flint protested, 'there's no need…'

'No problem, sir,' Kohlz said, then hissed, '*it's Gruss, sir. He's using a sub-etheric relay to communicate with someone inside the complex. I've been picking up strange vox-signals since we set out from the laager and I'm sure it's him*. You're welcome, sir.'

Glancing surreptitiously towards the Claviger-Primaris, Flint hissed back, '*You're sure?*'

'*Certain, commissar,*' Kohlz replied. '*But the signal's encrypted.*'

'Thank you,' said Flint as Kohlz carried the filth-encrusted storm coat off to wash it in the now-still waters of the weir's upper tier. Flint doubted the water was much cleaner than the coat, but it might do some good. Flint drew his bolt pistol and checked its mechanism was clear of the crap he'd had to wade through, causing several of the penal troopers to glance warily his way as they cleaned up or unwrapped ration packs. Flint used the distraction to study Gruss more closely, trying to work out if he might be talking into a vox-pickup hidden beneath the glossy, blank-faced visor of his armoured helmet. Of course he could, Flint thought, but did that mean he couldn't be trusted?

Perhaps the chief warden was simply communicating with his fellow clavigers, but if that were the case a personal vox would be sufficient and Kohlz would have been able to detect it easily. No, Flint thought. Far more likely Gruss was communicating with Lord Governor Kherhart, keeping his master informed of proceedings. Again, nothing intrinsically wrong with that, he thought as he glanced sidelong at Gruss while ostensibly cleaning the basket hilt of his power sword of slime. Studying the chief warden's stance, he certainly *could* be holding a conversation with someone over a secure vox-channel.

'Kohlz?' said Flint as his aide was finishing off with the storm coat. 'Anything from regiment?'

'No, commiss…' Kohlz started, then changed tack as he caught Flint's meaning. 'I'll check, sir,' he said as he crossed to where he'd set down his Number Four, its console protected from the liquid by a rubberised cover.

Flint strode casually over to Kohlz as his aide knelt down and lifted the cover from his vox-set. Through his peripheral vision Flint saw Gruss look sharply up.

Kohlz lifted the headset, holding one phone to the side of his cocked head as he worked the dials with his other hand.

'Anything?' said Flint.

'Trying to raise headquarters now, sir,' said Kohlz, then he hissed, *'There was a signal, sir, but it cut out suddenly.'*

'Commissar?' said Claviger-Primaris Gruss as he approached. 'Is there a problem?'

Flint pretended he hadn't seen Gruss approach, nodding in casual greeting and replying, 'No problem, just checking in with HQ.'

Gruss looked slowly about the interior of the tower. The brilliant light lancing down through the motionless blades of the air-scrubber was fading as the sun moved across the sky, but Flint read his meaning.

'We thought the open construction here might allow a decent signal through,' said Flint.

Gruss nodded slowly, and said, 'And did it?'

'Kohlz?' Flint said to his aide.

'Nothing, sir. This set doesn't transmit on the sub-etheric, but the higher bands are just hash.'

'I could have told you they would be,' said Gruss. 'Most of the generatorium's outer skin is covered by a demodulation grid. Individual nodes are deactivated to allow sanctioned signals through.'

'But unsanctioned signals get overridden with hash,' Kohlz finished. Gruss nodded silently in response.

'Why weren't we told?' Flint growled. 'How are we to contact the main force?'

'This facility,' Gruss replied, his metallic voice sounding oddly distorted as it growled from his armour's phono-casters, 'is rated amongst the most secure of its type in the sector. My primary duty is to keep it that way.'

'My question still stands,' said Flint. 'How are we to contact the main force?'

'Easily enough,' said Gruss. 'Using the code I will provide to deactivate the local jamming nodes.'

Flint suppressed a scowl, now convinced that the chief warden's use of a concealed sub-etheric transmitter was anything but innocent.

'Sir?' Corporal Bukin interrupted his chain of thought. 'Twenty minutes.'

'Thank you, corporal,' said Flint as the provosts began rounding up the penal troopers, rudely kicking awake those who had taken advantage of the brief lull to catch forty winks. 'Come on, ladies,' Bukin drawled as he stalked away. 'Beauty sleep's over!'

Becka was on point, ghosting through the shadows at the base of what looked like a ten storey-high crankshaft when a blood-curdling scream made her freeze. Her experience running with the narco-gangs far below Savlar Sink Nineteen kicked in. Better to stay still, she knew, better to melt into the shadows or play dead. That way, whatever was tearing apart whoever it was doing the screaming might not notice you.

The screaming cut out abruptly and it started raining. Not just a wet mist or the fine drizzle they'd first encountered as they pushed into Carceri *Resurecti*, but actually *raining*. Becka hated rain; after all, she'd grown up in a mine and never experienced it before escaping the world of her birth. To see it raining inside a generatorium installation was

Andy Hoare

something she considered totally wrong, as well as thoroughly uncomfortable. Plus, it ruined her hair.

Blinking runnels of oily, stinging liquid from her eyes, Becka squinted into the downpour. It was coming down in sheets that obscured almost everything beyond, but she caught sight of movement nonetheless. She waited, focusing on the dark patches as she felt a rumble pass through the rockcrete ground, up the metal of the crankshaft and into her hand resting gently upon its surface.

'Witch,' she hissed. 'Witch' was the term the inmates of Carceri *Absolutio* and several other chambers used to describe a class of walker used by the clavigers to keep the convicts in line. Based on the common Sentinel scout and anti-insurgency model used by the Imperial Guard and many planetary defence forces, the vehicle's proper name was the Dictrix-class. Instead of a heavy weapon it was armed with a neural whip that lashed outwards from a launcher resembling a primitive harpoon gun operated by the pilot in his caged cockpit. With that simple, non-lethal and supremely painful weapon, the pilot could control dozens of convicts with just the threat of its use.

Checking behind, Becka saw that the nearest member of the assault force was creeping forward some twenty metres behind her. It was Skane. She waved him back and made a hand signal only a fellow ex-convict would recognise, pantomiming the Witch's gait with two fingers.

As Skane waved his understanding and passed the message back down the line, Becka peered out from the crankshaft again. The downpour was clearing, as seemed to be the pattern in the weird, unnatural weather system evolving within the complex. As the last of the chemical rain splashed on the wet ground, a curling mist rose up through which the closest of the Witches stalked, each heavy step sending ripples chasing across the puddles formed on the rockcrete floor.

Its black-painted hull had been scrawled over with crude graffiti, and as its cockpit pod swivelled on its ball-joint waist a far more gristly form of decoration was revealed mounted on its sloped frontal armour. It was the former pilot, his limbs tied down with taut barbed wire. With a gasp, Becka realised that the man was still alive despite his wounds, his blood washing away as the last of the actinic rain flowed over him.

Becka's first instinct was to sneer at the fate of the claviger, but that ignoble reaction was soon eclipsed by the unfamiliar notion of pity. Scant weeks ago she might have fantasised about inflicting such ruin upon the body of one of the hated Witch pilots, but now, seeing it before her, the only hatred she felt was for those who had perpetrated the crime.

The Witch swivelled the other way and stalked off through the creeping vapour, and another stomped forward to take its place. This one was flexing its neural whip back and forth, the rebel piloting it obviously enjoying the sparks and hisses sent up as the cruel length cracked back and forth through the damp air. Just like the first, this one had its original custodian tied down with barbed wire across the front of its cockpit, though Becka couldn't tell if this one was still alive.

After a moment, the second Witch strode away, and a third followed after it. Only when she was certain it was safe did Becka report what she had seen to Vahn and the commissar.

Flint stooped as he ran, the mists parting before him as the shadowed bulk of an unidentifiable machine loomed up ahead. Gaining the shadow of the cover, Flint waited for Kohlz, Karasinda, Lhor and several others to catch up, then he motioned for silence. His breath was ragged, his lungs heavy with the sharp-smelling vapour building up from the crippling of the air-scrubbers. He could tell his companions were equally affected.

After a moment of quiet, he heard them. The clanking of hydroplastic-actuated mechanical legs, the grind of metallic claws on rockcrete and the background hum of a crystal battery generation unit marked the presence of the unseen walker as it stalked the mists to the left. It was hard to gauge distances, the white fog muffling sound and causing weird echoes. Many of Flint's troops were getting spooked.

'Lhor,' Flint hissed to the burly dragoon. 'You're on point. Go.'

The group was on the move again, and as they advanced Flint could hear the tread of more of the walkers as they moved through the carceri chamber. What they were doing he could only guess, probably hunting down loose convicts not part of the rogue colonel's uprising, or seeking out isolated claviger-wardens to brutalise and murder. Flint reminded himself that his enemy was, or had been, a trained officer of the Vostroyan Firstborn, and as such was fully capable of deploying his forces in a militarily effective manner. It was possible that Colonel Strannik had anticipated that the Guard would make an incursion into his territory, and the walkers were actively patrolling against such an attempt.

A hydraulic hiss roared close by, and Flint and his group swung around with weapons raised. A grey silhouette loomed through the drifting mist not twenty metres away, before lurching off just as suddenly as it appeared.

'Move,' said Flint. 'Quietly.'

He lingered as the troopers resumed their advance towards Becka's position, focused on the depths of the fog. 'You too, Karasinda,' he said to the last of the warriors. The combat medic was tracking her raised lasgun left and right, her face a mask of concentration.

'Medic?' said Flint.

Karasinda's eyes darted to Flint then back towards the mist. 'There's another one out there, sir,' she said.

'I've no doubt there is,' said Flint. 'So let's get moving.'

'I could take it, sir,' she said, her voice cold and flat. Coming from anyone else in the 77th Flint might have taken the statement for a ridiculous boast, but something about the medic's bearing and tone told him she believed what she said. Furthermore, so did Flint.

'Now's not the time, Karasinda,' Flint hissed, injecting a note of authority into his voice. 'Move out, now.'

The medic got the message, though Flint could tell she was reluctant. Finally, she lowered her lasgun and moved off behind Flint. He hadn't had the opportunity to study her service record yet, but he made a mental note to do so when the opportunity arose.

Following after Karasinda, Flint soon found the rest of the group massed behind the huge crankshaft, backs pressed against its casing as the troops took advantage of the brief rest.

'Report,' he ordered Becka, keeping his voice low in case the mists played tricks and revealed their presence to some unseen foe.

'Something like a dozen Witches, sir,' said Becka, adding, 'the walkers,' at Flint's quizzical look. 'I think they're moving from a sub-chamber a kilometre or so ahead and patrolling the southern reaches of *Resurecti*.'

'So they'll be back this way eventually,' Flint mused, as much to himself as to the Savlar woman. 'How long to make the circuit?'

'It'd take them twelve hours or so to run the complete lap, sir,' she said. 'But their crystal stacks have to be recharged every six hours of normal operation.'

'Can you find the sub-chamber from here?'

'Yes, sir,' Becka replied. 'It'll be guarded though.'

'That's why we're going there,' Flint replied.

Vahn could see arc lights shining through the white mist up ahead, each as fuzzy and bright as the sun rising over the fog-wreathed moors of home. Though the thick airborne vapour diffused the white light, it was almost blindingly bright and it hurt Vahn's eyes to look directly into it.

Halting beside a burned-out crate, Vahn sighted down the carbine's barrel and scanned left and right. The bulk of the sub-chamber loomed in the mist, and as his eyes adjusted to the glare he saw that the arc lights were mounted along a parapet walkway. The sub-chamber occupied a point where several dozen gantries and walkways converged at various heights, the void in the centre forming an almost totally enclosed space. It was from here that Becka had guessed the Witches were patrolling, and Vahn was leading the scouting mission to check it out.

'Anything?' Vahn whispered to Rotten, the Asgardian only just visible in the lee of the crate at Vahn's side.

'If it's where the Witches are based,' Rotten whispered back, 'there's no one home now.'

'Crew?' said Vahn.

'Can't see any,' said Rotten. 'But my guess is yes.'

'Agreed,' said Vahn. 'Wait here, Rotten,' said Vahn, preparing to muster his penal troopers to move in on the sub-chamber. 'I'll be…'

A piercing scream cut through the fog, the weird acoustics making it sound like the source was mere metres away.

'Crap!' hissed Rotten.

'Shhh!' Vahn hissed, swinging his carbine around towards the source and shrinking down into the small amount of cover afforded by the wrecked crate. The scream cut out, but as Vahn concentrated on locating its source he half-heard more sounds, like grunts and muffled threats.

The scream sounded again, and this time Vahn was sure of its source. Then it cut out to the sound of clinking chains, followed by a cruel laugh and the wet thud of a body hitting the rockcrete.

'Bastards,' Vahn growled, memories of the first days of the uprising coming unbidden to his mind. The colonel's followers had become fiends, murdering those who wouldn't join him with a feral glee the like of which Vahn had never before seen. The carceris, sub-chambers and vestibules had run red with spilled blood, and clearly, it hadn't ended yet.

'Argusti?' said Rotten, looking at Vahn with a mixture of concern and suspicion. 'What's up?'

'Where are the guys?' said Vahn.

'Vendell and Solomon are closing,' said Rotten distractedly. 'Skane and Becka are with the commissar... Why?'

'Just wondering what the odds are, that's all,' said Vahn as he plotted an approach to the sub-chamber. 'Flint wanted us to take a look, right?'

'Right...' said Rotten.

'So let's take a look.'

Not giving Rotten the chance to object, Vahn grabbed hold of the man's webbing and shunted him towards the sub-chamber. His eyes adapting to the bright light from the arcs overhead, he saw the form the sub-chamber took. True to his suspicions, the space where the gantries intersected had been fortified to create something that looked like a tower with dozens of walkways leading from it. The base of the tower was made from blocks of piled rockcrete, steel rebars jutting out at odd angles. Its sides were clad in chunks of metal plating suspended from the gantries.

And that wasn't all that was suspended from them.

Bodies, and somehow worse, body *parts*, were also strung from the gantries, thick black pools of clotted blood pooled on the rockcrete below. Vahn's knuckles turned white as he gripped his carbine. As another grunt of pain sounded from within the sub-chamber, Vahn decided that things were very much about to turn nasty, if he had any say in the matter.

Vahn, Rotten, Vendell and Solomon moved into the full glare of the overhead arcs as the mist thinned to the extent that any sharp-eyed sentries walking the gantries overhead would surely see them. Feeling suddenly vulnerable, he picked up the pace, dashing through the hazy space towards the towering structure, the others at his heels. Reaching its base, Vahn pressed his back against the rockcrete and ushered his fellow penal troopers onwards. Rotten reached his position and moved along the base of the wall to cover one approach with his carbine; Solomon did the same from the other side, his sniper rifle raised to his shoulder as he scanned the darkness through its powerful scope.

'We got any sort of plan?' scowled Vendell as he came to stand beside Vahn.

'Flint wanted this place checked out. We're doing it.'

'And we have to do it from close range?' said Skane as he looked left and right along the rubble-strewn base of the sub-chamber tower.

'Something's going on inside,' said Vahn. 'You can hear it.'

'And you want some payback, is that it?'

'Screw you,' Vahn snarled, just as another scream rent the air. 'You want out anytime just say it, Skane. I've had enough of this *gak*.' Turning his back on Skane, Vahn addressed the other two troopers. 'You guys with me?'

Rotten nodded, his disgust at whatever was happening inside the chamber clear to see. Solomon looked less certain, but nodded nonetheless.

'So?' Vahn said to Skane.

The Elysian didn't reply straight off, but listened a moment to the sounds of blunt instruments slamming into bare flesh. His face set in a grim mask, he nodded. Skane's thumb flicking his carbine to full auto was all the confirmation Vahn needed.

'Good choice,' he snarled, and moved off along the rubble-piled base surrounding the sub-chamber. As he edged around the uneven space towards the opening, he saw signs that Becka had been correct in her assumption that this was where the walkers were based. A power node rose from the ground near the entrance, fat couplings snaking from its terminals. Markings were stencilled onto the rockcrete, giving directions towards maintenance bays. What had once been a workshop and storage facility had been fortified by the rebels into a small bastion that could be defended from a major assault. But, Vahn grinned, he and his three companions weren't a major assault, and they had the advantage of surprise.

The sounds grew louder as Vahn closed on the entrance to the sub-chamber. The opening was large enough for one of the walkers to pass through, the structure reinforced by the chamber's new owners. A flickering orange light spilled out from within, and Vahn realised its source was some kind of open fire. Then the stink of burning flesh hit his nostrils, and he understood why.

'Get ready,' he growled to his fellows.

Pressing himself flat against the uneven wall, Vahn edged his way along the last few metres and leaned forward to peer within the sub-chamber. After the hazy white glare it took his eyes a moment to adjust to the shadowed interior, but when they did he saw clearly who was making the noise, and the smell.

A group of at least two-dozen rebel convicts were gathered around the remains of several dead clavigers. It was obvious that the rebels had been torturing the wardens, venting hate and bitterness nurtured throughout the long years of their imprisonment in Alpha Penitentia. Each gripped the instrument of his vengeance, from rusted chains to still-glowing pokers. Their fun at an end the rebels looked ready to disperse, and Vahn saw his opportunity.

Pulling back, Vahn opened a channel on his personal vox. Each of the troopers carried such a device, and with it they could communicate within the small force, though it was not powerful enough for longer ranged transmissions. So far, they had maintained vox silence, but Vahn decided now was the time to break that rule.

'Vahn to Flint,' he hissed into the pickup. 'Commissar, do you read me?'

His ear filled with hissing static for a moment, before Flint's voice came on the channel. 'Vahn? This had better be good...'

Getting straight to the point, Vahn replied, 'I have

multiple enemies clustered inside the sub-chamber. Send Lhor forward, commissar, I can–'

'Denied!' Flint's voice hissed back. 'We're not here to liberate, not yet anyway. We're here to watch, you know that.'

Frustration welling inside him, Vahn pressed on, 'Commissar, there are at least twenty of them, and…'

'And they'll be a hell of a lot more if we show our hand now, Vahn,' said Flint. 'You'll stand down now, trooper, or you'll face the consequences. Resume passive reconnaissance. Flint out.'

'Bastard!' Vahn hissed, fighting the urge to storm into the sub-chamber and open up on full auto. But even with the element of surprise, he knew it would be suicide; there were just too many rebels for the four penal troopers to deal with.

'Come on, boss,' said Rotten, taking hold of Vahn's shoulder, his expression showing he shared Vahn's feelings. 'Time to pull back.'

Vahn heard the rebels moving inside the sub-chamber, their cruel voices raised and he knew Rotten was right. At that moment he wasn't quite sure who he hated more – the rebels or his own commander.

TEN
Excoriation

'Vahn, report,' Flint growled into his personal vox. 'Report right now, over.'

The channel burbled and blurted a garbled response that may or may not have been Vahn's return transmission and Flint closed the link in disgust. He resented the need to use the vox in the first place, knowing that there was an outside chance it might betray his force's presence to the rebels, however remote that chance might be. 'Kohlz?' Flint said testily to his aide. 'Keep your set open, let me know the moment you hear anything.'

'Is there a problem, commissar?' said Claviger-Primaris Gruss as he approached. Flint suppressed an irritated rejoinder, annoyed with Vahn for the challenging of his orders, and with the chief warden for noticing it.

'No problem, Gruss,' said Flint. 'Just having issues with the low-pass carriers.'

Gruss nodded. 'Your scout element has pushed too far ahead and your vox-sets cannot penetrate the structural interference.'

'Something like that,' Flint replied flatly. 'My scouts have reached the sub-chamber housing the walkers,' he changed the subject. 'It's been fortified and it sounds like there's a substantial rebel presence guarding it.'

'Then we leave it to the main force,' said Gruss. 'As per mission parameters.'

'Indeed,' said Flint, feeling that the chief warden was somehow mocking him behind that glossy visor.

The force moved out, passing through the drifting banks of smog towards the sub-chamber Vahn had reported on. Soon, the fog thinned and the glare of white arc lights became visible up ahead, but just as soon it began to rain once more. Flint pulled his peaked cap down to cover his face and fastened his storm coat over his cuirass, though the oily downpour could hardly be kept out. As he trudged on, ever vigilant for signs of the enemy, Flint pondered the issue with Vahn. He'd thought the leader of the penal troopers a reliable, if hard to read soldier, but now he was showing signs of weakness. The scouts were pushing forward out of personal vox range, and Flint suspected it was a deliberate attempt to make communications between the two groups difficult. The next time Vahn found a group of rebels he thought he could take out, he might not ask for permission to engage. And that, Flint knew, could very well compromise the entire mission.

'Anything?' Flint snarled to Kohlz, his aide trudging along

beside him with the collar of his coat turned up to ward off the downpour. 'Any word from the scouts?'

Kohlz had his headset pressed tight to his ear in a vain attempt to keep the water out of its machine systems, and after a moment more listening to the churning garbage, he shook his head. 'Nothing, sir, just background hash.'

'What about the main force?' said Flint. He still hadn't heard a thing from the main bulk of the 77th, which should by now be ready to push into the complex once Flint's force located the rebels' stronghold. He knew the answer even before his aide shook his head in the negative.

The advance continued in smaller groups better able to make use of the cover afforded by the clumps of massive generatoria machinery. As he marched, the thought struck Flint that the interior of the installation was more akin to that of some grotesquely oversized engine, though he was beginning to suspect that the effect might be partly cosmetic, designed to dehumanise and brutalise the worker-convicts. Sometimes, he fancied he spied movement amongst the gears and shafts, as if the machinery were stirring. He couldn't help but dwell on what might happen to the small, soft bodies of the troopers were they to get caught up inside those gears and pistons. He knew they would be mashed to a pulp in seconds. The tech-masons who had built the place were true masters of their art, Flint thought as he cast off the grim thoughts the architecture conjured in his mind.

Marking the sub-chamber's position, Flint took the force in a wide loop around it. He knew his forces were easily sufficient to defeat the rebels manning the strongpoint, but equally, he wanted to avoid the alarm being raised were he to order a direct assault. Far better, he knew, to log the enemy's strengths and push on, ever deeper into their territory.

As the force infiltrated further, its members reported ever more gruesome signs of the rebels' activities. Great smears of blood and gristle stained the rockcrete ground, even the chemical rain failing to wash them away. One group had thought to take temporary shelter from the downpour in the lee of a vast piston housing, only to find the ground crunching beneath their feet. On closer inspection, the troopers had found the blackened remains of scores of bodies carpeting the entire area, and moved on quickly. Bukin's provosts discovered an open conduit stuffed with hundreds of mutilated bodies, the sight causing even those hardened individuals to blanch. As the force pressed on, its members became somewhat cold to the sights they were seeing, though Flint was ever watchful for signs of some individuals being pushed too far. They would either get angry, he knew, or they would crack, and it was his job to anticipate which.

'We're approaching another sub, sir,' said Flint's aide, snapping the commissar from his musings. Raising his hand to shield his face from the downpour, Flint saw that Bukin's provosts had reached another structure, this one taking the form of a slab-like blockhouse at least ten storeys high. The frontage was dominated by an armoured portal, and from the light cast up from the top Flint judged it was roofless.

'Gruss?' he said as the Claviger-Primaris appeared at his side, three other wardens close behind.

'Excoriation block, commissar,' the chief warden responded. 'I'm sure you know its purpose.'

Flint eyed the man's featureless visor with suspicion, barely able to curtail his lip from snarling in response to the comment. Gruss was correct in that as a commissar he was well versed in the Rites of Excoriation, but such methods were only ever used by the Munitorum as a last resort. Clearly, the masters of Alpha Penitentia made use of them, though for no reason Flint could fathom.

Little wonder the convicts had rebelled.

'Kohlz,' Flint addressed his aide, deliberately not answering Gruss. 'Anything from Vahn?'

Kohlz was fiddling with the controls of his vox-set, his face set in concentration. 'A sub-carrier communion, sir,' he answered. 'I can't read the transmission, but I can get a fix on where it's coming from.'

Squinting through the rain towards the distant excoriation block, a sense of dread came over Commissar Flint. 'Where?' he growled, his gaze settling on the armoured portal.

Kohlz followed Flint's gaze, before replying, 'Down there, sir. Somewhere...'

'Go!' Vahn waved Solomon forward as he covered the alleyway with his carbine. The Jopalli disappeared into the shadows between the carceri wall and the free-standing block and Vahn lost sight of him within seconds.

'Rotten, you're next,' he hissed. 'Get moving!' If anything, the Asgardian was an even better stealther than Solomon, melting into the darkness the second he moved into the alley.

That left just Skane.

'You up for this?' Vahn asked the big Elysian, just to be sure. There were still tensions between the two men, and now would be a bad time to air them.

'After what we saw back there?' Skane cocked his head back in the direction the scout group had come from. 'Abso-fragging-lutely.'

'Get moving then,' said Vahn. 'I've got you.'

Skane checked his weapon's charge counter one last time and then ran after the first two men. Skane was nowhere near as stealthy as Solomon or Rotten: he was the wrong shape and size for it for a start and his regiment's specialisation was entirely different. As a former Elysian drop-trooper, Skane was far more used to plummeting from a great height with only a grav-chute to save him from a messy end, or going into battle in the troop bay of a Valkyrie airborne assault carrier. Vahn grinned in wry amusement as he watched Skane move off down the alley, guessing that the Elysian was passing the other two troopers even if he couldn't see either. With one last look around him to ensure that no enemies lurked nearby, he followed after Skane.

Although Vahn thought of the space as an alleyway, it was really just a void between the cliff-like wall of the carceri chamber and one edge of the free-standing structure. The shadows swallowed him the moment he stepped into the space, the only light that of a hazy, orange illumination flickering far overhead. The ground was covered in detritus that crunched painfully loud under Vahn's tread. He slowed his pace and lightened his step, feeling the texture of the ground under his booted feet to ensure he didn't give his presence away any more than he may already have done.

The alleyway was around a hundred metres in length, and all that was visible overhead was a thin strip of orange illumination. Vahn forced himself not to look upwards, knowing that even that wan light might ruin his night vision. He slowed as he saw the bulky mass of Skane's back a few metres ahead, turning slowly to face back the way he had come, his carbine at his shoulder.

Movement. Vahn froze, the fold-down stock of his weapon pressed tight against his cheek. Whatever he'd seen, it had passed across the mouth of the alleyway at some speed but was now gone. Had it looked down the alley and seen them? He had no way to tell, but he wasn't going to stick around and find out the hard way.

Walking backwards with his carbine still trained on the opening, Vahn caught up with Skane, who had seen something was up and was waiting with his own weapon raised and his back pressed hard against the rockcrete. Skane didn't ask what was wrong, but Vahn raised his left hand and pantomimed a fast-walking figure moving from left to right with two down-turned fingers. Skane patted Vahn's shoulder to indicate his understanding.

Vahn ushered Skane onwards and in another few seconds he sensed more than saw the other two scouts not far ahead. He felt a tap on his leg and looked down to see

Rotten kneeling in the shadows. Vahn went down beside the Asgardian.

'There's an entrance round the corner,' said Rotten. 'Left of the end of the alley.'

Vahn realised that Rotten's deduction was based on the quality of the sounds bouncing around the chamber. Though he hadn't noticed it before, a low murmuring was steadily growing as the men pressed further on. Straining his ears, Vahn realised the sound was that of dozens of voices, moaning or whimpering in hushed tones. The sound dripped with misery, seeming to rise to a mournful dirge the more Vahn concentrated on it. He knew he had to find out its source.

'To the left?' Vahn whispered to Rotten as the other man appeared at his shoulder. Rotten nodded, and Vahn leaned out to take a look.

Another thirty or so metres along the wall, Vahn saw a tall opening. The same orange light that flickered high above shone from the portal, reflecting on the damp floor in front of it. But it wasn't just the light that emanated from the portal, the sound of misery spilled forth too.

Vahn scowled as he guessed that the sub-chamber was being used as a holding pen for those inmates who had dared stand against or flee from Colonel Strannik and his rebels. The murderous bastards had rounded them up and brought them here to await whatever vile end they decided to mete out. Vahn had seen it dozens of times in the weeks since the uprising and he was reaching the limit of his endurance.

'Vahn?' said Rotten. 'What's up?'

Vahn didn't answer straight away, but concentrated on the flickering orange light pouring through the portal and the sound emanating from the chamber within. From his hiding place, he couldn't see through the opening, but his mind was conjuring images of hellfire and damnation the most rabid preachers of the Imperial Creed would be hard-pressed to invoke.

'Vahn,' Rotten said again, placing a hand firmly on Vahn's shoulder.

'We're going in,' he hissed. 'Get ready.'

Rotten sighed. 'I knew you were gonna say that.'

'What?' said Solomon from further back inside the alley. 'What's up?'

'We need to see what's happening inside,' said Vahn as he turned towards his companions. 'And maybe do something about it.'

Solomon's mouth hung open for a moment as if he were about to object, then he nodded with resignation. Rotten looked grim-faced while Skane nodded his agreement with Vahn's statement.

Another wave of misery spilled from the orange-lit portal and Vahn stepped out of the alleyway into the open.

'Sir?' said Karasinda, squinting down her scope towards Excoriation Block 412. By her tone Flint could tell it was important. 'The tunnel mouth, to the right of the portal.'

Flint followed Karasinda's direction and saw a group of figures emerging into the open, carbines raised as they approached the opening.

'Vahn,' said Flint, to no one in particular. The medic didn't answer, but continued to track the scouts through her scope. 'What are they...?' he started.

'Enemies,' Karasinda hissed. 'Five, correction, seven, contacts at the portal.'

A group of rebel convicts were emerging from the guttering depths of the orange-lit portal, and the scouts couldn't yet see them. 'Damn it,' said Flint. 'Kohlz, you're going to have to—'

'I really wouldn't, commissar,' interjected Claviger-Primaris Gruss. 'If you transmit on that set in this chamber Strannik will know it.'

'How can you be certain?' said Flint, instantly suspicious.

Gruss paused as if caught off guard by Flint's question. 'Strannik has already transmitted various threats and demands using vox equipment captured during the initial uprising. Would you risk the rebels detecting the full extent of this operation?'

Flint stared into the blank, glossy depths of Gruss's visor for a moment. 'I'll do whatever needs to be done to complete the mission. Karasinda,' Flint turned his back on the chief warden. 'You have them in your sights?'

'Confirm target, sir,' said the medic, not taking her eye from her scope. 'I have Trooper Vahn in my reticle.'

'Stand by,' Flint growled, distracted by a new sound only just audible at the edge of hearing. An image from a battle fought two decades ago flashed into his mind: the plains of Delta Suthi, the survivors of his storm trooper detachment ambushed by the home-made stalkers of the isolationists...

'Sir?' said Kohlz.

'Wait,' Flint hissed as he turned sharply towards the source of the faint noise. Squinting into the damp shadows of the chamber he saw a glint of light as it caught on a shallow pool, ripples spreading slowly across its oily surface…

'I hear it too, sir,' whispered Karasinda as she swung her rifle sharply about, bringing it to bear on the darkness beyond the pool. All that was visible was a twisted mass of girders and debris.

'Bukin,' said Flint. 'Get the–'

The commissar never completed his order. At that moment a white light strobed sharply from behind, accompanied by a sharp *whip-crack* and the screams of several provosts and penal troopers.

'Enemy walkers!' Flint bellowed into his vox, the bead churning with a mass of angry static. 'Rally to me!'

The first of the Dictrix-class walkers pressed in from behind as Flint spun about. It was three times the height of a man, its angular, caged cockpit mounted on a pair of reverse-jointed mechanical legs. On one side of the cockpit was a harpoon-like weapon, into which was retracting the glowing white neural whip it had just unleashed upon the rearmost of Flint's force while they were distracted by what was happening up ahead.

It was that thought that saved Commissar Flint from the same painful fate. The second of the walkers burst suddenly through the mass of twisted girders, scattering debris in all directions as its cockpit tracked left and right in search of a target. The pilot saw Flint straight away and unleashed the massive harpoon whip in his direction. But Flint had seen it coming.

The darkness was lit blinding white as the whip fired straight forward out of its tubular launcher. Flint ducked as the air was split by the weapon's deafening crack and a moment later he was rolling across the floor as the whip scythed overhead. Though Flint had avoided the strike, so potent were the disruption charges surging along the whip that he felt the half of his body exposed to it burning as he rolled away, but others of his force weren't so fortunate.

A penal trooper not three metres away was struck across the chest and one of Bukin's provosts was caught across the shoulder. A third man, one of Dragoon Lhor's assistant flame troopers, took a glancing hit to an ankle as he dived clear. The effect on all three men was immediate. A disruption charge powerful enough to debilitate a bull grox surged through the whip, all three men screaming like the wailing souls of the damned as they went down. Even as the whip retracted, its victims' bodies went into violent spasm where they had dropped, each alive but very much out of the fight.

Knowing he had just seconds before the first Dictrix discharged its weapon a second time, Flint cast about for Dragoon Lhor, his flamer one of the few weapons that could take down the marauding walker. But Lhor was too far away to intervene before the walker fired again.

The half-forgotten battle against the isolationist stalkers flashed across Flint's memory once more and in an instant he knew what had to be done. The only way to avoid being gunned down by those, or any similarly constructed walker, was to get inside its reach before it could react...

'Engage it!' Flint bellowed as he powered forward, his gaze fixated on the machine's whip launcher. 'Get in close and take it down!'

Too shocked to react to Flint's order, most of those nearby stood transfixed while others simply dove for cover. Fools, he cursed, vowing to hammer home some discipline if he survived the next few seconds. The launcher on the walker's side glowed white as it charged its disruption systems, the cockpit swivelling towards Flint as he dashed across the open ground before it.

Then, it fired again.

This close, it was a simple matter for Flint to sidestep the attack, but its passage less than a metre to the left still inflicted burning pain down his entire side, ripping a snarl of anger from his throat. More screams from directly behind told him more of his troops had gone down, but by that point Flint had more pressing concerns.

Ducking left past a clanking mechanical shin, Flint found himself directly beneath the walker's cockpit. Up close, its pneumatic articulation seemed crude and ill-maintained, but just one slip could spell death if the pilot tried to stamp down on him. The walker lurched right and Flint guessed the pilot had seen the danger. Its metal limbs squealed and hissed but Flint caught another sound in amongst the cacophony. It was a warning, delivered just in time.

Flint dove forwards straight between the walker's legs as the neural whip snapped back into its launcher with a shockingly violent discharge of arcing disruption energy.

Glowing corposant streaked outwards from the launcher to chase up and down the metal legs, the sight highlighting what Flint had to do next.

'*Emperor grant thy servant strength,*' Flint quoted the *Dictum Commissaria* as he threw himself forward and up, gripping hold of an access handle on the side of the cockpit. '*That I might deliver thy judgement to the guilty!*'

Gripping tightly, Flint hauled himself upwards and hooked a leg about the front of the boxy cockpit. The Dictrix lurched violently sideways as it was thrown suddenly off balance and in a second Flint found himself face-to-face with the pilot, shielded behind the corroded mesh of his cockpit cage.

The man's eyes bulged wide in surprise as he saw an Imperial Guard commissar appear mere centimetres away. He drew backwards and the walker did likewise as he all but forgot the control column bucking in his hands. Flint hung on for dear life as the machine spun about, almost toppling before its self-righting mechanisms cut in and the pilot wrested control back once more.

But before the pilot could shake his tormentor from his machine's back, Flint let go of one hand and with a feral snarl drew his bolt pistol. The man saw his doom and hauled violently on the column, forcing the commissar to redouble his grip or be thrown clear and no doubt crushed beneath its splayed mechanical feet. But it wasn't enough. As a storm trooper, Flint had tallied four confirmed stalker kills in the swamps of Delta Suthi. He might be twenty years older, but the method was unforgettable.

Hauling his bolt pistol around as the walker span crazily about, Flint grit his teeth against the growing centrifugal force. At the last, he levelled the pistol straight at the pilot's face, the man screaming a valedictory curse that would ensure his soul was damned for an eternity.

'By your own confession be judged!' Flint spat as he squeezed the trigger. The pilot was dead before the bolt detonated, the explosion sending up a cascade of brain matter and bone shards as Flint kicked back against the cockpit and tumbled through the air to get clear of the madly spinning, out of control walker.

The impact on the hard, wet ground drove the air explosively from his lungs but Flint was soon scrambling backwards and away as the Dictrix went down in a tangled mess of tortured metal and kicking mechanical limbs. At the last, the machine's self-righting mechanism gave up and the limbs disengaged with a mechanical sigh.

'Sir?' the voice of Dragoon Kohlz came from somewhere off behind. 'Are you…'

But Flint never heard the rest of his aide's question, with the now still wreckage of the walker being kicked violently aside as the second machine appeared overhead, bearing down on the commissar's prone form. With a hiss of pneumatics, it raised one leg, ready to bring it slamming down on its intended victim…

A single las-bolt rang out from the darkness, striking the second machine's pilot straight between the eyes. The walker's leg froze in mid-air and Flint rolled clear as the entire walker toppled backwards and crashed to the floor, lifeless.

Flint knew without looking who had fired that shot. Wherever the medic Karasinda had learned to shoot, it certainly wasn't in the Vostroyan defence militia.

Vahn heard the rebels before he saw them, his instincts kicking in before his conscious mind had a chance to voice an objection. In a single motion, he swung his carbine down on its sling and tucked it in behind his right arm. An instant later the rebels stepped out of the portal and turned to walk off in the opposite direction.

In the two or three seconds it took for one of the rebels to register Vahn's presence, the other three penal troopers had clocked what was happening and stowed their own weapons. In an instant, the four press-ganged penal troopers became rebel convicts, for as long as they could get away with it at least.

'Hey…' the rearmost rebel growled as he caught sight of the penal troopers.

'What?' Vahn said brazenly, walking forward as if he had every right to do so. 'What?' he repeated, his three fellow troopers spreading out behind him. He cast a furtive glance into the flickering depths of the portal but all he saw were flames spouting from crude barrel fires.

'What you doing here?' the largest of the rebels snarled, hooking his thumbs into his belt as he looked down at the strangers. The man was almost as massive as the Catachan they had encountered during their escape attempt. The mess that had at one time been his face showed all the signs that he was some kind of pit fighter. The man's bald cranium was pitted with metal studs, as were his knuckles. Definitely a pit fighter, Vahn thought, and a nasty one at that.

Vahn thought on his feet. 'Got a message for Bing,' he said, plucking the name of a convict-worker he had once shared a geotherm sink work shift with from his memory. 'He inside?'

The pit fighter thought on it for a second, Vahn preparing to sweep his carbine upwards from behind his arm should the other man come to the wrong conclusion.

'Dunno,' the pit fighter said. 'Who's the message from?'

'From the top,' said Vahn. 'That's why we came four-handed.'

The insinuation that Vahn was acting on behalf of the uprising's leader had the desired effect on the pit fighter, yet several of his companions looked unconvinced. One, a wiry fellow who looked like a particularly ugly simian hybrid decided to face-off with Solomon.

'I seen you before?' Monkey Man snarled right into Solomon's face.

Solomon looked down at the rebel with barely concealed disgust, but he held his tongue, aware that one wrong move could bring the whole thing to a very messy end.

'We don't got time for this,' said Vahn, pointedly addressing the pit fighter rather than Monkey Man. 'You gonna let us pass or not?'

Behind his back, Vahn flicked the safety off of his carbine and his three companions did likewise.

The two Dictrix walkers were defeated, but Commissar Flint was in a foul mood. Those struck down by their neural whips were back on their feet having been dosed up with an unhealthy stimm-shot by Karasinda, who was observing the scene at the sub-chamber through the scope of her rifle.

'Looks like Vahn's going inside, sir,' Karasinda reported. 'Orders?'

Flint ground his teeth as a hundred possibilities rushed through his mind at once. What if Vahn and his fellow scouts were overcome and made to talk? What if the two dead Dictrix pilots had reported his force's presence? The rebels would learn of the 77th's mission and maybe even their strength and deployment. Or perhaps Vahn was on the verge of betraying the 77th? After all, he'd meant to escape the penal generatorium but had ended up getting himself and his friends press-ganged into the Imperial Guard. Maybe he was having a second go at it.

'Is he going willingly?' Flint asked the medic.

'Yes, sir, I'd say he is. I won't have a clear shot for much longer though.'

'Stand down, Karasinda,' he ordered, deciding despite himself to place the entire mission in Vahn's hands. If you let me down though, Flint swore, I'll go in there and execute you myself...

It took Vahn's eyes a moment to adjust to the dark as he and his companions entered the sub-chamber. The vast space resembled the inside of a cooling tower, barely lit by guttering barrel fires, the smoke and embers rising upwards towards the opening above. Vahn's earlier suspicions were soon proved correct – the sub-chamber was being used as a huge holding pen. The multiple barrel fires were strung together with heavy, barbed chains that formed the outer perimeter of a paddock in which several hundred moaning prisoners were held. The sight of inmates chained to one another and unable to move further than a metre brought bile to Vahn's throat. To make things even worse, many were dead, their weight still useful to the rebels to restrain those forced to endure the horror of being tethered to a bloated, stinking corpse. And above it all, the low, mournful dirge of human suffering swelled and echoed around the curved walls of the chamber, echoing upwards along with the darting embers of the barrel fires.

'*Pash…*' Solomon cursed. 'Why is it–'

'Quiet!' Vahn hissed, checking that none of the rebels had overheard Solomon's outburst. Pit fighter and Monkey Man were talking conspiratorially and there were at least another twenty rebels guarding the prisoners, but with the barrel fires raging in the darkness it was all but impossible to be sure of their numbers.

'We can't do anything,' said Skane as he came to stand beside Vahn. 'I wish we could, but…'

'I know,' Vahn replied bitterly. 'But we at least need to log this place, make sure the following forces do something about it. Then…'

'Bing's not here,' Pit Fighter interrupted as he strode up to Vahn. 'Mash says he's with Khave's crew.'

Vahn fought to contain his surprise that his earlier ploy had paid off, finding himself suddenly faced with a new opportunity. 'Where?' he tried his luck.

'Carceri control,' the pit fighter replied. 'Khave's been ordered to attend the colonel after his frag-up over in *Didactio*. You'd think a big lad like him would be able to stop a bunch of runaways, but apparently not...'

The Catachan. He was talking about the leader that would have ruined Vahn's escape attempt mere days before had it not been for Flint's intervention. Evidently, this Khave's failure to stop Vahn and his companions escaping had earned the wrath of Colonel Strannik.

'Carceri control, you say?' said Vahn, scanning the scene of misery beyond the guttering barrel fires once more. 'Then I think we should go pay them a visit.'

It was only as Vahn walked back out through the sub-chamber's portal that he realised he'd been had.

'You looking for me, stranger?' a phlegmy voice rasped. 'Heard you got a message from the colonel.'

The owner of the voice was a grotesquely obese individual attended by a mob of goons armed with lengths of iron bar and wickedly serrated shivs. No one had any business getting that fat, thought Vahn, not in a prison where food was a luxury and most of the inmates were chronically malnourished. The man's skin was pale and waxy, his bare torso a mountain of heaving fat. His face was a twisted, mashed up mess and his eyes and mouth were little more than folds amongst layers of flesh.

'Bing, huh?' Vahn nodded slowly, reading what was about to unfold. There must have been at least two-dozen rebels up front, while Pit Fighter and Monkey Man, along with at least a dozen more were still behind inside the sub-chamber. But most importantly, only a handful of the rebels appeared to be carrying firearms, and most of those were improvised blunderbusses or practically useless breech-loaders.

Vahn swung his carbine around on its sling, bringing it from behind his arm to point directly at the flesh mountain. In an instant, Skane, Rotten and Solomon had done likewise.

'Cover the rear,' Vahn told Solomon and Rotten.

Amazingly, the obese rebel leader didn't seem in the least bit intimidated by the las-weapons aimed squarely at his body. Perhaps the rebel was stupid enough to think he had the mass to absorb a few shots, Vahn thought, preparing to find out.

'This ain't gonna finish how you think it will,' the obese man rasped. Heavy footsteps sounded from behind as Pit Fighter and Monkey Man had joined the party.

Something inside Vahn was getting dangerously close to snapping. 'To be honest, I don't really give a crap how it ends. But you're right,' he added. 'It *is* ending...'

'Vahn?' said Skane, his voice low so the rebels couldn't hear him.

Vahn was about to continue his death wish taunt when something in Skane's tone made him pause. 'What?'

'Don't look,' the Elysian whispered. 'Eleven o'clock, three hundred metres.'

'Don't look?' hissed Vahn. 'How do you expect me...'

'Don't!' Skane hissed urgently. 'Not if you want them to...'

A flash of colour off in the shadows along the cliff-like rockcrete wall of the carceri chamber caught Vahn's eye despite Skane's warning.

'What the…' said the obese rebel leader.

A las-bolt hammered out of the mists and slammed into the leader's meaty shoulder. A puff of flash-boiled blood mushroomed upwards and a look of dumb, quizzical surprise crossed the man's face before he toppled forward with a dull thud.

Three more las-bolts lanced out of the fog, three more rebels falling to the ground, before anyone thought to react.

'Move!' Vahn roared, diving to his right as one of the rebels unloaded a blunderbuss directly at him. The air was filled with a mass of scything shot. Miraculously, Vahn and his companions avoided the blast as they dived across the ground.

'Four,' Solomon counted as he squeezed off a sniper rifle shot all but un-aimed. The weapon was never intended for use at such close quarters, but even firing from the hip Solomon took a rebel clean between the eyes and sent his brain matter vomiting from the back of his cranium.

In a moment Vahn was up and pushing the gangly Jopalli before him as he scrambled to get clear of the killing zone. He fired his carbine into the mob as he moved, catching one rebel at the elbow and causing his severed arm to cartwheel backwards through the air, and another in the stomach causing him to double up as he dropped.

'Rotten!' Vahn yelled, spinning around as he cleared the immediate crossfire. The other two men were close behind, but the Asgardian wasn't clear yet, pausing to let off more shots to cover his companions' withdrawal. 'I appreciate the thought,' Vahn shouted. 'But it's time we were somewhere else, get moving!'

Rotten looked almost disappointed as he squeezed off one last burst before upping and running. A shotgun blast split the air he had just vacated and tore up the ground he had been standing on.

'Thanks,' Rotten laughed madly as he overtook Vahn. 'Where now?'

The rebels were scattering in all directions and dozens of their fallen were sprawled across the ground. Most of the survivors were making for the safety of the sub-chamber and those without the sense to do so were being gunned down mercilessly by the closing Guard force.

'Wait,' said Vahn. 'Crap…'

'What?' said Rotten as he shot down another fleeing rebel. 'Vahn?'

'They're heading back to the pens,' he said.

'Seven,' said Solomon as he lined up and fired, his sniper rifle kicking back into his shoulder with its fierce recoil. 'The prisoners?'

'The prisoners,' said Vahn, scanning the carceri chamber. 'Where's Flint?'

'Over there!' said Rotten, pointing towards the source of many of the incoming las-bolts. The majority of the rebels had by now reached the sanctuary of the sub-chamber and the weight of fire was lessening. 'Right flank, by the gear shaft.'

A group of troopers were firing from the cover of an over-sized gear casing. Commissar Flint could be seen directing their fire and Corporal Bukin was further along the line, loosing shot after shot at the retreating rebels as he led his provost section in a wide flanking manoeuvre. Then Vahn saw the flash of colour again, and realised it was Becka, her acid green mohican visible through the drifting tendrils of airborne vapour. 'Becka!' he yelled. 'Tell Flint there are multiple prisoners inside that sub!'

Becka waved her confirmation that she had heard him. 'And tell him we're getting them out!'

'He's what?' Flint snapped as the Savlar finished relaying Vahn's message.

'He's getting them out, sir,' Becka repeated, glancing nervously back towards the sub-chamber portal. The firing had died right down, reduced to the occasional solid slug unleashed indiscriminately from the shadows of the opening. Stray rounds were still zinging around and the gear shaft didn't offer nearly as much cover as Becka would have liked.

'I heard what you said,' said Flint. 'What the hell's he playing at?'

This time, Becka didn't answer. 'Can I go now, sir?' she said, her discomfort in the presence of a commissar obvious to see, even with half of her face obscured by her ever-present rebreather.

'Go,' said Flint. 'Muster the penal troopers under Corporal Bukin and be ready to move out at my command, understood?'

'Well,' Flint turned to Claviger-Primaris Gruss. 'It looks like Trooper Vahn has made a somewhat precipitous decision...'

'You'll be executing him in due course,' replied the chief warden.

'What?' said Flint, distracted for a moment from the plan forming in his mind. 'Execute him?'

'For disobedience, commissar,' said Gruss. 'And for compromising the mission.'

'He may not have done that, Claviger-Primaris,' Flint replied. 'We might be able to salvage something from this yet.'

'You can't be...' Gruss started.

'Serious?' Flint cut him off. 'I'm serious, Gruss. Vahn went in there for a reason, came out, and now he wants to head straight back in again, even in the face of *that*.' He jerked his head towards the entrance as a torrent of gunfire sounding like a dozen tree branches being snapped at once burst from the portal. 'I don't *like* him, and Emperor knows I'd put a bolt-round through his temple myself. But,' Flint concluded, 'in this, I'm deciding to *trust* him.'

Gruss's blank-faced visor held Flint's gaze for a moment before he shook his head in evident resignation. 'Where do you want my men?'

Flint considered the question, weighing the options. Gruss's clavigers were equipped with far superior armour than any of Flint's troops, and that would be vital in an assault. In addition, they carried combat shotguns ideal for a close quarters storming action.

'I need them taking that portal,' he replied, knowing he was asking a lot. 'Agreed?'

'Agreed, commissar,' said Gruss. 'I'll make preparations,' he said, before departing to brief his men.

Seeing Gruss departing, Kohlz tapped his headset and gestured towards the chief warden's back. Flint got the message, but had more immediate concerns. With Vahn leading the scout element back towards the sub-chamber portal Flint saw no choice but to intervene before things got completely out of hand.

Drawing his power sword in one hand and his bolt pistol in the other, Flint gathered up the remainder of his troops, including Lhor with his heavy flamer.

'I want you going in with the wardens,' Flint ordered Lhor as he broke cover and worked his way through the snaking mists towards the provost section. Lhor looked like he was just about to voice a complaint at serving alongside the penal generatorium's staff, but he shut his mouth at Flint's venomous glance. 'Do it.'

Stooping as he ran across the open space between towering piston casings, Flint ducked into Bukin's position. The chief provost had cleared his flank, as evidenced by the sight of a dozen or more dead rebels littering the open ground in front, pools of blood spreading out around each.

'Cover the wardens, Bukin.' Flint ordered. 'And Vahn reports there are prisoners inside, so play nice.'

Bukin looked mildly hurt but any objection was forestalled by the sound of armoured boots pounding the rockcrete behind him. Claviger-Warden Gruss and his men appeared, ready to carry out Flint's order to storm the opening.

Another ripple of gunfire sounded from the portal, stray shots spanging from the metal casing Flint and the provosts were sheltering behind and sending up a shower of angry sparks. The commissar peered around the edge and caught sight of a hugely muscled rebel armed with a primitive blunderbuss standing in the opening, blood covering his bare torso.

'Ugly mother…' said Bukin, puffing on his cigar before plucking it from his mouth and grinding it against the metal piston casing to extinguish it. Dropping the smouldering stub into a webbing pocket, he said, 'That one's mine, sir.'

Flint ignored Bukin's boast and nodded to Gruss. With a command that Flint couldn't hear, Gruss ordered his wardens forward out of cover and into the open. The clavigers set their shotguns against their chests, lowered their helmeted heads and charged forward across the corpse-strewn open ground.

The instant the clavigers were out in the open the rebels opened fire. Rough cast solid slugs and a hail of scatter-shot spat out from the opening, most of it missing its target but some slamming into the wardens' hardshell. One warden staggered as a slug struck his bulky shoulder armour, but in a moment he was continuing in his advance, stepping over the corpse of a fallen rebel to rejoin the line. A second claviger took the brunt of a shotgun blast, the hammer blow almost casting him from his feet. Incredibly, he straightened up and carried on towards the objective, his armour having absorbed the worst of the impact.

'Up!' Flint bellowed, raising his power sword high and then chopping it downwards to indicate the axis of advance. Breaking cover, he sprinted forward after the claviger-wardens, ensuring that Dragoon Lhor was following close behind. Corporal Bukin shouted his own battle-cry, something that definitely wasn't approved by any of the texts Flint had studied, but it had the desired effect. The provosts echoed Bukin's shout and powered forward along with the remainder of Vahn's penal troopers.

'Loosen up!' Flint shouted as the line advanced. As the clavigers closed on the opening, Dragoon Lhor took position, his heavy flamer ready to disgorge into the portal and incinerate any rebels sheltering within. As the wardens closed to firing range they set their shotguns at their hips and at Gruss's bellowed order opened fire. The thunderous fusillade made a mockery of the rebels' crudely improvised firearms and bodies twisted and fell or were torn to shredded rags as shot after shot was pumped into the opening.

Flint's warriors roared in savage celebration at the spectacle, and it wasn't just the soldiers of the 77th that did so. The penal troopers, until recently subject to the clavigers' brutal stewardship, bellowed just as loudly. Clearly, the sight of the rebels being cut down was enough to overcome whatever misgivings the former convicts might have harboured at fighting alongside Gruss's men.

'Lhor!' Flint shouted as he closed on the sub-chamber's outer wall. 'Ready?'

The burly dragoon grinned and lowered his anti-glare goggles over his eyes as he followed behind the clavigers. At Gruss's signal the line of wardens parted to make room for Lhor, and the weight of return fire increased as the defenders realised what was coming their way. Shots rang out from the opening, but Lhor ignored the torrent of lead screaming in his direction despite the risk that he would be transformed into a human torch if his fuel tank was struck and ignited.

'Give him space!' Flint ordered the nearby Firstborn dragoons. None, he realised, had seen a heavy flamer discharged at close range, but by the reaction of the penal troopers most of them had. The dragoons ducked away from Lhor as he set his feet wide, lifted the flamer and opened the valve wide. A raging cascade of burning chemical death spurted forth and arced right into the sub-chamber's opening, incinerating the few defenders who had remained to guard it. Lhor washed the burning jet left and right, backwash billowing up and out of the portal in great raging sheets of fire. Though Flint was at least ten metres away from Lhor when the dragoon opened up, the heat was tremendous, forcing the commissar to turn his face away as he gritted his teeth and screwed his eyes tight shut.

'Disengage!' Flint shouted, and Lhor closed off the heavy flamer's valve. A cloud of greasy black smoke mushroomed upwards and flames sizzled from stray gobbets of flamer fuel. The fire that had engulfed the portal had burned itself out and no more movement was visible there.

Lhor lifted his goggles, his face now entirely black apart

from the circle around each eye. From the look of sheer joy on his face, Flint knew he would have trouble getting the flamer off Dragoon Lhor after the battle. Even before Flint could wave the force onwards again, Gruss's clavigers were storming the portal. Though the opening was wide enough to allow five or more men to pass through at once, the wardens, experienced in such actions, split into two assault parties one taking each side of the opening.

'Bukin!' Flint called as he came to the wall and knelt down. 'Take a multiple right and back them up!' Acknowledging Flint's order, Bukin peeled off to the right as he dashed across the open ground, waving two-dozen provosts and penal troopers ahead of him.

'Everyone else,' Flint bellowed, 'With me!' Two-dozen other troops clustered in behind Flint, and at that moment the wardens pressed in through the opening. They went through in two stacked groups, the front men ducked down while another two leaned in over his back to present as small a target as possible to any defenders left inside. A shot boomed out and a warden grunted as he fell to the ground. Another stepped forward and took his place as a third dragged the convulsing form clear.

The entire portal exploded in smoke as the clavigers opened fire as one. Massed combat shotguns roared and the wardens pressed in and were gone. 'For the 77th!' Flint shouted, rising and waving the troops onward. On the other side of the portal, Bukin made an equivalent shout to muster the penal troopers and the two groups rushed forward into the opening.

The ground around the portal was a bubbling mass of blackened rockcrete and flesh, and Flint felt something close around an ankle as he stormed through after the wardens. The twisted and blackened arm of a still-living rebel grasped upwards in an attempt to drag Flint down to share his grisly death. Flint sneered with disgust and swept his power sword downwards in a savage arc, severing the rebel's arm at the elbow. Even as the man's face twisted with hatred and pain, Flint levelled his bolt pistol and put a round right into the rebel's open mouth, blowing out the back of his neck and severing his head.

'Keep going,' Flint growled at the penal troopers who had backed up behind him. 'But watch your fire!'

Plunging into the darkness, Flint looked around for more enemies, his bolt pistol raised as he tracked it in a wide arc. The interior of the sub-chamber reminded him of some mad artist's vision of eternal damnation, the only illumination provided by the guttering barrel fires and the flash of the wardens' combat shotguns as they gunned down the cornered rebels.

Flint's eyes started to adjust to the hellish gloom and he saw the prisoners. There were hundreds of them, emaciated wretches cowering inside the ring of flame formed by the chain-linked barrel fires. Denied cover from the shots winging back and forth over their heads, the prisoners pressed themselves to the ground or cowered behind what little cover was afforded by the corpses of their dead fellows. While most made every possible effort to hide, some were becoming so maddened by the unfolding scene that they strained futilely at their chains in an effort to break their bonds. Sickened by the grim spectacle, Flint determined to end it, straight away.

But before he had the chance, a savage bellow filled the cavernous space; the prisoners cringed with what Flint could immediately see was a deeply ingrained fear response. The source of the terrible sound was an obese rebel leader, his shoulder a burned mess of ruined flesh, held out amidst his surviving companions at the far side of the holding pen and backlit by raging flames. He roared his defiance at the incursion into what must surely have been his personal fiefdom.

'He's mine!' Bukin called out to his men as he led them forward. Flint was just about to grant the chief provost permission to engage when a figure appeared behind. Vahn stalked towards him, his dreadlocks silhouetted against a raging barrel fire and his eyes glinting with menace.

'No,' Vahn growled. 'That's Bing, one of the colonel's bosses. We need that one alive.'

Hearing Vahn's words, Bukin hesitated, and looked to Flint for confirmation. Though the chief provost dearly wanted to take the obese rebel down, if Vahn was right, the man had to be spared, whatever his crime.

'Agreed,' Flint growled. 'The rest are yours, corporal, but take that one alive.'

The far side of the chamber erupted in gunfire: a brief competition of combat shotguns and las-weapons against blunderbusses and breech-loaders. The exchange was over in seconds, and could only have one winner.

'Well?' said Flint ignoring the last of the gunfire.

'Well what, sir?' he replied.

'Who's in charge here, Vahn?' Flint said, his voice low and dangerous.

'Huh,' said Vahn. 'That'd be you, I guess, *commissar.*'

'Correct,' said Flint, his point made. 'So what's so special about this one?' he said as Bukin returned leading the obese rebel leader in front. The man was huge, his shoulder wrecked and his bare torso smeared with his own blood. His face was a crumpled, twisted mask of bitterness, initially aimed at his captor but redirected towards Flint the instant he saw the commissar's unmistakable uniform.

'He knows where Strannik is,' said Vahn. 'Carceri control, they said.'

'Does he now?' said Flint, meeting the man's hateful, porcine eyes. 'He'd better speak up then, hadn't he?' he said as he racked the slide on his bolt pistol.

The rebel leader sneered, his flabby lips peeling back to reveal black teeth. 'You ain't no competition for the colonel, mister,' he said. 'Nothing, not a thing you could do to me would be anywhere as bad as what he would do if he found out I'd blabbed. I ain't tellin' you a thing.'

'Is that so?' replied Flint, glancing around at the crowd of troops gathering about the confrontation. It was clear the rebel meant every word and the simple threat of summary execution wouldn't suffice. A nasty little germ of an idea forming, he cast his eye over each of the onlookers, discounting the Firstborn and settling on a knot of penal troopers watching sullenly. Solomon looked like he'd rather be somewhere else, but that appeared to be his normal state, while Karasinda was dressing a light wound to Stank's left arm. Vendell and Skane were scowling, their hatred boring into the rebel. But neither of them was regarding the man with anything like as much unfettered bitterness as the Savlar, Trooper Becka.

A cruel grin twisted Flint's lips and he leaned in towards the rebel. 'You might not fear me,' he whispered, his voice low so the other man had to strain to hear his words. 'But I'm just a commissar, so I've only been indoctrinated into the first seventeen procedures of the Rites of Excoriation. I know I could flay the skin from your body and you'd still be more scared of your colonel, so that leaves me with just one option.'

The man's leer faded as he followed Flint's nod towards Becka. Slowly, the Savlar drew a serrated combat blade from a thigh-high leather boot and ran a thumb along its lethally sharp cutting edge. As she lifted the blade to examine it in the flickering firelight, a thin line of crimson appeared across her thumb.

'She's not indoctrinated into any of the Rites,' Flint said even lower. 'Not officially at least. Where she's from, they make it up as they go along. Plus, she's a she, and that means she knows more about inflicting pain on a man than you or I could ever imagine…'

'May I, commissar?' Becka said coyly, right on cue.

'Not fair, sir,' whined Bukin, causing Flint to suppress a snort of amusement. 'I said he was mine.'

The rebel's eyes darted towards Bukin, then back to Becka. It was clear which he was more afraid of. 'He's all yours

Trooper Becka, but not here. Listen up!' Flint called out. 'We move by sections starting in two minutes, one minute intervals. Muster at grid three-three-nine. Understood?'

The assembled troops grumbled their understanding as Bukin's provosts started mustering them into sections. Within a couple of minutes the first group was moving out to the map reference Flint had indicated, and he was looking around the charnel pit of the sub-chamber.

'What about them?' said Vahn, nodding his dreadlocked head towards the holding pen beyond the barrel fires and the hundreds of prisoners cringing inside. 'They're the reason I came back.'

'I noticed,' said Flint, though they weren't the reason *he* came back. 'Did you plan this far ahead?'

Vahn smirked slightly, and admitted, 'Not really, commissar.'

'Well,' said Flint, holstering his bolt pistol as he made to follow Becka as she led the rebel leader away. 'Do something, and quickly.'

Grid three-three-nine was a twisted mass of conduits Flint's force had passed through on its way towards the excoriation sub-chamber. It had been chosen as a muster point because it offered a defensible position the entire force could lay up in. Pipes several metres across rose from the rockcrete ground, some snaking away across the surface, others running directly upwards and disappearing into the overhead murk. Some seemed to writhe around one another like mating serpents and none of them had any discernable purpose.

Nevertheless, the sound of liquids and gases rumbling through the large, corroded pipes was audible as Flint waited for Vahn to catch up having dealt with the freed prisoners.

'Anything?' Flint asked Dragoon Kohlz, who was hunched over his vox-set in the shadow of the conduit.

'I'm getting a carrier wave, sir,' the aide replied. 'I can attempt communion on your say so, though I can't guarantee I'll get a good signal.'

'Good work,' said Flint, knowing that Kohlz was right in not attempting to establish two-way communication just yet. Even if it worked the rebels might detect the signal and then the infiltration force's presence and disposition would be betrayed.

'Can you keep the carrier wave fixed until we need to call the main force in?' Flint asked.

'I can try sir,' said Kohlz. 'It's a risk though. As Gruss said, the structure is shielded and I could lose the wave any time.'

'Speaking of the Claviger-Primaris,' said Flint, his voice low. 'Anything?'

Kohlz glanced around the muster point to ensure that the nearest of the clavigers was out of earshot. 'Nothing showing up, sir, but I'm on it.'

'Good,' said Flint, clapping his aide on the shoulder as he turned at the sound of someone approaching. The mists had come down again and ambient illumination was almost at whiteout, but Flint could just about make out a figure walking directly towards his position.

'Contact ahead,' Flint heard medic Karasinda hiss through the personal vox-net. 'One target.'

'It's Vahn,' Skane replied over the net, and by the dark halo of dreadlocks around the figure's head, Flint could see that Skane was correct. 'Stand down,' Skane ordered the medic, and she lowered her lasgun, reluctantly, it seemed to Flint.

A moment later, Vahn had climbed over the conduit and was standing before Flint. 'Well?' the commissar asked.

'I freed them,' he answered.

'Where to?' Flint asked.

'I didn't ask,' said Vahn. 'They were in a bit of hurry to get moving.'

So long as they don't interfere with the mission, Flint thought. The last thing he needed was a body of freed convicts getting in the way. Besides, they would soon be returned to captivity once the rebels were defeated.

'Anyway,' said Vahn, looking around at the troops waiting to move on. 'We ready to get going?'

'As soon as Becka's finished up,' Flint grinned coldly. 'I got what I needed and left her to her fun.'

'Always knew your lot were cruel bastards,' said Vahn. 'But that's just–'

Vahn's words were cut-off when a blood-curdling scream rang out from deep amongst the nest of twisting pipes. The scream turned to a sob, and the sob to an unintelligible plea for mercy. Flint and Vahn shared a look of sympathy even for the vile rebel. Becka's attentions were anything but gentle.

A moment later, Trooper Becka appeared from the nest of conduits the Savlar was using as an ad hoc interrogation cell.

'Anything to add?' Flint asked. Having gleaned the

location of the rebel colonel's strong hold early in the 'conversation', he doubted Bing had anything further to add, but it was worth trying.

'I may have broken him, sir,' Becka sneered. 'But what he told you was the truth, I'm sure of that.'

Vahn smiled grimly at that, but Flint pressed the trooper for more.

'Can he lead us to the rebels' hiding place?' asked Vahn.

Becka tilted her head playfully, and replied, 'He won't be leading anyone any place, not for a while anyway.'

'We don't need him to, I got the location,' Flint said. 'We know where Colonel Strannik's holed up.'

'Where?' pressed Vahn.

'He said the rebels have set themselves up in a control facility in the air scrubber chamber,' said Flint, drawing his data-slate and invoking Major Herrmahn's tri-D map of the complex. The slate came to life and the image of Carceri *Resurecti* revolved slowly in its centre.

'There,' said Flint, pointing out a grid reference high atop the northern face of the chamber's wall. 'If I was the colonel, that's where I'd be too.'

Flint had already studied the map and calculated the quickest route to the atmospheric processors. A honeycomb of tunnels led through the wall face but he judged it would be costly to lead an assault through them. Too costly for the small force he was leading.

'We confirm that's definitely where they are, then we exfiltrate and call in the regiment to launch a full assault on that position.'

'Fat boy *said* that's where they are…' said Becka.

'I know,' Flint held up a gloved hand to forestall Becka's complaints. 'But I need visual confirmation before I call in the regiment. Understood?' Not that he needed her to understand, but Becka was one of the more competent of the penal troopers and he'd need her for the next phase of the mission.

'Five minutes,' Flint announced, loud enough for all of the troops nearby to hear. 'Section leaders, check ammunition distributions and get everyone ready to move out.

'This is it,' he growled. 'This is what we get paid for.'

'We get paid?' Becka muttered to Vahn as the commissar stalked off. 'No one told me…'

ELEVEN

Heart of Darkness

Becka squinted up into the clouds staining the vaults high above. It was raining again, and not just a fine drizzle. The closer the force got to the cooling tower and its crippled scrubbers, the worse the weather. She sneered in amusement at the thought of weather inside a prison, but it was the truth. The chamber's roof space was in effect an artificial sky, and that sky was now dominated by boiling black clouds that looked for all the world like they were about to explode in lightning.

'Becka, you okay?' said Vahn over the personal vox-net. 'You want someone else to take point?'

She didn't answer straight away, but scanned the vista up ahead, cautious for the presence of more rebels. The infiltration force was approaching the northern wall of Carceri *Resurecti*, and that wall was now looming from the haze, pale and glistening, like the tallest cliff face rearing from an ocean. The base of the wall was still lost to almost oceanic fog, while the very top was wreathed in darkness and churning clouds. Inbetween was several hundred metres of slab-like, cyclopean rockcrete, studded with thousands of small openings, each a cell portal.

The sight made Becka shiver, for she knew that high atop the wall was the rebels' fortress. And inside it, Colonel Strannik, the insane butcher who had orchestrated all of the bloodshed she had witnessed over the last few weeks. And that, she knew, was where the commissar was now saying they had to go.

'Becka?' Vahn repeated, the gain on the transmission pumped up so that his voice squawked painfully loud in her ear. 'You reading me, Becka?'

Becka slowed as she walked, tracking her carbine slowly left to right. 'Here, Argusti,' she replied. 'What's up?'

There was a pause, during which Becka squinted into the drifting mists as she blinked the rain out of her eyes. The downpour was definitely getting worse, the entire surface of the chamber floor looking like one huge, shallow lake. The air was darkening too, what little natural light that was able to shine down through the upper levels being cut off by the steadily thickening cloud layer. Then, Vahn's voice came back.

'I don't like this, Becka,' he said.

'Hah!' she snorted inside her mask. '*You* don't like it?' I'm the one on point, she thought.

'I mean it,' he said, his irritation obvious in his voice even over the static-laced personal vox-channel. 'Something's up.'

'Repeat last,' said Becka as the channel burst with distorted interference. 'You're breaking up, Vahn.'

'I said,' Vahn repeated, 'something isn't right.'

Becka glanced back the way she'd come. All she could see was rearing machinery and massively over-scale chains hanging down from above, slick with rain and wreathed in coils of mist. She'd got too far ahead and would have to slow to allow the remainder of the force to catch up. 'You sure this channel's secure?' she said.

'As sure as I can be, Becka,' he replied. 'I can see things going very wrong, and I want us ready for it.'

'By *us*, you mean the *convicti*,' she said. 'Not the guard, right?'

'Right,' Vahn replied. 'I don't know what it is, but be ready, okay?'

'Okay,' she replied as she spied a figure approaching through the mists back the way she'd come. She rapid-blinked to clear the rain from her eyelashes and saw that the figure was the Claviger-Primaris, Gruss. She waited a moment, allowing him to close up the line of march, then turned to resume her progress. Just before she turned her back on the chief warden, however, Becka got the impression from his head movements that he was talking to someone, though she couldn't be sure.

Having closed on the base of the northern wall, Flint had decided it was time to split the force up into smaller groups. At this point, force security was less of a concern than fulfilling the mission, and they would have more chance of doing so if split into sub-units.

The upper reaches of the wall were lost to shadow and mist, and its surface was honeycombed with portals, each leading back into a complex network of tunnels and chambers. According to the former convicts, the tunnels afforded dozens of different routes upwards and just as many dead ends. At the very top was the chamber that housed the crippled scrubbers, a chamber which, if the obese rebel leader were to be believed, housed the rogue colonel's stronghold. Chances were those tunnels would be well guarded, certainly well enough for any lookouts to detect the approach of Flint's force and warn their fellows to lock down their defences. By splitting into smaller groups, Flint hoped to bypass at least a few of the lookouts and increase the chances of getting a confirmed fix on Colonel Strannik.

Flint watched as the last of the ten-man multiples tramped off towards the wall, each allocated a different route up to the air scrubber chamber. Most of the squads were made up of the newly inducted penal troopers, but Flint had assigned one of Bukin's provosts to lead each. He doubted any of the former convict-workers would be especially keen to switch sides but he had to make sure none would decide to make for some dark corner and wait the battle out. Gruss had led his squad of clavigers away, leaving Flint with Bukin, Lhor, Hannen, Kohlz and Karasinda.

'Everyone ready?' said Flint, lowering his night vision goggles.

A chorus of affirmatives confirmed they were, and Flint led his squad through its assigned portal. Immediately, they encountered signs of the rebels' atrocities, the walls splashed with long-dried blood. Someone had used the blood to scrawl crude graffiti along the length of the tunnel, and Flint's lip curled in disgust as he read the first few words.

The statements daubed in blood were telling, offering clues into the mental state and motivations of the rebels and their leader. Flint was alert for signs of outside influences at work in the complex, perhaps aliens, or worse, having inspired the uprising. The *Dictum Commissaria* warned commissars of the signs of domination by such forces, and Flint was well versed in detecting such taint. Though he doubted alien interference, he was genuinely concerned that the servants of the Archenemy, Chaos, might be behind the uprising and that the rogue colonel might be some manner of demagogue or high priest of the Ruinous Powers. He had looked for the telltale signs of such corruption, but had yet to see any direct evidence, though there was plenty in his surroundings to disturb him. The uprising, Flint had cautiously concluded, was the result of hubris and ambition and the refusal to yield to duty, and nothing more sinister.

The floor became increasingly strewn with debris the higher the squad advanced, and it was soon an effort to avoid crunching on the litter underfoot. At one point Flint halted to examine a pile of bones scattered across the tunnel floor, deciding that a corpse had been stripped of its flesh by some manner of vermin, the gnawed remains left strewn all about. The air was musty and the temperature was rising. The humidity increased as the squad moved deeper into the tunnels and Flint's chest stung with the taint hanging in the air that he breathed, sharp pains stabbing his chest with each breath. Soon, he was forced to don one of the Firstborn's standard issue rebreathers, designed to be proof against the choking pollution of Vostroya's industrial nightmare landscape. The rebreather made the going easier, though combined with the bulky night vision goggles, Flint felt encumbered and somehow more vulnerable than before.

The tunnel corkscrewed and twisted through the rock-crete cliff face with no apparent logic until Flint had all but abandoned any attempt to track progress on Major Herrmahn's tri-D map. The purpose of the tunnels was far from clear too, for they appeared cut from the rock-crete instead of being built that way. While most of the complex's myriad tunnels and passageways were lined with kilometre after kilometre of pipes and cabling, these were not, suggesting they'd been carved by the inmates themselves as if in an effort to create a refuge from the overwhelming weight of the vast space of the open carceri chamber beyond. If that was the case, Flint could well sympathise, for the chamber's sheer scale was oppressive in the extreme, the unnatural weight of the void overhead thoroughly crushing.

Ten minutes into the ascent, Flint's squad came upon the first of many junctions. Cautious of an ambush Flint sent Lhor and Hannen forward, ready to unleash a devastating burst of heavy flamer fire should any enemy show themselves. None did, and the squad continued its climb, the going getting all the more rough as they progressed.

After another few minutes, Kohlz started to notice odd signals reverberating through the airwaves and the short-range personal vox-net that linked each warrior was completely shut down by the tunnels. There was now no way of coordinating the actions of the different squads as they each climbed upwards through the dank darkness towards the air scrubber chamber and the rebels' stronghold. Truly, the mission was at its most vulnerable, and its success rested entirely in the hands of the God-Emperor.

'This is such a load of crap,' Vendell moaned as Vahn's group picked its way along a corpse-strewn length of steep climbing, pitch-black tunnel. Thankfully, the squad's provost watchdog, a man called Katko, was either hard of hearing, concentrating on other things or he just didn't care for any of the penal troopers' complaints.

Vahn was on point, leading his squad through the labyrinthine tunnel network. He'd insisted on taking the lead position, mainly as a statement of intent to show the squad, and in particular Provost Katko, who was boss. The provost didn't seem that bothered and had barely uttered a word to the penal troopers since being given command over them.

'How much further?' muttered Solomon from behind Vahn. 'This is getting old.'

'Quit your moaning, will you?' Vahn growled. 'Just for once...'

'It wasn't moaning,' Solomon whined. 'I mean, we should be getting near the scrubber chamber, shouldn't we?'

Vahn slowed, examining the darkness up ahead through

the grainy green vista afforded by his night vision goggles. He could see no visual clues of the squad's location at all, but Solomon was right. They'd been climbing for some time and must be approaching the objective.

Vahn held up a hand for quiet as he advanced along the corridor, stepping cautiously over more scattered debris. Even through the mask of his rebreather, he was aware that the air was getting warmer and heavier, and the walls glistened with moisture as if sweating.

'Hear that?' Vendell whispered from directly behind Vahn. How the Voyn's Reacher could hear anything with a missing ear Vahn couldn't tell, but he paused nonetheless, straining his hearing to pick up whatever Vendell had heard.

'What?' said Solomon. 'I don't hear–'

'Shhh!' Vahn hissed. He could hear something too, the low grumble of a generator or some other form of machinery. The sound of raw power arcing through the air crackled and seethed nearby, but Vahn couldn't discern the source. The damp air became charged, the hair on the back of his neck standing on end. The other members of the squad looked at one another uncertainly, until Katko pushed forward, his shotgun raised.

'Get moving,' the provost growled.

Resuming his advance, Vahn felt the renewed conviction that something was definitely wrong. Before, his concerns had been centred on the involvement of the clavigers and what might happen if the mission went badly awry, but now something else gnawed at his subconscious mind. He slowed again, signalling a halt with a raised hand.

Solomon looked ready to complain, but shut his mouth when he saw Vahn was serious. He knelt, signalling the squad to do likewise, and scanned the rough-hewn, rock-crete walls. Seeing nothing out of the ordinary up ahead, Vahn panned along past the squad.

'Crap…' he whispered.

'What?' said Solomon, before Katko pushed past him and repeated the question.

'Wait a second,' said Vahn. He skimmed a hand across the damp wall, feeling the texture. The air buzzed as if charged with energy, and the sound rose in pitch as his hand swept higher.

'Crap,' he repeated.

Provost Katko placed a hand on Vahn's shoulder and made to pull him around.

'Get your hand off my shoulder, friend,' Vahn growled. 'This ain't the time to…'

'You'll tell me what's got you spooked,' Katko said, his unshaven face closing on Vahn's. 'Or I'm taking over and you're on a charge.'

'You want to know what's up?' said Vahn, a note of derision entering his voice. 'Look straight up.'

Katko swore under his breath.

'What?' Solomon repeated. 'Can't anyone just tell me what's…'

'We've just walked right through an operational power shield,' said Vahn.

Solomon's face resembled a fish gasping for air as he looked to Vahn, wide-eyed and open-mouthed. 'How…?

'Must be configured for one-way passage,' Vahn explained, though he deliberately withheld the source of his assertion. 'We pass through the other way, we get fried.'

'Crap…' said Solomon.

Flint's squad was passing along a wide landing strewn with shattered bones and scraps of torn clothing when Bukin stooped down suddenly, examining the ground. Flint gestured for the squad to hold and everyone went firm.

'Someone's been through here,' Bukin hissed, holding up a scrap of discarded food. Flint couldn't tell what the food had been, and didn't really want to. 'And recently,' Bukin added, sniffing distastefully at the morsel.

Flint pressed forward with his bolt pistol raised, clapping Bukin on the shoulder to indicate he should continue. They were nearly there, Flint was sure of it – it certainly felt like they'd climbed several hundred metres of sloping tunnel towards the upper reaches of Carceri *Resurecti*. His leg muscles were burning and his lungs stung. Every now and then the tunnels had converged with others, and several times the squad had thought it had caught glimpses of others as they worked their way upwards. Each time, the point men had waited as footsteps echoed weirdly through the passageways, but aside from the occasional silhouette or darting shadow, hadn't come close to encountering one another.

'One of ours?' Flint whispered as he and Bukin moved cautiously towards the end of the landing. He doubted it, but had to check.

'No, sir,' Bukin said as he held up the morsel of discarded

food, an expression of disgust twisting his face. 'Not even Vahn's mob would eat this…'

'Agreed,' said Flint as he caught sight of the slimy object Bukin was holding. 'Proceed, with caution.'

'And besides,' added Bukin. 'Can't you smell it? This place *stinks* of mutant.'

He was right. In amongst the reek of decay and destruction was that same underlying taint that had, now Flint considered it, always been present. It was that almost familiar, but indiscernible cocktail of biological corruption and chemical pollution, permeating the very air Flint breathed.

Flint nodded and Bukin led the squad to the end of the landing where a smaller tunnel branched off, rising steeply as it corkscrewed upwards through the rockcrete. It was too dark to see much, but Flint could certainly hear something. Voices.

Not risking giving the squad's presence away, Flint gestured for a cautious advance. Edging slowly forward Flint lowered his rebreather, freeing himself of its constriction and reduced airflow. Immediately, the dank, chemical-laced air rushed into his lungs and he almost gagged. The higher up the carceri chamber's wall the squad advanced, the worse the air quality. How many of their fellow convicts must the rebels have slain in the preceding weeks to produce such a reek, he thought? What diseases must even now be swarming in the unclean air he was breathing?

Pushing onwards, Flint felt a stirring in the rank air and sensed a wide, open space at the end of the narrow passageway just beyond the turn, dirty light oozing in from beyond. The space the passageway opened into was low and broadly circular, lit by columns of harsh daylight lancing down from directly overhead. The roof was formed by a rotor several hundred metres in diameter, its multiple blades, each the size of a heavy bomber's wing, streaked with washes of garish corrosion. This then was the air scrubber that when operational kept the air moving through Carceri *Resurecti*. The light streaming downwards between the massive fan blades cast the scene in harsh shadows, but the air was stale and rank, held immobile since the scrubber had shut down. However, it wasn't the rotor that had caught Flint's baleful eye, but the figures occupying the chamber beneath it. There were hundreds of them, perhaps thousands, the scrofulous ranks filling the entire chamber. Rebels. An *army* of rebels.

'Saint Nadalya's mercy...' Bukin mouthed.

Flint shouldered past the chief provost to get a better view and he bit back a bitter curse as he took in the spectacle before him. The rebels were mustering, not as a huge, unruly mob, but as an organised body of troops. As he looked on, Flint saw squads organised into platoons, and platoons organised into companies. The voices he'd heard before must have been the last of the rebels gabbling as they settled into position, but now, silence descended on the massed ranks. The rebels were standing to attention, almost like proper, drilled and trained soldiers.

Then it came to him. They *were* proper, drilled and trained soldiers. If the convicts assimilated into the 77th were anything to go by, the majority of the rebels must be erstwhile members of the Imperial Guard or other bodies such as planetary defence forces. Granted, they'd been expelled for transgressions too severe for the regimental provosts and commissars to deal with, but nonetheless, many must have been well used to military discipline. The rebels were scruffy and ill-equipped, but there was no doubt they were being drilled as soldiers. It made sense. If the infamous Colonel Strannik was in charge, he'd be using rigid military discipline to keep the murderous scum under his command in line.

And then, Flint saw the huge figure of the Catachan come into view as he passed through a downward-shining beam of wan daylight. The man was a mountain of scarred and tattooed gristle, his oversized frame barely contained within his ragged combat fatigues. His left shoulder was bound in crude bandages, the result of the bolt pistol round Flint had clipped him with during their last confrontation. His face was cast in harsh shadow by the light source directly overhead, emphasising his heavyset features. But by that light, the Catachan's face was revealed as bruised and his lip was split, as if he'd been savagely beaten sometime in the last few hours.

Trained by the Commissariat and a veteran of dispensing similar justice, Flint knew for certain that the Catachan hadn't been set upon by any of his fellow rebel convicts. None would have been able to take him down and if they had he'd no longer be in a position of command. No, the Catachan had submitted to the beating, administered by, or at the command of, the only man with the power to do so – the renegade Colonel Strannik.

As Flint watched, the Catachan walked the length of the first rank, his steely gaze sweeping over the men lined up before him. Even the toughest of those men shrank before the Catachan's gaze, his eyes smouldering with menace. Flint recognised the signs of a man recently humbled by a superior and who needed scant excuse to enact his vengeance on those weaker and further down the pecking order than himself. Clearly, this was the only form of discipline that would keep such men in line.

As the Catachan reached the end of the first rank, Flint saw movement at the far end of the chamber. A shape appeared through a hatch in the far wall, silhouetted against the harsh column of light shining down from above. But the form was far from that of a normal man, even though Flint could barely make it out from his hiding place. It was twisted and distended, and moved with a hideous shuffling gait. Its every step was imbued with unbreakable threat and sullen menace.

Silence descended on the assembled rebel convict soldiers, the single figure cowing hundreds of his underlings by his very presence. Flint couldn't make out the face, but he knew instantly exactly who the figure was.

'Strannik,' Vahn hissed, ducking back into the mouth of the stairwell he and his squad were hiding in.

'You're sure?' said Katko. 'You're absolutely sure that's our target?'

'That's him,' Solomon gulped before Vahn could answer. 'You don't forget that bastard in a hurry...'

'I'm *sure*,' said Vahn. 'Solomon's right. Once you've seen that murdering scum up close you don't forget, even if you'd rather.'

'Then we extract,' said Katko. 'Inform the boss and call in the regiment.'

'You forgetting something?' Vahn growled. 'We're going nowhere. Not the way we came at least, not with that power shield operational.'

Katko's face twisted in frustration and he sighed as he looked back down the stairwell. 'You know a better way?'

'There was a junction a hundred metres down,' said Solomon. 'We could take that and hope–'

'Hope it bypasses the power shield?' Katko interrupted the Jopalli. 'That's a pretty big ask.'

'It's the only way,' said Vahn. 'Unless you know how to deactivate the shield trips.'

'No?' Vahn pressed, hefting his carbine and preparing to head back down the stairwell. 'Then it's the junction. Come on.'

'Target confirmed,' Flint growled beneath his breath. 'Kohlz?'

Flint's aide failed to answer, and in a moment, he knew why. Something was happening in the chamber, and that horribly familiar stink was back, now stronger than ever before. But it wasn't just a taint that filled the air, Flint realised as the hairs on the back of his neck stood on end. A charge was building, one he hadn't experienced in a long time, not since going into combat alongside the Imperial Guard's dreaded battle psykers at the height of the Siege of the Iron Bastion. The air thickened, the light bending in ways no tech-savant could possibly explain. Time stretched and became distorted, so that a single breath took an age of screaming torment to inhale and exhale while a billion thoughts flashed through Flint's mind in the same span of experience.

If the effect upon Flint was drastic, those in the chamber beyond were affected a thousand times worse.

As one, every rebel in the chamber staggered to his knees. Hands clamped over ears as the crimson glint of spilled blood twinkled in amongst the shadows. Two thousand and more pairs of knees slammed into the hard floor and those hands not struggling to contain rapidly expanding grey matter thudded hard to the ground. A cacophony of torment erupted as rebels moaned, wailed or vomited, even the Catachan reduced to a helpless form splayed at his master's feet. Waves of malevolence washed outwards from the colonel and as each one broke against the ranks of his followers the rebels were forced into ever-greater acts of obeisance. Foreheads ground into the dirt in abject supplication until the skin was rasped off to reveal the bloody, white bone beneath.

All the while, the figure of Colonel Strannik, his features thankfully obscured by the shadows of the chamber, drank in the enforced adoration of his personal army. Hatred welled inside Flint's heart as he struggled to break the spell, the words of every catechism he had ever learned spilling through his mind in an instant.

The moment stretched on forever, Flint's perspective

altering in every possible way. He caught a hint of movement in the periphery of his vision, though it was gone by
the time he could fix his gaze upon it, his reactions glacially
slow. Another burst of movement darted across the centre
of his vision and he thought he caught the sight of a ghostly
skull face imprinted upon the strained reality before him. It
was almost as if a shoal of oceanic predators was circling the
shadowed form of the colonel, as if drawn to him, though
Flint couldn't tell if it they were circling around him like
hunters, or if they were answering his call for obeisance.

Then it ended. The colonel lowered his spread arms and
uttered a groan of hideous release. Where minutes before
his army had been arrayed in perfect ranks, now it was a
sprawling mass of writhing, bloody limbs. What blasphemous display of dominance Flint had just witnessed the
commissar could not fully explain, for it defied all logic.
The rebel leader had wilfully reduced his own warriors to
mewling, puking victims of his psychic brutalisation simply
to demonstrate his power, and for that, he was damned.
Colonel Strannik must surely have been a psyker, an
abominably powerful one at that, and his control over his
subjects was total.

Even as Flint composed himself, the rebels were recover-
ing; men and women staggering to their feet as the colonel
turned and made his way from the chamber. Soon, the
Catachan was staggering to his feet too and lashing out at
his underlings, bullying the ranks into some semblance of
order.

There must be two thousand of them, Flint estimated, and

most were armed, with weapons looted from slain clavigers. That put the rebels on a rough par with the 77th in terms of raw manpower, but the calculation was nowhere near that simple. The Vostroyans were better equipped, that much was true, but then the rebels were on home territory. The 77th would be assaulting a prepared position and the rebels were both experienced and cornered, a lethal combination in Flint's experience.

Right now, the odds were stacked in the rebels' favour, unless Flint could bring the regiment down on their heads, hard and fast, before the enemy could react.

'Sir?' said Flint's aide as he knelt down beside him, his voice cracked and strained.

'Time to call the regiment, Kohlz,' said Flint. 'Do you still have that carrier signal?'

Kohlz worked the dial at his headset, evidently grateful for a distraction from what he had just witnessed and experienced. Very soon however, his expression darkened.

'Kohlz?' said Flint.

Kohlz fiddled with the controls for a few moments longer, then looked up at the commissar. 'The signal's gone, sir. It's being blocked.'

'Who by?' said Flint. 'Who would–'

'There's something else, sir,' Kohlz added. 'Another signal.'

'Who,' Flint pressed, glancing impatiently back towards the mustered rebel army. 'Quickly...'

'I can't tell, sir,' said Kohlz. 'It's encrypted, high level. I can't break it with this set.'

'Sir?' Bukin interjected before Flint could press the matter further. The chief provost's face was almost completely drained of colour and he appeared to have aged at least a decade. 'I really think we should be moving out, sir.'

Flint looked back into the chamber, the distant form of Colonel Strannik shambling away on mechanical callipers. 'What the...' he mouthed.

'Sir?' Bukin insisted, pointing towards a large group of rebels starting to move out, directly towards Flint and his force. 'They are on the move, sir.'

'Understood,' said Flint. 'We're moving out too, but only when I say so. Bukin? Gather up all the frags you can. We're not leaving without a parting shot.'

Vahn was the last out of the stairwell having allowed Katko to lead Solomon, Vendell and the rest away from the air scrubber chamber. He leapt from the stair onto the landing beyond, scattering debris as he dashed after the last of the squad. As he ran Vahn fought to recall the route they'd taken and find the path that avoided the area seeded with power shield trips. His mind was all but shot by the warp craft that bastard colonel had unleashed, and he was running on a noxious cocktail of instinct and adrenaline. He cursed inwardly as he ran along the dark corridor, his night vision goggles robbing him of depth perception so that several times he almost tripped or slammed into the trooper in front. He cursed Colonel Strannik, he cursed Alpha Penitentia, and he cursed Commissar Flint. A terrible sense of entrapment was welling inside him, the rebel army behind and the power shield somewhere up ahead.

Katko had halted the squad, his hand raised for silence.

'What?' said Vahn as he skidded to a halt, almost knocking into Solomon.

'Shh!' the provost hissed. 'I thought I heard...'

'There!' said Solomon, un-holstering his laspistol, his sniper rifle next to useless in such cramped environs.

Vahn strained his hearing until he heard it too. Footsteps. Lots and lots of footsteps...

'They're coming!' Solomon gulped. 'The whole *pashing* lot...'

'Get moving,' Vahn ordered, shoving Solomon ahead. 'It's the third branch on the left, but watch out for more trips, got it?'

As the squad moved on and the sound of hundreds of tramping feet echoed madly about the rockcrete tunnels it became clear that Solomon was right, the rebel army was definitely on the move. Each time he halted Vahn imagined the rebels gaining ground, but in truth he couldn't tell if they were actually pursuing or just moving out. Then, he heard the first of the gunfire.

The distinctive *whip-crack* of a las-bolt sounded from somewhere nearby. The sound rang through the tunnels and rebounded in such a way that Vahn had no way of discerning its source. Then another shot rang out, followed by an angry shout and Vahn thought the source might be a tunnel branching off not far ahead.

Katko had his Mark III raised and pointed into the dark mouth of the side tunnel. Vahn pressed himself against the wet tunnel wall and leaned in to peer along the side passage.

A shot rang out, impossibly loud in the narrow tunnel, and powdered rockcrete spat in Vahn's face. He ducked back instinctively, swearing loudly as he rubbed the grit from his eyes.

'That was a knock-off piece,' Vahn growled as he cleared his eyes and raised his weapon to his shoulder. 'Return fire!' he shouted as he leaned around the corner.

Vahn and Katko swung into the tunnel mouth as one, their weapons scanning left and right for a target. The tunnel was barely wide enough for one man to pass along it and its floor glistened with moisture running down from its walls. The passageway turned twenty metres ahead, and Vahn and Katko both saw the rebel figure as he cleared the bend, a bright smudge of pale green through the grainy vista of the night vision goggles.

Both men opened fire as one. Katko's shotgun blast took the rebel square in the chest, while Vahn's las-bolt struck him in the throat. The rebel flew backwards, twisting and flailing as his chest cavity emptied itself across the ground.

The weapons' discharge filled Vahn's vision with pulsating static, the goggles' viewfinder fouled by the sudden brightness. Vahn jerked his head back and flicked the goggles onto his forehead, his vision replaced with almost pitch-black.

At that exact moment, Katko fired down the tunnel a second time, the report of his shotgun almost blinding. His target was a second rebel edging along the bend in the tunnel and stepping gingerly over the remains of his comrade. Katko's blast took the man in the stomach and he tumbled forward, his improvised firearm clattering across the ground before him. The instant Vahn's eyes recovered from the sudden flash he squinted down the barrel of his carbine just as a third rebel appeared.

This one was smarter than the first two, and he stooped as he threw himself forward, a claviger-issue shotgun raised towards Vahn and Katko.

But Vahn was ready, and the rebel passed right into his iron sights. He squeezed the trigger and the carbine spat its las-bolt straight and true, right into the rebel's forehead, explosively vaporising the man's head.

A mass of angry bellows betrayed more rebels massing beyond the bend in the side tunnel. It was time to get moving.

'Go!' Vahn shouted as he unclipped a frag grenade from his webbing. Katko grinned wickedly and was gone. Vahn flipped the fuse to three seconds.

As Vahn stooped to roll the grenade along the tunnel's wet floor, another shot blasted from its depths, striking the wall where he had been standing less than a second before. Mouthing silent thanks to the God-Emperor, Vahn sent the frag skidding across the ground and dived clear of the opening.

Another shot hammered out of the side tunnel as the rebels swarmed down its length, then a savage curse echoed from its depths. Mad laughter erupted from Vahn's mouth as he hit the ground at the exact moment the grenade detonated. The blast tore everything in the side tunnel to shreds and the overpressure hammered down the main passage-way, throwing Vahn and the rest of the squad forward as flame and black smoke erupted all around.

His hearing replaced by a high-pitched whine, Vahn staggered upright, feeling his arm grabbed by another trooper. It was Solomon and he was saying something, but Vahn's ears were still ringing after the explosion. 'What?' he shouted. 'I can't hear…'

Then Vahn's hearing returned in a wave of noise, the once eerily quiet tunnels now echoing with gunshots and shouting.

'…the side passage!' Solomon was saying, pointing along the passageway with one hand as the other dragged Vahn along. 'Katko's found it!'

Realising what Solomon was trying to tell him, Vahn staggered forward and caught up with the provost, who was aiming his Mark III down another passage. 'This the one?' said Katko. 'You reckon its safe?'

'No,' Vahn laughed humourlessly. 'But I don't see we have much choice, do you?'

'What we waiting for then?' he said as he pressed into the passage that Vahn hoped would take them back down towards the carceri chamber floor and avoid the power field trip they had encountered on the way up.

Katko disappeared into the darkness and Vahn waved the other members of the squad after him. Having checked behind him one last time, he ducked into the passageway and followed after them, the black smoke of the grenade's detonation roiling down the corridor in his wake.

'If I find out it was one of ours that fired first,' Flint shouted to Bukin as he and his companions powered down the corridor, filthy puddles splashing around them, 'I'll shoot him myself.'

'Not if I get there first, sir,' Bukin shouted back as he ran, his waxed moustaches trailing behind. A muffled explosion sounded somewhere in the labyrinth of tunnels not far behind, the combined force of the dozen or so frag grenades Flint had rigged as a trap for their pursuers. He'd learned that trick on Gethsemane stalking the rebels' notorious cannibal death-squads in the equatorial war zones, and had used it several times since.

The tunnels concentrated the blast so tightly it sounded to Flint like a mass-yield nucleonic detonating at his back, backwash flames licking at his and Bukin's ankles as they pounded down the tunnel. The explosion must have slain dozens of rebels.

'Commissar!' Karasinda shouted from up ahead. The medic had discovered something sprawled across the wet tunnel floor. Flint skidded to a halt and Bukin quickly moved to cover their rear.

'What...' said Flint as he looked down at the ground.

'More like *who*, sir,' Karasinda said.

'Looks like one of Vahn's mob, sir,' said Kohlz, his words coming out in ragged bursts as he fought to regain his breath after the mad flight. 'Tobos?' he said. 'Or something like that.'

The shape at Karasinda's feet had been a man, but now it was little more than a lump of charred meat, the stink of seared flesh filling Flint's nostrils. The combat medic appeared entirely unmoved by the sight or by the smell, but Kohlz was on the verge of throwing up.

'Move ahead, Kohlz,' Flint told his aide to avoid him being violently ill. 'But be careful for–'

'No, sir!' Karasinda barked, her gaze sweeping up the tunnel wall and along the ceiling.

'What?' Bukin called back, angry that he couldn't see what was going on.

Kohlz froze. 'What?'

'Listen,' Karasinda hissed.

Flint did so, and there, beneath the muffled sounds of gunfire echoing through the rockcrete, he heard a high-pitched hum.

'It's a generator,' said Flint, craning his neck as he swept the shadows above. 'Something like a Terminus-pattern…'

'Kohlz,' said Flint. 'Step back, very slowly, now.'

The aide stared dumbly back, then followed Flint's gaze to look directly overhead. There, set into the rockcrete, was a small brass hemisphere, glinting dully in the low light of the tunnel.

'Crap,' said Kohlz.

'Now!' Flint hissed. 'Slowly, Kohlz…'

Kohlz swallowed hard and tensed, setting one foot gingerly behind the other as he edged backwards, his eyes fixed on the brass power node. The humming increased in pitch and volume with each step, and then a searing white arc spat outwards, passing through the space where Kohlz had been standing and grounding itself in the wet rockcrete floor.

Finally clear, Kohlz spluttered, 'What the hell is that?'

'It's a power shield,' said Flint. 'One way, by the looks of it.'

'Terminus-pattern, as you said, sir,' Karasinda confirmed. 'One more step, Kohlz, and you'd have ended up like that,' she jerked her head towards the burned corpse sprawled nearby.

'So what now, sir?' Bukin called over his shoulder.

'We find another way down,' said Flint. 'Get moving.'

Another explosion sounded from down another side passage as Vahn dashed across its mouth, a billowing cloud of dust and vapour swallowing him for a moment before he burst through the other side and pounded down the passageway after Trooper Solomon. Even at full tilt they were less than halfway towards the chamber floor. Once again Vahn was starting to feel cornered, and when that happened, people often got hurt.

The tunnels were turning into a warzone, though they were so intertwined and complex that Vahn's squad had yet to cross paths with any others from their force. But they had heard them sure enough, the las-bolts, shotgun blasts and grenade explosions of the Imperial Guard competing noisily with the discharges of the myriad looted or hand-cast weapons used by the rebels. They had heard angry shouts and grunts of pain, and orders bellowed back and forth. On several occasions Vahn had been positive that one of his fellow penal troopers was just around the corner, only to find no one there. Once, a grenade had rolled out of a side passage and Vahn had only just dived clear as it detonated, lacerating his back with painful, yet ultimately non-lethal, fragments of shrapnel. He found no trace of who'd thrown the grenade.

A curse sounded from up ahead and Vahn only just threw his arm across his face as a blinding white light filled the tunnel. The air erupted and bolts of seething energy danced across the moisture coating the floor and walls, crackling and spitting as the air filled with ozone. A hot, greasy shock wave powered up the tunnel, throwing troopers aside or slamming them into the walls.

Then it all went quite and the stink of burning meat assaulted Vahn's senses. Someone swore loudly, and someone else vomited even louder.

'Sound off!' Vahn shouted, his vision still swimming with livid nerve light.

'I said...' he shouted, before he heard the first of the squad call his name. As Vahn's vision cleared he guessed what had happened and shouldered his way to the front of the squad.

A smoking corpse was strewn across the floor, battledress and armour burned away to reveal blackened and cracked skin. It was Katko, and he'd run straight through another power shield trip.

'No one move,' Vahn said through grated teeth as he quickly scanned the walls. It didn't take long to locate the hemispherical brass nodes secreted in the rockcrete.

'What now?' said Solomon, his face pale and his eyes wide as he glanced back up the tunnel the way they'd come. Muffled sounds of combat drifted back from the darkness.

'We double back to the last branch,' said Vahn. 'Press on 'til we meet up with the rest.'

'Or not,' scowled Vendell. Several of the other penal

troopers nodded while others cast nervous glances between Vahn and Vendell.

Here it comes, Vahn thought.

'We don't *have* to link up with the rest,' Vendell said. 'Do we? We got a whole generatorium to get lost in, if we want.'

Vahn drew himself up to his full height as the sound of closing pursuit echoed through the tunnels. Squaring off against Vendell, he looked down his nose at the man's upturned face.

'We've done this already,' Vahn growled as he met the smaller man's glare. 'Now is a *really* bad time to kick off, Vendell.'

The other man's face twisted in a nasty leer as he gave thought to pressing the point, but when no one else seemed willing to join him he relented. Vendell stepped backwards and stalked a few paces back up the passageway.

'Okay,' he called back. 'We'll do things your way. But I ain't taking point,' he nodded back towards the smoking corpse of the provost.

Vahn sighed as he shoved Vendell aside and took position at the head of the squad to lead the former convicts back the way they'd come.

Flint and the rebel came around the corner at exactly the same moment, but the commissar was quicker and far better armed. His power sword plunged through the man's guts, its glowing tip lancing upwards to emerge between the shoulder blades. The rebel was dead before he even knew he'd been struck, and Flint pulled the blade free to let the corpse fall forward and slam into the rockcrete floor at his feet.

A las-bolt whipped down the tunnel, dispelling the shadows in the blink of an eye before slamming into the shoulder of another rebel. Flint threw himself sideways against the wall, drawing his bolt pistol as he did so. Karasinda fired again, her next shot dropping the second rebel.

A shotgun boomed in the darkness, filling the passageway with smoke and fire. Bukin racked the slide of his shotgun and fired again, shouting incoherently at enemies closing on the rear beyond Flint's sight.

The tunnel up ahead was filling with rebels, but there was no other way down. Gritting his teeth, he levelled his bolt pistol and stepped around the corner. The space in front was some kind of landing, three or four side passages joining together and rebels streaming out of each. Flint's first shot caught a rebel in the side of the head, the initial impact sending the man cart-wheeling backwards to crash into two others before the bolt buried in his cranium exploded and showered them both with shards of bone and grey matter.

His lip curling in disgust as he jerked his pistol left, Flint's second shot struck another rebel and severed the arm that was raising a heavy gun jack's piece, sending the ugly pistol clattering across the wet floor.

By the time the rebels were organised enough to fire back, Flint was already moving. Sidestepping right, he avoided a burst of automatic fire that chewed into the wall he'd just been standing in front of. His third shot took the firer clean in the centre of the chest, the bolt exploding as it plunged through his heart. The rebel's death spasm caused him to empty his weapon's entire magazine in less than a second, a wild spray of bullets stitching death across the landing and felling three more rebels.

An instant later, Karasinda and Kohlz were at Flint's side, pumping fire into the mass of rebels spilling out of the tunnel entrances. Though cut down like chaff, their numbers seemed endless and it was only a matter of time before Flint's group was overwhelmed.

'Lhor!' Flint called out. 'Front and centre!'

The burly dragoon emerged from the portal, Hannen at his side with a spare fuel canister in each hand. Lhor's face was a greasy black mess, his eyes and teeth shining white as he grinned insanely.

'Stand clear!' he drawled, and Flint, Kohlz and Karasinda ducked back to avoid the worst of the backwash.

The heavy flamer erupted in searing chemical fire, the nozzle set to a wide aperture. A wall of fire washed outwards in an unbearable torrent, the front rank of the rebel mob simply scoured away. Those rebels further back were engulfed in seething flames and transformed into screeching human torches, though the screams of pain were mercifully attenuated. The rebels towards the back of the mob, those who had might have thought themselves safe from immediate harm, suffered the most, as gobbets of flaming promethium splashed over their bodies. It burned through clothes and skin in seconds to melt fat and bone to liquid as they bellowed in pain and threw themselves to the floor in a futile attempt to douse the all-consuming flames in steaming puddles.

'At them!' Flint bellowed over the roar of burning corpses as he waved the squad forward. The landing had been transformed into a vision of damnation, the floor a mass of guttering flames and smoking chunks of flesh. A shot rang out from behind as Karasinda put a las-bolt through the head of a rebel who hadn't had the sense to die just yet. Glancing back, Flint suspected it was more an act of military necessity than one of medical compassion.

As he pressed towards a portal on the opposite side of the landing, Flint's throat started to fill with thick, black smoke, and he coughed to clear it before lifting his rebreather over his mouth and taking a deep breath. The mask filtered the worst of the smoke, but it couldn't keep the stench of burning flesh out.

Advancing through the burning charnel house, Flint came to the nearest of the portals and leaned in to check the way ahead. The tunnel was dimly lit by a wan light source shining from below, and Flint realised it must open up into the carceri chamber. They were almost free of the labyrinthine tunnels.

'Sir!' Karasinda shouted, her voice so urgent Flint froze, his subconscious telling him what was wrong before he fully realised what was happening. He looked upwards, and saw set in the rockcrete a small, brass hemisphere, its surface spitting white arcs as the air filled with a deep, sub-sonic hum.

'Back away, sir,' the medic called out. 'Slowly.'

'Stupid mistake,' Flint growled under his breath as he backed carefully away from the power shield node, watching as it sparked and guttered as if reacting to his movement. As the light at the base of the steep tunnel receded as he backed away, he cursed his stupidity and thanked the Emperor for Karasinda's alertness.

'Which way?' said Kohlz as he looked towards the other portals leading off into more tunnels. None of them appeared to be heading in the same direction as the one Flint had been about to plunge into. They were so close, but the power shields must have been placed to herd them into deadly killing zones as they fled towards the safety of the open carceri chamber.

Soon after taking point Vahn found an almost sheer, spiral stairwell leading straight downwards and threw caution to the wind as he descended into its lightless depths, taking the steps three or four at a time as the sound of pursuit rang out from above. He was placing his faith in the stairwell not being seeded with more power shield trips, for the ones they'd encountered so far were all set in straight corridors.

'We must almost be there!' shouted Solomon. Vahn was thinking the same thing and despite the sound of heavy footsteps and angry shouts ringing from high above he slowed up, his carbine raised as he approached what must have been the last few turns of the spiral stairwell.

'What the hell is that *stink*?' said Solomon, lifting his rebreather to cover his nose and mouth. 'Smells like...'

Vahn held up a hand as he crept around the last turn

and Solomon shut up. The dank air was filling with greasy black smoke illuminated by a flickering orange hell-light. As he descended the last few steps, Vahn heard the sound of crackling meat and popping fat. He made the signal to be ready for contact with an unknown number of enemies up ahead.

Counting down to zero with the fingers of his raised hands, Vahn took a deep breath and stepped neatly out from the stairwell…

…and stopped dead as he found himself staring down the barrel of Corporal Bukin's Mark III.

'What took you?' Bukin leered.

Vahn lowered his carbine, which he had been about to discharge in Bukin's face, and breathed out, his blood thundering in his ears. He looked around the landing he found himself in, his lip curling at the sight and smell of the guttering corpses feeding the fires that raged all about. Commissar Flint and his aide were approaching, while Karasinda, Lhor and Hannen covered the other entrances opening into the area.

Ignoring Bukin's jibe, Vahn called across to the commissar, 'We've got company, no more than a minute behind!'

'Understood,' Flint shouted back. 'Lhor, cover the stairs, Vahn, get your squad covering the other mouths.'

As Vahn waved his squad out of the stairwell, Dragoon Lhor approached, a savage grin lighting his soot-blackened face. It looked to Vahn like the logistics man was enjoying his new role rather too much.

'Everyone back,' Lhor growled as he test-fired a short huff

of burning promethium and placed his feet wide at the entrance to the stairwell. 'This is gonna hurt.'

Lhor waited a moment longer as the sound of heavy footsteps descending the spiral stairs grew louder. Then, he opened the nozzle, angled the heavy flamer upwards into the stairwell and let out a three second burst that arced upwards in a seething torrent of flame, silhouetting him against the raging inferno. Even against the roaring flame, Vahn heard the banshee wail of men burning alive, and he held up a hand to shield his face from the searing backwash.

'Vahn!' Flint shouted over the roar. 'Have you seen any other groups?'

'No, commissar,' Vahn said. 'But we saw Strannik, positive ident.'

'Us too,' said Flint. 'Now we need to reach the regiment.'

'Problem?' said Vahn, knowing something was wrong.

'You could say that,' Flint muttered as he leaned inside the tunnel that the medic Karasinda was guarding and squinted up at the shadowed ceiling. 'You've encountered the power shields, I take it.'

'Yeah,' said Vahn. 'We...'

'Hey,' said Bukin. 'Where's Katko?'

Vahn opened his mouth to answer, but an explosion somewhere overhead rocked the landing and brought rock-crete dust showering down on the warriors.

'Dead?' said Bukin.

'Walked into a power shield. I'm...'

'Stupid *khekker*,' Bukin growled, ducking his head into the tunnel mouth that Flint had just looked down into. 'Always was. Anything, sir?' he said.

'Can't tell,' Flint growled back, scowling as another grenade explosion shook the rockcrete and brought another drift of dust pattering down. 'Looks like we might have to take the unsubtle approach.'

'Blast through?' said Vahn, his eyebrows raised incredulously. 'I guess that could work...'

'I wouldn't recommend it,' said a new voice, and every warrior on the landing spun around as a black-clad figure appeared at the mouth of the side tunnel that Kohlz was supposed to be watching. Flint's aide swung his lasgun up sharply, but the figure caught its barrel and pushed it firmly away.

'Gruss,' said Flint, as the Claviger-Primaris came into the open, his squad of wardens emerging behind and spreading out. The commissar looked far from happy to see the head warden. 'We've tried that passage,' Flint nodded towards the portal. 'There's a power shield down there.'

'This is our domain, commissar,' Gruss's voice sounded from his armour's hidden phonocasters. 'Despite what the inmates might believe.' Looking around the corpse-strewn, guttering landing, he added, 'Are you coming or not?'

'Wait!' Flint snarled. The two men squared off against one another, the tall commissar looking down into the chief warden's glossy, black visor. The guttering corpse-fires cast baleful reflections but nothing of the man's face was visible. 'You knew about the power shields?' Flint said, his voice low and dangerous.

'Of course, commissar,' Gruss matched Flint's tone.

'And you didn't think it worth informing me?' Flint barked.

'Certain information regarding this facility's security measures is–'

A deep, rumbling quake shook the landing and great chunks of rockcrete tumbled from the ceiling along with clouds of billowing dust. Neither Flint nor Gruss moved, though it was clearly time to get out, and quick.

'Everyone!' Vahn bellowed over the explosion's aftershock as he darted for the mouth of the tunnel the clavigers had just emerged from. 'Move!'

None needed telling a second time. Another deep rumble shook the rockcrete chamber and Vahn made to leave. 'You coming or not?' he shouted to the commissar and the chief warden.

The two men continued to stare at one another a moment longer, then each stepped backwards, the stalemate broken.

A moment later all three men were heading towards the open space of Carceri *Resurecti*.

Commissar Flint blinked as he emerged into the carceri chamber, a strobing wave of nigh blinding white light arcing down from directly overhead. He raised an arm to shield his eyes from the pulsing glare and saw that the light was sheet lightning, flickering in the black clouds high in the chamber. The air was charged and heavy and the instant Flint stepped out into the open he was drenched by the fine, relentless drizzle.

Several dozen warriors were emerging from nearby openings. Even though they'd found their own way around or through the Terminus field trips they must have suffered casualties, their numbers drastically reduced.

'Commissar?' Dragoon Kohlz pointed towards a group of penal troopers clustered around a portal further along the chamber wall. 'It's Skane's multiple, sir. Looks like he's having trouble...'

'I'll give him trouble,' Flint snarled, drawing his bolt pistol. Flicking the safety off his pistol, he blinked as the lightning flashed again and the rumble of thunder ground overhead.

Movement, in the shadows perhaps a kilometre away. The lightning flashed again and Flint caught the sight a second time, figures clustered around the base of a towering drive head. The instant the lightning was gone his vision was replaced by seething after-flash. He lowered his night vision goggles and concentrated on the shadow at the base of the massive drive.

'Emperor's mercy,' he breathed.

'Sir?' said Kohlz, appearing at his side. 'What's... Oh *khekk*...'

'Bukin! Vahn!' Flint bellowed. 'Get everyone ready to move out, right now!'

The two men turned and followed his gaze. With the next flash of lightning they saw what Commissar Flint had seen. A mass of rebel convicts was spilling around the base of the towering machinery and was even now charging outwards across the rain-lashed rockcrete floor of the carceri chamber.

The water that spilled across the surface was transformed into a fine mist by the pounding of a thousand and more feet and a hateful roar was slowly rising as the rebels crossed the open space.

For a moment, Commissar Flint stood transfixed by the sight of so many enemies surging forward towards his small force. Scenes from a dozen and more battles flashed across his mind. In its own way, each was just as desperate and uneven, yet somehow, he had walked away from them all. He had walked away from them because he was schooled in the dictates of the Commissariat, raised on the words of a thousand holy men. All their teachings distilled down into a single principle – the Emperor protects. When all else appears lost, a true servant of the Emperor knows that whatever else befalls him, he shall sit at the right hand of the Emperor for all eternity.

But not just yet, thought Flint. Not while there's a mission to complete, a regiment to call in and a warp-spawned mutant uprising to crush.

Vahn, Bukin and the provosts herded the troopers into order and made ready to move out at Flint's word but several of Skane's group were making to head off on their own along the chamber wall in the opposite direction. The big Elysian was engaged in a bellowing altercation with another of his squad, the two men's words lost to the crash of thunder and the growing roar of the onrushing rebel host. Snarling, he racked the slide of his bolt pistol. 'What's the problem here?' he barked over the rumbling of thunder. 'We're leaving, now!'

'We ain't going with you!' shouted the man Skane had been arguing with. 'We ain't.'

'Barra!' Skane snarled. 'Don't do this.'

'Why the hell shouldn't we?' the penal trooper bellowed. 'We're leaving! We'd rather take our chances on our own!'

Flint raised his bolt pistol and levelled it squarely at Barra, mere centimetres from his forehead. The man froze, his eyes fixed on the gaping barrel before him, and his companions stopped where they were. The sound of the onrushing rebel horde grew louder by the second, but right now, the only battle Flint cared for was the contest of wills between Barra and himself.

'Barra,' said Skane, his voice low but insistent. 'Do as he says. It's the only way.'

Flint's eyes bored into the other man's and his finger tightened on the trigger of his bolt pistol. Barra blinked, knowing full well that Flint would enact his field execution if he had to, that he was trained to do so, and had performed the act dozens of times before. The sound of the baying rebel horde grew louder still, the first shots from crude, improvised firearms rippling up and down the front rank. Stray shots zipped through the air and impacted on the rockcrete chamber wall, making Barra flinch.

Commissar Flint didn't even blink.

'Barra…' Skane hissed.

'Frag!' Barras exclaimed. 'Okay, we're coming,' he said to Flint.

The commissar jerked his bolt pistol to the left and fired. The body of a fleeing penal trooper tumbled to the ground, his back blown open in a ragged mess. The fool had tried to flee under the cover of the confrontation, but Flint had seen every trick in the book and acted accordingly. Flint lowered the smoking weapon and returned his gaze to the other man.

'That was your last warning,' he said, loud enough for the whole group of would-be deserters to hear. 'For all of you.'

'Get them together,' said Flint. 'And if any give you trouble, you know what to do. They've had their warning. Understood?'

Skane nodded grimly and turned his attention back to the onrushing mob. The sight reminded Flint of the death-wave tactics used by the Gethsemane rebels, each bellowing with incoherent anger as they all but tripped over one another in their thirst to close the gap and descend upon their foe. But these were no hate-fuelled fanatics. These were simple convicts, but they appeared to have descended to the level of mindless savages.

Flint knew he had scant time to issue his orders. 'Move back the way we came, Vahn first, by squads,' he said, his eyes fixed on the nearest group of rebels which was now closing to within five hundred metres. 'Bukin, you and I are leading the rearguard.'

And that was all Flint had time to order as the first of the rebels closed towards the effective range of the lascarbines carried by the penal troopers. The first las-bolts lanced outwards, slamming into the horde and sending up puffs of red blood mist as rebels staggered and fell. More blasts spat out, felling more rebels, but those who followed simply trampled over the dead and the wounded alike, the horde's momentum unaffected.

'Move out,' Flint shouted to Vahn, clapping him on the shoulder. The penal trooper and his squad were gone in a second.

'Skane!' Flint called. 'Go!' The Elysian's squad dashed off along the wall close on the heels of Vahn's group. Flint's eyes narrowed as he watched Trooper Barra move out but he had other things to worry about.

'Becka,' Flint shouted to the next group along. 'Go!'

The Savlar made what Flint assumed was intended as a salute and shoved the nearest of the group she was leading, pushing the man after Skane's squad. Flint almost chuckled as he caught the gist of the curse words she was snarling at her squad to get them moving. Almost.

'Stank!' Flint barked to the last group of penal troopers. Stank's squad was pouring a torrent of disciplined fire into the oncoming horde, which Flint judged to be closing on four hundred metres with no signs of slowing up. 'You're next, move!'

The troopers of Rotten's mob squeezed off one more burst each, then stood and dashed off after Becka's squad.

'That leaves just us, sir,' Bukin shouted over the combined roar of the rebel horde and the crash of thunder, slamming a fresh twenty-round magazine into his Mark III. 'And them,' he jerked his head towards Gruss and his squad of clavigers.

'They can look out for themselves,' Flint snarled, now entirely distrustful of the Claviger-Primaris and his motivations. Frankly, Flint couldn't care less if Gruss left or not.

Nevertheless, Gruss and his wardens were heavily armed and armoured and they knew the territory well. In addition, they appeared to have knowledge of hidden security measures and that made Flint distinctly uncomfortable. Evidently, he would have to suffer the clavigers' presence a while longer.

With the rebel horde closing, Flint decided it was time to be somewhere else. He bodily pushed Bukin forward to get the squad moving. Though Flint's small force was massively outnumbered by the horde of rebels he knew he had one major advantage – the small size made it easy to outmanoeuvre the enemy and to lose them in amongst the clusters of oversized machine plant. The low light conditions and the mist and rain made that objective easier too, and within minutes Flint's squads were gaining ground, each stopping to cover the one following on behind in a classic display of light infantry tactics that Flint knew his schola progenium drill abbot would have been proud of.

Within ten minutes Flint's force was pushing south across the carceri chamber floor and the storm raging in the eaves kilometres overhead was steadily growing. Sheet lightning seethed deep within the boiling, grey clouds and the rain lashed down in a violent torrent. Flint maintained his position at the rear of the column, ensuring that no stragglers got separated from the force and keeping an eye on the pursuers even as the horde lost coherency and broke down into dozens of smaller groups. The rebels were scouring the carceri chamber for the interlopers, bawling their frustration as loud as the storm raging above. The screams and cries echoed weirdly through the charged air, reverberating from the massive engine casings and towering manifolds strewn across the chamber floor. Several times, one of those groups closed on the rearmost squads and Flint had to lead vicious counter-attacks to slay the pursuers before their presence was betrayed to the bulk of the rebel horde. Flint's power sword hissed and spat in the downpour, the blood of his enemies washing away with the rain each time his squad clashed with the savage rebels.

It was only when the column had finally put a kilometre between its rearguard units and the pursuers that Flint had could take stock of the situation. An hour into the pursuit the storm reached an unprecedented severity, rivalling violent and natural atmospheric phenomena Flint had witnessed on a variety of worlds. Ducking into the cover of an overhanging conduit to speak to his aide, he had to shout to make himself heard.

'We need to get through to regiment!' he bellowed into Kohlz's ear as the two took temporary shelter from the driving downpour and the relentless pursuit. 'Have you got the carrier signal back yet?' he said.

Kohlz hefted the heavy vox-set from his back and set it down at his feet, peeling back the canvas cover to reveal its controls. For several long minutes he worked its dials and levers, the horn pressed tight to his ear and his rain-slicked face a mask of concentration.

After another minute, Flint said, 'Well? Come on Kohlz, we really don't have the time…'

'I'm not getting a thing, sir,' said Kohlz. 'I don't know if it's the storm, the installation's structure or if we're being jammed, but I'm sorry, commissar. I can't get a signal. I think we're on our own.'

TWELVE
Rearguard

For three gruelling hours, Flint led a tense rearguard action against the pursuing rebels, rallying troops verging on panic but stopping the retreat turning into a full-scale rout on several occasions. Flint saw no choice but to lead his force back through the carceri chamber, which seemed somehow twice the size it had on the way in, towards the insertion point. If he couldn't call in the location of the rebels' stronghold, there was no point in doing anything other than fight back to the regiment, but the commissar raged inside that the mission was unravelling with each passing minute.

Though the retreat was conducted with commendable discipline, Flint knew from experience that many of his troops were on the verge of collapse. Most had been fatigued even before battle had erupted and the pace of the retreat had been necessarily relentless. To slow up for just a moment would have invited disaster and Flint and the provosts had been forced to motivate the troops to keep moving and fighting by every means at their disposal.

Thirty minutes into the retreat, Flint's force had taken its first casualty. A blunderbuss had been fired from a gantry high above and by sheer fluke found a target. One of Stank's troopers, a man by the name of Skelt, stumbled and fell, his companions assuming he'd tripped over some piece of the debris scattered across the rockcrete floor. Turning back to aid his companion, Stank had cursed loudly when he saw the wound torn in Skelt's neck. The man had died before Stank could help him, the blood washed away across the ground in the torrential downpour.

Less than five minutes later a dozen rebels leaped down from a gantry that Vahn's squad had been passing under, swarming down the heavy chains hanging from the walkway to splash heavily to the wet ground. Without even breaking stride, Vahn opened fire as he charged the enemy, unleashing a burst of semi-automatic lascarbine fire that cut down three of the snarling rebels before a brutal melee erupted. As the last of the rebels fell dead to the floor, Vahn saw that two of his own squad had fallen too and three more had sustained wounds that would slow them all down as they pressed back towards the extraction point. Vahn and the unwounded members of his squad helped their fellows on, refusing to abandon them to the murderous attentions of the pursuing rebels.

Flint himself had been forced to draw his sword on several occasions, and each time he had used the opportunity to provide an example to the men and women under his command. It was a commissar's duty to lead from the front, to do exactly what the troops were being asked to do, and to watch for signs of doubt or cowardice. On one occasion a group of rebel convicts had emerged from an oily sump Flint's force had been dashing past, one of them catching hold of a penal trooper's ankle and pulling the man down into the black depths. Even as the waters thrashed and foamed blood red, a dozen more rebels emerged, their bodies coated in oil that glinted every colour in the spectrum as it ran to the ground. Flint beheaded the first with a sweep of his power sword and was gratified to see the body erupt in blue flame as the sword's generator touched off the flammable liquid clinging to the man's form.

Shouting a line from the *Adoration of the Techno-Magi*, Flint unleashed a roundhouse kick that propelled the flaming body through the air and sent it plummeting into the chemical sump. A moment later, the entire lot went up in a raging column of blue flame, consuming those rebels yet to emerge, as well as what remained of the penal trooper. The rest of the ambushers were cut down easily as they broke and fled, cut-off from their escape route.

Though the ignition of the chemical sump had slaughtered untold numbers of the ambushers, the resulting conflagration had provided a beacon, to which countless more were drawn. Howling atavistic war cries or screeching ululating cries of delirium and bloodlust, the rebel convicts pressed in from all directions, forcing Flint to cut his way through a tide that threatened to drag him down from behind.

When a trio of Dictrix walkers surged forward through the

mob, the rebels scattered lest they got caught in the lashing attack of its neural whip. Flint knew there was no way his small force could face three of the hideous machines, and certainly not with thousands of screaming maniacs closing on them all the while. The Emperor was surely watching, Flint saw, as the walkers mistimed their attacks and caught dozens of their own compatriots in their arcing whip strikes. Those struck convulsed where they fell, and there were so many of them that the walkers were forced to wade through a carpet of twitching flesh and bone in their desperation to close with the fleeing Imperials.

Incensed by the sight, more of the ground-pounding rebels turned on the walker pilots, swarming up the machines' flanks and dragging the crews out by force. The last Flint saw of the machines was a pilot being torn into at least six separate chunks of meat by the baying, vengeful horde. As if to confirm the God-Emperor's benefaction, no others among the enemy appeared able to re-crew the walkers, and with the horde in utter disarray, Flint's small force was able to escape.

Three hours in the mist and rain up ahead slowly thinned to reveal the kilometre-high precipice of the southern wall. The column finally closed on the armoured portal that led through to the sluice chamber with its stinking weirs and raging torrents flooding in from the overloaded sinks every twelve minutes. Part of him was relieved to reach that milestone on the march back to the extraction point, but another, the greater part, was almost consumed with anger at the thought that the mission might be compromised by something as simple as the inability to transmit the rebel's location to the main force of the regiment.

But, as the ragged column approached the far end of Carceri *Resurecti* and Flint plotted the next phase of the forced march, he recalled something of the details of the structure, revealed to him by Claviger-Primaris Gruss the last time they were there…

Distracted by his chain of thought Flint almost missed the group of rebels emerging from the ventilation gate in the side of a huge, corroded manifold. Karasinda shouted a warning and Flint dove to the left, only just avoiding the first of the shotgun blasts that hammered through the air towards him.

A moment later, Flint, Kohlz and Karasinda had thrown themselves into the shelter of a collapsed actuator housing, the rebels' fire hammering loudly into the metal and sending up a shower of angry sparks.

'We're cut off, sir!' Kohlz shouted over the sound of shotgun pellets pounding the other side of the housing. 'And we're last in line!'

Karasinda raised her lasgun to her shoulder and leaned calmly sideways out of the cover. She squeezed off three aimed shots and ducked back as a torrent of return fire scythed through the space she'd just vacated.

'We'll be fine,' Flint said, slamming a fresh magazine into his bolt pistol. 'Ready?'

'Ready, sir,' Karasinda replied, her voice as cold as her eyes.

'Kohlz?' said Flint, seeing that his aide was reaching the

limits of his courage and endurance. Another shotgun blast hammered into the cover and Flint judged by the angle that the rebels were working their way around to the left. They would soon be in a position to unleash a lethal torrent of enfilading fire. 'I need you alive for this, got it?'

Kohlz swallowed hard and nodded, resolving not to let Flint down. 'Got it, sir,' he said, fumbling for his lasgun.

'I'm serious,' Flint growled. 'I've got a plan, a way to call the regiment in. But I need you functional. Understood?'

Kohlz saw that Flint was serious and the message got through.

'On three, then,' said the commissar, patting his aide on the shoulder and nodding to Karasinda. 'Three!' he said, and dove out of the cover on the opposite flank the rebels were heading in on.

Karasinda's lip curled as she unleashed a burst of covering fire, catching one rebel in the gut and sending the rest diving for cover. 'Go,' she told Kohlz calmly, then followed as he dashed after the commissar.

His blade hissing in the damp air, Flint pounded towards the corroded structure the rebels were still emerging from. A dozen las-bolts lanced through the air as Karasinda covered his charge and another two rebels went down screaming. A moment later, Kohlz opened up too, his first shot decapitating a screeching rebel.

Flint reached the manifold at the exact moment a rebel propelled himself out and landed heavily in front of the commissar. This one must have been twice the size of his fellows, his chest and arms so massively over-muscled they reminded Flint of an abhuman ogryn. But the glint of oily metal augments in amongst the bulging musculature told Flint the man was no stable strain of mutant.

Flint skidded to a halt and brought his power sword up into guard position. The fighter leaned forward and roared, his mouth gaping wide as he bellowed an utterly incoherent war cry. Flint looked into his opponent's eyes and saw nothing very much there. The mountain of corded sinew had been created purely as a fighter. Flint guessed it needed help just feeding itself.

'Abomination,' Flint growled as he sidestepped left to circle the monstrosity. 'You are nothing natural, nor the work of the Omnissiah.' A passage from the *Dictum Commissaria* came unbidden to his mind and he found himself reciting the opening lines of the Twelfth Absolution of Saint Jark. *'From the work of the heretic, Emperor lend us strength…'*

The monstrosity growled as if it recognised the curse levelled against it. It lunged forwards clumsily, a fist the size of most men's skulls hammering through the air. The blow was clumsy and easily sidestepped, but had it struck home it would have pounded Flint's body to paste.

'From the horror of the beast of iron made man,' Flint continued the Twelfth Absolution. *'Let my heart be steeled…'*

Flint allowed the creature to advance towards him as he backed away, drawing it into the open where he knew that Karasinda and Kohlz could intervene if he needed the help. His mind raced as he sought a way to end this, quickly. With the rebels in pursuit, he had no time to tarry in a pointless confrontation.

The monstrosity growled, baring teeth of rusted iron and pounded both fists down into the ground simultaneously. The rockcrete cracked, showering rank water and making the corroded manifold it had climbed through tremble.

Though he had to end this, Flint knew that one false step would see him dead.

'Come on then…' Flint snarled, looking to taunt the monstrosity into making a wrong move. He swung his power sword lazily as if to mock the muscled beast. A howl echoed from somewhere far behind and the beast glanced towards the sound. That was all the opening Flint needed.

Darting forward, Flint lunged with the very tip of his power sword and cut a long, if shallow wound across his opponent's rippling chest muscles. The creature roared and stumbled back as the skin across its pectorals peeled backwards to reveal the glistening red musculature beneath. Simple enough to get inside the monstrosity's guard, Flint thought, but the wound hadn't slowed it in the least.

Quite suddenly, Flint's enemy reversed its backwards movement and twisted its torso at the waist, bringing its right fist up as it did so and hammering the air with a pile-driver punch that Flint only just avoided.

Ducking as the fist pistoned over his head, Flint raised his sword two-handed and drove it into the flesh of the beast's forearm, using his enemy's strength against it. The sword spat arcs of raw power as its generator shunted lethal energies into the blade's edge and the beast howled as it pulled its fist clear. At the last, Flint reversed his grip and pulled the sword towards him, the blade slicing out through the creature's wrist, its entire forearm cut in two and hanging in useless strips of ragged muscle.

The creature stumbled backwards and slammed into the huge corroded manifold, making it tremble as if about to fall. It bellowed, but now its cry was not just of anger but of pain and sheer, dumbfounded incredulity that another being could make it bleed.

Shots sounded from somewhere behind and a part of Flint acknowledged that time was almost up. Karasinda and Kohlz weren't far away, their weapons raised as they tracked enemies Flint himself couldn't see. 'Get moving!' Flint ordered, then flung himself aside as the mountain of muscle and anger that was his opponent threw itself forward with both its arms raised above its head and its face a mask of inhuman rage. Flint knew in that split second that here was his chance, but if he mistimed his attack he would be dead; those arms, each as big and strong as a power lifter's hydraulic claws, hammering down upon him.

He lunged, scything his power sword two-handed across the beast's stomach. The flesh split as the power field parted molecules asunder. The creature staggered backwards as it voiced a scream like twisting, tortured metal. Flint gritted his teeth and drove the blade onwards, hewing muscle and bone until the creature's innards ripped apart. Long, looping guts shot through with cabling flopped out at his feet and he sprung backwards to avoid the torrent of coiling viscera.

The monstrosity finally realised it was dead as it toppled backwards against the manifold. Sliding downwards, its head slumped against its massive chest and made one last huffing sigh.

'Sir?' said Kohlz. 'What the crap *was* that?'

It took the commissar a moment to regain his breath, but when he did, he answered, 'Something that had no business existing, Kohlz. Not even in a place like this,' he added, looking around the hellish place. The portal to the sluice chamber was only a few hundred metres distant and he guessed that the rest of the column would be closing on it even now. An ululating howl from somewhere behind pressed home the urgency of getting a damned move on.

Flint soon found out that the clavigers had hung back. Rounding the base of a huge storage tank he found them as they guarded the flanks against potential attackers. Flint barely suppressed a growl as the thought crossed his mind that Claviger-Primaris Gruss may have *waited*, but he hadn't *intervened* in a combat that could have cost the commissar his life.

'Are you the last, commissar?' Gruss demanded as Flint reached his position and stopped, his breath coming in ragged gasps.

'Only recidivists and traitors behind,' said Flint, looking past the chief warden's shoulder to the huge armoured portal. His troops were visible as they secured the entryway, bright light shining through it. *White light*, Flint thought, realising that the chamber had been lit by harsh white daylight from above the last time they had travelled through it – how much time had gone by since then, he wondered...

'Commissar?' said Gruss, his voice metallic and distorted through his armour's phonocasters. 'Are you wounded?'

'What?' Flint said, the exertion of the last few days threatening to catch up with him. 'I'm fine,' he said, realising just why Gruss had asked. He was covered with the blood of the thing he had killed by the manifold. 'None of it is mine.'

A few more minutes later Flint and his companions were walking through the great armoured hatch into the sluice chamber. At his back, Carceri *Resurecti* appeared to be coming alive with grim, shrill screams, some of anger and bloodlust, others of savage pain. The sound reminded Flint of his time fighting secessionists on the frontier world of Farout, where the enemy encampments were consumed by raucous anarchy each night. It was louder even than the nocturnal chorus of the death world of Chbal, where as a young storm trooper he had once been unfortunate enough to spend an entire terrifying month.

'Taking it out on each other,' said Vahn as Flint passed. The penal trooper was leaned against the inner wall of the portal, his face etched with weariness as he gazed back into the depths of the massive carceri chamber.

Flint grunted, distracted as he walked through the portal into the towering space of the sluice chamber. As before, it was illuminated stark white by a column of daylight shining directly down from the open space at the very top of the chimney-like interior. Just like before, the air was filled with the vile stink of billions of litres of polluted, irradiated water.

'Kohlz?' Flint called as he craned his neck upwards and covered his face to protect his eyes from the glare.

'Remember what Gruss said about the jamming nodes set into the generatorium's structure?'

Kohlz hesitated, his brow furrowing, before he replied, 'Yes, sir. He said he could deactivate them when we needed to transmit to the main force.'

'You believe him?' Flint said, lowering his voice so that none of the wardens could overhear.

'Sir?' said Kohlz, not getting it. 'I don't...'

'What're the odds?' Flint pressed, weariness creeping into his voice. 'How likely is it that if I asked him to deactivate the jamming nodes he'd find some excuse not to?'

Kohlz thought on it a second, then answered 'I might take that bet, sir.'

'*I* wouldn't, dragoon,' said Flint, his gaze searching the open space far above, before tracking downwards the two hundred metres towards the slimy bottom of the sluice channel.

'Sir?' said Kohlz, concern and confusion etched on his face. 'What's up, sir?'

Flint fixed his aide with an almost sympathetic stare. 'How are you with heights, dragoon?'

'Sir?'

'Sorry, Kohlz,' he said to his aide. 'Gambling's against regulations.'

'Unfortunately, commissar,' said Claviger-Primaris Gruss as the sound of raging water grew in volume from the weir at his back. 'I am unable to deactivate them. The rebels must have corrupted the machine-spirits, or aggrieved them in some manner.'

Flint and Kohlz caught each other's eye and the aide's discomfort grew. Flint took a deep breath as he scanned the chamber walls closely, studying the lurid streaks of corrosion and decay etched into the rockcrete. An ancient and rusted ladder was set into the wall, climbing upwards hundreds of metres, but to reach it one would have to cross the sluice channel, which was even now filling with surging waters as the overflow systems far below filled up.

Gruss followed Flint's gaze. The commissar looked sharply away from the distant ladder towards the area where the secreted chute and the entrance to the hidden tunnel was located. Gruss took the bait.

'We have no choice, commissar,' the chief warden stated flatly. 'We must extract via the infiltration route and summon the regiment in person.'

Yes, thought Flint, that would suit you nicely. But why? What was the Claviger-Primaris up to? Was he just trying to keep the 77th out of the penal generatorium to save face so that the eventual glory of retaking it would be his? Or was there something else at play, he wondered, something far darker...

'We'll have missed our chance by then,' Flint snapped back, frustrated. 'It'll take hours to extract, and longer to lead the regiment back in. By that time the rebels will have scattered. Strannik won't be where he was and we'll have to track him down all over again. He's got the entire installation to get lost in – we were lucky this time, but we might never find him again.'

'Then I'm sorry for the wasted effort,' Gruss replied, his phonocasters increasing in volume in order to be heard over the steadily growing roar of the rising sluice tide. As the three men looked on, the chemical sludge at the bottom of the channel swelled, objects that could only be bodies bloated with corpse-gas and pollution bobbing on the surface as the tide rose. The rockcrete platform they were standing on began to tremble, lightly at first, but soon building to something approaching a low-level quake. It was obvious this flood would be far more violent than the last.

'It won't be wasted!' Flint shouted over the roar of water.

'What?' the chief warden shouted back, even his augmented voice all but swallowed up by the sound of the surging tide.

'The effort won't be wasted,' Flint shouted back, looking upwards towards the open top of the chimney structure. Both men followed his gaze as the waters broke, billions upon billions of litres of water surging down the sluice channel in a raging tsunami so loud that no more conversation was possible for the next few minutes. Uncounted items of debris were swept along in the torrent, bloated, decaying bodies intermingled with thousands of tonnes of rubble and other unidentifiable waste.

As the waters finally receded, the worst of the tidal wave having passed, Flint smiled grimly, though not with any cruelty.

'Sorry, Kohlz,' he said to his aide.

'No!' protested Kohlz as the waters finally washed away, the bottom of the sluice channel glistening with millions of tonnes of stinking silt and garbage. 'I can't sir, I…'

'You won't be going up alone,' Flint said, glancing around the faces of the other troopers. Every one of them looked away, distracted by something only they could see. In truth, he'd already chosen the troopers who would be making the climb with Kohlz.

'Stank!' Flint barked. 'Front and centre.'

A groan sounded from behind and Trooper Stank pushed through the crowd, shouldering Solomon roughly aside as the gangly Jopalli tried unsuccessfully to suppress a chuckle.

'Solomon,' said Flint. 'You too.'

Solomon's face dropped and he turned white as his mouth gaped open. 'You heard me, *indenti*,' Flint growled. 'The Emperor's got a job for you. He's got a job for all three of you. Now listen up…'

'I really didn't sign up for this!' Trooper Solomon shouted back at Kohlz as he ploughed through the knee-high chemical filth at the bottom of the sluice channel.

'We've been through this. You didn't sign up at all,' Rotten snapped back. 'None us *signed up* for any of this crap…'

'Keep it down,' said Kohlz, his face flushed as he struggled with the heavy vox-set. 'If the commissar hears you talking like that he'll–'

'I don't care, ' Rotten replied petulantly as he struggled to pull one leg in front of the other, the sheer effort making him breathless. 'A bolt-round to the head would be a welcome break from *this*.'

Kohlz grit his teeth and carried on, deciding not to waste breath bitching about the task the three had been given. Despite his outward stoicism however, Kohlz was seething inside. He'd served the commissar diligently since his arrival and this was his reward. Ordered to cross an eighty metre wide sludge flow, climb several hundred metres up a rusted ladder, then cling to the upper reaches of the cooling tower structure while attempting to operate the heaviest pattern vox-set manufactured in the entire sector. Solomon was right, he thought – he really didn't sign up for this.

Since the last time the force had been this way, the channel had filled even deeper with chemical sludge dredged up from the outflows far beneath Alpha Penitentia by the sudden rise in water levels caused by the crippling of the air scrubbers across the entire complex. No one could say how many decades, even centuries worth of outflow had collected in the sinks and was now swelling to the surface, but the slime seemed to Kohlz like a gruel of congealing, decomposed matter distilled in a faintly-glowing suspension that must have curdled in the darkness far below for an age.

The smell was so strong, so vile that even the Firstborn's standard issue rebreathers could not keep it out, and they were designed to withstand the worst of the acrid, scorched metal stink of Vostroya's polluted surface. The rebreather was constricting Kohlz's breathing, making him even more light-headed with exertion. But he dared not remove it, for the stink bubbling up with his every step was so bad it made him gag even with the mask on. Without it, he knew he wouldn't make it across.

'Half...' Solomon stammered before taking a gulping breath through his mask, '...way.'

Keep going, Kohlz told himself, his every step made leaden and slow by the constant sucking of the actinic chemical slime. He forced his head up as he ploughed on, making sure the three were on course for the ladder set in the rockcrete of the opposite wall. Locating the corroded rungs, he wondered again how the commissar could possibly be sure they wouldn't come loose the moment any pressure was put upon them. Then an even worse thought struck him – what if they came loose when the three men were halfway up the wall...

'Six minutes!' Rotten called out breathlessly. 'Come on, guys, pick it up!'

'I'm *pashing* well...' Solomon started, breaking off mid curse. 'Wait,' he stammered. 'What was...'

'Get moving!' Kohlz shouted as he realised what was happening. 'The pressure's rising. The intervals are getting shorter!'

Even before he could draw breath to bemoan this new twist of cruel fate, the rockcrete floor beneath the river of stinking sludge started trembling. Kohlz felt the stirring of titanic forces transmitted up through the ground and he knew that the next flood would be an order of magnitude worse than the last. Even as panic rose up inside, Kohlz heard the warriors assembled on the now distant platform at the top of the weir complex shout out. But he couldn't hear anything of their words above the sound of his raging breath, the thundering of his blood and the rising torrent.

Kohlz swore loudly as he realised the mire around his knees was swelling with water, its consistency thinning as the waters rose up from the overflow sinks far below. Bubbles of acrid gas broke on the surface, splattering the three men with gobbets of reeking muck, and the surface shifted as the sound of a raging flood grew.

'Seriously, guys!' Solomon wailed. 'We're not gonna…'

'Shut the hell up and keep moving!' Kohlz yelled. They were closing on the opposite bank and the lowermost of the corroded metal rungs was in sight.

As the sludge thinned to a luminescent gruel the going got easier and soon the three men were splashing desperately towards the ladder. Even as they closed on it, a great roar went up behind them…

The iron gate slammed shut with a deep, resounding crash and the dozen warriors who'd pushed it too heaved on the huge bolt mechanism, locking the gateway shut.

'You think that will keep them out, sir?' Bukin asked Flint with evident scepticism.

'No,' said Flint, his answer making Bukin grimace as he chewed on the sodden remains of his cigar. 'But we'll be gone long before they break through.'

As if to test the veracity of Flint's statement, the gate boomed as something heavy impacted against the other side. The gate was constructed of twenty-centimetre thick armaplas and reinforced with heavy crossbars, but it bowed inwards under the pressure nonetheless.

'What the *khekk*…' Bukin mouthed.

'Present!' Flint bellowed, waving the nearest of the troops into a firing line before the massive gate. There was a pause during which more warriors rushed to join their fellows, and soon almost three-dozen lasguns were levelled on the gate.

Then the impact sounded again and a mist of fine rock-crete powder drifted down from above. The metal of the gate buckled and a muffled roar went up from the other side. It sounded like an entire army of rebels was gathering on the far side of the armoured hatch and something even bigger than the monstrosity Flint had slain was throwing itself against the gate.

'Mutants,' Corporal Bukin sneered, his nose wrinkled in disgust. Flint had smelled it too, but in truth the taint was now so prevalent it permeated the entire place.

'Gruss,' Flint demanded as the Claviger-Primaris waved his wardens to join the firing line. 'Tell me what that is,' Flint demanded. 'I faced something big outside, but *that* must be twice its size.'

Gruss turned his blank-faced visor towards the hatchway at the exact moment a third impact caused it to buckle even further. The troops on the firing line cast nervous, sidelong glances at one another, several swallowing hard.

'Gruss?' Flint pressed.

'I don't know, commissar,' the Claviger-Primaris snapped.

'I think you do,' said Flint.

'What?' he growled.

'That thing I fought out there,' said Flint. 'That was no inmate, no Guardsman serving out a penal sentence. That was something else and I don't believe it could exist right under your nose without you having some idea of its presence.'

The hatchway boomed again, the loud report echoing through the sluice chamber. The troops in the firing line shuffled nervously, their eyes darting between the violently shaking gate and the confrontation developing between the commissar and the Claviger-Primaris.

Gruss squared off against Flint and several of his wardens broke off from their places in the firing line. 'Are you accusing me of something, commissar?' said Gruss, his voice low but carrying across the platform even over the howls and roars coming from the other side of the portal.

'I'm asking you a question, Claviger-Primaris,' Flint snarled back. 'What the hell are they, and how did they come into being?'

'Sir?' Flint heard Bukin mutter from behind him. 'I think...'

'Not now,' Flint replied. 'Gruss?' he pressed.

'Sir,' said the chief provost insistently. 'I really think...'

Flint risked a quick glance towards the armoured portal. 'Mercy...' he muttered. A fracture had appeared in the slab-like armaplas and movement was visible beyond.

'Prepare to address!' Flint shouted, then lowered his voice and said to the Claviger-Primaris, 'We're not done, Gruss.'

If Gruss heard Flint he didn't respond, instead joining his

fellow wardens, his plasma pistol levelled two-handed at the compromised hatchway.

Even as the sound of rising liquid swelled from the sluice channel behind, the sound of another massive impact striking the portal boomed forth. The force steeled itself to face whatever was trying to hammer its way through.

Kohlz's hands closed around the corroded rung set into the crumbling, run-off-streaked rockcrete, the rising chemical river swelling below him. He hauled with every ounce of his strength, his weight feeling like it was doubled by the water soaked into his battle-dress and the heavy Number Four strapped to his back.

'Get a move on, will you!' Rotten called from below, the glowing waters now at his waist. A deep, resounding rumble sounded from back across the channel and a wave crashed into Rotten, almost knocking him over. Kohlz knew he had to get himself higher up the ladder to allow the trooper to get clear of the rising flood.

He pulled even harder, his muscles burning, and the rung slipped suddenly with a pattering of loose rockcrete chips, but it held despite its sudden instability. The torrent increased in volume and Kohlz grasped for the next rung, hauling himself hand over hand until the lower rungs were clear. Finally, Rotten had the space to climb up.

With Solomon leading the way the three men climbed upwards, the channel filling to overflowing with the chemical filth dredged up from the stygian sumps beneath Alpha Penitentia. The smell was awful, the flood accompanied by gales of sharp-smelling gas. The waters were oily and black, and lumpen forms were carried along by the relentless, swirling currents. Many of the forms were clearly corpses, some fresh, no doubt convicts slain in the uprising in the last few weeks. Others were shrunken and pale as if preserved in formaldehyde for countless centuries, washed up from the depths by the rising torrent and held together by little more than ropey sinew.

As the tsunami reached its climax all further thoughts were drowned out by the deafening crescendo. Kohlz concentrated on placing one hand before the other and hauling himself upwards blindly, his eyes screwed tight against the stinging spray. Several times he felt his feet engulfed in crashing waves and knocked by debris washed along and he prayed that Rotten was able to hold on for he must have been submerged as the flood waters crashed down the sluice channel.

Then the waters had receded and Kohlz opened his eyes. Rotten was still clinging to the rungs, his battledress sodden and his rebreather torn away by the force of the flood. The Asgardian had only managed to hold onto his lascarbine by looping its sling around his elbow while he held onto the rung for dear life. One side of his face was bruised livid purple where the weapon had been battered against his face by the torrent.

Rotten looked surprised that he was still alive and Kohlz was shocked how high the three men had climbed in their bid to escape the torrent. A wave of vertigo washed over him and his vision swam for they'd somehow climbed almost fifty metres. The bottom of the channel was returning to its former state, a sea of glowing, reeking sludge settling on the rockcrete, coils of noxious vapour creeping upwards from the bubbling mass.

Redoubling his grip on the corroded rung, Kohlz forced himself to look upwards and he was immediately dazzled by the white glare blazing through the open roof. Forcing himself to look into the nigh-blinding light he saw that Solomon had managed to cling on too, then sought to judge how much further the three had to climb. He cursed as he realised they had climbed less than a quarter of the way. The view overhead was a dizzying shaft of slab-sided rockcrete chimney, the circle of sky like a blazing singularity at its summit.

'Solomon?' Kohlz called up to the Jopalli. 'You okay? We need to get moving!'

At first, Solomon's only reply was low, petulant muttering, but then the Jopalli said, 'What?'

'Get moving!' Kohlz snapped, rapidly losing his patience. 'You're on point and we're going nowhere 'til you get your arse shifted!'

'Why *me*…' Solomon muttered. 'Why is it always *me*?'

Flint shielded his eyes against the glare as he stared up at the three tiny figures working their way painfully slowly up the ladder towards the distant, open roof of the sluice chamber. Another impact sounded on the portal and the scream of tortured metal tore his attention back to more pressing concerns. The gash in the buckled plate had widened and now a pair of massively oversized, gnarled hands gripped on its jagged edges as if to tear them further apart.

'Front rank!' Bukin bellowed at a nod from Flint. 'Three rounds, fire!'

The dozen or so kneeling warriors of the front rank opened fire as one, the air filling with the flash of las-fire, smoke and the stink of ozone. The bolts lanced into the gash and the massive hands disappeared in a burst of sparks and smoke. A bellowing howl of rage sounded from the other side and something at least as large as an ogryn plunged its entire arm through the tear, right up to the shoulder, and groped for something, anything, to grab hold of and haul back through the gap.

The firing line opened up with a second fusillade, a dozen las-bolts slamming into the hugely muscled arm and sending up a puff of greasy, flesh-stinking smoke. But the limb was huge, its sinews as strong as corded iron and its stone-hard flesh seemingly able to absorb even multiple direct hits.

The kneeling troops fired their third fusillade and this time several of the fingers, each as thick as a man's forearm, were severed. The thing howled and the arm pulled back, though Flint saw more movement through the dark wound in the armoured portal.

'I have seen mutants, killed mutants,' Bukin muttered to himself. 'But what the hell *was* that?'

Though he knew the question was largely rhetorical, Flint answered the chief provost nonetheless. 'It's not just a random mutant,' he said. 'It's something bred, hybridised and enhanced with some form of heretech. It's been deliberately created down in the lowest depths of the geotherm sinks. And it looks like it'll get through before help does.'

'A hybrid?' Bukin looked far from convinced. 'In a *penal* facility, sir? No one breeds such things in a *khekking* prison...'

Flint glared pointedly at Claviger-Primaris Gruss, who was barking orders to his wardens. 'They do if no one stops them, Bukin,' he said.

'Wouldn't *he* stop it, sir?'

'He might if he were in charge.'

'But he is not, sir?'

'Doesn't look like it, does it. I've seen enough of this hellhole to guess something of what's been going on,' said Flint, his gaze fixed on the back of the Claviger-Primaris's helmet. The roaring of the horde beyond the armoured gate resounded through the sluice chamber and made it unlikely Gruss would overhear anything. 'It looks to me like Lord Governor Kherhart isn't in charge at all, and neither is Gruss. It looks to me like this Colonel Strannik is the real leader around here and that he's been running this place like his own personal kingdom for years.'

'Makes sense, sir, I suppose,' Bukin replied, raising his voice over the crash and boom of another impact against the portal. The metal buckled still further as a massive shoulder rammed into it, accompanied by the jubilant howl of the rebels amassing to swarm through the instant the gateway ruptured.

'Listen,' he said, glancing upwards at the distant climbers.

'With that thing leading the assault, we both know there's no way help's getting here before that door gives out.'

Bukin nodded grimly, evidently having reached a similar conclusion. 'Your orders, sir?' he said.

Flint thought on it a moment longer, considering and rejecting a dozen options in an instant. 'We have to hold them here as long as possible,' he said, considering the length of the sluice channel and the distance to the secret infiltration tunnel. 'There's no way we'd get the whole force back down in the time between the floods.'

Bukin nodded. 'Unless we went in small groups, sir.'

Flint raised his eyebrows in question, and the provost continued, 'Break them down into smaller sections, sir, say, five, ten troopers. Move fast, get down the chute before the flood comes.'

Flint considered Bukin's suggestion but he instantly saw a flaw. 'By the time there's just one section left the gateway will be all but broken down. They'd have to face the horde alone. It would be suicide.'

'That might not be such a bad thing, commissar,' Bukin growled, looking pointedly towards Claviger-Primaris Gruss. 'Depending on who the last section was, if you see what I mean, sir.'

Once again, Flint felt justified in having selected Bukin as his chief provost, and grateful they were on the same side. But as devious as Bukin's suggestion was, Flint knew it wasn't workable. 'I appreciate the sentiment,' Flint grinned as he replied, 'But I don't see how Gruss would go for that.'

'No,' he continued. 'We have no choice but to make our

stand here. Hold out as long as we can.' His gaze settling on the many and varied items of flotsam lodged in the upper section of the weir a plan came to mind. 'Get a detail together. If we're staying put we'd better make ourselves at home.'

By the time Kohlz and his companions reached the halfway point in their climb all three were so fatigued they had long given up on bemoaning their fate. Their every effort was focused on the simple act of placing one hand on the next rung and hauling their aching bodies ever upwards. As they climbed higher Kohlz realised the folly of looking down the way they had come, vertigo threatening to make his hands clamp around the metal rung so tightly they might never be prized off.

Taking a deep, rasping breath, Kohlz pulled his right foot up and set it on the rung, the act made all the harder by the weight of the water sloshing around his boots. He grunted as he set his weight on the rung and pushed upwards, grabbing hold of another with his free hand. A deep rumble sounded below and he thought for a moment that another flood was about to come raging along the sluice channel. Then he realised another wasn't due for several more minutes.

The rumble sounded again and the sound of voices raised in anger drifted upwards from the platform at the top of the weir where the rest of the force was mustered. He'd heard firing ten minutes earlier but hadn't seen any sign of the gates being compromised. Now, it sounded like they had been flung wide open and the rebel horde was pressing in.

Kohlz wished he hadn't looked, his vision swimming before he could locate the platform. He felt his grip on the rung slipping. He screwed his eyes tight shut and hooked his free arm around the next rung, catching himself before he could slip.

His blood thundering in his ears and his last ration pack threatening to come back up the way it had gone down, Kohlz concentrated on the climb, his eyes screwed shut as he got back underway once more. Though slowed by the need to grope blindly for each and every rung, he found after a while that his progress got back underway and the sounds from below receded. When the next flood powered down the channel he was able to keep going, ignoring the spray lashing his face.

As the last of the flood roared away down the channel, something grabbed hold of Kohlz's wrist. He cursed and pulled back as he opened his eyes, a shadowed figure with a bright light behind it looming over him. He panicked and lashed out at the shadow with one hand and almost lost his grip entirely. Then the grasping hands took hold of him again and pulled him bodily forward.

'Kohlz!' someone shouted. 'It's me, calm the *pash* down!'

Kohlz found himself spread-eagled on a flat rockcrete ledge, bright light filling his vision and cold air stinging his face. After the interior of Alpha Penitens the light seemed so bright it threatened to blind him and he struggled to throw a forearm over his face as he fought to work out what had just happened.

'Saint Katherine's arse,' another voice exclaimed. 'If anyone ever asks me to do *anything* like that again,' it continued, 'Just shoot me...'

His senses returning, Kohlz sat up, his head swimming as he took in the sheer scale of his surroundings. Solomon appeared over him again, leaning down to offer a helping hand standing up. 'Thanks,' Kohlz said as he and Solomon clasped forearms and he was pulled to his feet.

The sight before Kohlz's eyes was almost enough to send him screaming back down the ladder to the relative comfort of the interior of the penal generatorium. Though Kohlz was foundry-born, raised in the cathedral-size manufactoria of Vostroya, he had never stood on such a vantage point as this. The three men had emerged onto the flat, open rim of the chimney-like structure of the cooling tower, which itself was but a small spire on the side of the vast form that was Carceri *Resurecti*. They were hundreds of metres up and the surface of Furia Penitens formed a cyclopean panorama all around.

The wastes stretched southwards for kilometre after kilometre, hundreds of ancient craters appearing like minor pockmarks from so high up. In the far distance, made hazy by the effect of aerial perspective, the distant mountains rose upwards over the horizon, their white-capped peaks jagged and cruel.

A cold wind made Kohlz squint and brought tears to his eyes. His skin stung, his system having grown used to the chemical humidity of the interior. Turning east, he saw that the distant mountains rose to sweep in over the horizon, spilling across the surface towards the complex. The rearing, blocky forms of other carceri chambers were clustered all about, and Kohlz felt something of the true scale of the penal generatorium as he considered how large the interior of each chamber truly was.

Turning north, Kohlz was confronted with the slab-like flank of the central spire towering so far above that its very top was lost to the seething clouds that guttered and pulsed with their weird inner light far overhead. In that instant, Kohlz felt utterly insignificant, small and weak. Another gust of wind caused him to stagger backwards a few steps and Solomon caught him before he got dangerously close to the open roof and the huge drop to the sluice channel below.

'Come on,' Solomon shouted over the howl of the wind. 'We've got a job to do!'

Kohlz nodded several times as he looked around for a place to set his Number Four. He shrugged the heavy vox-set off his back and prayed to the immortal God-Emperor of Man that it hadn't been damaged on the climb up.

While Kohlz set about his task, Solomon and Stank went about providing him with cover. Rotten unslung his carbine and took position over the ladder, squinting into the shadows below as he tried to work out what might be transpiring in the depths around the portal. Solomon stalked out onto the circular, guard-less space around the chimney and knelt as he looked out across the roof of the carceri chamber from which the chimney projected. The roof was largely flat, though strewn with a multitude of smaller, ancillary vents and spear-like antennae that must have been the jamming nodes that blocked the signal from within the complex. Some looked like extensions of the massive, unidentifiable machinery that so dominated the interior of the complex while others were most likely geotherm ventilation shafts.

As Kohlz searched furiously for a viable channel, a sense of dread settled over him just as Solomon knelt suddenly and raised his sniper rifle to his shoulder to squint down its scope. At first nothing was visible apart from the irregular grey surface; pipes, vents and slab-like projections jutting from it at seemingly random angles. Then something moved behind a ten-metre tall funnel.

'Solomon?' said Kohlz. 'What is it? What have you seen?'

Solomon didn't answer at first, his only reaction a tightening of his stance as his aim jerked left and tracked a target that Kohlz couldn't see. The Jopalli's finger tightened on the trigger and the weapon bucked against his grip, its report swallowed up by the howling wind.

'Eight,' Solomon mouthed.

The air filled with light and smoke as the firing line unleashed another salvo into the breach, forcing the mutant-hybrid-thing back once more. Flint added the weight of his bolt pistol to the fusillade, firing a well-placed mass-reactive shell into the centre of a howling face that appeared briefly at the wound in the gate. The bolt exploded with a shower of blood and gristle. The enemy forced temporarily back for what felt like the tenth time in as many minutes, Flint ejected the spent magazine from his pistol and slammed a fresh one into place.

The platform was a scene of fevered activity as those warriors not assigned to the firing line struggled to construct a makeshift barricade from the flotsam and jetsam gathered from the churning sluice channels. Initially, Flint hadn't been especially confident that the work detail would locate any materials of any great use but his hopes had stirred when the first of the detail returned dragging great lengths of heavy boarding behind them. Though not as tough as the flak board used to construct temporary field fortifications, those the troops had found were nonetheless useful enough. They must have been used in the fabrication of holding pens somewhere else in the complex. The plan was for the firing line to remain in place as long as possible while the makeshift barricade was erected behind them, and then to fall back to its cover once the breach in the armoured hatch was torn so wide that the troops couldn't hold the rebels back any longer.

It might just work, Flint thought, so long as Kohlz could get the message out to the regiment and they could hang on long enough for help to arrive. The barricade was taking shape, a mass of misshapen boards and ragged stanchions lashed together with random lengths of cabling and barbed wire.

With a howl of tortured metal the mutant monstrosity was back once again, its arms, now bloody and scorched from the mass of las-fire they had absorbed, reaching through the ragged tear. The mighty hands braced against the jagged sides and pushed outwards as Bukin bellowed for another salvo. The short distance between the firing line and the breach filled with bright darts of las-fire and billowing smoke, forcing the arms to retract as the mutant howled in rage and pain. It was driven off, but the breach was that little bit wider. Very soon, it would be wide enough to allow the rebels to press through.

'Bukin!' Flint shouted. 'Hold the line.'

Dashing across the platform to the edge of the uppermost weir, Flint came across a group of five men struggling to haul a large metal crate up towards the barricade. The waters were strewn with all manner of debris, including the dark forms of dead things looming under the oily surface. He made a mental note to ensure every member of the infiltration force was treated for contamination when, or indeed if, they made it back to the regiment.

Another impact struck against the hatch and Flint stepped down towards the weir, striding knee-deep into the luminescent liquid. He grabbed hold of the leading edge of the huge metal container and added his strength to the effort to drag it from the water. In another minute or so Flint and the men had hauled the crate from the weir, dragged it across the rockcrete platform and lodged it at the end of the barricade.

'That'll have to do it,' Flint said breathlessly. As if in confirmation the hatchway shook and the entire door buckled inward violently. The piston-like bolt snapped in two and the separate parts spun off across the rockcrete floor.

'Bukin!' Flint shouted. 'Get ready to pull the firing line back. They'll be through any moment.'

As Bukin took his place behind the firing line, Flint located Dragoon Lhor and his assistant. 'Sir?' said Lhor, his face still black with the backwash from his flamer.

'How much fuel do you have left, Lhor?' Flint asked. Flint suspected Lhor would be sleeping with his heavy flamer by his side from now on so attached to the weapon had he become. 'I may have a job for you.'

Lhor frowned as he replied, 'Not a lot, sir. One good blast in this flask, then one more load before I'm out.' Lhor's second was now carrying just a single fuel flask, the tank strapped to his back ready to be swapped out when Lhor had exhausted the one he was using. The two looked distinctly disappointed that their role as flame troopers might soon be ended with the last fuel flask.

'Understood,' said Flint. 'I want you forward, covering the retreat when it goes off. One blast through the breach at the exact moment Bukin orders the line back. Got it?'

Lhor nodded grimly as he hefted his flamer. 'Got it, sir,' he said before the two headed off towards their station. Flint drew his bolt pistol and braced it against the parapet of the barricade as another impact struck the hatch, scattering shards of metal and rockcrete across the space before the portal.

'Bukin!' Flint yelled over the tearing of metal and the roaring of the rebel convicts. 'Stand by!'

'Twelve!' Solomon counted off his latest kill between gusts of howling wind. The crack of his sniper rifle was whipped away by another gale, but Kohlz was focused on the console of his vox-set.

'Repeat!' he shouted over the howling wind. 'Call sign Crimson Eagle to last sender,' he shouted. 'Repeat last, over.'

The earpiece churned with static and howled with painful feedback, but Kohlz was sure he could hear a voice in amongst the hash. The console's dials indicated someone was transmitting, but the structure of the installation, the atmospheric conditions and no doubt the effect of the complex's internal jamming nodes were combining to interfere with the signal so badly he could barely keep a lock on the transmitting station.

'…aquila, over,' the voice said in a moment of relative quiet, the background static receding for a few seconds. 'Repeat, authenticate aquila, over.'

Thank the Emperor, Kohlz mouthed, fumbling to pull a small tactical data-slate from a pocket inside his coat. Invoking the authentication key, he quickly scanned the code table and identified the proper response. 'Authenticate Beati, Nine, over,' Kohlz transmitted.

The channel howled and churned as he waited for a response, barely registering that both Solomon and Stank were now rapid-firing down at the chamber roof. Finally, the response came back, 'Confirm authentication. Kohlz?' the voice continued. 'That you?'

Kohlz smiled as he realised he was talking to Corporal Drass, a well-liked member of the signals platoon.

A shot whined through the air nearby and he ducked instinctively. 'Drass?' he said urgently. 'Flint wants the regiment forward, as soon as possible. We've located the enemy stronghold, over.'

Another shot whined through the air as a dozen or more figures darted across the roof from cover to cover as they closed on the chimney spire. Solomon tracked the nearest enemy but he made cover before he could fire.

'No need, Kohlz,' Drass replied, the channel fizzing and popping as he spoke. 'Graf Aleksis got bored waiting for you. He's ordered the entire regiment forward already, over.'

What? thought Kohlz, his mind racing. That wasn't the plan. 'Repeat last, Drass,' he replied. 'The regiment's already inbound?'

'Not just inbound, Kohlz,' said Drass. 'We're deploying now. That's why this signal's so poor. We're not in the open wastes, we're already breaking in, over.'

A bark of mad laughter came unbidden to Kohlz's lips as he finally realised what had happened. Aleksis, Emperor bless the old bastard, must have got tired waiting for the infiltration force to report back and ordered the main force forward. It was against the plan, which stated flat out that if Flint's force couldn't identify the rebel stronghold then the regiment wouldn't be going anywhere. Thank the Emperor for *gakked* up plans, Kohlz thought.

'Understood,' Kohlz replied. 'Transmitting our current coordinates now, over.'

Kohlz sat back as the vox-set churned out the location of the infiltration force, daring to hope that things might not end quite so badly as it had looked like they might.

At the edge of the platform, Solomon's sniper rifle barked again. 'Lucky thirteen,' the Jopalli said, oblivious to anything other than the righteous slaying of the Emperor's enemies.

'Firing line!' Flint bellowed over the howling of the rebels. 'Prepare to fall back!'

The mutant battering ram had torn a great gash in the armaplas hatch and the entire door was on the verge of being forced inwards. 'Lhor!' Flint shouted, raising his power sword above his head. 'Now!'

On Flint's order, Lhor dashed forward with Hannen close behind and took position beside the breach. Raising the flamer towards the wound in the armoured hatch, Lhor braced himself as he looked back towards the commissar. Flint brought his power sword down in a chopping motion, and Lhor opened up.

The Vostroyan angled his fire so that the stream of incandescent promethium arced through the breach and exploded against the first object it struck. That object, by the Emperor's beneficence, turned out to be the mutant monstrosity. The thing bellowed like a wounded bull grox but instead of going down it charged forward as if the pain enveloping its senses drove it on with redoubled determination. The breach now resembled a gateway to some hellish dimension, a flaming portal through which the screams and howls of the damned competed with the raging of infernal conflagrations and the rending of metal. The flaming mutant thing braced its arms against the inner edges of the breach and pushed outwards with every ounce of its strength, its muscles cording and its vile face twisting with agony and rage.

Lhor and Hannen staggered back as the huge hatch finally buckled and gave way explosively as the two halves crashed inwards.

'Get clear!' Flint bellowed to the two dragoons. 'Firing line, back!'

Damn it, Flint seethed, cursing the mutant's seemingly preternatural vigour. Lhor's burst of heavy flamer fire should have reduced it to greasy ash, yet still it came on. And now the gate was open and the hordes beyond were massing to press through.

Lhor shrugged the spent fuel flask from his back and the two men bolted. The firing line was up and moving too, the warriors pausing every ten metres or so to turn, kneel and fire a quick burst of semi-automatic las-fire into the mutant and the howling convicts around it. Flint's bolt pistol barked as he added his fire, the sound almost swallowed up by the enraged bawling of the mutant.

The creature staggered under the weight of fire, its torso twisting as rounds hammered into it, but still it came on. In a moment it had clambered over the broken remains of the armaplas hatch and was finally able to draw itself to its full height. The beast was as wide at the shoulder as it was tall, standing almost three metres at the hunched-over shoulders. Like the creature Flint had encountered earlier, its massively overlarge, flame-wreathed arms were augmented with metal pistons, cabling and rebars, all adding to its already unnatural strength. Its torso was a mass of augmented muscle and its head appeared to be that of a man, its features dominated by a pugnacious brow, heavy jaw and small, porcine eyes. Those eyes were alight with uncomprehending, feral pain and entirely devoid of even a glimmer of lucidity.

Flint fired again, the bolt hammering into the creature's collarbone and exploding to leave a smoking crater but otherwise failing to slow its progress as it stumbled forward into the open. There was a roar and dozens of rebels pressed through the smoking portal, spreading out and charging on even in the face of a wall of concentrated las and shotgun fire. Dozens were gunned down before travelling more than a few metres forward. Dozens more clambered over the still-writhing forms of the dead and the dying.

As the last of the firing line vaulted over the barricade and took their positions behind it, Flint realised that something drastic had to be done. Things looked desperate, but he'd been in such seemingly hopeless positions before. Visions of the Fall of Nova Tellus flashed through his mind, the final days of that epic campaign etched in his mind forever. The razing of the shrineworld of Volupia had taught him that faith was the greatest weapon that any servant of the Emperor had in his arsenal. As a commissar, Flint knew well how to wield it.

'Warriors of the Emperor!' Flint bellowed, drawing himself to his full height so that all could see and hear him. 'Our Lord on Terra watches! Deliverance is at hand! We need but stand, and fight!'

The troops at the barricade set their weapons to their shoulders and redoubled their rate of fire, a wall of las-bolts splitting the air and scything down rebels without mercy.

But the mutant beast staggered on, its every step shaking the rockcrete platform. The first glimmer of doubt appeared in the warriors' eyes.

'We fight for the Emperor!' Flint bellowed over the staccato *crack* of massed las-fire rippling up and down the barricade. 'We fight for Vostroya!' Knowing that only a portion of the force were from that world and were instead former convicts of Alpha Penitentia, each from a different world, Flint added, 'We fight for deliverance!'

'Deliverance!' Bukin echoed, bellowing over the cacophony of war.

'Deliverance!' three-dozen more voices echoed Flint's war cry, the light of zealous duty glinting in their eyes and chasing away any doubt.

The mutant beast staggered to a halt, its imbecilic eyes glowering at the barricade. They came to rest on Flint and its drooling mouth twisted into a cruel sneer. Clearly, the mutant thing had taken Flint's war cry for a challenge, and one that it fully intended to answer.

The beast shrugged its massive shoulders, flexing its muscles even as the last of the burning promethium guttered out. Its skin was a blistered, bubbling mass, burned away in many places to reveal raw glistening muscle as well as tarnished steel beneath. Its blackened form gave off creeping tendrils of smoke as it moved. The stink of burned flesh was so powerful it stung the back of Flint's throat.

Then, it charged.

Flint only barely registered one of his subordinates, probably Bukin, bellowing for all weapons to be brought to bear

on the mutant as it charged across the rockcrete towards
Flint. As its momentum increased it lowered its shoulders
like a drunken ogryn, bearing down on its rival, scores of
black las-wounds appearing across its form as it came on.
The commissar barely had time to react but in the few
seconds he guessed he had before the beast flattened him
he knew he had to draw it away from the barricade. If he
couldn't, it would smash the entire structure aside and the
battle against the remainder of the horde would be lost.

'Come on then!' Flint shouted directly at the mutant as
he leapt back from the barricade. A massively oversized
arm swung out to cleave the air where he had stood but a
moment before, a trail of smoke stinking of burning flesh
and metal billowing in its wake.

The beast roared and bent double as its tormentor evaded
it. Using all four limbs as pistons, it leaped into the air and
came down on top of the barricade, warriors scattering in
shock as it stood there swinging its mighty arms left and
right. One man was too slow, his head crushed down into
his shoulders by a brutal overhead impact while another
was caught by a swinging arm and propelled twenty metres
through the air to land in the glowing oily waters of the
uppermost level of the weir.

Seeing the flailing warrior splash into the water gave Flint
an idea and he turned and ran for the water's edge, yelling
for the other troops to keep up their fusillade as he went.
Las-fire strobed behind as he pounded the platform, the
ground trembling as the mutant leapt from the barricade
and powered after him.

Flint turned at the water's edge and raised his power sword. The mutant slowed to a halt, thinking it had him cornered, but the ground was still trembling and Flint knew why. He swung his power sword in contemptuous sweeps, baiting the mutant to come onward.

The beast fixed him with its beady, vacant eyes, and took a step forward, clenching and unclenching its fists as if imagining them wrapped around Flint's neck.

'Monstrosity!' Flint snarled, comparing this creature to the one he had faced previously. He'd thought that one superhumanly strong and unnaturally overgrown. This thing before him was twice as muscular and larger still. It was a grotesque anathema of the human form, and his heart swelled with hatred as it advanced. 'You have no right to exist in the Emperor's Imperium,' he shouted over the increasingly loud rushing of the waters at his back. 'I condemn you, beast!'

The creature bent forward and roared in Flint's face, its breath a wind as noisome as the chemical waters of the sluice channel. It took one step forward, the rockcrete ground shaking, and Flint's blade lashed out, scoring a wound only a hair's-breadth wide, but a hand's span deep, in its arm. The beast squealed, the sound quite innocuous coming from such a massive bulk of muscle and flesh, then lashed out with its other arm.

Flint sidestepped, his ankles suspended over the precipice as the waters rose. The weirs were filling rapidly as the sluice channel flooded and the roar of an oncoming tsunami filled Flint's ears.

The commissar ducked as another punch drove through the air over his head, the mutant surging forward until it too was right at the water's edge. Flint sprang sideways and the mutant twisted to follow his movement. In that instant Flint had the beast exactly where he wanted it. Powering forwards, he rolled under the creature's grasping arms and as he came up behind it, cut savagely behind with a back-handed swing of his power sword. The blade cut deep into the mutant's hamstrings, flesh vaporising and cables sparking as both parted.

The monstrosity roared, arching its back as its legs gave way beneath it. 'Now!' Flint bellowed as he dove clear.

Though his voice was barely audible over the roaring of the torrent now surging down the sluice channel those nearest him had heard. They opened fire on full auto, unleashing a fearsome salvo into the creature's back. It staggered forward on ruined legs, crashed to its knees and toppled forward into the now churning waters. In an instant, it had vanished beneath the raging waters.

The last Flint saw of the mutant monstrosity was a hand, rising once from the sucking waters to grasp for the edge of the platform before being pulled under by the current and swept away down the sluice channel.

A flash strobed from behind and Flint spun to face the ruined portal. The warriors at the barricade were firing at full pelt, the report of their las-weapons swallowed up by the raging flood echoing around the massive sluice chamber. Dozens of rebels were dying but dozens more were pressing forward through the gate to assault the barricade.

Drawing his bolt pistol once more, Flint rejoined his warriors. Soon, he was pumping round after round into the seemingly endless wall of screaming flesh surging towards the barricade.

'Fifteen,' Solomon muttered as he put a las-bolt right between the eyes of a screaming rebel. 'Kohlz, Stank, go!'

Neither did as Solomon shouted, instead standing their ground at the chimney rim as they poured fire down into the rebels swarming across the carceri chamber roof. 'I said–' he started to repeat.

'Okay!' Stank shouted back, his voiced raised over the *whip-crack* of solid slugs coming in from the rebels below. The fire was poorly aimed and the weapons incredibly inaccurate but stray rounds *spanged* off of the corroded metal and cracked the rockcrete cladding all around them. 'Kohlz, you first.'

'Why *me* first?' Flint's aide yelled back as he continued to fire, his indignation clear in his voice even over the discharge of his weapon.

'We're only here to cover *your* arse!' shouted Solomon. 'Get moving, will you?'

Solomon lined up another shot as a group of rebel convicts dashed along a raised gantry a hundred metres below. Though the angle was poor he squeezed off a shot to keep them busy, the sniper rifle bucking hard against his shoulder. The las-bolt struck a guardrail and sent up a shower of sparks, causing the convicts to scatter for cover. Glancing over his shoulder, Solomon saw that Kohlz was hefting his bulky vox-set over his shoulders and securing his carbine for the climb down.

'You're next!' Solomon shouted to Stank.

The Asgardian grinned. 'What's got into you, Solomon?' he said before unleashing a three-round burst towards a group of rebels taking up position behind a ventilation funnel. 'How come you're so keen?'

Solomon had no time to respond and even if he had, the heavy stubber opening up on them would have drowned out his words. Where the hell the rebels had got hold of a heavy auto piece like that he had no idea but the chimney rim suddenly felt ten times more exposed than it had a moment ago as hand-cast slugs sang through the air all around.

Stank dropped and Solomon thought for a moment his fellow penal trooper had bought the farm. But a moment later the Asgardian was crawling towards the ladder that Kohlz had disappeared down a few moments before. Not a bad idea, Solomon thought as he too dropped to his stomach and brought his sniper rifle up to scan for the enemy heavy weapon crew. The instant he was down, the air above his head was filled by the angry buzz of dozens of heavy stubber rounds. Guessing roughly where the weapon crew must be positioned he squinted through his scope and tracked across the rockcrete roof, the viewfinder blurred before he found his range.

'You coming, Solomon?' Stank shouted over the hail of incoming bullets as he lowered his legs onto the ladder's upper rungs. 'Or you determined to play the hero?'

Having located the flashing barrel of the heavy stubber Solomon ignored his friend. It was protruding from a mass of pipes and exposed cabling and all he could draw a bead on was the business end of the weapon. The firer was out of his field of vision somewhere inside the mass of confused cover.

'Solomon?' Stank repeated. 'Come on!'

Holding his breath to steady his aim as the stubber chattered angrily away, Solomon shifted his aim, settling the cross hairs over a point above and slightly to one side of the flaming barrel. He might not be able to see the rebel manning the heavy weapon, but he could guess where he was.

A heavy round split the air near Solomon's head, the sheer force of its passage stinging the exposed skin of his upper face. Knowing he might be dead in a heartbeat Solomon took the shot.

The rifle kicked and the pipes cracked apart in a shower of fractured metal. The heavy stubber fell silent as the barrel tipped upwards, the last of the burst it had been firing cutting through the air above.

'Sixteen!' Stank shouted. 'Now can we just get the frag out of here?'

Don't look down, Solomon told himself. Just don't look down.

Having claimed his sixteenth tally in the effort to pay the Emperor back for the blessing imparted upon Solomon's home world, the Jopalli had followed Kohlz and Stank back down the ladder. He was elated that Kohlz had been able to contact the regiment and that help was incoming even now, but as he fought to keep his grip on the wet, corroded rungs, reality was rapidly reasserting itself. People, he realised, had been trying to kill him…

A muffled explosion sounded from far below, the noise of battle drifting up from the gate. Solomon concentrated on the climb, muttering to himself as he went. The sound of las and shotgun fire intensified and someone was shouting. Was it the commissar? He couldn't be sure but the tone sounded right for the Imperial Guard's morale officers – confident, inspiring, and just daring you to ignore it so they could put a bolt shell through the back of your head.

As the descent continued Solomon realised that the steadily growing, subsonic roar of another flood was swallowing up the sound of battle. Now, he looked down.

Stank had halted ten metres below and looped his arms tightly around a rung. He was looking straight downwards but Solomon couldn't see past him.

But before Solomon could find out what was causing the hold up, the sluice channel exploded. If the flood had been bad before, now it was cataclysmic. The outflows surged upwards and where before the waters had come in a tsunami now they came in a solid line of geysers. The luminescent waters erupted straight upward and in an instant Stank was engulfed. A nanosecond later, Solomon's world turned cold black and his only thought was to cling as tight as he could to the iron rung. The waters surged upwards, buffeting him against the rockcrete wall and he felt the rung loosen under the incredible force, threatening to pitch him into the hundred-metre tall spout and carry him away to his doom. The roaring of a billion litres of water filled his ears, drowning out his shout of denial.

Then the waters were gone and it felt to Solomon like the force of gravity had slackened. Coughing actinic liquid from his mouth he blinked his stinging eyes and looked downwards. 'Stank?' he shouted over the receding roar. As he blinked his eyes clear he saw his friend's sodden form still clung to the ladder, the churning waters a hundred metres below. 'Stank, are you and Kohlz okay?'

The Asgardian looked up but he didn't reply. His eyes said it all.

Flint's aide was gone, carried away by the sheer force of the surging waters.

THIRTEEN
Deliverance

The 77th Vostroyan Firstborn Dragoon regiment was finally on the move. Dozens of armoured vehicles were advancing through the tunnels and chambers of the generatorium, months of tedious practise suddenly translating into something very real indeed.

Graf Aleksis was leading the advance in the manner of his illustrious ancestors – from the forefront, riding in his command vehicle. For years, Aleksis had served in the staff cadres of numerous different Vostroyan Firstborn regiments, always near the centre of power but never quite close enough to claim it for himself. When the previous iteration of the 77th Dragoons had been wiped out at Golan Hole, destroyed pursuing a mission dictated not by the Departmento Munitorum chain of command, but by the Techtriarchs of Vostroya, a small part of him had rejoiced. He had seen that chance to finally claim the power he so craved, and he had called upon every shred of influence his status with the clans granted. Though the price had been steep, Aleksis had bought himself the one commission he so dearly craved – a colonelcy in a Firstborn regiment.

But Aleksis was not the power-hungry petty noble he might have seemed to the unschooled. He was a scholar too, a man well versed in the glorious histories of the Vostroyan Firstborn. Unlike many of his kin, he had some understanding of the roots of the home world's ten millennia old tradition of sending its firstborn male children to fight in the Imperial Guard. Once, he knew, though he dared not speak of it even to Polzdam, Vostroya had failed the Imperium, turned her face from the Emperor and refused to send troops to fight in His wars, claiming that the men were needed to meet the armaments production quotas. In the aftermath of an ancient war only known to most by way of myths, legends and dire warnings, Vostroya renewed its oath of fealty, promising that its firstborn sons would serve for all time as an act of racial contrition.

Aleksis knew these things, and he cared deeply about the ramifications they implied. His immediate forebears had showed weakness at Golan Hole, allowing their loyalties to become divided in a cruel repeat of what had happened ten thousand years ago. Weak, stupid men had led the glorious 77th to defeat, *khekking* on the long, glorious history of Vostroya.

No more, Aleksis growled, his gorge rising the nearer the Chimera approached to the war zone. *No more dishonour, no more vainglory*. The ignominy of Golan Hole will be wiped from the annals, and a new 77th will rise to replace its predecessor. His grip on the overhead rail was so tight his knuckles were turned white. The Chimera bucked violently and Aleksis redoubled that grip to remain upright, before the vehicle settled back on its suspension as it ground north-west through Vestibule 41.

'Sorry, sir!' the driver called over the intercom. 'There's debris everywhere. The forward tracks are saying its getting denser further in.'

'Understood,' Aleksis replied. 'Keep your eyes to the front, please, driver.'

Huffing his impatience, Aleksis lowered the periscope and thumbed on the night sights. He silently mouthed the requisite prayer as he set his face against the rubberised surround. The Chimera jolted again as it careened over an especially large and solid piece of debris and Aleksis banged his forehead against the metal casing.

Suppressing the urge to reprimand the driver, Aleksis waited a moment before sighting through the periscope. The viewfinder was grainy and shot through with machine hash, a side effect, so he was informed, of the installation's machine systems. The view plate showed the wide, arched tunnel of the vestibule, pale lumen strips zipping by intermittently overhead. Even in the low light conditions, Aleksis could make out graffiti scrawled across the walls. His lip curled with distaste as he caught random words as he passed – *Emperor, deny, choke, resist.* A dark shape loomed suddenly out of the darkness and clattered against the pintle-mount overhead. A body, Aleksis saw, reduced to little more than bones, strung from the ceiling on long, rusted chains.

The graf's first proper taste of regimental command was not shaping up to be the glorious endeavour he had looked forward to.

'Report,' Aleksis said through gritted teeth, folding the periscope up into its housing.

Behind Aleksis sat Lieutenant-Colonel Karsten, his chief of operations. Aleksis knew Karsten to be a proficient officer and one of the few in the regiment to have some measure of genuine command experience. The man had served in the Vostroyan defence forces and had proved himself worthy of his commission during the badland uprisings of 932. Some regimental commanders might have seen Karsten as a rival and relegated him to some obscure post far from the glory. Much to the consternation of several others, Aleksis had resisted that temptation and ensured Karsten's experience would be of use.

'Reconnaissance tracks have reached junction designate X-delta-nine, sir,' Karsten replied smartly, his eyes not leaving his glowing strategium terminal. 'Moderate resistance, small arms, nothing they can't handle, sir.'

'Understood,' Aleksis replied, scanning his own command console. The multiple screens displayed reams of data, so much that it took a conscious effort to filter out the extraneous information. That was what officers like Karsten were there for, to take the strain and allow him to command.

'Additional,' Karsten announced, his hand pressing his headset to his ear as he concentrated on an incoming message. 'Signals report contact with Flint's force. Stand by...'

Aleksis hooked his arm over the back of his seat and turned to face his operations chief. The chatter of a stubber sounded from somewhere up ahead, muffled by the Chimera's hull and almost drowned out by the growl of its engine. Come on, Aleksis thought.

'Confirmed,' Karsten said. 'We have Flint's coordinates.'

'And?' Aleksis pressed. 'Has he located the rebels' stronghold?'

'Unknown at this time, sir,' Karsten replied. 'It sounds like Flint might be in a spot of bother.'

'Does it now,' said Aleksis, smirking slightly despite himself. 'So he might appreciate a little help?'

The operations chief grinned back, a mischievous glint in his eye. 'He might that, sir.'

'Inform all sub-commands, Mister Karsten.' Aleksis ordered. 'Plot us a route to Flint's location. Lead us in.'

Commissar Flint's pistol barked and the rebel convict dragging himself up over the barricade was thrown backwards with a smoking crater punched in his chest. Even as the rebel cartwheeled backwards through the air, his arms flailing and a gory tail of displaced viscera trailing behind, he screamed such blasphemies against the Emperor that Flint was all but driven to put a second bolt into him just to silence him. Then the bolt exploded, and the remains were lost to the press of the horde. Within seconds another had taken the rebel's place.

The next rebel to face Flint was every bit as rabid as the last, and the clotted, dirty wound across his forehead told the commissar he was one of those who had been forced to make obeisance to the colonel in the chamber high above. That recognition took but a second to implant itself upon Flint's consciousness, and it was followed an instant later by an impression of something deeply… wrong in the rebel's eyes. They were almost alight, though not with anything so conventional as illumination. Rather, the light of the warp shone behind the wildly staring orbs and it threatened to reach out and entrap Flint's soul with its pernicious grasp.

'Back!' Flint growled, only just avoiding a blow from the rebel's serrated meat cleaver blade that would undoubtedly have decapitated him had it struck. 'Lost and damned! Slave to darkness! Back!' he bellowed, recalling the words the *Dictum Commissaria* reserved for the most diabolic of foes.

The rebel snarled as he squatted like some feral beast upon the barricade, his crude weapon drawn back for a second blow. The fell light of the warp sparked from his eyes and he opened its mouth as wide as it would go, then opened it more. The yawning, fang-lined chasm seemed to swell before Flint's eyes, and part of him was aware that the man must be touched by the creatures of the beyond and drawing somehow on the power of their darkling realm. The lips peeled back still further, revealing first the teeth, then the gums, then, with a hideously wet tearing sound, the glistening musculature beneath the skin of his face.

'In the name of the God-Emperor of Mankind…' Flint

uttered, and the creature drew back, hissing, even as some weirdling illumination guttered and sparked in the wet depths of its gullet. Drawing strength from his faith and the fact that the enemy seemed weakened by the very same weapon, Flint redoubled his spiritual assault. The words of a regimental priest he had once seen face down a charge from an alien monstrosity the size of a Scout Titan sprung unbidden, though not unwelcome, to his lips.

'Die!' the priest had bellowed, and so too did Flint. 'In the name of Him on Terra, I command thee to die!' Now those words were echoed from the distant past by Flint's invocation of a man who had himself died seconds after uttering them. 'Die!' he repeated, focusing every ounce of his faith and his hatred of the Emperor's foes into that one, single word.

The spell was broken and Flint's bolt pistol was raised before he even realised he was wielding it. Without conscious effort, the barrel was thrust into the abomination's gaping mouth, the creature clamping oversized fangs down around it in a vain effort to avert the inevitable.

'Emperor!' the words of the Litany Against the Mutant came to Flint's lips. 'Let your undeniable light burn on the misshapen and the twisted!'

Absently aware that several warriors nearby were joining in the recitation, Flint continued. 'Let me see them with pure sight!'

Now still more voices joined the commissar's as he completed the litany. 'And purge them with righteous fire!'

When it came, the bolt pistol's report was both deafening

and spectacular. The blast dissolved the rebel's head in a shower of biological filth that all but blinded the commissar with blood and fragments of pulped grey matter. As he blinked his eyes clear, Flint saw the body tumbling back down the barricade and into the seething mass of rebels. The energy that had carried the rebel and his fellows up the barricade seemed to ebb, and the tide recoiled, if almost imperceptibly.

The barricade was holding, but Flint knew that couldn't last. The small force was fighting like true servants of the God-Emperor but with their backs against the waters of the upper weir there could be no retreat. The last time the channel had flooded the waters had swelled right up and over the upper level, swamping the area before the gate in stinging backflow. Even now, with the flood receded, the force was fighting in ankle deep water.

Another rebel threw himself atop the barricade but instead of maintaining the impetus of his charge he paused a moment to wave his fellows onwards. Once more, an all but imperceptible flicker appeared in the man's eyes, the daemon-haunted warp threatening to break through into the material realm. Flint saw his opening and lashed out with his power sword, taking the man in the ankles. The blade's seething edge parted flesh and bone with barely any effort and the man let out a scream like that of the damned. He collapsed backward to land atop a handful of his fellows and Flint's section of the barricade was momentarily clear.

Taking advantage of the brief respite, Flint ejected his almost spent bolt pistol magazine and replaced it with what he realised was his last spare. At this rate, by the time relief arrived he'd be long dead. That grim thought reminded Flint of his aide and the mission he must by now have completed and he turned to look down the stepped tiers of the weir pools and out across the sluice channel. The waters in the sluice channel were at their lowest ebb and on the verge of rising once more. The overflow was getting ever more frequent and soon the entire area would be inundated. Movement at the base of the slime-coated weir ramp caught Flint's eye as two figures struggled upwards. Both were coated in chemical filth and giving off a coiling miasma of vapour but they were clearly his men.

'Kohlz?' Flint called out. The two men struggled onwards, their fatigue obvious in their every step.

Militarily, it mattered not at all which of the dragoons had returned, only that they had completed their allotted task. With a mild shock however, Flint realised in that moment that he did care. These were his troops, and they were fighting not just for the Emperor, their regiment or anything else. They were heeding his words and following his example, he was almost overwhelmingly proud of them.

The battle at the gate raged on, the sound of gunfire echoing out over the waters and Flint knew he had no time to waste in sentimentality. Renewed gunfire boomed from close behind, the loudest reports those of the wardens' shotguns, the clavigers fighting side by side with the penal troopers they had guarded not so long before. Though he was needed back at the barricade Flint had to know the result of the mission.

Finally, the nearest of the men stumbled up the last few metres and hauled himself up onto the lip. Flint reached out a gloved hand and helped the man up. Only when he wiped his face clear of a portion of the filth caking his features was it revealed as Trooper Stank.

Bending double, Stank stumbled up onto the lip. With his hands on his knees he threw up a great gout of luminescent liquid. Flint left him to it and proffered a hand to pull the next one up. From the man's gangly frame it was clearly the Jopalli, Indenti Solomon.

'Kohlz?' Flint said flatly as he helped Solomon up onto the lip.

Solomon started to speak, then spluttered and like Stank before him coughed up a stream of garish liquid. Stank straightened up as Solomon spewed his guts across the wet rockcrete and answered the commissar's question. 'We got separated on the way down, sir.'

'Separated?' Flint repeated, guessing the trooper's meaning straight away. The last overflow had been the worst yet and the geysers that had erupted from the sluice vents had reached halfway up the chimney at least.

'Did he get through?'

'Yes, sir,' Solomon said, straightening up. 'The regiment's already inbound, sir.'

'Time to contact?' Graf Aleksis barked, not taking his eyes from the dozens of icons flashing across his command console.

'Estimated five minutes, sir,' Karsten replied. 'Lead tracks report increasing resistance but nothing coordinated.'

'Yet,' Aleksis muttered to himself as he oriented his position on the glowing tri-D map on his main viewing slate. The dull *crump crump crump* of an autocannon firing from one of 1st Company's Chimeras sounded from close by, followed a moment later by a sharp explosion. The graf's blood was up and he was starting to enjoy himself. For so many years he had watched other, lesser men write their names in the histories of Vostroya. Now finally, he was the one wielding the auto-quill.

'Time to get into the fight, then,' he growled, reaching above his head to unlock the Chimera's turret hatch.

'Sir?' Karsten's voice came over the vehicle's intercom. 'Might I suggest you leave that to someone...'

Aleksis ignored his chief of operations and pushed the hatch upwards so that its two halves clanged loudly on the upper armour.

'If Lord-Marshall Supovka had stayed on his command barge at the Siege of Thaltor, do you think the Blood Angels would have delayed their drop? Hah! If General Kolskoi had not led the assault on King Tancred's fortress from the command deck of his Leviathan, do you think that fate would have granted him another day before the death of that entire world?'

Warming to his subject, Aleksis dredged up still more examples from the annals of Vostroyan military history. 'What of the 109th at Kvalgron, or Battlegroup Volga at Horthn IV, or Lord-General Royanz in the death-glades of Nashe's World?

'No?' Aleksis pressed when Karsten dared not advance any more objections. 'Quite right,' he said, pulling himself up through the open hatch. The noise of the outside world flooded in and threatened to overwhelm the graf's senses with a cacophony of clattering tracks, gunfire and roaring engines. Pulling himself up, Aleksis seated himself high in the turret and took hold of the twin-gripped pintle-mounted stubber. He took a deep breath but grasping for his rebreather he immediately wished he hadn't.

The air stank, and not just of the engine fumes of the vehicle in front. It was tainted and damp, thick with corpse-gas and pollution. It was an unutterably vile cocktail of chemicals and decay. The armoured column was grinding its way along the barrel-vaulted tunnel of Vestibule 39 and according to reports was closing on the main entrance into the vast generatoria chamber called Carceri *Resurecti*. The bulk of the headquarters company was rolling along at full speed, smashing aside the piles of debris scattered all about. Ahead of them, the 'armoured fist' Chimera-borne infantry of 1st Company were approaching the chamber entrance while the other four battle companies were following behind the HQ. With the air-scrubbers disabled, the air was so thick with mist and the exhaust fumes of dozens of vehicles that visibility was reduced to less than a hundred metres.

Aleksis activated his vox-pickup and opened a channel to his company commanders. 'All commands, this is Cobalt Lead,' he said identifying himself by his designated call sign. 'This is it, gentlemen, the first battle honour of many.

The 77th Firstborn shall this day be *reborn*! You have your orders, follow them and glory is ours. Cobalt Lead, out.'

A series of affirmatives flooded back over the vox as the company commanders joined in with their commander's show of bravado. Listening to their oaths and affirmations, Aleksis was proud and suddenly very aware of his place in history. The 77th had served for countless generations and won hundreds of battle honours but Aleksis and his fellow intake of officers had much to prove.

The crackle of gunfire brought the graf's attention back to the head of the column as it passed under the archway and pressed into Carceri *Resurecti*. The Chimeras of 1st Company's armoured infantry platoons spread out as they ground into the chamber with turrets tracking left and right as they unleashed a torrent of autocannon, multi-laser and heavy bolter fire on an enemy Aleksis couldn't yet see. Hull-mounted weaponry added its weight to the fusillade and individual vehicle commanders were manning the pintle-mounts atop the turrets. Soon, the entire firing line was shrouded in the discharge of dozens of heavy weapons, the rolling smoke lit from within by continuous, strobing muzzle flares.

It was a stirring sight, making Aleksis eagerly tighten his hold on his stubber's twin grips as his Chimera trundled towards the archway. His blood pumped hard as the sounds of battle increased, the back and forth updates of his subordinate commanders a constant background buzz in his ears.

As the Chimera passed under the archway, the buzz cut

out as Lieutenant-Colonel Karsten engaged his override. 'Sir? I really must insist you allow someone else to…'

A sudden movement in the shadows to the right caused Aleksis to swing the stubber around on its mount. A figure wrapped in trailing bands of ragged fabric rose from a pile of stinking rubbish and raised a purloined heavy combat shotgun to its shoulder.

Aleksis found himself staring down into the gaping barrel of a weapon obviously taken from the dead hands of a pious servant of the Emperor and knew utter contempt for his foe. But before he could draw a bead the man pulled the shotgun's trigger.

The blast was deafening, but to his total shock Aleksis was unharmed. It seemed that time itself was frozen like a clock hand unable to move past the hour. The rebel convict groped for a reload but before he could retrieve a fresh cartridge Aleksis snapped out of it. Squeezing the stubber's grips hard, he ground his thumbs into its trigger plate, gritting his teeth against the anticipated recoil and the sight of his foe being ripped to shreds by the close range burst…

…but nothing happened. The two men locked incredulous gazes and the rebel's face twisted into a feral sneer. The Chimera ground on, the driver oblivious to the one-on-one battle for life and death being enacted outside. The rebel darted forwards, tensed his rag-clad body and pounced upwards towards Aleksis.

Acting purely on instinct Aleksis reached to his belt and withdrew his laspistol, an heirloom weapon carried into battle by seven generations of his line's firstborn sons. He might never have fired a heavy stubber in anger but he was well practiced in the noble art of duelling and the pistol was like an extension of his very body.

With a flick of his thumb the safety was off. With a squeeze of a finger the weapon spat an incandescent blast that for an instant chased away the shadows beneath the archway. The las-bolt struck the rebel at the very apex of his leap, his hands twisted into atavistic claws and struck him a glancing blow to his left shoulder. Momentum carried the rebel forward, slamming him into the Chimera's side armour, but instead of slumping down, its side his arm was caught in the tracks as they clattered over the topside of the nacelle.

The Chimera ground on and the mortally wounded rebel, now screaming as he saw his impending death, was dragged along with the track. In a moment he was lost to the graf's view and the scream cut off abruptly with a sickening crunch.

A moment later, the Chimera passed out of the archway, and into the staggering vastness of Carceri *Resurecti*.

'Warriors of the Emperor!' Flint bellowed over the roar of the rebel horde. 'Deliverance is at hand!'

His bolt pistol spat its last burst as it stitched a line of exploding craters across the bodies of a wave of rebels clawing their way over the barricade. Flint had never seen such hatred in his foe, even when facing the most fanatical of the insurgents on Gethsemane. The rebels had been whipped up into a frenzy beyond anything Flint had ever encountered and were on the verge of overwhelming what remained of his force.

His bolt pistol spent and with no spare magazines to hand Flint dropped his weapon, unable to spare the second of precious time it would take to holster. As another pair of rebels clambered over the barricade his power sword was up and blood was flying.

Even amidst the anarchy of hand-to-hand combat Flint knew well enough that the position was untenable and would fall within minutes. The roar of the rebel horde was so loud it echoed back through the sluice chamber and by its pitch and volume the enemy were as good as number-less. Fallen rebels were piled up before the barricade, the dead and the dying hideously intertwined as those follow-ing after used the broken bodies as a ramp to assault the Imperial position. Countless more were pressing through the ruined hatch, pushing the rest forward by the sheer mass of the endless tide.

'There's no end to them!' Flint heard a penal trooper nearby shout, the unmistakable edge of panic in his voice. 'We have to fall back!'

'Nowhere to fall back to, lad,' Bukin bellowed in response. That didn't help.

'Shut the hell up,' Flint shouted at Bukin. 'And let me do my job.'

The defenders were on the verge of a rout, yet, as Bukin had so crudely put it, there really was nowhere to go with the surging waters of the sluice channel cutting off any retreat or redeployment. Though the regiment was inbound there was no way of knowing when they might arrive as the lost Kohlz had the only high-powered vox-set. In such situations, Imperial commissars had two means of motivating the troops – *make* an example or *be* an example. Punish fear or overcome it.

Flint hauled himself onto the barricade where everyone, friend and foe, could see him. Immediately, a dozen screaming rebels surged towards him and he was forced to hack all about in a crude arc just to keep them at bay. Most recoiled from the scything blade while those not quick enough or unable to push back against the pressure behind lost limbs and lives.

'At this, our moment of need!' Flint bellowed over the roar of the enemy and the crack of lasguns discharged at impossibly close range, 'The Emperor casts his gaze upon us!' It was the twenty-ninth Catechism of Duty, which the drill abbots had taught the adolescent Flint and his fellow progenia so many years before. The words came to him without conscious effort yet the troops needed more.

'We are the instruments of the Emperor's will!' he invoked the twelfth chapter of the catechism. 'Through our deeds his enemies are felled!'

This is it, Flint thought, the moment of truth. As the rebel hordes roared and surged forwards once more, he decided to commit his fate to the God-Emperor in whose glory he was raised. In so doing he would set such an example to his warriors that the impossible odds facing them might seem as nothing.

Flint leaped off the barricade and into the chaotic mass of frothing enemies.

The mist parted in coiling vortexes as Aleksis unleashed a stuttering rain of heavy stubber rounds at the silhouetted rebel horde. With the turret weapon adding its weight of fire to his own he could barely even hear the weapon that jerked and bucked in his grip. The vast chamber had come alive with the fury of battle as groups of rebels emerged from side passages and floor vents to throw themselves at the 77th as the Chimeras ground across the debris-strewn floor. Bones crunched under his vehicle's treads as Aleksis ordered his driver onwards, plunging through the dense mists enshrouding the entire chamber floor.

'Have at it, you bastards!' Aleksis yelled with savage battle lust, his voice inaudible over the roar of the engines of dozens of Chimeras and the constant report of their weapons. 'For the Grey Lady!' he invoked Nadalya, the patron saint of his home world. 'For the 77th renewed in glory!' With a loud, metallic *clack*, the stubber's ammo feed dried up and he hauled on the release that freed the hopper. Even as he slammed in a fresh box and cranked the belt home, a massive shape loomed out of the mists towards his vehicle.

It was too close for the turret to engage but Aleksis brought the stubber to bear on the fresh target, this time ensuring its action was clear. His eyes widened as the huge shape resolved into something only vaguely resembling a humanoid body, its proportions grotesquely exaggerated by some unwholesome and probably forbidden process.

'*Mutant*,' he growled, suddenly reminded of the stories of the twisted creatures that dwelled in the ruined industrial badlands of Vostroya's northern polar regions. 'Filthy, dirty–'

The rest of his tirade was snatched away as he pressed his thumbs hard into the heavy stubber's trigger plate. The weapon erupted in his hands, its stabilised mount only barely able to contain its savage recoil. A hundred rounds and more scythed through the air and hammered into the mutant's upper torso. Though the air was still too hazy for the graf to see his target clearly or to judge the effectiveness of his fire, it staggered under the weight of the stream of rounds, its arms thrashing about as if the bullets were bothersome insects it was trying to swat away.

Incredibly, the mutant monstrosity wasn't cut down by the opening burst. It bellowed, splitting the air with a shrill cry unlike that of any natural creature. It lowered its shoulders and rushed on through the mists. Aleksis kept his thumbs on the trigger plate as the form became fully visible through the mists, a prayer for deliverance forming on his lips.

The beast's vile features twisted in savage rage, its naked body a mockery of the human form. Its head was set low between the rippling slabs of its shoulders and its over-muscled arms ended in forearms and fists the size of barrels. Its legs were bent at the knee and undersized compared to the rest of its body, lending it a hunched gait and its skin was smeared with oily filth.

Worst of all, Aleksis caught sight of corroded machine augmetics protruding from angry purple wounds in amongst its seething muscles and he knew that such a creature was unsanctified by the machine priests of the Adeptus Mechanicus and therefore impure.

Aleksis unloaded another long, steady stream of heavy rounds, hammering them one after another into the knotted muscle of its chest. Yet, now the thing was in motion, nothing appeared capable of stopping it.

Nothing perhaps except thirty-eight tonnes of armoured transport travelling at full pelt straight over it.

The Chimera crashed into the mutant at around seventy kilometres per hour. The beast roared as if challenging a rival and brought its massive fists hammering down onto the glacis plate the instant before impact, inflicting a pair of huge dents before it was dragged under the bow and the vehicle ground overhead.

It was far from dead; Aleksis could tell that from its shrill and frenzied cries as it receded behind, punctuated every few seconds as another Chimera ground over it. But the column was closing on the portal leading from the carceri chamber to the area beyond, where according to reports, Flint's beleaguered force was holed up. The seething mass of rebel scum pressed in around the wrecked gateway into that chamber was all the confirmation Aleksis needed that the commissar and his troops were there.

'All commands!' Aleksis shouted into his vox-set as he cranked the heavy stubber's mechanism. 'Close on target as per orders.'

'In the name of the 77th!' he added as he opened fire on the rearmost of the horde. 'Cut them down!'

Flint's entire world was swallowed up in the press of bodies, limbs thrashing in all directions as rebels sought to pull him down. Flint's power sword burned white hot as he swept it in a great arc. Bodies were sliced open as the power field split flesh and spilled organs across the rockcrete ground. Limbs were severed and rebels fell at Flint's feet yet still more foes came on.

Flint gave himself utterly to his duty as a commissar, certain beyond any shred of doubt that the words he had spoken moments before were true. The Emperor was watching and Flint was most certainly the instrument of His will. He was divine retribution, the manifestation of the judgement that should have been visited upon the wretched denizens of Alpha Penitentia long ago. He hacked and sliced and parried instinctively those attacks the rebels launched against him. His blade cut all other weapons in two, its power field scything through the crude weapons wielded against him. His arm rose and fell what must have been a hundred times and more before he eventually became aware that the press of bodies was lessening. The tide was receding and the ever present muted roar was changing into something very different.

It was turning into a cry of terror and woe.

Reality came crashing back in and Flint found himself standing in the midst of dozens of bodies. The rebels were backing off towards the portal and the safety of the carceri chamber beyond and the space before the hastily erected barricades had been reclaimed. Firstborn, penal troopers and claviger-wardens alike had followed Flint's example and vaulted the obstacle to take the battle to the surging enemy.

Flint was about to issue the order to run the last enemy down when the sound of heavy weaponry opening fire sounded from the carceri chamber beyond. A cacophonous roar of multiple types of weapons rang out and the last of the rebels surging through the portal were cut down. The wrecked hatchway was soon clogged with ruined bodies.

The sight of so much blood made Flint look down at his own body and only then did he realise that he'd sustained scores of small wounds in his insane battle against the rebel horde. His cuirass was scratched and dented in countless places and the tails of his heavy leather storm coat were ragged and torn. His breeches were cut open and soaked in blood, his own and that of his enemies, and his peaked cap was gone having been lost at some point in the battle.

At the last, the blunt prow of a Chimera armoured transport ground over the bodies and halted on the far side of the portal. An officer with golden epaulettes at his shoulders stood high in the turret manning the pintle-mount. 'Aleksis?' Flint muttered. He could scarcely believe the regiment's commanding officer was manning the overhead weapon of the lead vehicle.

Flint looked sidelong at Bukin as the chief provost appeared at his side. The other man was a ragged mess and covered in as much blood as the commissar. 'Get the force together,' Flint ordered. 'This is far from over.'

As Bukin fished a fresh cigar from a webbing pouch, Flint added, 'And get someone looking for my hat.'

FOURTEEN
Consolidation

Over the next few hours the 77th Firstborn cleared the southern extent of Carceri *Resurecti* with ruthless efficiency, the un-blooded dragoons soon earning their first kills amongst the corroded machine edifices and along the creaking suspended gantries. But the rebel convicts were on home ground and made the Firstborn pay for every square metre they took. The bulk of the rebel horde scattered into scores of smaller bands as the Chimeras pushed outwards in a solid line of growling ceramite that secured a large area of the chamber in the first hour. While the undisciplined mass was broken up easily enough the smaller bands soon proved a lethal prospect to locate and engage amidst the twisted machinery and gantries of the chamber. A series of running battles soon developed as dismounted infantry pushed up into the spider's web of walkways criss-crossing the air. The dragoons soon discovered the rebels were using the vast lengths of heavy chain suspended from the roof to move from one level to another, descending through the ever-present mists to launch devastating rear attacks on units passing by.

Despite his fatigue and the grumbling of his warriors Flint insisted on leading the counter-attack to secure the lowermost of the overhead gantries. This was the first occasion he had climbed up onto the rusted walkways and he was disgusted by the number and nature of the trophies attached by hooks and chains to the guardrails. One walkway was festooned with a long line of grinning skulls, the flesh crudely flensed from the bone. Great loops of long-dried intestine hung from another like a grim version of the seasonal decorations sometimes seen at the Feast of the Emperor's Ascension.

Stealth was all but impossible for while the mists provided visual cover, the tread plates and grilles underfoot were so corroded they creaked and split as troops passed, the metallic grinding echoing weirdly through the fog. On one length Flint found thousands of teeth scattered across his path. Despite his best efforts the teeth cracked horribly underfoot. Seeing movement up ahead and suspecting an ambush, he led his force on another route and the ambushers were caught in the flank and slaughtered to a man.

Even when Flint and his small force weren't engaging the vicious bands of rebel convicts that haunted the upper walkways the sounds of battle resounded all around. The stuttering roar of turret-mounted autocannon was an ever-present accompaniment to the action to clear the southern extent of the chamber. Sometimes the clamour was explosively loud from directly beneath the walkway along which the force advanced, at other times it sounded several kilometres distant. The mist was so dense in places it appeared that Flint was leading his force along a gantry that passed over the clouds themselves and that the ground was many kilometres beneath.

Then it started raining harder than it ever had before. The mists were blown away in the span of minutes and a hot, tainted wind started up. The vox-channels burst into life as desperate queries flew back and forth between the different units. Yet the signals were so distorted by the installation's structure and by the freakish weather that few got through.

None of the 77th had ever experienced such a downpour for they were foundry-dwellers and everyone knew it didn't rain inside buildings. Yet here they were, inside a generatorium complex almost the size of a hive with each of the vast carceri chambers developing its own, interrelated climate without the moderating systems of the air scrubbers and cooling towers.

Some regions experienced hugely disproportionate increases in air pressure while others were subject to sudden drop offs. The juncture between each chamber became the site of a great, raging battle between unnatural elemental forces that caused howling winds and driving rains to concentrate along unbearably dense weather fronts. The longer vestibule tunnels linking each carceri chamber were hit the worst for they funnelled what felt like entire tornadoes along their lengths and soon became impassable to any unit not mounted in armoured transports with the hatches buttoned firmly down. Several of the regiment's lighter-equipped units were cut-off as the vestibules became too dangerous for them to pass along. The reconnaissance platoon, mounted in its open-topped Salamander transports, was forced to take shelter in a sealed-off meat storage chamber that despite the lingering stench had, thankfully, been stripped of its former contents. The light walker troop, mounted in its Sentinel scout walkers, was so battered by the winds as it probed Vestibule 47 that the pilots had to abandon their machines. These were found later wrecked by rebels moving unseen through the complex's labyrinthine tunnel systems.

By the end of the day, if such a measure of time had any relevance by that point, Flint was forced to pull his penal unit out of the line for fear of the troopers simply collapsing from fatigue. Instructing Vahn to get the unit fed, rested and rearmed, he and Bukin made for the temporary command post Graf Aleksis had erected in the midst of a cluster of vent-sinks three kilometres into Carceri *Resurecti*. As the pair were about to enter the circle of grumbling command vehicles, Vahn caught up with them.

'I thought I told you to get the unit down,' Flint shouted over the driving rain.

'I did, commissar,' the trooper answered. Even over the wind and rain, his voice sounded as tired as Flint's. 'They're down.'

Flint halted and turned on his heel to face Vahn. 'Then why aren't *you*?'

'Because, sir, like you said earlier, we're not done here yet.'

Flint's eyes narrowed as he regarded the man before him. Vahn looked a mess, but then they all did after so many hours fighting through the rank depths of Alpha Penitentia. Vahn's battledress, a mix of his convict fatigues and Vostroyan issue armour, was encrusted with the chemical filth they had all had to wade through crossing the sluice channel and it was ripped and torn in multiple places. His waist-length dreads were matted and dirty, his general state far from acceptable, even on campaign.

With a wry smile, it occurred to Flint that some commissars he had served alongside would have executed Vahn on the spot for presenting himself to them in such a state. The trooper must be serious, he realised.

'What's up?' Flint asked. 'Why are you here, Vahn?'

The trooper glanced towards the bustling command post, then back at Flint. 'I wanted to make sure we're still in this, sir,' he said.

Flint noted a cold glint in Vahn's eyes as he spoke. He knew what it meant.

'You want this,' he said. 'You want… payback?'

Vahn didn't answer straight away, but shuffled almost nervously. He looked like a man placed on a charge despite the fact he was in the opposite situation.

'Yes, sir,' Vahn eventually replied. 'The guys and me,' he continued. 'We've got a lot of stuff to settle.'

'With the rebels?' said Flint.

'With Strannik,' Bukin interjected from beside Flint. 'That right, son?'

'Vahn?' Flint pressed.

'Yes, sir,' Vahn finally replied. 'If the regiment's going after him, we want in.'

'*Who* wants in?' Flint asked. 'You, or the rest?'

'All of us, sir,' Vahn replied, nodding back the way he had come. Flint followed the gesture and saw Vahn's fellow penal troopers sheltering from the rain beneath a low gantry, looking on from a distance. 'We all want it.'

Flint nodded slowly then answered, 'Understood. You'd better come along then.'

The command post was a circle of Chimeras belonging to the headquarters company's various sub-units, including specialised command, signals and service tracks. Staff officers and tacticae advisors went about their business, setting up or manning augur transponders and vox-terminals bristling with antennae masts and revolving sensor dishes. Canvas awnings extended from the rear of each Chimera to keep men and equipment from getting drenched in the stinging rain but it was impossible to keep the worst of it out. The sound of explosions and gunfire was clearly audible even over the relentless rain, the battle to push into the vast carceri chamber raging as hard as ever just a few kilometres north.

Pulling down the rim of his peaked cap, which one of Bukin's men had located under the body of an eviscerated rebel convict, Flint located Graf Aleksis. The commanding officer of the 77th was conducting an orders group beneath the shelter at the rear of his command track.

'...echelon to laager at reference point zero-delta-nine

with recovery section and three squads from 4th Company. Go,' Aleksis was saying as Flint and his two companions arrived. The officer the graf had been speaking to saluted and dashed off and Flint stepped smartly into the vacant space leaving Bukin and Vahn to stand uncomfortably hunched in the rain beyond the awning.

'This operation has now escalated from a policing and suppression mission to something far more serious,' Aleksis continued, obviously glorying in the escalation he was describing. 'I can no longer guarantee the Munitorum will get their Penal Legion from this place. Frankly,' he concluded as Flint edged to the front of the gathering, 'our objective is now to defeat these rebels, no matter the cost.'

A dozen heads turned towards Flint and at that same moment a distant explosion rumbled through the chamber from the direction of the front line. How different the officers all looked after a few hours in the field, how their once starched uniform jackets and peaked officers hats were now drenched by the stinking rain and creased from sitting in the back of a Chimera for a while. A little humility would do them good, Flint thought as the heads turned back towards Aleksis, most pointedly ignoring the commissar.

Flint listened as Aleksis and Polzdam issued a stream of perfectly routine orders, growing increasingly impatient as he waited to hear anything of the assault on the enemy stronghold the commissar's force had identified what felt like days earlier. Several times the graf was forced to raise his voice over the dull crump of distant explosions.

Eventually, Aleksis concluded his address and asked the assembled cadre if anyone had any further questions.

'I do, graf,' Flint spoke up over the sound of rain hammering the topside of the awning. Once again, several dozen heads turned in his direction. 'When do we clear the rebel leadership out? We know where they are, but they may not be there long.'

'A good question, commissar,' replied Graf Aleksis. 'And one I do not yet have a proper answer to. If you would…'

'Graf,' Flint interjected, his gorge rising. Having fought through hell and not slept for days he was in no mood for diplomacy. 'Why not?' he demanded, his voice low and dangerous.

'I am instructed to wait before the final assault is launched,' Aleksis replied bitterly.

'Instructed?' Flint repeated incredulously. 'Instructed by whom?'

'Commissar…' Lieutenant-Colonel Polzdam interrupted, evidently uncomfortable with Flint's tone. 'I really must insist–'

Aleksis held up a hand to silence his second-in-command and Polzdam shut up, though he continued to glower at the commissar bitterly. 'Please,' he said. 'The commissar has every right to know, as does everyone.'

'Go on,' Flint scowled, knowing he wasn't going to like what he was about to hear.

'This operation has certain… limitations placed upon it,' said Aleksis, raising his voice over the growing rumble of an approaching transport track.

'What limitations?' said Flint, his eyes narrowing. Despite his ire he had an inkling that this was nothing of the graf's doing. The question was, what would Aleksis do about it?

'We are here to aid the authorities of Furia Penitens in regaining control of this installation,' Aleksis continued, raising his voice over the growl of an armoured vehicle's engine. 'We have a duty to consider the wishes of those authorities.'

It was immediately obvious which authorities Aleksis was referring to. The sound of clattering treads made him and the rest of the gathered officers turn in time to see a vehicle slow to a halt just outside the awning.

The vehicle was a Rhino armoured transport, a smaller and boxier vehicle than the Chimeras used by the Firstborn, though its armour and many other characteristics were generally superior. The vehicle's slab-like sides were streaked with rain and its upper surfaces were misted over completely with the back-spray from the heavy downpour. The flash of a distant explosion glinted from the rain-slicked armour and illuminated the crest of the world's ruling body. The vehicle's every surface was covered in complex heraldic motifs, Imperial eagles bearing keys and death's-head skulls behind portcullis gates. Flint recognised the motifs and even as the side hatch swung down to thud into the wet rockcrete he knew who would disembark.

'Gentlemen,' said Graf Aleksis. 'Due respect, please.'

The officers moved backwards to clear a space under the awning as movement stirred inside the open hatch. The Vostroyan officers doffed their caps but Flint kept his firmly on his head. A brass rod emerged jerkily from the opening and was followed a moment later by a second, the pair feeling forward like a blind insect using its antennae to discern its surroundings. A moment later, the hideously gnarled hands holding each stick appeared, followed by the rest of Governor Kherhart.

Lord Kherhart was attired in a ridiculously impractical robe of office that must have been even older than him and that looked on the verge of collapsing to a ragged heap of scraps. The robe was made of the rarest black void silk and must once have glittered like the starfield after which it was named. About his shoulders Kherhart wore a cloak of silver fur, the hide of some exotic beast Flint couldn't identify. On his head he wore a periwig at least three times the size he had worn when last Flint had seen him. His face was twisted in concentration as he manoeuvred himself down the Rhino's hatch using the brass sticks as support. Finally, the governor stood beneath the awning and he squinted myopically. With both hands occupied gripping the walking sticks he was unable to raise his lorgnette to his eyes in order to see clearly.

The governor lurched suddenly forward, angling his face up towards Captain Bohman, the chief signals officer. 'Aleksis! You will tell me what is going on, right now!'

Bohman stood rigidly to attention and stuttered, 'Bohman, sir. This is Graf Aleksis.'

'Quite,' the governor spat before swinging his head around to face Graf Aleksis.

'My lord, I...' Aleksis began before Kherhart cut him off

with a brass walking stick jabbed in the chest. If it weren't for the graf's body armour he might have sustained a nasty, sucking chest wound.

'Look what you've done to my domains!' Governor Kherhart shrieked, the sudden and unexpected outburst making several of the gathered officers flinch. 'I approved no more than a reconnaissance and now look! The entire place is in anarchy!'

'With respect, my lord,' Flint interrupted, 'it was like that when we got here.'

'And who are you?' Kherhart rounded on Flint. He leaned right forward, his impossibly wrinkled face pushed uncomfortably close as he looked Flint up and down. 'Commissar is it, eh?'

'*Regimental* commissar,' he answered. 'Flint.'

'Well, Commissar Flint,' Kherhart sneered. 'You and Aleksis here and all of the rest of you can just clear out of my facility, do you understand?'

'Clear out?' Aleksis blurted before Flint could respond, causing the governor to swing back around to face him. 'The commissar here has located the rebels' lair, my lord. We were hoping you would acquiesce to an immediate assault upon it, so that we–'

'No!' Lord Kherhart screeched in response. 'I will not *acquiesce*! You will leave here, this instant, do you–'

The remainder of Lord Kherhart's words were drowned out by a sharp explosion nearby. The blast wave ripped at the canvas awning and fragments of shrapnel pattered from the hull of the graf's command track. The officers ducked for whatever cover they could find while Claviger-Primaris Gruss appeared out of nowhere accompanied by several other wardens and formed a protective circle about the governor. A moment later the chief warden was bundling his master back towards his transport and was lost to Flint's sight.

'Bukin?' Flint bellowed, striding out from under the awning to be greeted with the sight of a huge, orange fireball blossoming upwards just a few hundred metres away. 'What the hell was that?'

The chief provost was nearby, Vahn at his side as staff officers ran to and fro. 'Looks like one of our tracks went up, sir,' he shouted over the raging of flames, the wind and the rain. 'Must be rebels in the wire!'

'Vahn,' Flint shouted over the rising pandemonium gripping the command post. 'Muster your men and get them here. Go!'

Vahn nodded and was gone, leaving Flint with Provost Bukin. 'Can't say I'm surprised,' he muttered.

'Sir?' said Bukin, shielding his eyes from the rain as he squinted towards the roiling flames and the column of black smoke rapidly rising into the air.

'He's counter-attacking,' Flint shouted.

'Who is, sir?' Bukin bawled in response.

'Strannik,' Flint shouted. 'That's what I'd do!'

Another explosion blossomed nearby and a Chimera less than fifty metres distant lifted into the air, flipped onto its side and came to rest on its back with flames consuming both fuel tanks. Muzzle flares lashed out of the darkness overhead as figures appeared on gantries that the head-quarters security platoon had declared secure. Flint saw Vostroyans cut down where they stood, unaware of the danger from above and he shouted a warning to get behind cover. Las-fire erupted all around, competing with the deep, resounding boom of combat shotguns and handmade jun-kers. A great roar filled the air, a sound Flint had grown all but accustomed to during the battle in the sluice chamber. It was the sound of a horde of rebels attacking in numbers greater even than they had back then.

Vahn reappeared with the remainder of the penal troop at his back. The soldiers were struggling to pull on armour and backpacks only recently set down and most appeared not to have slept a wink.

'What the...' Vahn started as he came to a halt beside Flint and Bukin. 'Oh frag...'

FIFTEEN
Revelation

With an explosive release of stinging luminescent liquid, Kohlz awoke, rolling onto his side and vomiting the chemical gruel across the rockcrete floor. Every muscle in his body screamed with pain and his bones felt like they'd been pulped. Still, he wasn't quite convinced he was actually alive until the painful dry heaving finally ended and his eyes stopped streaming long enough to see clearly.

Hauling himself up onto his elbows, Kohlz realised that the ridiculously heavy Number Four vox-set was still strapped firmly to his back. Punching the release catch at the centre of his chest he shrugged the hated thing off and let it drop hard to the ground as he struggled painfully to his feet.

'Where the hell...' he started as he looked all about. He was at the base of some manner of shaft, a small circle of light visible twenty metres or so above. He'd come to rest on a slim ledge at the side of a sluice channel, the filthy waters having deposited him there safely against all the odds.

Safely, except that to escape he would have to climb yet another set of corroded rungs. For a brief moment Kohlz seriously considered just sitting back down and waiting this one out but the idea was a fleeting one that soon left his mind. Besides, he thought, aside from the vox-set he had no one to talk to.

'Oh fu...' he began, realising that he'd dropped the vox-set so heavily it might no longer be functional. His heart suddenly pounding at the thought of being left alone at the bottom of the drainage shaft, he bent over the Number Four and folded back its canvas protective covering. 'Come on...' he implored the device.

Throwing the main power rune he was greeted by the sound of churning static. 'Thank the Grey Lady!' he blurted out deliriously. 'Thank Her I wasn't dumb enough to get a Number Twelve...' There was no way he could get a signal where he was, but at least the vox-set was functioning. He was as certain as he could be that he'd be able to transmit from the top of the shaft.

Then Kohlz heard something out of place, a sound from high overhead that brought his head up slowly towards the circle of light that formed the mouth of the shaft. 'What the hell...' he muttered, straining to hear more over the rush of water and the hiss of static. Cocking his head, he concentrated on the noise. It sounded disturbingly like an odd combination of animalistic grunting and the creak of old leather.

Something Trooper Solomon had said many times over the last few days came to Kohlz's mind as he bent over, deactivated the vox-set and shrugged it back over his shoulders. 'Why me?' he mumbled as he cautiously took hold of the lowest of the ladder rungs. Given that the last one he relied upon had given up on him and cast him into a raging flood and almost drowned him in the process, he tested it first, making sure it was firmly set in the rockcrete.

Reasonably satisfied, Kohlz climbed slowly up the dark shaft, concentrating all the way on the sounds emanating from above. The higher he climbed the louder the noises became until he was dreading actually seeing what might be causing them. His body had yet to even start to recover from the harm done to it by the flood and he was sure he'd be covered in livid bruises when all this was over and by the time he neared the top his muscles were screaming for respite. At the last, he halted just below the lip, his ears filled with the hideous sounds.

Swallowing hard, he raised his head and peered out.

The sight that greeted him made him wish he'd taken his chances with the sluice and been washed further on into the bowels of the geotherm sinks. He was at the northern end of Carceri *Resurecti*, that much he could tell by the sight of the cliff-like wall and the many openings through which the force had climbed previously to infiltrate the stronghold up above. From out of those openings came a steady stream of hideously deformed figures, some massively large and machine-augmented, others small and twisted. Hundreds, probably thousands of the creatures were staggering and trudging south across the open ground and the sound Kohlz had heard earlier was their mute mumbling and the flexing of their vile musculature.

'Mutants…' Kohlz breathed. Hundreds upon hundreds of mutants, dredged up from the darkest bowels of the geotherm sinks.

'These must be the ones we saw in the stronghold!' Flint yelled into his vox-pickup as he ducked into the cover of a burned out Salamander, its shattered armour still radiating heat. 'They're properly armed with weapons taken from the clavigers,' he continued. 'They aren't the cannon fodder we faced at the sluice chamber!'

'Understood, commissar,' Graf Aleksis's voice came back through Flint's earpiece, barely audible through the interference and the constant barrage of gunfire all around. Yes, Flint was sure of it. The rebel convicts attacking the regiment were well armed and they were organised into squads and platoons, just like the formations Flint had seen during the infiltration of the stronghold.

That being the case however, Flint was wondering where the rebel colonel, Strannik, might be.

Leaning out from behind his cover Flint sought to decipher the enemy's deployment, to fathom the centre of the formation's mass and where its commander might be directing it from. The scene before him was hazy with the weight of rain pounding the ground and the light levels were at an all time low, yet he could make out dark shapes running from the cover of one machine edifice or pile of debris to the next.

One group was engaging First Company almost a kilometre to the west. Another, larger mass was probing towards the east where its leading edge was contacting Third and Fourth Companies along with elements of the support echelons. If I were the overall commander, Flint thought, and I had nothing in the way of vox, I'd be… over there, advancing in the lee of that twenty-metre tall piston housing.

'Vahn?' Flint shouted back towards the penal troopers huddled behind a line of tracked supply wagons belonging to the assault pioneer platoon. 'Get ready to move out!'

'Come on, come on, come on…' Kohlz muttered as he worked the dials and switches of his Number Four. Hanging from the ladder just below the lip of the shaft with hundreds of vile mutants swarming past scant metres away, it really wasn't easy.

'Come *on!*' He repeated through gritted teeth. A line of red lights turned green, telling him the set had achieved machine communion with a transmitting station. 'Yes!' he hissed as he raised the horn to speak.

But before he'd said a word his headset phones spat into life and a voice cut through the static-laced feedback.

'…aren't willing to do as I say, cousin,' the voice said. Kohlz froze and lifted his thumb from the transmit rune. 'He refuses to honour his familial duty, thanks to that damned commissar…'

That got Kohlz's attention and he worked the dials to get a clearer channel.

'Very well,' a second voice replied. 'I anticipated such a

turn of events. I have mustered the… inmates, of the under-sinks. They are inbound now.'

'Are you…' the first voice stammered. '…are you sure that's, er, wise…?'

'*Cousin!*' the second voice hissed, the tone coldly intimidating to Kohlz even though he wasn't its target. 'You will listen to me and you will heed my words, do you understand?' When there was no reply the voice continued. 'I do not care if every one of my followers is slain, I do not care if this entire complex burns down around me, but I have told you, I shall not submit to them. I cannot, and not just for my sake, you know that, Kherhart, it's for the sake of the entire damned line, understood?'

Kherhart? Kohlz was stunned. The first voice was the governor of Furia Penitens. Not just the lord of Alpha Penitentia, but the Imperial Commander of the entire world.

So who then was he speaking to?

'Understood, cousin Strannik,' Kherhart replied, his voice petulant and defeated. 'Then I see I have no choice but to leave if you are set on your course of action.'

Strannik? Kohlz almost lost his footing on the ladder and was forced to grab hold of another rung. He almost dropped the vox-horn in the process, his breath short and his blood pounding in his ears.

'Do what you must, kinsman,' Strannik replied. 'Be gone. I am unleashing the under-sink host now. Our traitorous kinsman and his regiment won't know what hit them, cousin. Within the hour, they'll be dead. Every last one of them.'

* * *

'Khave,' Vahn hissed from the shadows at Flint's side. 'He's mine.'

'The Catachan?' Flint replied as he leaned out from his hiding place behind a huge storage tank that had been torn open by multiple heavy bolter rounds. 'Then make it quick, we don't have time for personal vendettas.'

'Understood,' Vahn replied and a moment later he had the detachment up and running. Flint could see the unfettered hatred etched on the face of each penal trooper as they dashed by his position. It was clear that the penal troopers were kept going far beyond the point of exhaustion by a motivating force Flint hadn't yet considered. It wasn't duty or honour that was keeping the ragtag group going – it was hatred. Hatred of every rival convict that had been part of the uprising they themselves had chosen not to participate in.

Out of a population that had numbered in the tens or hundreds of thousands before the uprising, that small group represented the last few souls who had, for whatever reason chosen not to surrender to the bloodshed and anarchy that the rebel Colonel Strannik had unleashed upon Alpha Penitentia. He'd thought they were following *him*. Instead, as they charged past with their carbines raised and mouths roaring unspeakable oaths of vengeance, Flint decided *he* would follow *them*.

Flint broke cover and joined the mad charge towards the enemy lines. Bukin bellowed something from behind but he ignored the chief provost. Then Bukin was beside him, he too surrendering himself to the mad rush.

As Flint steeled himself the first shots rang out. Vahn and

his fellow penal troopers fired their carbines from the hip as they advanced at full pelt through the rain and many had attached bayonets in preparation for the charge hitting home. Flint's world was reduced to a tunnel of las-fire and rushing bodies and the blinding white lances of the carbines were soon competing with a heavy weight of return fire. The detachment had the advantage of surprise but as it closed on its target, the Catachan and the rebels he was leading started to recover and fire back.

The first of the penal troopers went down. A scream of frustration and pain split the air so loudly it competed with the *whip-crack* of carbines and the thunderous report of the rebels' crude firearms. The man fell at Flint's feet and he had no choice but to vault over him. Landing heavily, his power sword instinctively raised to the guard position, he found himself face to face with the Catachan.

The enemy roared, filling the air with a blasphemous curse and swung his shotgun like a heavy club. Flint ducked back from the clumsy attack but before he could advance another came in. The Catachan was far quicker than a man of his bulk had any right being.

Flint parried without thinking and his power sword's white-hot, monomolecular edge scythed the improvised club clean in two. The Catachan's already ugly face twisted into a hideous mask of hate and he flung the two halves of his ruined weapon to the ground with a savage curse.

The charge was hitting home all around Flint, Vahn's penal troopers surrendering themselves to the hatred and fury that had built up within them since the first slaughter-filled days of the uprising. Facing off against the Catachan, Flint glanced quickly left and right and saw the troopers engaged in bitter, one-on-one fights to the death.

He saw Becka strike an ape-faced rebel hard in the side of the head with the butt of her carbine then reverse the weapon in her hands to stab the bayonet savagely up into her enemy's guts. The Savlar screamed something in the man's face as he fell at her heavy-booted feet, comparing his features to those of a simian and casting aspirations on his parental legitimacy.

Trooper Skane, the big Elysian, was wrestling with a huge enemy with metal studs crudely mounted in his bald skull and other scraps of metal protruding from his heavily mus-cled body. The two men were soon locked in a death-grip only one of them could possibly win. Skane's foe pulled back his head, the whipcord muscles of his grox-like neck tensing like steel cables. An instant later he drove his stud-ded head straight towards Skane's but the Elysian was ready and rolled sideways at the last possible moment. The rebel's head slammed into the wet rockcrete ground and sent up a spray of rainwater mingled with blood.

Trooper Vendell, the one-eared Voyn's Reacher, had cast his carbine aside and was sat astride a screaming, desper-ately squirming rebel. His knees clamped around the man's head as he drove his thumbs down into, and through, the eye sockets.

Trooper Stank, the Asgardian, had been cut across both cheeks by a crude, serrated knife wielded by an impossi-bly skeletal but preternaturally fast rebel convict. But the

Asgardian was faster and fuelled by a thirst for vengeance his opponent could never match. Stank twisted sideways and in a flash his enemy's blade was in his hand. Another flash, of steel and blood, and the knife was in his enemy's throat right up to the hilt.

Even Solomon, the lanky Jopalli *indenti*, was there in the thick of it along with over two-dozen more penal troopers whose names Flint had yet to learn. Solomon had his beloved sniper rifle slung over his back and had drawn a laspistol with which he was gunning rebels down at shockingly close range.

Flint looked around for Vahn but the Catachan lunging forwards snapped his attention back to the fore. He drew his power sword back and tensed his body in preparation to strike when he was pushed hard from the side.

'He's mine!' Vahn shouted, drawing a curse from Flint's lips as the commissar was knocked almost off of his feet.

'What the hell?' Flint snarled, turning to see that Vahn was already engaging the Catachan. His dreadlocks streaming behind him like a ragged mane, Vahn screamed and drove forward with his bayonet-tipped carbine. The Catachan ducked left and by his own move, Vahn had expected him to duck the other way. A meaty fist came out of nowhere and slammed into the side of Vahn's head and he only just managed to roll with the blow sufficiently to avoid it breaking his neck.

Seeing that Vahn was outclassed, Flint began circling around toward the Catachan's blind spot. Vahn growled a stream of incoherent curses but he had the sense to circle around the Catachan in the opposite direction to Flint.

But the Catachan wasn't stupid, despite all appearances to the contrary. He did exactly what Flint would have done in the same circumstances, and dived forwards onto Vahn before Flint could get behind him. The last blow must have dazed the penal trooper for he reacted too slowly to dodge the Catachan's two-handed grasp for his neck. He went down screaming, his mouth twisted into a savage, animalistic snarl as he dropped his carbine and attempted to lever his enemy's girder-thick wrists away.

No chance, Flint thought, knowing the Catachan would snap Vahn's neck within seconds.

'Vahn!' Flint bellowed over the chaos of battle and the pounding rain. 'Twist!'

Not waiting to see if Vahn had understood, or even heard, his order, Flint reversed his grip on his power sword's basket hilt and lunged forwards, the Catachan's rippling back firmly in his sights. He caught a glimpse of Vahn's face, his eyes bulging from pain or panic, he couldn't tell which.

With a snarl, Flint drove his power sword into the Catachan's back, forcing it through the mass of sinew and muscle. As the blade plunged into the man's innards Vahn twisted and an instant later the sword was sunk all the way to its hilt. With a shout, Flint twisted the blade and drove it straight upwards, through the Catachan's upper torso, and out of his right collarbone.

His torso split in two, a fountain of blood spat upwards as the two halves peeled apart. Gore spattered at Flint's feet and the body finally collapsed, its eviscerated organs tumbling forth.

'Frag!' Vahn spat, looking up at Flint from the butchered corpse on the ground between them.

'Commissar Flint?' The commissar heard in his ear.

'What?' said Flint as he fought for breath, his heart pounding after the exertion of the deathblow.

'That was...' said Vahn as he fought to regain his own breath having been choked almost to death.

'Commissar Flint?' the voice repeated.

His mind catching up and his head clearing of the battle lust that had driven him through the last few seconds, Flint raised a hand to silence Vahn.

'Flint here,' he said into his vox-pickup. 'Who's there?'

'Dragoon Kohlz, sir,' the voice said. 'Commissar Flint, you've got multiple...'

'What?' Flint demanded, thinking for a moment the confusion of combat and the pounding rain had addled his mind. 'Repeat last, over.'

'I said, this is Dragoon Kohlz, commissar. Listen, please, I don't have time to explain, sir, but you have multiple mutants closing towards you, and–'

'Mutants?' Flint demanded, recalling the two abominations he had already faced.

'Yes, sir, mutants,' Kohlz pressed. 'Thousands of–'

'Mutants...' Flint growled. '*Filthy* mutants...' Glancing around, Vahn's penal troopers had slaughtered the majority of the Catachan's fellow rebels and the rest were scattering. But Flint knew it wouldn't last long.

'Vahn, Bukin!' he shouted. Vahn looked half dead. Bukin looked like he'd been enjoying himself. 'Get the detachment ready to move out, right away,' he barked, wiping blood and rain from his eyes with the back of his hand.

'Where are we going, sir?' Bukin replied.

'We need to find the colonel,' Flint said. 'Right now, or this is all over.'

It took Flint and his small force the best part of twenty minutes to locate Graf Aleksis and his staff, and as he did so, Kohlz filled in the spaces in his report and provided a running description of what he was seeing. By the time Flint had pushed his way through the bustling staff manning the graf's command post he had a good idea what was going on and he was utterly livid.

'You won't deny it?' he thundered at Graf Aleksis, his rage incandescent. 'The leader of this rebellion is,' he paused for breath, 'is your own *cousin*?'

'I will not deny it, Commissar Flint,' Aleksis replied, his command post falling silent with shock. In a moment, only the rain pounding the awning overhead and the sound of ominously close gunfire was audible. 'He is, as you say, my cousin.'

'And when were you going to tell me this?' Flint raged. No wonder, he seethed inwardly, the archive on Strannik was sealed.

'In truth,' the graf replied defiantly as he faced off against the furious commissar, 'I was hoping to deal with the matter without sullying my clan's good name.'

'Your clan's…?' Flint spat incredulously, the ignominious fate of the 77th's predecessors forcing its way into his consciousness. 'You gave me your word, graf. You swore you would not repeat the sins of your forebears and allow your loyalties to be split–'

'I understand your reaction, commissar,' Aleksis insisted, 'But rest assured, I have every intention of bringing my… cousin, to account for his deeds.'

Flint was about to retort with a barbed reply when he saw something in the graf's expression that made him hold his tongue. He nodded for Aleksis to continue.

'This sort of thing…' Aleksis started, uncertainly at first but with increased resolution as he spoke. 'It is normally dealt with by way of certain… formalities.'

'Meaning?' Flint replied.

'Meaning,' Aleksis went on, 'we of the Anhalz Techtriarchs prefer to keep our own house in order, and not involve outside parties.'

Flint fixed the graf with an ice-cold stare, weighing up the man's future on the balance of his words. 'You do realise, graf,' he growled, his words punctuated by the heavy rain, 'that I could have not just your regiment for this. I could have your life.'

Aleksis held Flint's gaze a moment, before replying. 'Yes, commissar. I am very much aware of the extent of your powers.'

In that moment, Flint's mind was made up. 'Then prove it.'

'I intend to, commissar, believe me. I intend to clear this entire damned installation of every last rebel scum lurking within it,' he growled, his voice low and vengeful. 'It was one of my clan that started this and so it is I who must end it,' he concluded.

'This Strannik,' Flint replied. 'If he's one of your Techtriarch clan, why is he here, in Alpha Penitentia?'

A number of the senior officers looked to one another uncomfortably and Polzdam opened his mouth to object. But Aleksis raised a hand to forestall any interruption and answered Flint's question. 'He's here because he deserves to be, commissar.'

'Meaning?' asked Flint, growing impatient to end the discussion with the abominations Kohlz had reported closing all the while.

'You have read that the 77th was destroyed at Golan Hole, that there were no survivors,' Aleksis said darkly.

'Sir!' Polzdam interjected.

'No!' Graf Aleksis rounded on his executive officer with a savage burst of anger. 'This cannot go on! It *shall* not go on. Commissar Flint will have the truth of it, and you shall not say a word more, unless you want me to call the provosts, understood?'

Polzdam fumed silently, but said no more.

'The records of the Battle of Golan Hole state that every last member of the 77th perished...'

'The records lie?' said Flint.

'The records were doctored. One individual survived.'

'Strannik,' Flint said coldly.

'*Graf* Strannik,' said Aleksis. 'My kinsman, and my predecessor as colonel of the 77th Vostroyan Firstborn.'

'How?' Flint asked. 'And why was he imprisoned?'

'How, I cannot fully explain, though I suspect his crimes extend beyond the moral. I believe that he has manifested certain... abilities, deemed blasphemous by the creed we all share.'

'So he's a mutant,' said Flint. 'Are you suggesting he's manifested psychic powers too?' If that was the case this mission might not be completed without the intervention of an Ordo Hereticus strike force, and that would escalate matters by an entire order of magnitude.

'Possibly,' said Aleksis. 'I cannot be sure. But as to the second part of your question, he is here because he has sufficient rank to have the death sentence such crimes should lead to commuted. He is a traitor and a coward. His actions led to the destruction of the 77th, and he is a mutant and an unsanctioned psyker. Believe me, I intend to settle this–'

'And the prison governor is his kinsman,' Flint interrupted.

'Indeed,' Aleksis replied dejectedly.

With time running out and it being futile to press the matter further, Flint changed tack. 'Graf Aleksis,' he announced, loudly enough for every officer nearby to hear clearly. 'We have a mountain to climb, and an abominable enemy to defeat if any of us are to see the daylight again.'

'I suggest you gather your officers, Aleksis, and issue a warning order. I suggest this regiment gets advancing, sir, right now.'

Dragoon Kohlz had been following the mutant horde for what felt like hours, always close enough to be sure of its course yet never so close that his presence might be discovered. Had he been seen, he would have been torn limb from limb or eaten alive by the unutterably vile creatures of the mutant horde. The young Firstborn's deeds went unrecorded, for there was no one else there to write up a citation. In balance however, this was a good thing, for there was one deed that Kohlz would never want written up in any form of communiqué.

Kohlz had tracked the horde for over an hour and had only just avoided detection by a gang of stooped, ghoulish fiends with mouths dripping with congealed blood when the familiar silhouette of a Vostroyan Firstborn warrior loomed in the shadowed entrance of a waste grinder, just like the one the infiltration force had been forced to travel through hours before. The shaggy fur headgear and the long, crimson coat were unmistakable, and it was all Kohlz could do to stop himself calling out to his kinsman.

It was fortunate indeed that he didn't, for the twisted ghoul creatures appeared to have picked up the other Firstborn's scent and were looping back to investigate. Kohlz ducked into the cover of a wrecked flatbed cargo hauler and was just about to open a channel on the personal vox-net when he realised the identity of the trooper emerging from the tunnel. It was Dragoon Slavast – better known in the ranks of the 77th as 'Slug'. Immediately, the bruises earned at the hands of Slug and his goons just a few days before started throbbing as bitterness and shame at the beating he had received swelled inside.

His eyes narrowing as he watched, Kohlz saw that Slug

wasn't alone. He was leading his squad and several of the meatheads were further inside the tunnel, struggling with boxes of heavy ammo. Obviously they had been tasked with bringing fresh ammunition to the fighting units, but they were shirking that duty like the cowards they truly were.

Kohlz lifted his thumb from the vox-switch, deciding against warning his fellow troopers of the imminent danger. Even as he watched from the shadows, the ghouls closed across the open chamber floor, and it was only at the last that Slug caught sight of them.

Instead of standing and fighting like they had been trained to do, the squad fell back into the tunnel, compounding their crime of cowardice with that of dereliction of duty as they dropped the ammunition and fled.

With a blood-curdling shriek, the ghoulish mutants dashed by Kohlz's hiding place, so close he could see the pallid translucency of their shrivelled, filth-encrusted hides. An instant later, they were pressing cautiously into the waste grinder, sniffing the damp ground as they followed the scent of Slug and his fellows.

His mind suddenly clear, Dragoon Kohlz broke cover and dashed for the opening of the waste grinder. A moment later he was by its mouth, the sound of shouting emanating from within. It sounded very much like Slug and his goons were attempting to call for help over the personal vox-net, and a blinking telltale on his set confirmed it.

Whichever station was receiving Slug's distress call, it was never completed. Kohlz slammed his fist down upon the waste grinder's activation rune, causing the toothed, metal walls of the tunnel to stir into sudden motion. A roar like that of a million gears shifting as one blasted from the tunnel mouth, followed a moment later by the twitching gristle that had once been the ghoul-like mutants and the half a dozen Firstborn, mingled together into a steaming gruel of mangled flesh and shattered bone.

Kohlz slammed his fist down on the rune a second time, the gears disengaging with a wet, metallic rumble. Hefting his heavy vox-set, he resumed his pursuit of the mutant horde, resolving never to say a word of Slug's fate.

SIXTEEN
Judgement

The charge of the 77th Vostroyan Firstborn Dragoons was, as Graf Aleksis had said it would be, a glorious thing indeed. Dozens of Chimeras formed into a line several kilometres wide straddling the centre of the southern end of Carceri *Resurecti* and advanced through the driving rain to meet the mutant horde head on. The vast darkness of the carceri chamber was lit as bright as day as the Chimeras' heavy weapons opened up on the shambling, howling mass of abominations seething across the floor. Heavy artillery, following the main push in bounding advances, lobbed hundreds of high explosive shells overhead, their passage as loud as a freight conveyor and their detonations sending limbs and greasy, black smoke arcing high into the air.

Commissar Flint was riding high in the turret of one of the HQ Company's Chimeras, every one of the regiment's armoured vehicles advancing and every one of its guns blazing away at the horde up ahead. The acid rain stung his eyes and the already polluted air was tainted further by the discharge of so many weapons. The roar of engines made communication all but impossible in his exposed position, but Flint no longer had need to communicate. Kohlz had given him the last piece of information he needed.

Following in the wake of the horde, an act of extreme courage for which Flint had already decided his aide would be commended, Kohlz had maintained a continuous reconnaissance. Eventually, he had located the target Flint had ordered him to find and reported his sighting back to the commissar.

Colonel Strannik.

As the line of Chimeras closed to within a hundred metres of the enemy, Flint finally got a close look at the creatures the force was up against. The shambling mutants were obviously related to the two he had faced already, yet those two must have been the more controllable of the mass for the rest appeared a riot of screeching, thrashing limbs and gaping maws. Each was at least as tall as an ogryn but represented no stable abhuman strain. These mutants were grotesquely malformed, each limb a different size. Some hauled themselves along on massively oversized arms, their legs so atrophied they couldn't even walk. Others were all barrel-shaped, contorted torso, arms and legs jutting out at improbable angles. Some had limbs protruding from entirely the wrong point of their bodies, creating the overall impression of a wall of disjointed muscle and flesh surging across the chamber floor.

Flint bellowed a prayer to ward off the foulness of genetic corruption, most of his words snatched away by the rush of air and the roar of bullets but enough of them getting through to his vox-pickup that the rest of the regiment could hear and take heart. Captain Bohman, the chief of signals, relayed Flint's words through the regimental vox-net and every dragoon in the 77th Firstborn heard him as they charged towards their foe.

As the range closed, Flint opened fire with his pintle-mount, keeping up his tirade of zealous invective even though he couldn't even hear his own words. The heavy stubber spat a stream of fire towards the line of mutant flesh and he was gratified to see torsos exploding and limbs cartwheeling overhead. Soon Flint could make out individual faces and he was struck by an almost overwhelming sense of revulsion. He had reached the conclusion that these mutants must have bred, or been bred, in the deepest, darkest geotherm sinks beneath the penal generatorium, though from what corrupted stock he had yet to discover. The heat that drove the generatoria was derived from the radioactive decay of sub-surface minerals, so perhaps that had something to do with the obscene process. Whatever the cause, their very existence was a blasphemy against the God-Emperor of Mankind. Once more, Flint would be the instrument of judgement.

Finally, the charge of the 77th Vostroyan Firstborn Dragoons struck home. The wall of steel met the wall of flesh and battle was joined.

The Chimeras ground through and over the first ranks of

the teeming mutant horde, crushing hundreds to gristly pulp within seconds. But despite the devastation those mutants not slain in the first few seconds threw themselves forward without fear or hesitation as if compelled beyond reason to tear down all that was pure and unsullied by corruption in the world. Flint angled his heavy stubber almost straight down, firing continuously with no need to aim. An ocean of thrashing limbs and rippling muscle surged beneath him, grossly distended claws reaching up like breaking waves to pull him down. The sound was nigh deafening and the stench was beyond description. It was like the mutants had gestated within an irradiated, amniotic sack swelled with chemical fluids in which a million corpses had slowly rotted and their otherwise naked bodies were smeared with all manner of unimaginable filth.

The Chimeras ground onward into that undulating sea of mutant flesh, firing hull and turret weapons without pause. Top hatches swung outwards by prearranged order and the men and women of the 77th rose from the armoured troop bays and took position atop their transports. Lasguns, flamers, plasma guns and grenade launchers were discharged at all but point-blank range, often right into the howling faces of the enemy who were attempting to swarm up and over the Chimeras.

Gunning their engines against the sheer force of the press of mutant bodies, the drivers pressed on. Though a seemingly crude tactic, the attack was in essence a classic heavy cavalry charge. The drivers were under orders to press on at all costs, to break through the horde before turning around and hitting it again. They couldn't stop, for to do so would be to shed momentum and then all would be lost. Even when dragoons were pulled screaming from fighting compartments to be dragged into the horde still they couldn't stop. Even when vehicles were swamped and disappeared beneath a wave of thrashing corruption, they had to keep on going.

Almost as soon as the armoured assault crashed home it was breaking through the other side of the mutant horde. Flint spun the cupola about just in time to witness the bloody path his Chimera had crushed through the mass of bodies disappear as the mutants pressed in. Several nearby Chimeras were overrun by howling mutant abominations and the dragoons within torn limb from limb, but there was nothing he could do – the plan was all.

Ahead of the advance was an open area of the carceri chamber floor dominated by a high platform resembling an oversized gallows. Fittingly, the platform was the control pulpit for the surface-to-orbit weapons battery that had shot Flint's drop-ship down what seemed like weeks earlier. It was Flint's target, because Kohlz had reported it was where Colonel Strannik waited, watching and directing his blasphemous horde as it surged across the chamber.

Flint drew his bolt pistol and checked its action. He'd only had the time to scare up a single spare magazine. Let that be sufficient, he prayed to the Emperor. Let your will be done…

Reaching a prearranged phase line, the entire wave of Chimeras and other armoured vehicles slowed and by companies turned back to face the way they had come. The only vehicle that didn't halt was Flint's, which carried himself, his aide, Vahn and the best of his penal troopers. The driver followed his orders to press on for the towering weapons control platform at all costs. Flint holstered his bolt pistol and dropped through his hatch into the Chimera's red-lit troop bay.

A dozen faces looked back at him, their expressions grim but determined.

'Ready?' he shouted over the roar of the Chimera's engines.

'Go!' Vahn barked as the Chimera's assault ramp slammed into the ground. An instant later, Becka, Solomon, Vendell, Skane, Stank and the rest were charging out of the vehicle's troop bay and into the rain and the all-consuming darkness outside. At a nod from Commissar Flint, Vahn followed his fellow penal troopers out into the open area beneath the target platform. Weapons control, the rebel colonel's seat of power and, so Flint had ordered, the site of his execution.

The air was alive with unreal etheric energy, seething arcs chasing up and down the metal structure of the weapons control platform. It was as if the tower was the very epicentre of the storm, though it was far from calm. The air was so charged the hair on the back of Vahn's neck stood on end and his skin itched maddeningly.

'Move!' Vahn bellowed, knowing they had no time to waste. Already, the line of Chimeras was opening up again, pouring fire into the raging horde, which had changed direction and was surging back towards the regiment's lines.

Within minutes, what had been the horde's rear rank and was now its leading edge would crash against the Imperial Guard lines and the slaughter would begin afresh. The 77th was wreaking bloody ruin on the mutants but it couldn't stand forever.

Vahn's squad rushed the base of the control tower, rebel convicts emerging from amongst its girders and conduits. Becka was by his side the whole way, an avenging angel of scorn and fury. The penal troopers opened fire, discharging carbines from the hip as they ran for the metal steps leading upwards. A snarling brute of a man emerged from the shadows and lunged straight for the commissar. Karasinda, who Vahn hadn't even realised was nearby, put a las-bolt through the rebel's left eye without breaking stride. A dozen more rebels were cut down within seconds, and soon Vahn's squad was pounding up the open metal stairwell, carbines raised into the darkness above as they advanced.

His heart racing, Vahn mounted the steps, Becka just a step behind as the tread plate rang at their passing. Commissar Flint was close behind, his power sword drawn and a prayer that could be heard even above the roar of gunfire and rain on his lips. Vahn and Becka took the stairs three at a time, the need to end this madness all but consuming them. Vahn's hatred for those who had led the uprising drove him on despite his fatigue until finally, he and his fellow penal troopers mounted the last few steps and charged out onto the carceri control platform.

Gale force winds buffeted Vahn as he stepped out onto the open space, rain lashing his face mercilessly. Squinting

against the onslaught he realised the platform was far
higher than he had imagined from the base, rearing above
the sea of mutant flesh far below. It was long and narrow,
the far end obscured by the rain and a mass of machinery.
Weapons control stations lined the central space, but all
were long dead, their machine-spirits extinct and none of
their original custodians alive to operate them. He cast
around for his target with his carbine raised and a figure
appeared out of the rain in the centre of the platform, its
features obscured by shadow.

No, Vahn realised. Not by shadow. By a blank mask.

'Gruss…' Becka hissed in warning, the other penal troopers loosing their own curses as they emerged from the
stairwell and spread out behind Vahn.

The Claviger-Primaris stood defiantly in the centre of the
wind- and rain-lashed control platform but made no reply.
Instead, he raised his right hand and levelled his snub-nosed
plasma pistol past Vahn to a target behind the penal trooper.

'Commissar Flint,' Gruss said, his voice amplified above
the raging storm by the phonocasters mounted in his black
hardshell armour. 'Leave this place now. You hold no
authority here.'

Bitterness threatening to overwhelm him, Vahn looked
sideways as Flint stepped up to stand beside him and Becka.
'What…' he started, before Flint interrupted him.

'Gruss!' Flint shouted over the wind and the rain. 'Stand
aside. It's him I've come for. He's Guard, and this is Commissariat business.'

Flint stood his ground even though the Claviger-Primaris had the plasma gun pointed straight at his head. In truth, Flint didn't expect the chief warden of Alpha Penitentia to surrender Colonel Strannik, but he needed time to formulate a plan.

'How is this any of your business?' Gruss spat, his pistol tracking Flint as he edged sideways to get a better view of the figure that lurked at the end of the platform some distance behind the Claviger-Primaris. 'Last chance, commissar,' he said, jerking his pistol for emphasis.

'You don't want to do this, Gruss,' Flint said, stalling for the last few seconds of time. 'Your duty is to the Imperium, not to this corrupted clan.'

'What *clan*…?' Flint heard Vahn stammer from behind him. '*Corrupted*…?'

'The Anhalz Techtriarchs of Vostroya,' Flint growled. 'And all their damned progeny.' With that he made a sweeping gesture that took in the entire floor of the carceri chamber and the thousands of abominations swarming across it. 'A noble clan I'm sure,' he continued. 'But one with more than a few *secrets*, wouldn't you say?'

'All you had to do,' Gruss snarled, his voice distorted by his armour's systems. 'All you had to do was let *us* deal with it…'

Flint saw what would happen next and he dove suddenly to his right. An instant later a searing ball of plasma screamed by overhead, the leather of his storm coat's back blistering so intense was the heat. He struck the metal of the platform's surface right at its edge and for an instant was staring straight down towards a mass of thrashing, mutated limbs as the horde crashed against the 77th's lines far below.

A las-bolt whined by as Karasinda opened fire on Gruss. Flint rolled back from the edge of the platform and leapt to his feet, drawing his power blade as he did so. Gruss was moving back along the thin arm of the platform towards a mass of weapons control stations, writhing cables and unidentifiable machinery at its end. In just a few seconds the chief warden's plasma pistol would be recharged and he would unleash another potentially devastating shot. This time, Flint doubted he would miss.

It was now or never. Flint raised his power sword and pressed along the increasingly narrow arm of the control platform, the wind and rain threatening to pitch him into the ocean of mutated blasphemy raging far below. He heard the unmistakable high-pitched whine of the plasma pistol reaching full power. A shadow emerged from behind the mass of machinery at the very end of the arm, and Flint ducked.

At that moment, the driving rain redoubled in force and Flint lost his footing, slamming to the surface of the platform, which by now was little more than a narrow gantry. He hit the metal so hard the air was driven from his lungs. Grasping desperately for purchase he almost lost his grip on his power sword, catching it an instant before it could drop into the chaos of the battle far below.

Vahn pressed after the commissar, edging out onto the narrow arm at the exact moment the commissar fell hard to the surface. In that instant Vahn was sure Flint was dead, but somehow the commissar kept hold. Gruss had fled towards the end of the arm but as the penal trooper dashed forwards with his carbine raised and ready he saw the Claviger-Primaris appear from behind the machinery at the very end of the arm.

His plasma pistol screeching, Gruss sighted on the prone form of the commissar. Vahn snarled with savage battle lust – Gruss hadn't seen him. Snapping his aim to track the Claviger-Primaris even as his finger closed on the plasma pistol's trigger, Vahn opened fire.

The las-bolt caught Gruss in the right shoulder and spun him around. The incandescent burst of raw plasma lanced through the rain into the darkness overhead. Gruss staggered backwards, fighting to keep his footing on the narrow arm.

Vahn lined up a second shot, determined to finish this hated enemy who was to him and his fellow penal troopers the symbol of all he had suffered throughout his incarceration in Alpha Penitentia. But his aim was spoiled as Commissar Flint surged to his feet in a blur of trailing leather storm coat.

Vahn cursed as he sidestepped. He hoped to get a better angle but Flint and Gruss were already engaged in deadly combat. Flint's blade swept in hard but Gruss stepped back deftly despite his wound, kicking out as he did so and almost catching Flint's knee. Had the attack struck home, Flint would have been forced to the deck but it was a feint. The Claviger-Primaris was attempting to keep Flint at a distance.

'By the authority vested in me by–' Flint's voice boomed, before he was interrupted.

'You have no authority *here*!' Gruss cursed, the pain of his wound evident in his voice. 'Only Strannik!'

'Then you add the sin of idolatry to that of treachery,' Flint cursed, advancing as Gruss staggered backwards with one hand over his wound. 'The Emperor is our creator, our lord, our father and our judge. *I* am the instrument of his judgement!'

Flint drew back his power sword, its edge white hot and hissing in the driving rain and swept it around and down in a blinding arc. The Claviger-Primaris appeared to stand transfixed for one frozen moment. Then his body came apart in an explosive welter of blood and gore tumbling the way Flint's power sword had almost fallen but an instant earlier.

But Flint didn't pause to savour his victory. Before Gruss's remains had even struck the ground far below he was advancing once more. Soon, he was closing on the very end of the arm protruding out over the battle.

At the end was a nest of tangled, pulsating conduits and rust-streaked machinery that must once have been the command pulpit for the surface-to-orbit defence battery that had so nearly downed Flint's drop-ship. It was adorned with the remains of its previous operators and custodians, and in amongst the gristly flesh-and-bone throne was Colonel Strannik.

Flint had known his enemy would exhibit some form of mutation but he could never have anticipated the utter physical blasphemy that confronted him in the pulpit at the end of the platform's arm. The colonel was a mass of pulsating flesh and distended limbs, his sagging body supported by a mechanical contraption of metal legs and callipers. Folds of stretched flesh were partially clad in the filth-encrusted remnants of a uniform, which Flint recognised as the remains of that of a regimental commander of the Vostroyan Firstborn. It was the same as the uniform worn by Graf Aleksis.

The colonel's face was a sack of writhing, purple flesh and his cranium was hideously distended as if his skull were struggling to contain the grey matter squirming within. The hideous familial resemblance to the mutants below was horribly plain to see. Flint was assailed by a wave of hate and nausea as he came to a halt, the colonel fixing him with eyes plainly touched by the soul-searing madness of the warp. Flint knew in that instant that the creature before him was some form of terrible patriarch, the sire and the master of the thousands of mutants below. Worse, he was exerting some form of control over them, their screams of anger and bloodlust hideously synchronised with the sickening pulse of his swollen cranium.

One of the colonel's distended, claw-like hands was hovering over a control rune set into an arm of his blasphemous throne. Fighting waves of madness, Flint focused on the rune and a nearby pict-slate, his mind struggling to interpret its significance through the palpable aura of warp-witchery.

'Emperor's man...' the colonel sneered through horribly

swollen lips, his eyes bulging as if inflated by corpse gas. 'You're too late...'

Flint's vision swam as darting, half-seen forms from stygian depths of the Sea of Souls threatened to break through the weakened skin between reality and the warp. Ghostly figures with slavering maws and grasping talons swooped down from above, serpentine bodies wrapping themselves suggestively about the supine body of the colonel. Flint was unsure whether or not the traitor noble could perceive the forms and the damnation they represented. Then, his tortured gaze settled on the shape revolving in the centre of the pict-slate and his blood turned to ice in his veins as he realised what it represented.

'Yes, Emperor's man...' Colonel Strannik drawled, his Vostroyan accent audible even through the bubbling corruption that laced his voice. Projected on the screen was a targeting reticule, and it was centred on the drive section of the *Toil of Kossia*. 'Soon, you and your lackeys will be trapped here, with *us*...'

Flint's ears filled with the howling of the damned as more ghostly figures rose up from the beyond to dash and dart about the end of the platform. Summoning the last reserves of his faith and his sanity, he saw that Colonel Strannik was entirely unaware of the leering, drooling gargoyles, and that one fact granted him the strength he needed to overcome the otherwise paralysing waves of utter, unfettered insanity and corruption radiating outwards from the mutant patriarch.

The howling of the damned reached a deafening crescendo

as the colonel's finger stabbed downwards towards the rune that would launch the surface-to-orbit missile and destroy the *Toil of Kossia*, stranding the 77th Vostroyan Firstborn on a world seething with obscenity and damning them all to an ignominious slaughter.

Flint vowed that would not come to pass.

Bracing himself against a psychic wavefront so fierce the ragged tails of his leather storm coat billowed at his back, Flint drew his bolt pistol and with an unprecedented effort of will racked the slide.

Levelling the pistol towards the colonel's grossly pulsating head, Flint delivered his judgement.

'*Graf* Strannik,' he snarled. 'By the authority vested in me by the High Lords of the Adeptus Terra, I hereby call you to account for the sins of mutation and warp-craft.'

Flint's bolt pistol barked once and the colonel's head exploded in a fountain of sickly gore. Far below, the mouth of every single mutant abomination and every single enslaved rebel convict opened wide and emitted a piercing scream of grief and pain. The horde faltered and the Firstborn redoubled their fire. Then, the real killing started, and the sluice channels far below the complex were turned red with the spilled blood of countless thousands of traitors to the God-Emperor of Mankind.

'Let Him on Terra be your judge,' Flint concluded.

Unseen by Commissar Flint or anyone else, a lone figure dressed in the crimson of the Vostroyan Firstborn had taken position just below the control platform, nestling herself in amongst the girders of the tower. With deadly grace and an economy of effort bordering on the preternatural, she levelled her ornate, hand-wrought lasgun and squinted down its master-crafted scope. The targeting reticle settled over the stooped and wizened form of Governor Kherhart as he scuttled for the imagined haven of one of the claviger-wardens' secret access tunnels. For Kherhart however, just like Strannik and his vile progeny, there would be no escape. He had been entrusted with the rank of Imperial Commander, given power over an entire world, and he had betrayed those who had granted him that station.

Unlike his kinsman Strannik, Kherhart never saw his fate. He believed he could escape right up until the moment his head vanished in a pall of red mist as Karasinda, or rather the agent of the Emperor's justice who had taken on that name, pulled her trigger and ended his treachery for all time. When the regimental rolls of honour were later compiled, the very existence of a combat medic by that or any other name was strangely absent, those few who had known her assuming she had fallen in that final, glorious battle against the mutant horde of Colonel Strannik.

EPILOGUE
Last Words

Commissar Flint deactivated the data-slate and turned from the huge, multi-paned viewport of the *Toil of Kossia*, the world of Furia Penitens hanging in the black void beyond. The commissar having executed the renegade Firstborn Colonel Strannik, Aleksis had finally acquiesced to granting Flint access to his regiment's archives. Aleksis hadn't been offered much choice.

The files secreted away in the deepest levels of the archives filled Flint with disgust and made him realise something of the true nature of the Firstborn regiment in which he had been called to serve. Colonel Strannik, he learned, had been hiding the fact that he was a mutant for many years. His attempts to conceal it had led to the disaster of the Battle of Golan Hole, and after that, his mutations could be hidden no longer. When they became fully manifest and his corruption had got out of control his kinsmen had been forced to embark upon a course of action they hoped would hide their clan's shame. Instead of being handed over to the League of Black Ships along with the psyker cull all worlds were required to gather, Strannik had been granted sanctuary with another of his line, Governor Kherhart, far, he hoped, from prying eyes. He'd established his own private domain of brutality and filth in the lowest reaches of Alpha Penitentia, his rule warranted and guaranteed by his familial link to the installation's governor.

What happened next would likely remain the subject of conjecture for years to come, or else be sealed away by bodies keen to avoid the unwelcome and unfamiliar glare of scrutiny. The mutant colonel's sin had spread and over several decades a population of abominations had gestated in the penal generatorium's lowest levels. Perhaps because the geotherm processes utilised the heat emitted by irradiated minerals far below the surface, the taint of the warp had mingled with that of genetic corruption and birthed the mutant army the 77th had confronted. Flint had no doubt that the agents of the Holy Ordos of the Emperor's Inquisition, especially those of the warp-hunting Ordo Malleus, would be investigating the matter.

Another question that nagged at Flint, despite the fact that he had more pressing concerns, was the use to which Strannik had intended to put his army, if he had any intention at all. Had the mutant colonel intended to declare the entire world of Furia Penitens his own personal domain? Had he harboured some dark, treacherous desire to take his army off-world? The matter might never be fully uncovered, Flint knew, but he had no doubt that the Inquisition would be seeking the truth as a matter of urgency. He almost pitied any rebels subjected to the Inquisitions' investigative methods. Almost.

The situation was only uncovered when the Munitorum demanded a Penal Legion be raised from the population of Alpha Penitentia, to be shipped out to the Finial Sector to combat the uprisings afflicting that region of late. Colonel Strannik, it seemed, had been unwilling to surrender his subjects and must have known that the mutation afflicting so many would have been discovered had he done so.

How many rebel convict-workers would be left for the formation of a new Penal Legion was another question, but one Flint cared very little for. He'd be quite happy if every rebel in Alpha Penitentia was purged as a precaution against the spread of genetic deviancy, regardless of the need to reinforce the Finial Sector.

As Flint handed the slate back to Kohlz the hatch to the observation chamber opened inwards and Graf Aleksis stepped through. 'That'll be all, dragoon,' Flint dismissed his aide.

'Graf Aleksis,' Flint nodded, clasping his hands behind his back and turning to look out of the lancet-arched viewport towards the planet below. Another stray thought flashed across his consciousness – just how far removed was Graf Aleksis from the abominable Strannik, genetically speaking? Did the graf harbour any latent mutation or psychic potential?

'I've been expecting you,' said Flint, his eyes narrowing in suspicion.

'You have read the archives, I take it?' Aleksis said, taking his place at Flint's side as he too looked out into the glittering void and the world below. His aristocratic bearing gave him the appearance of power, yet Flint saw the line creasing his brow.

'I have,' said Flint. 'Is there anything you would like to add?'

'Yes, Commissar Flint. I wish to make something perfectly clear to you in case you are in any doubt. I have made my choice. I have chosen my duty to the Emperor over my duty to my clan.'

'But?' Flint pressed, seeing that Aleksis was troubled.

'But,' Aleksis continued, 'there will be a price to pay. For us both.'

'Then we're in this together, graf,' said Commissar Flint as he turned back to the viewport. 'Whatever price there is to pay, whatever is coming, the 77th Firstborn meets it as one. This regiment is far, far from full combat effectiveness, despite its first victory. Chain of command, morale, discipline – all are in dire need of my attentions.'

'Aye, commissar,' Aleksis answered. 'The 77th owes you much. It is renewed, redeemed. We stand ready to emulate and to exceed the deeds of our forebears, now the shame of Golan Hole is redressed.'

Let's hope it is, thought Flint, holding the graf's gaze for a moment as he considered, then just as quickly rejected, his previous thought regarding the man's lineage and whether or not he might harbour some hidden genetic corruption.

'The regiment is as much yours as it is mine.' Aleksis

smiled, adding, 'Even those ragamuffin penal troopers you insisted on drafting in. I pray we shall all serve together for the glory of Vostroya, and of the Imperium.'

The deck beneath the two men's feet began to tremble as the *Toil of Kossia's* massive plasma generators were stoked steadily up toward full power, unimaginable reserves of energy shunted towards the drives as the vessel prepared for its journey back to the system's outer jump point. Already, the regiment had received an astropathic communiqué detailing its next deployment. Flint was relieved to note the orders had been delivered via the Departmento Munitorum chain of command, and not the damnable web of intrigue that had resulted in the mess the 77th had just won through.

'Indeed,' Flint replied. As the distant roar of the plasma drives steadily grew the final line of one of the Imperium's most dearly cherished litanies – the Warrior's Catechism of Worship – came to mind.

'We ask only to serve...'

ABOUT THE AUTHOR

Andy Hoare works as a writer for Games Workshop. Currently employed by Forge World, he also worked for eight years developing games and background material for Warhammer and Warhammer 40,000 in the main design studio. As a freelancer, he has a number of novels, roleplay game material and gaming-related magazine articles to his name. Andy lives in Nottingham with his wife Sarah and way too many cats.

READ IT FIRST

EXCLUSIVE PRODUCTS | EARLY RELEASES | FREE DELIVERY

blacklibrary.com

Available from

GAMES WORKSHOP

blacklibrary.com
and all good bookshops